BLOOD KNIGHT

VAMPIRE SLAYER

BOOK ONE

Cover Art by Yanai
Cover Design and Internal Layout by Edie Skye

KDP Edition.

ISBN-10: 8884112155
ISBN-13: 9798884112155

Books by Edie Skye

The Titan Mage series
Titan Mage (#1)
Titan Mage Ruin (#2)
Titan Mage Dragon (#3)
Titan Mage Rising (#4)
Titan Mage Apocalypse (#5)

Titan Mage Side Quests
The Hot Springs Episode (#1)

The Blood Knight Series
Vampire Slayer (#1)
Scepter of Bone (#2)

The Monster Girl Tamer Series
I Power Up With Every Monster Girl I Defeat! (#1)

BLOOD KNIGHT

VAMPIRE SLAYER
BOOK ONE

EDIE SKYE

CHAPTER ONE

"HEY, CLARKE?"

"Hmm?"

"I know this is out of the blue, but have you ever played Dungeons & Dragons before?"

J.B Clarke sat in the Engineering and Science building's study hall, his brain fogged with the musty stench of the decades-old building his college was too cheap to update, despite its exorbitant tuition fees. It had fallen deeper into fog over the past few hours, immersed in a grueling software problem as part of his database coursework. So when Emma called upon his brain to switch gears, it was a struggle—but soon he ungummed his brain cogs and flicked his eyes up from his laptop to meet hers across the table.

Emma cocked a playful eyebrow, which managed to coax Clarke's mind fully out of its code-induced stupor.

"A while ago," he said cautiously, not sure what was behind her question. "Some of my friends were into it back in high school, but I haven't played since I graduated. Why?"

"No reason, really. You just seemed the type."

"The type?" Now it was his turn to raise an eyebrow.

Their professor had divvied up the class into random pairs for this assignment, which involved two students tackling each problem together. That meant they were supposed to divide the scope of their code between them and develop an interface to mesh their work back together.

Clarke had hoped to be paired with one of his acquaintances from the class—he hadn't been at Chester Creek University long enough to develop any new close friends—but he'd ended up with Emma, a girl he'd exchanged no more than three words with before this assignment.

Not that he minded! He'd take about *any* excuse to get to know her better, and it just so happened one had landed in his lap.

It was a testament to the brain-dulling, soul-sucking nature of his surroundings that he'd managed to be distracted from her at all.

Emmaline "Emma" Rose possessed what Clarke thought of as an "abundant" figure. Her burgundy leather jacket, black miniskirt, and gray-and-black striped stockings each seemed to strain against all those curves, especially the high and heavy thrust of her breasts, almost as if her clothes were under immense pressure from the inside, ready to burst open from all that barely-contained femininity.

Her face was equally attractive with large, dark eyes behind horn-rimmed glasses and a generous—often smiling—mouth, all framed by a cascade of long, raven-black hair. The glasses gave her a "sexy geek" vibe.

"Well, are you?" Emma asked.

There was no judgment in her voice. No condescension or disdain. Just a soft, friendly form of curiosity.

Clarke had been a little nervous about how to approach Emma after class, worried about coming across as either too forward or too business-like. They were classmates assigned to the same problem; it would have been awkward for him to hit on her right out of the gate. Conversely, he didn't want to keep things *too* formal. This *was* a golden opportunity to get to know her better, after all!

Fortunately, Emma had beaten him to the punch. She'd broken the ice outside class with a great programming joke: *A SQL query goes into a bar, walks up to two tables and asks, "Can I join you?"*

He'd have to remember that one.

"Why do I get the feeling this question didn't come out of nowhere?" Clarke asked.

She flashed a brief smile. "Well, this place is *boring*, for one. And actually, one of my friends likes to GM. She put together this custom campaign, but we're short one player. You interested?"

"I—"

Clarke paused to consider how best to reply. A girl—a *smoking hot* girl—was inviting him to join her and her friends—her *very possibly smoking hot* friends—for a night of pen-and-paper roleplaying. There was no way he could turn this down!

Careful though, he told himself. *Don't come across as too eager. Ease up to an eventual "yes."*

"Depends," he replied guardedly. "What gaming system are you using?"

"Pathfinder 3.5. You ever hear of it?"

"I have," he replied, his mind flashing through countless hours playing.

"Ashley likes to use Pathfinder as a base for all her custom scenarios."

"Ashley?"

"One of my friends. She stopped by our table earlier."

"You mean—" He almost said *the blonde that looks like a supermodel,* but instead replied, "the blonde dressed all in white. Long hair? Shiny hairband?"

"That's her. My other friends—Sammy and Brooke—also play. Normally, the three of us would be enough, but Ashley *insists* we have four players for this one." Emma leaned forward and gave him a crooked, knowing smile.

"She can be stubborn like that sometimes."

"Well, if she put in all the time and effort to make her own scenario, then yeah. I can see why she'd be picky about how you played through it."

"Which brings us back around to my question." She leaned back and draped an arm over the back of her chair. "Interested?"

"Sure. When and where?"

"This Saturday at my apartment. We generally start arriving around five, have something to eat, then pull out the dice around six—six thirty. I'll email you the address. It's about twenty minutes from campus."

"Great. I assume I'll need to put together a character?"

"Not for this one. Ashley has prebuilt characters for all of us. That's part of the reason why she needs a specific number of players."

"For the story?" Clarke asked.

"You guessed it!"

"What can you tell me about the scenario?"

"It's urban fantasy, so the setting is modern day but with all these secretive magical elements thrown in. You'll be playing a blood knight in hiding. They're a hybrid class, sort of like a ranger or druid. Ashley gave the class a mix of magic and combat abilities. *Very* versatile."

"Sounds fun. I've always enjoyed playing hybrid classes. More options make for more engaging roleplay."

"See?" She extended an open palm toward him. "I knew you were the type!"

"Yeah, I guess you had me figured out," he replied, returning a bashful smile. "Should I bring anything to the session?"

"Just a copy of your character sheet and some dice, though I have spares if you need some."

"No, I have my own."

"Figured you would." Emma gave him a friendly wink. "I'll email you the character sheet along with the address. Just need to get it from Ashley first."

"Thanks, but I was actually asking about food or drink. I don't want to mooch off your hospitality or anything."

"No worries there. The four of us—now *five* of us—take turns covering the pregame meal, and it's Brooke's turn this week."

"Got it, and thanks for the invite. You can expect me at five, rules and dice at the ready."

"Great! Looking forward to it!"

"What about you? What's your character like?"

"Oh, me?" Emma placed a demure hand over her chest. "I'm playing a succubus."

That Saturday, Clarke arrived at Emma's apartment a few minutes before five with a ring binder clutched in the crook of his arm and a dice bag hanging from his fingers. Of the housing options available around campus, this was clearly one of the higher-end ones—not fancy, exactly, but sleek and new with pleasant facades that looked like they saw few raucous, vomit-strewn parties or drug deals, which was more than he could say about his own cheap place. He knocked on the door with his free hand.

The door cracked open, and Emma peeked her head out.

"Hey, Clarke!" She gave him with a warm smile. "Come on in."

"Thanks."

She swung the door wide, and he stepped in, taking in the apartment. It was larger than the cubbyhole he called home—and cleaner, too—with comfy recliners and a long couch arranged around a low coffee table. Artwork hung on the walls in thick, black frames depicting a mix of anime and movie characters. *Frames.* She definitely lived a step above him.

"Thanks for the invite, again." He set the binder down on the granite counter that separated the kitchen from the living room and tried not to look overly curious as he returned his attention to the binder. "It feels like ages since I scratched that pen-and-paper itch."

"Don't mention it."

"Though, I do have some *slight* concerns."

"Like what?"

"Well …" Clarke opened the binder and thumbed through the hundred or so pages. "I wasn't expecting quite this many custom rules."

"Yeah," Emma replied, her eyes laughing. "Sometimes Ashley can go a bit overboard."

"Where's she find the time for all this, anyway?"

"Who knows? But you know how it is. If you're passionate about something, you find the time."

"I guess so. Just wondering if her grades suffer because of her hobby."

"Nope. Quite the opposite, in fact. She gets straight A's every semester, and I'm pretty sure she takes more hours than either of us."

"You know her major?"

"Ma-*jors*, actually. Political science and history."

Clarke's eyes widened. "She's getting straight A's with a dual major?"

"Yep."

Clarke shook his head. He flipped back to the front page, which contained the bulk of his character stats.

Emma glanced down at the page. Something must have caught her eye, because her brow furrowed.

"Uh, Clarke?"

"Yeah?"

"That's not your real name, is it?"

Clarke sighed internally. *Here we go.*

"I'm afraid so."

"But ..." She made a disgusted face. "There's no way."

"I wish that were true," he replied in a tired manner that attested to many similar conversations he endured in the past.

"I thought Clarke was your first name."

"That would have been nice, but no. It's my last name."

"Come on." Emma pointed to the name at the top of his character sheet, as if that would reveal some secret, *really* real name beneath it. "You're pulling my leg."

"Wish I was."

"But no one's parents would be that cruel!"

"You'd *think.*"

J.B. Clarke gave her a sad smile, because his full name was Joffrey Baratheon Clarke. His mother—bless her enthusiastic fantasy-loving heart—had discovered George R.R. Martin's A Song of Ice and Fire a few years before he'd been born and had "really liked the name's ring."

His father—bless *his* heart—hadn't put his foot down, which led to him being named after a contender for "worst human being in fiction."

It wasn't all bad, though. Back then, most people didn't have a clue who Joffrey Baratheon was, and the name shortened to the much more palatable J.B., though his parents had settled for Joff most of the time. However, his namesake's anonymity had vanished once HBO turned the books into a popular TV series and thus elevated the character from "worst human being in fiction" to "worst human being in fiction, for whom people cheered when he died and then rewound to watch it again."

And then the teasing began.

And kept going.

And going.

And fucking *going*.

Clarke couldn't have been happier when the show tanked in its last season so disastrously that literally *no one* wanted to talk about it anymore. Even a *global pandemic* couldn't get people to rewatch its dumpster fire of an ending.

That said, his parents had been less than sympathetic when he'd confronted them about his namesake, stressing that they had no way of seeing into the future and it could have been worse. They even shared the supposedly true story of a woman who'd wanted to name her newborn daughter "Vagina" because she'd never encountered the word before the obstetrician used it and because, "Thas jus tha purdiest word I eva hurd!"

Clarke shivered involuntarily. Yes, it could have been worse.

"Actually," he continued, "I'm wondering how Ashley knew my name, because it seems you didn't tell her."

16

"Nope. News to me."

"Will she let me go by 'Clarke' in the campaign?" He tapped a note on the page. "Because this part says we're playing alternate versions of ourselves in the scenario."

"Oh, I'm sure Ashley will," Emma replied with a carefree wave of her hand.

"Will what?" came the unexpected response from the opening door.

"Hey, Ash! Speak of the devil."

The newcomer gave Emma a cross look. "You know I don't like that joke."

"Must be why I keep using it, then," Emma teased in a good-natured manner.

Ashley Smith rolled her eyes as she eased the door shut, then crossed the room with long-legged strides, high heels clicking on the hardwood. She'd dressed in all white again, this time with a short neck scarf to accent her sleeveless button-down shirt. She'd left the first three buttons open to provide a tantalizing glimpse of deep, firm cleavage. Her long, blonde hair practically gleamed in the light, held back by a metallic hairband.

She smiled at Clarke, but the expression held all the warmth of a business transaction. Clarke fought an urge to check his phone, almost certain she'd arrived at *exactly* 5:00 PM. She struck him as the severely punctual type.

"I'm Ashley." She extended a slender hand, which

he shook, and found she was all business there, too. "I'm glad you could make it."

"Me, too," Clarke replied, not sure what else to say, and trying to keep his eyes from wandering toward her plunging neckline. (Which was *not* business-appropriate.)

"So, what are you sure I'll allow?" Ashley asked.

"He wants to shorten his character name." Emma tapped her finger on the character sheet. "Just chop off the first two parts."

Ashley leaned over the page, then glanced up at Clarke.

"You don't want to use your given name?" she asked, sounding somewhat perplexed.

"Not really."

"Why not?"

"Uh …" Clarke frowned at her. "Isn't it obvious?"

Ashley's eyes darted to the character sheet, stayed there for long, confused seconds, then zipped back up to Clarke. She seemed ready to ask another question, but then something softened in her face, and she shrugged.

"If you're not comfortable with it, then use whatever you like. I only thought starting with everyone's real names would make the scenario more immersive." She gave Emma a knowing glance. "After all, if tonight goes well—"

The door swung open violently. A tall, athletic woman barged in, four pizza boxes balanced atop one hand with absurd grace compared to the rest of her, especially when she shouted:

"Hey, bitches! I brought the meats!"

The second newcomer was almost as tall as Clarke, who was no slouch in the height department, though her shoulders weren't nearly as broad, and her chest possessed a great deal more … topology than his. Still, the toned muscles visible on her arms and bare midriff spoke to an active lifestyle. Or curriculum. Or both, perhaps.

She'd tied her thick, wavy mane of brunette hair back into a ponytail and wore a baggy gray T-shirt cut off at the bottom to reveal her firm stomach, its design and lettering too faded to make out. Her jeans gave a similar impression of comfortable wear and tear with a few rips around the knees.

Her sharp, intense eyes caught his, but then widened suddenly, and she froze midstride, almost launching the pizzas forward before she stabilized them with her free hand. Her expression—initially loud and boisterous—became almost mousy.

"Oh. You're already here."

"That I am," Clarke replied dryly.

"Uh … Hi? I'm Brooke. Brooke Hawthorne."

"Clarke. Nice to meet you."

"Yeah, uh." Brooke held the boxes out as if offering them as an apology. "I brought pizza."

"I'll take those." Emma grabbed the pizza boxes and began arraying them on the kitchen counter.

The rich, savory smell of hot cheese, meat, and marinara tickled Clarke's nose, and his stomach grumbled in anticipation. Emma and Ashley busied themselves setting out paper plates, napkins, plastic cups, and a selection of colas at one end of the boxes. Brooke eventually unfroze from her awkward pose, gave Clarke a bashful glance, then grabbed a plate and began loading it up with pizza slices.

Clarke grabbed his own plate and surveyed the selection: three large pizzas consisting of pepperoni, meat lovers, supreme (also piled high with enough meat that the rare veggies would have cowered in fear if they'd been sapient), one medium pizza split into half pepperoni and half cheese, and a bag of breadsticks and marinara dipping sauce.

"The meats indeed," Ashley noted with a sour glance over the options.

"The cheesy one is for you," Brooke said. "See? I kept you in mind."

"And what about our guest? You consider him, too?"

"I—" Brooke paused with her mouth open, then frowned. She faced Clarke. "You're not a vegetarian, are you?"

"Nope."

"Any allergies?"

"None I'm aware of."

"You like pizza?"

"No, I *love* pizza, and the more meat the better."

"Fantastic! I was worried there for a minute." Brooke's face brightened. "You'll fit right in."

"The point," Ashley said firmly, "is you should have asked *before* you bought the food."

"Whoops." Brooke shrugged before adding another slice to her plate.

"Hey there, girlfriends!" said a petite figure from the doorway.

"Hey, Sammy!" Emma waved at her. "Would you mind locking the door? We're all here."

"Sure thing."

Clarke realized he'd seen Sammy a few times around campus, though he'd never spoken to her. In fact, it was hard *not* to notice her, since she favored loud clothes and even louder hair, which seemed to be a different color every time he laid eyes on her. She wore a hoodie stylized with splotches of fluorescent paint, the hood pulled back to reveal a pixie cut of vibrant red hair blending toward purple at the tips.

She walked up to Clarke. "You Clarke?"

"That's right."

"Samantha Eloise." She extended a gloved hand. "But you can call me Sammy. All my friends do."

21

He shook her hand. "A pleasure to meet you, Sammy."

"You ready to kick some vampire butt tonight?"

"*Shh!*" Ashley snapped. "Spoilers!"

"Oh, come on." Sammy rolled her eyes as she grabbed her plate. "He already knows. You put it right there in your twenty-thousand-word lore dump."

Clarke kept very quiet.

"I suppose you have a point there." Ashley placed a single cheesy slice on her plate, struggling to disentangle the gooey strands gracefully. "You did read all the lore, right?" she asked, her voice tinged with uneasy hopefulness.

"I …" Clarke sighed. "Okay, I'm going to be honest here. I didn't realize there was going to be quite so much material when I started printing it out. All I did was skim it before I drove over."

Ashley sank in her seat a little and, oddly, her hair-band seemed to darken a few shades. It must have been a trick of the lighting.

"Don't give him that look." Sammy flopped into one of the recliners and took a large bite from a bread-stick. She continued speaking with her mouth full. "All I did was skim it, too. It was either that or fall asleep halfway through."

"Hey, now," Ashley protested. "It wasn't that dry."

Sammy snorted out a laugh.

"Well, I liked it." Brooke plopped down into one of the chairs. "I think it's a good primer for people new to the, uh, setting."

Clarke guessed she'd been about to use a different word there at the end, but he didn't give it more than a passing thought.

Ashley sighed and joined them around the coffee table.

With all the recliners taken, Clarke sat down at one end of the couch, fully expecting Emma to pick the other end.

She didn't, instead choosing to sit in the middle close enough for their hips to press against each other. Clarke felt a jolt of almost electric excitement surge through him at the unexpected contact. He glanced over at her, and she smiled sweetly back.

"Something wrong?" she asked.

"It's nothing." He was about to start eating when he noticed Emma hadn't brought a plate. "Not eating with us?"

"I'll snack on something else later."

"Not a fan of pizza?"

"It's not that. I love a good slice of pizza as much as the next girl. I just have these"—she twirled a hand around as if searching for the right word—"dietary restrictions."

"Ah."

"I can only handle so much junk food before I get hit with these cravings and need something more, umm, nutritious to fill me up."

"Got it. Say no more."

Sammy chuckled around a fat bite of breadstick. He had no idea why.

CHAPTER TWO

"YOU GAZE DOWN THE DECREPIT ALLEY," Ashley said, "your eyes adjusting to the moonlit gloom."

"Except for me," Brooke pointed out. "Because I have dark vision."

"Yes," Ashley sighed more than said. "Except for you. The alley—"

"What do I see?"

"You *all* see an empty alley that stretches back and then forks where the abandoned warehouses meet a high concrete wall covered in graffiti. Soaked cardboard boxes and rotting wooden pallets litter the path ahead, as do a few bags of trash scavenged long ago by rats." Ashley looked up meaningfully. "Or something else."

"My money's on something else," Sammy said, the crust of a pizza slice hanging from her lips like a fat cigar.

"Moonlight glistens on the damp, rain-slicked walls, and a faint, unpleasant stench lingers in the—"

"What sort of stench?" Brooke interrupted.

Ashley slumped her shoulders.

"Girl, does it really matter?" Sammy asked.

"I don't know. Could. Might be a trap."

"Give me a perception check," Ashley said.

Brooke rolled her D20 then checked her character sheet. "Nineteen."

"The smell is emanating from the mounds of feces atop the garbage."

"So, literally piles of shit?" Sammy asked.

"But what kind of creature took the dump?" Brooke asked. "*That's* the important question."

"Another perception check, please," Ashley asked wearily.

Clarke leaned over to Emma and whispered, "Are Brooke and Ashley always like this?"

"Sometimes," she whispered back.

Emma turned back to the free entertainment. Her hand grazed across his thigh, and he sucked in a quick, quiet breath. She'd been touching him a lot. Nothing overt. Nothing that couldn't be waved off as an accidental brush.

But consistently.

She's interested, he thought. *She's got to be.*

After all, if she weren't, why not sit at the far end

VAMPIRE SLAYER

of the couch? He'd given her plenty of space, but she'd plopped down right beside him and hadn't been shy about it. So much so that he found himself struggling to focus on the game at times. Though, despite this, their efforts to work through Ashley's story had gone well so far.

True to her word, Emma played the succubus, complete with a plethora of empathic abilities that allowed her to gauge the intent of various NPCs, if not actually read their minds. She'd taken to the role with gusto, already seducing two of Ashley's nonplayer characters before "pumping" them for information in what Clarke admitted was rather arousing dialogue between the two girls.

Brooke was clearly meant to be the melee bruiser of the party, playing to her werewolf strengths, though she possessed a wider range of abilities than he'd expected. For example, her shapeshifting allowed her to take intermediate forms, enabling her to dip into her werewolf advantages while retaining most of her human appearance. At the moment, she possessed wolf ears and a tail—both hidden by her attire—as well as claws that could slice through steel like it was damp cardboard.

Sammy played as a sort of slime/doppelganger hybrid, which made her an excellent scout and assassin. She couldn't mimic any person or object at will; she needed to prepare her transformations ahead of time, much like a classical D&D wizard had to memorize spells. That said,

27

her slime form allowed her to ooze past just about any obstacle, and her touch attack could inflict a variety of unpleasant status ailments.

His own character came with a healthy mix of combat abilities and utility spells. Fifty *pages* of abilities, some of which struck him as grossly overtuned for the enemies they'd faced so far. Not that he was about to complain; sometimes it was fun being ridiculously overpowered.

The ladies seemed to appreciate having a blood knight along for the campaign—or at least their characters did—since they'd showered him with in-game flirting. There'd even been a bit of "penetration" involved, though since it had been with Sammy's character while in her gelatinous form, he wasn't sure it counted. "Technically," his dick had been inside her, but his pants had stayed on the whole time.

So, yeah. Probably didn't count.

Brooke's in-game attitude had surprised him the most. He'd wondered if her reserved demeanor would carry over to the game, but it clearly hadn't! She'd crawled out of whatever social shell had materialized earlier, enjoying the game with incredible gusto. She and Ashley were once again engaged in a verbal sparring session, so Clarke took the lull to flip through his spell list again, perusing the expansive options.

Meanwhile, Sammy rose to refill her plate yet again.

At the start of the evening, Clarke had wondered how the five of them would finish off four pizzas without leaving a mountain of leftovers, especially since Emma had declined any and Ashley had picked daintily at her single slice, but it turned out both Brooke and Sammy were voracious eaters. He'd expected Brooke to have a healthy appetite, given her impressive stature and whatever workout routine had toned all those muscles, but *Sammy* could pack the pizza away right alongside her.

Clarke hadn't been keeping track, but he was almost certain the petite redhead had consumed *more* slices than Brooke, and that was saying a lot.

He had no idea where Sammy was hiding all that food; he expected most people with a similar diet would resemble bowling balls after a while, but Sammy's lithe build and slender arms scoffed at the notion. Maybe she had a really high metabolism? He wasn't about to ask. After all, what would he say?

"Hey, Sammy? What's your secret to not turning blimp-shaped from all that food?"

It was probably best to keep those thoughts in his head.

"But what about—" Brooke continued before Ashley interrupted her.

"The time you've wasted dithering about the alley has not gone unnoticed. Three figures approach you from behind, all clad in long black coats, their faces shadowed by wide-brimmed hats."

"Where did *they* come from?" Brooke demanded crossly.

"They emerged from the gloom."

"That's it? There's an empty parking lot behind us. Shouldn't I get a perception check or something?"

"You were too engrossed by the alley." Ashley glanced around the table. "*All* of you were."

"Oh well." Sammy set her plate down and crashed into her recliner. "Sucks to be us."

"Are they baddies?" Brooke asked. "Do they look like baddies?"

"You and you"—Ashley pointed to Clarke and Emma—"can both tell they're vampiric thralls. You can sense the control spells on them."

"I warn the rest of the party," Clarke said.

"The lead figure reaches into his coat. He seems to be drawing a weapon."

"Screw that!" Brooke snatched up her dice. "I grab whatever he's going for and then beat him to death with it!"

Ashley gave her a look of tested—and *frayed*—patience.

"You're too far away. Everyone, roll for initiative."

The clatter of dice filled the room.

"Crap!" Brooke sank back in her seat. "I rolled a two!"

30

"Seven," Sammy reported. "Not what I was hoping for."

"Nine for me," Emma said.

Clarke checked his die and then his character sheet. "Is my initiative modifier supposed to be this high?"

"Yes," Ashley replied. "The bonus comes from your Mana Attunement perk. You're naturally sensitive to changes in the surrounding magic."

"Then I have a twenty-seven."

Sammy whistled.

"You go first," Ashley said. "Followed by the thralls."

"Right." Clarke began flipping through his spells. "Do I see anyone besides the first three?"

"No. Just them."

"And are they spread out or bunched up?"

"Bunched up near the mouth of the alley. They're blocking the way out."

"Then I'll cast …" He kept flipping until he came across a familiar page. "Right. I'll spend three hit points to cast Blood Freeze on the entire group."

"Nice!" Emma beamed at him. "Your spell should disable them for the rest of us."

"That's what I was going for."

"Hell, yeah!" Brooke thumped a fist. "You go, Clarke!"

"Hold on. The thralls each get a saving throw." Ashley rolled three dice behind her Game Master screen. "And all three twitch in silent pain before they drop to the ground in ragged, helpless heaps. A crowbar clatters against the pavement."

"Can I pick that up and beat them to death with it now?" Brooke asked with an eager, toothy grin.

Ashley narrowed her eyes. "Once it's your turn."

The warehouses turned out to be teeming with vampiric thralls and familiars.

"Whew!" Brooke gave her brow a theatrical wipe. "That was a toughie!"

"I like how you ripped off that one guy's leg," Sammy said, "and then used it as a skewer. I didn't realize someone's foot could pierce through a ribcage, let alone *two*."

"It can if you throw it hard enough!" Brooke declared proudly. "How about you? You done with that hellhound?"

"Yep." Sammy let out an exaggerated burp and patted her stomach. "I'm good."

"I hate to be a downer," Clarke began, "but wasn't there supposed to be a vampire in here?" He looked around the table. "I mean, that *is* the reason we came—"

"It's an ambush!" Ashley rolled a fistful of dice and studied the results. "A cloud of black vapor descends from the rafters and coalesces into a large, hooded silhouette in the middle of the party. Forks of green lightning snap outward from the figure as it descends, striking each of you. Everyone give me a reflex check minus your dex bonuses. Except for Clarke; he can keep his."

"Aww, come on!" Brooke grabbed her D20. "What for?"

"Because the rest of you have been caught flat-footed. He was the only one on guard for the vampire, and none of you bothered to look up."

"*Fine,*" Brooke huffed and rolled her die. "Crap."

"Look on the bright side." Sammy flopped back and stretched her arms over her head. "Can't be worse than what I rolled."

"Wanna bet?"

"Your saves?" Ashley asked.

Sammy blew out a breath. "Critical fail."

"Same here."

"What?" Emma asked. "*Both* of you?"

Sammy and Brooke nodded, almost in unison.

Emma rolled then checked her character sheet.

"That's an eight. Is that high enough?"

"All three of you are paralyzed and suffer"—another fistful of dice clattered behind her screen—"twelve points of damage."

"Ouch!" Emma updated her sheet. "Another hit like that and I'm done for."

"Tell me about it," Brooke said. "I'm not doing so hot either."

"Shush," Ashley said. "All of you are too paralyzed to talk."

"What about me?" Clarke asked. "I rolled a seventeen."

"Yeah, you're fine." Ashley gave him a dismissive wave. "And even if it hit you, your Sanguine Shield is still up." She sat forward in her chair. "The figure drinks in the last of the smoke, which flows low and fast across the concrete floor to his feet. His eyes glow a faint, malevolent green as he raises a huge black sword, its uncanny blade casting an aura of darkness."

"Well, that's not good," Sammy said.

"Shh," Brooke whispered out the side of her mouth. "We're still paralyzed, remember?"

"I remember. I just don't care."

Clarke thumbed frantically through his spell list.

"The vampire charges Clarke and swings. Black energy scintillates behind the arcing blade." More dice rattled behind Ashley's screen. "The attack breaks through your shield, and you take seventeen damage."

"Oof." Clarke marked the damage. "I'm almost dead."

"Your turn," Ashley said, her tone low and ominous. "Right."

"Just remember," Brooke said, "you're probably the only thing standing between that vampire and a total party kill."

"Sure looks like it." He flipped to a page where he'd folded the corner over earlier. "Okay, I'm going all out. First, I'll summon my thirstblade. Next, I'm going to use Sacrifice to boost its attack power with all my remaining hit points. Except for the last one, of course."

"Of course," Ashley said.

"And then I'm going after the vampire."

"Roll to hit."

Clarke picked up his D20 and was about to roll when Emma placed her hand atop his. A tingle of excitement jolted up his arm at her soft caress, and he paused and turned toward her.

"I think," she began with a sly smile, "the situation calls for the big guns."

"I'm pretty sure that's what I'm doing."

"I don't mean in the game." Emma presented a metal D20, held in the tips of her fingers. "Why don't you use my lucky die? I only bring it out for special occasions. It hasn't failed me yet."

Clarke had to stop himself from letting a condescending smirk slip. Some of his friends from high school had employed bizarre rituals to "purge" their dice of bad luck, from putting dice in the freezer when they performed poorly to smashing them to bits while the survivors "watched." He found their efforts ridiculous back then and that attitude hadn't changed.

Math didn't care about your "luck," and there was no such thing as hot or cold dice, but that didn't mean he doubted Emma. To the contrary, he knew some dice performed better than others. Not because of luck, but because they'd been manufactured poorly. This was especially true for D20s, where some of the cheaper offerings could be a little … egg-shaped, leading them to roll higher or lower than the statistical averages.

Clarke set down his D20 and accepted Emma's "lucky" die. It felt surprisingly heavy as he rolled it around in his hand. The numbers were black except for the green 20 and the red 1.

"Thanks."

She leaned close enough for Clarke to feel her breath against his ear.

"If you save us, I'll be *very* grateful."

"Aren't you still paralyzed?" Clarke asked.

"Who said I was still in character?"

A knot formed in Clarke's throat, and sudden excitement strained against his jeans. They might have been in relative public, but something in her tone of voice was very *not* public-appropriate. (He couldn't say he minded, though.)

"You going to roll or not?" Sammy asked.

Emma stuck her tongue out at Sammy. He wasn't sure how long *he'd* been paralyzed.

"That's enough from the peanut gallery," Ashley scolded. "But seriously, please roll."

"Okay. Here goes." Clarke let the die slide off his hand. It tumbled over his papers, then onto the wooden tabletop, hit a knot in the surface, rebounded in a different direction, then finally began to settle.

The red digit caught the light.

Not good! He found himself cringing, every muscle in his body tense.

The die teetered between the 1 and the surrounding numbers, then finally—with a surprisingly sharp judder—landed on the 19.

"Whew!" Clarke exhaled, suddenly feeling light-headed for some reason. The moment passed, and Emma patted him warmly on the thigh.

"That's a hit," Ashley said. "Roll for damage."

Clarke did so, adding over a dozen D6's, one for each hit point consumed by the Sacrifice spell.

"That'll be—"

"Your blade cleaves effortlessly through the vampire's neck, and his head flies off his shoulders in a spray of blood. The sword's shadow-light flickers away as it slips from his hand. It clatters to the ground, and his headless corpse takes one step forward, two, then crumples into a lifeless heap. Your living sword drinks in a portion of the vampire's power, and you regain your lost vitality."

"Nice!" Clarke erased the damage numbers from his character sheet.

Ashley paused, eyeing each player in turn. Sammy raised a curious eyebrow while Brooke jittered excitedly in her seat.

"Also," she said at last, "all of you are unparalyzed."

"Woohoo!" Brooke threw up her arms in triumph before the other two could chime in.

CHAPTER THREE

Ashley brought the session to a close shortly after the vampire's defeat, and the evening began to break up. Sammy left first, filling one of the pizza boxes with leftovers and heading out with *yet another* crust hanging from her lips. She said her goodbyes at the door and let it ease shut behind her.

Clarke bagged his dice while Ashley folded up her GM screen and Brooke stuffed a greasy pizza box with her own leftovers. He rose and joined Emma and Brooke by the kitchen counter.

"Can I help with anything?" he asked.

"Sure, if you don't mind," Emma said. "Can you stay to help me clean up?"

"No problem," he replied, his pulse quickening with a sense for where the evening might be headed. Emma had just subtly arranged for the two of them to be alone. "Always happy to help."

"Well, I'm outta here." Brooke grabbed her box and grinned mischievously at Emma. "Enjoy your dinner!"

"Oh, I'm sure I will."

Clarke frowned as Brooke left. He'd picked up on an unusual undercurrent to the brief exchange, as if the two women were party to an inside joke, but he had no idea what it could be. What was so strange about Emma's diet? Or did Brooke, too, have some idea of where the evening was headed?

"What'd she mean by that?" he asked, half playful, half genuinely curious.

Emma smiled coyly and shrugged it off without answering.

"I'm heading home, too," Ashley said, her reference books and GM screen tucked under an arm. "Let me know how it goes."

"Will do!" Emma replied brightly.

Clarke's frown deepened, but he also didn't let it bother him. He was moments away from being alone with the beautiful young woman who'd been subtly pawing him all evening. There were *all kinds* of ways the evening could improve.

He waited for the door to shut one last time, then turned back to Emma.

"So, how can I—"

Emma's lips met his with ravenous force, and her tongue pressed between them hungrily.

Well, he thought. *That answer came fast.*

His lips parted to accept her advance, almost automatically, almost without thought, and soon his hands found her narrow waist. She wrapped her arms around his back, pulling him close, the generous swell of her breasts pressing against his chest.

Clarke considered himself a fairly reasonable person, but at the touch of her lips, her tongue, her arm, her chest—all reason abandoned him, leaving only a core of voracious, almost animalistic want. He needed her, more than anything he'd ever sought in his entire life. His existence had been filled with a string of gray, drab events up until this moment, but now the press of her body had suffused his mind with light and color and the sweet, sweet scent of her.

His hand found the back of her neck. They broke for a quick, shared breath, and then their lips met again.

No words were exchanged. None were needed.

But a kiss wouldn't sate him. Not here, and not now. Not after *this.* He yearned for more. So much more.

So much it hurt.

Oddly, it occurred to him that this didn't feel *normal*—as if something alien to his mind were compelling him to act with such aggression—but he also didn't care.

She seemed to sense the urgency of his desire and guided them back to the couch, where they sank into its massive cushions, her astride him, his loins eager to be freed. He explored her body, hands slipping underneath her skirt, tracing around to encompass her firm, shapely behind.

She giggled as she ground her hips against his, and he let his hands flow across the contours of her body, up and up, under her shirt and across pale, supple flesh to finally grace the lacy contours of her bra.

"Yes," she moaned against his mouth, and then broke their kiss and arched backward. She crossed her arms and lifted her shirt in one fluid motion to expose her constrained breasts, then undid the hook at the back.

Her twin, perfect mounds bounced free, and she tossed the garment aside. He took hold of one with a firm hand, squeezing and kneading her flesh while his mouth found the other's erect nipple.

Emma sucked in a sharp breath through clenched teeth, then let out a hissing exhale as his tongue played across her areola. She rose off him a hair and reached down, finding his zipper. She freed his lust, let it spring forth, then traced her fingers up across its veiny girth.

"Now there's what I've been after," she uttered breathlessly.

Before he could even think about what she'd just said, she pulled her panties aside and sank down on him. The hot, wet folds of her sex accepted him effortlessly, even as the walls squeezed in with delicious tightness.

"Fuck!" Clarke exclaimed, his mind ablaze with desire and the need for release.

Emma only smiled in reply, and her mouth met his once more. He grasped her hips, and she rocked back and forth atop him, urging his excitement onward, upward, guiding him through a crescendo of pleasure.

Her long, black hair showered across her bare shoulders, skin glistening with sweat. He cupped one of her breasts, squeezed, felt her grateful moan across his own lips, and rocked upward, thrusting into her to meet her grinding.

His crescendo peaked.

Exploded.

All of existence vanished except for her body, and he shot his lust up into her.

"Yes!" she cried, back tensing, arching, her head flung back, dark wings unfurling to either side of—

Wait. What the fuck?

Clarke shook his head. Some semblance of rational thought returned to him, and he took in the two small, bat-like wings that had somehow spread from Emma's back.

"Whew!" She collapsed forward and kissed the nape

of his neck. "That was scrumptious! I *really* needed that!"

"Uh, Emma? I'm not sure how to break this to you, but you've got something on your back."

Her entire body tensed again, but not in an erotic way this time.

"On my back?" She asked. The two wings twitched. "Right. Uh, I probably should have told you this before we fucked."

"Told me *what?*"

She sat up and regarded him with a serious-but-nervous face. This despite the fact he was still deep inside her and still, more or less, ready for round two.

"I'm a succubus," she stated in a clear voice.

Clarke grimaced, then leaned to one side to take in the little wings. They looked like cheap props—sexy, but certainly not big enough to support a body in flight. Wait, why was he even thinking that?

He met her gaze once more.

"Sure, you are."

"Look, I know this is unexpected, but it's the truth."

Clarke gave her a doubtful eye. "Is this some sort of roleplay kink?" He held up a hand before she could respond. "Because if that's what starts your engine, I am all for it!"

"I'm being serious here."

"So am I!" he replied, but the concern in her eyes

suggested they weren't being serious about the same thing, and he sensed round two slipping away.

"Here, I can prove it to you." Emma spread her arms grandly, and the wings grew, unfurling beyond the width of the couch. "Behold! I am a—"

Clarke wasn't sure what kind of emotion was building in him at that sight—wonder, horror, confusion, the sense that he had stumbled into a part of his world that he hadn't known about and wasn't ready for—

But all of that crashed away when one of her wingtips clonked against a lamp on the end table, and it teetered dangerously.

"Oh, shit!" She scrambled off him, dove across the couch, and managed to catch the lamp before it fell. She planted it back on the end table, then folded her legs underneath her and sat beside him.

Clarke—now with complicated emotions in places other than his drafty erection—considered her wings more seriously.

"How did you do that?"

"I can control their size and even make them disappear." She smiled bashfully. "Except, I sort of lost control there for a moment."

"Are they …" He reached a hand toward one wing, but then hesitated.

"Go ahead. No need to be shy." She extended a

wingtip toward him. "I'm a succubus. Touching me is kind of the point."

He reached out and touched the dark, translucent flesh and found it to be both soft and surprisingly warm. Its elastic surface reminded him of the skin of a balloon, but more alive with muscles. Light from the lamp shone through, revealing a complex tracery of veins.

He drew a finger across the top, and Emma shuddered.

"Sorry. That tickles." Her wings shrank until they were almost comically small.

"Definitely not a prop."

"Nope."

"You're really a succubus?"

"Yep."

"Then …"

With some effort, Clarke managed to stuff his erection back into his pants. Emma watched him do that with a slightly forlorn expression, and maybe he was a bit forlorn about it too, but the past sixty seconds of his life had opened up an entire tree of questions, and none of them were best asked with his dick out.

"Then," he continued, "did you just suck out part of my soul?"

"No way. That's just vampire propaganda."

"Vampire … propaganda?" he echoed, his brow furrowing once more.

"Yeah, vampires control most major media outlets," she said as if it were the most normal thing in the world. "Hollywood, books, the arts, and much, much more."

"They *do*?"

"Yep. That's why vampires are so overpowered in books and movies and stuff." She rolled her eyes. "And why succubi have such terrible reputations—because that's how vampires depict us. What we *actually* do is elevate the lifeforce of anyone we couple with, and then *both* parties reap the benefits. Don't you feel invigorated right now?"

"I ..." Clarke took a moment to consider his own physical condition. "Now that you mention it, I feel like I could run a marathon."

"See? Everyone wins when a succubus gets it on!"

"Wait a second." His brain spun. He had to put this in terms he could understand, if only for the comfort of familiarity. "So, you can literally buff people by fucking them?"

"I know! Isn't it awesome?" She crossed her arms under her breasts. "Stupid vampires and their stupid lies. A lot of demihumans have bad reps because of them, but succubi get it worse than most."

"Hold on a second. Demi*humans*?" Clarke asked, struggling to keep up with the avalanche of revelations. "As in plural? There's more to all this?"

"Quite a bit, actually." She smiled slyly and crawled toward him on her hands and knees. "But why don't we leave the questions for later?"

"I don't know. They seem rather important."

"True, but how about we enjoy each other a bit more first?" She traced fingers across his thigh. "I know you want more."

"You're not reading my mind, are you?"

"More like your mood. It's a succubus thing."

"So, an empath, not a telepath."

"Exactly." She leaned close and whispered. "I'm especially sensitive to sexual urges."

"Just like in Ashley's …" Clarke paused, a thought coming to him, followed by even more questions, which were all set aside when Emma reached into his pants and pulled him loose.

Clarke *did* have more questions—but also, a succubus' hand was on his dick, and while his brain had complex feelings about the situation, the rest of him had other priorities.

She stroked to greater firmness, then bent down, and took him into her mouth.

"Fuck!" he gasped.

Girls had gone down on him before a few times in his life. Not often, but enough for him to possess a frame of reference; in his experience, the most any of them could take was about half—whether due to a lack of skill or because of his size.

Emma swallowed him down to the root all in one

go. She stayed there for a few seconds, his dick lodged deep in her throat, then slowly eased back off until just the tip remained in her mouth. Then her hungry eyes fixed on his, and she began a series of slow, luxurious slides up and down his member.

Clarke let out a content exhale and rested his head back, savoring the attention, reveling in her skill. She worked his shaft for what seemed like a delicious eternity, but in fact only lasted a few minutes, all the while coaxing him toward the edge of a second climax.

She let his dick pop free of her lips, then kissed the tip and rose. She pushed down her skirt and panties, leaving only her striped stockings and high heels on, then sank back into the chair opposite him and spread her legs, a hand underneath each thigh pulling her legs wide.

"It's been so hard waiting for this," she moaned. Her black, leathery tail curled up between her legs. "You may not realize it yet, but you're something both rare and special. I could feel it the moment I first laid eyes on you."

The tip of her tail coiled back and stroked down her glistening, pink slit.

"It's been excruciating for me." Her cheeks reddened, eyes moist with dreamy desire. "It took all my self-control just to be in the same room with you. I pleasured myself *so* many times after class, fantasizing about you, wishing for this moment."

Clarke stood up and nearly ripped his shirt off. He removed his pants and kicked them aside.

"Make love to me," she asked, almost begging. "Sate me, knowing full well what I am."

Her words banished any uncertainty Clarke had about the situation. He cupped a hand behind her neck and drew her lips toward his. They kissed again, though this time slow and soft, each of them savoring this strange sense of intimacy born of her confession. His tongue explored her mouth, and hers his, all while he reached down and guided his erection to her hot, dripping sex.

And then he drove himself into her, down to the hilt.

Emma broke their kiss and groaned. She bit her lower lip, a wicked smile curling her mouth. Their eyes met again, and Clarke began to thrust in and out of her at a steady rhythm, each stroke deep and firm and complete, his pace quickening as his loins tensed.

Her breasts heaved with each powerful thrust, and her tail wrapped around his waist as if to coax him deeper. She let go of her legs and drew him close, perspiration beading on their bodies.

Clarke pounded her with relentless abandon, his own endurance surprising him. He didn't know where this sudden font of strength welled up from—Emma's influence, perhaps?— but his muscles refused to tire as he drilled her again and again and again.

"Yes!" she gasped, her eyes alight with sensuous joy. "Keep going! I'm so close!"

"Me too," he growled. Their faces almost touched as he slammed into her, inches away from his own climax.

"Uhhhh!" She wrapped her legs around him, every muscle shuddering from the joy of release. "YES!" she exclaimed, almost in tears now. "FUCK!"

Clarke buried himself deep in her, his mind and body erupting at the same moment, filling her womanhood as a pure, beautiful bliss eclipsed his mind—

—and in that moment, something within him snapped.

Like the strained link of an old, rusted chain suddenly shattering into a thousand metal shards.

Something roared to life inside him.

In his head.

Through his body.

And across his skin, manifesting as green flames that didn't burn.

Unseen hands lifted them up off the chair, and both he and Emma floated through the air.

"Wha—what?" Clarke looked around, his limbs scrambling, those heatless flames hugging his body. "What just happened?"

"You did!" Emma's wings grew and flapped twice, steadying her. "Oh, I knew you could do it!"

"Do what?" Clarke asked urgently. The strange green fire was beginning to wink out. "What are you talking about?"

"You broke through the suppression spell!"

"That's great, I guess," he replied, feeling both frazzled and lost, "but would you mind letting me down first?"

"I can." She offered him a hand, which he took. "But I'm not the reason you're floating through the air. *You* are."

"I'm ..." Clarke pulled himself toward her, and she embraced him in midair. He was about to say something, but then paused in contemplation. The last few moments replayed in his mind: the awesome sex, something snapping within his mind, the eerie fire, them floating through the air.

Emma had mentioned it was his doing.

But that can't be right, he thought. *There's no way I could ...*

And then he found it, like a pebble under the tapestry of his mind. A disruption—no, a *presence* that hadn't been there before. He reached out to it within the confines of his own thoughts, took hold of it.

And *wielded* it.

He floated down to the floor, and Emma joined him with a cheerful clap.

"Wow, you're a natural!" she said, her voice full of genuine awe.

The green flames were gone now, but into their absence flooded a thousand new questions, least of which, again, was *What the fuck?* Somehow, he managed to voice it with more calm than he felt:

"Mind explaining what's going on?"

"Sure!" She smiled sweetly. "But you'll need to be patient. This could take a while."

"I have all night."

She guided him back to the couch and snuggled up next to him, her arm across his chest, thigh pressed against his. He doubted this was necessary, but she seemed to like it, and he didn't mind having her close.

"The short version is: You really are a blood knight," she said.

"You mean like in the campaign?"

"Yep! I picked up on your abilities at the start of the semester, but I could also tell they were being suppressed. Not much of a surprise there, to be honest."

"With a spell?"

She nodded.

"You mean like—" He almost said "like magic?" but then considered his current situation, seated beside a succubus after having floated placidly through the air. The question seemed both dumb and wholly unnecessary.

Emma tilted her head, waiting for him to continue.

"So, I can use magic?" he asked.

"You bet!"

"And I can fly, too?"

"More like float, at least for now. Seems you accidently used a Power Graft spell on me. That allowed you to absorb a small portion of my magic."

"Sorry?"

"No, no! Don't be." She rubbed a hand over his broad chest. "I didn't lose a thing, and you got to exercise one of your core powers. It's all good! And, truth be told, that spell wasn't the first you cast. Remember my 'lucky' die?"

"Yeah."

"Well, it's actually *un*-lucky. It's weighted to favor rolls of one. But your magic kicked in while we were playing. *You* pushed it to a higher number, even if you didn't realize it. Minor Telekinesis is one of your cantrips."

"Now that you mention it, that roll did seem a bit wonky. And I was a little lightheaded right after." He grimaced, struggling to absorb all this new information. "So, that … suppression spell you mentioned is gone now, right?"

"Yep! That green light we saw? That was it flaring out."

"What sort of spell was it, exactly?"

As if I have any frame of reference! he thought.

"What you had is called a vampiric Antimagic Hex. You probably acquired yours at an early age, well before puberty, which is when most people's abilities *should* manifest." She shrugged. "The vampires are thorough like that."

"You mean some vampire hexed me while I was a kid."

"Well, that's what they *used* to do. Nowadays, they

use social media to propagate their control spells."

"They *what?*"

"Didn't I mention this? Big Tech is managed by vampires."

"No, you didn't. Is that why I could never find your Facebook account?"

Emma grinned. "You looked?"

"Well—of course!" Clarke spluttered. He wasn't sure why he was so embarrassed by it, given what they'd just done, but what the hell. It had been a long evening.

"One of the reasons." She smiled, then snuggled closer to him. "Also, social media is where people go to pick fights and get themselves fired. I'd steer clear of it even if vampires didn't control the whole thing."

"I guess I can't argue with that." He sighed. "So, you managed to dispel the hex holding me back?"

"*We* dispelled it! Together!"

"During sex?"

"Well"—she batted her eyes at him—"I *am* a succubus. Sex magic is sort of my thing."

"Point taken."

"Plus, the campaign helped, too. Ashley wove some spells into the narrative to help soften up the hex."

"Yeah, about that." Clarke shifted around so he could look her in the eyes. "How much of her campaign is fiction?"

"Very little."

"So, Brooke and Sammy are, what? Demihumans, too?"

"Yep! See, you're getting it."

"I take it they're not succubi, though."

"Nope!"

"Which means Brooke's a werewolf."

"She prefers to be called a wolf girl."

"I'll have to remember that. And that means Sammy's a slime."

"Slime *girl*."

"Got it. What about Ashley?"

"She's a celestial."

"A celestial? You mean like the creature type in Pathfinder?"

Emma nodded cheerfully.

"That means she's, what? An angel or something?"

"Actually, we're not entirely sure. And neither is she, to be perfectly honest."

"How's *that* work?"

"Well, her halo got busted when she portaled to Earth, so she's been out of contact with her plane of origin. Her memories got a bit scrambled in the process, too. Probably as a result of vampiric hexes placed on transplanar travel. *Anyway*, she's using her halo as a headband until it regenerates."

"Incredible," Clarke breathed, shaking his head.

"We're all pretty sure she's here to help us with the vampires, though. She's the one who broke my hex, and then the two of us helped out Brooke and Sammy."

Clarke raised an eyebrow. "How, exactly?"

"Oh, I think you know." Emma ran her fingers lightly across his abs, then danced a bit lower. Clarke found his mind suddenly filled with images of steamy demigirl sex.

"I think I do."

"Oh, this is so exciting!" Emma snuggled up to him once more. "Now that you're here—and we have access to all your awesome blood magic—we can finally start a *real* campaign against the vampires!"

"Yeah," Clarke agreed without thinking, before the meaning behind her words fully registered. Before he realized she wasn't talking about a pen-and-paper campaign anymore.

His eyes widened in surprise.

"Wait. What do you mean 'real'?"

CHAPTER FOUR

COUNTLESS QUESTIONS FOUGHT for attention in Clarke's head. What had he stumbled into, and where did it end?

"You're talking about a *real* campaign against the vampires?"

Emma began to nod, but then her head bob turned into an epic yawn.

"Oh, wow." She shook the tail end of the yawn away. "It's really hitting me."

"What is?"

"I feel a food coma coming on." She patted her stomach.

No, not her stomach. A bit lower than that.

"You were absolutely scrumptious, but I'd like a bit of a lie down. Mind if we get cozy in bed?"

"Sure."

Emma rose from the couch, every inch of her glorious, naked body presented to him as if she were a feast for his eyes only, her wings peeking out behind her slender shoulders, her long tail whipping back and forth. She took his hand, led him into the back of her apartment, and opened what he presumed to be her bedroom door.

He wasn't sure what he expected at this point. What did succubi prefer to sleep on? Hell if he knew. Maybe a four-poster bed with black, gothic curtains surrounded by flickering candelabras?

The reality was rather mundane. And, if he was being honest with himself, a little disappointing.

It was just a bed.

A very ordinary, very practical bed.

The comforter was pastel pink.

Emma slipped under the sheets, shuffled to the side, and held her arm out invitingly. Clarke joined her on the bed, and she cuddled up to him, tail coiling around one of his legs. She pressed her cheek against his chest, smiling contently as if he were the best pillow ever.

Clarke wrapped his arms around her, but stopped when she let out a sudden squeak.

"Careful with the wings. They tickle."

"Sorry. You're my first succubus."

"You sure about that? A strapping guy like you?"

"Pretty sure I would have noticed the extra bits."

She closed her eyes and nuzzled his chest.

"So … about this campaign you mentioned."

"Later." She breathed in deeply. "That food coma's hitting hard."

"You sure we can't talk for a little longer? I just found out vampires and demihumans exist! I've got, like, a million questions I want to ask."

Clarke waited as her chest rose and fell rhythmically against his.

"Emma?"

She let out a sputtering exhale and then began to snore.

Emma snored like a buzzsaw.

It was kind of cute. Until it wasn't.

Clarke's mind buzzed with a different kind of noise: the cacophony of thoughts that refused to be silent. His entire world had been turned upside down and inside out over the course of a single evening, and he did *not* want to wait till dawn for more answers.

But he did wait. He let Emma slumber peacefully, her limbs and tail entangling him, and eventually he found himself dozing off.

He awoke the next morning to a most curious—and

pleasant—sensation centered around his groin.

"Mmm."

He stretched under the comforter, eyes blinking from the soft morning light glowing through the draped window. He rubbed the sleep out of his eyes, becoming more alert with each second, more cognizant of his surroundings.

He blinked once more and arched his neck enough to take in the bed.

The comforter formed a mound over his legs.

And it was bobbing up and down.

Clarke grabbed the edge of the comforter and tossed it aside.

Emma met his gaze with sultry eyes, his dick deep in her throat.

"Good morning, Beautiful," he said.

"'Oogh 'ornin'." Her wings fluttered in what might have been a handless wave.

"I guess this brings new meaning to 'bed and breakfast,' doesn't it?"

Emma chuckled around his shaft, then pulled up off him. She kissed his tip and traced gentle fingers down its length.

"You don't mind, do you?"

"Not one bit." He held out an open palm. "Please, enjoy your breakfast."

"Yay!"

She swallowed his shaft all the way down to the base, and then slowly rose up off it. Clarke closed his eyes and rested his head back on the pillow, relishing the sensations. She brought him to the edge of climax then managed to hold him there, almost as if she were savoring the anticipation of release before finally taking him deep, pushing him over the precipice.

He poured his hot, thick excitement down her throat, and she swallowed every drop.

"So good!" she exclaimed, grinning ear to ear. She sat back, straddling his legs. "So damn good! We need to do this more often!"

"You won't get any complaints from me."

"And don't think I've forgotten you." She climbed off him and rose to her feet at the foot of the bed. "One good breakfast deserves another. How's bacon and waffles sound to you?"

"Like a fantastic idea."

"Great! Give me a few minutes to get everything ready. You take your showers in the morning or evening?"

"Normally evenings." He flashed a quick, unashamed smile. "I was preoccupied last night."

"You and me both! Why don't you get a shower then? The bathroom's right through that door. I should have breakfast ready around the time you come out."

"Sounds great, Emma. Thanks."

Clarke tossed aside the comforter. He collected his clothes from the living room and headed for the shower.

The savory aroma of bacon greeted him when Clarke came out of the bedroom, his hair damp and unruly, though the rest of him was dressed and presentable.

"Hey, there!" Emma waved her spatula at him from behind the kitchen counter. She'd put on a black-and-white striped T-shirt and a black pleated skirt, which made her resemble an escaped convict plucked from an old movie. Or maybe a strip club. A white apron capped off the ensemble, complete with cheerful balloon text on the front.

It read "Kiss the Cook," because of course it did. Her wings and tail were nowhere to be seen.

"Hey, yourself." Clarke leaned against the threshold, a half-smile on his lips.

"What's that look for?"

"Just surprised you're not pulling a 'naked apron.'"

"Not with bacon grease to contend with." She smiled at him. "But I'll keep that in mind for future meals. You bring your appetite?"

"Absolutely."

"Good, because I made lots!"

Emma used tongs to heap the hot bacon onto one of

two plates then set both onto the counter. Clarke's eyes widened when he saw his. A triple-decker waffle served with a dollop of whipped cream on top, drizzled with maple syrup and garnished with fresh strawberries. The bacon was thin and crispy with a sheen of fat sizzling on the surface.

"Chocolate chips in the waffles?" Clarke asked, settling onto one of the stools.

"Yeah. Don't you like chocolate?"

"No, I *love* chocolate."

"Oh, good." She placed a hand over her chest and let out a relieved sigh. "You had me worried there for a second."

"Worried about what?" Clarke asked, picking up his knife and fork.

"That you might not like the food."

"Emma, please." He began to cut into the waffle stack. "You just woke me up with the best blowjob of my life, and followed that with a freshly cooked meal." He placed a forkful of waffles and whipped cream into his mouth and chewed. "Which is *delicious!*"

"Yay! Glad you like it."

"Trust me, Emma. After last night and this morning, it's going to take a lot more than ingredients I don't like to sour my opinion of you." He took another indulgent bite. "Though I do still have questions about the *rest* of last night."

"I still want everything to go well." She leaned forward on the counter, offering him a deep view of her cleavage. "You may not realize this, but you're the lynchpin to our campaign."

"The one against the vampires who control the world."

"That would be it."

"So, about that …"

"You have questions, I know. And I'll do my best to answer them, but some stuff will need to wait until we're all present. Also"—she pushed off the counter and untied her apron—"mind if I grab a quick shower first? I like to take mine in the morning. Helps me wake up."

"Sure. Go ahead." Clarke indicated the triple-decker waffle. "I'll be a while."

"Thanks!"

Emma hung up her apron and rounded the counter. He grabbed his phone out of his jeans and was about to check the news when she placed a hand on his shoulder.

"Clarke, quick note."

"Yeah?"

"You might want to switch your phone off. At least until Ashley can look it over and work her magic."

"Why? Are vampires going to check my browser history?"

"Probably not, but it doesn't hurt to play it safe."

"Fair enough." Clarke switched off his phone and pocketed it.

"That was easy. I thought you might argue about the phone."

"Hey, I'm just going with the flow. At least, until I get some answers." He gave her a meaningful look.

"Coming as soon as I finish my shower. Also, why don't you practice some magic while you wait?"

"Sure, but how? Do you have—I don't know—a spell book or something?"

"Oh, right! Almost forgot!" Emma hurried over to the coffee table, still with dice and papers scattered over it from last night. She grabbed the three-ring binder he'd printed out and planted it on the counter next to him. "Your spellbook, good sir!"

"Seriously?" Clarke gave the binder an incredulous eye.

"Yep! Ashley made sure your spells were accurate, so go on and give them a whirl." She paused before glancing worriedly around her apartment. "But maybe steer clear of the heavy hitters. I don't want to lose my deposit."

"No magical blasts while inside your apartment. Got it." He opened the binder and leafed over to the spell list. "Can all demihumans use magic?"

"Not all of them, but most can. Each species has different strengths and weaknesses."

"Like your sex magic."

"Exactly!"

"Are there a lot of different species."

"Oh, *tons*! Why, just at the university, you can find fey, elves, orcs." She crossed her arms and looked up. "A lot of orcs on the football team, now that I think about it. Also, there are several breeds of shifters roaming around, a few red or silver dragonkin, and even a mermaid, if you can believe it! Don't know why her parents sent her to school this far inland. I wouldn't recommend dating her, by the way."

"Wasn't contemplating it, but okay. I'll keep that in mind."

"Trust me. She's not worth the trouble. The first question you'll get is 'How long can you hold your breath, Sexy?' Even I wouldn't touch that, and I'm a succubus!"

"You mentioned dragonkin. Any genuine dragons roaming around?"

"Not anymore. They're all dead."

"Why? What happened to them?"

"The usual. They were hunted to extinction centuries ago. Mostly by humans enthralled by vampires. The bloodsuckers don't like competition, and the dragons were definitely competition."

Clarke felt an unexpected pang of loss at that. It was one thing to learn that the vampires were feeding on humans. Horrible as it was, it was also a predictable part of the whole vampire gig, which was probably why he hadn't been all that disturbed by it yet. He knew his emotions would catch up eventually.

This, though, was just weird enough to register a reaction. Without even knowing it, he'd lived in a world that once had dragons in it—*motherfucking dragons!*—but the vampires had killed them all before he could even be *aware* of their wonder. He was still wrapping his mind around what the vampires' influence meant in practical, everyday terms, but if they could obliterate something as amazing as dragons, what else had the world lost because of them?

"Anyway, you enjoy your meal." She gave his shoulder a quick pat. "I'll be right back!"

Her perkiness felt incongruous, relative to what was going through his head, but it did remind him of another question:

"Emma? Just one more thing before you go."

"Sure, but just the one."

"What exactly *is* a blood knight?"

"Oh, that?" She smiled. "Why, they're vampire slayers, of course!" She gave him a wink before disappearing into the bathroom.

"How's the practice going?" Emma asked, returning to the kitchen counter with her hair freshly blow-dried.

"I was able to move the butter tray without touching it."

"You were? How far?"

"Only about a foot off the counter and back."

"That's fantastic!"

"Are you being sincere? I can't tell."

"Hey, everyone's got to start somewhere, and we just busted your hex. I call moving the butter a big win!"

"Sure, but 'Mover of Butter' doesn't quite scream 'vampire slayer,' now does it?"

"One step at a time, Clarke. One step at a time."

"Mind if I ask another question now?"

"You can ask *all* the questions!" She sat on the stool next to him and crossed her legs. "Just no promises I'll have the answers."

"That's fair, I suppose." He closed the ring binder. "I'm still trying to wrap my head around all this. So, there are demihumans mixed in with humans."

"Yep."

"And those demihumans come in a wide variety of species."

"Very wide."

"Then are there whole families of demihumans? Whole sub-societies? Are your parents succubi?"

"Well, technically, my dad's an incubus. But, yeah. You're pretty much on the mark."

"Then does Brooke come from a family of werewolves? And Sammy from a family of slimes?"

"Yes to the first. No to the second." Emma waved her hand vaguely. "It can get complicated. And personal. Better to ask them yourself if you're curious."

"Okay. But the important part is there are whole demihuman families, many of which can use magic."

"Right you are."

"But humanity doesn't know they're there?"

"Because of the vampiric control spells," Emma said with a nod.

"And they also use hexes?"

"Yep. Like the one you had."

"Which was preventing me from using my blood magic?"

"Exactly."

"Then can other humans use magic, too? Or are blood knights unique?"

"No, there are other human mages. Witches and warlocks are the most common, but there are others. They tend to stick to themselves and keep their heads down."

"And the vampires don't go after them?"

"As long as they don't cause trouble. Vampires may control the world, but they can't be everywhere at once. Vampiric spells and hexes are powerful, but they're not foolproof." Emma rubbed a hand across his thigh, her eyes suddenly smoky. "As we so recently demonstrated."

"Do the hexes affect demihumans the same as

everyone else?"

"Not as strongly. The magic is optimized to work on humans, so it's naturally less effective against other species. How effective depends a lot on the spell and the race. For example, I could barely hover before Ashley removed my hex."

"Then what keeps the demihumans in line?"

"Intimidation. Power. You name it, the vampires use it to keep us demihumans down."

"Sounds like drawing a vampire's attention is a bad thing."

"Can be. No doubts there."

"Which is what you and the other ladies want to do?"

"*We-e-e-e-ell* … yes and no."

"That's not much of an answer."

"Okay, yes, we want to stir up trouble." She held up a finger. "But we have a plan."

"I hope it's a good one." Clarke pushed his plate aside and shifted to face Emma. "So, what kind of vampires are we dealing with?"

"What kind …" She blinked. "Oh, right! Sometimes it's easy for me to forget you don't know."

"There are a lot of fictional vampires."

"Right, right. Well, for starters, you can take all the usual weaknesses—garlic, silver, holy symbols, etcetera—and throw them all in the dumpster. They don't work."

"Vampiric propaganda?"

"More like misdirection. Garlic especially. That's a big in-joke amongst vampires, from what I hear. They like it when the 'cattle' seasons themselves, especially the Italian vampires."

"And by 'cattle,' you mean humans?"

"Yes, unfortunately."

"Then, they do drink human blood?"

"Yep."

"What about demihumans?"

"They feed on, too, though demihuman feeding is rarer."

"They prefer the blood of regular humans?"

"Preference isn't the right word. It has more to do with politics than diet. They don't want to antagonize the demi-cattle, if you catch my meaning, so they feed almost exclusively off the general populace. The rare vampires who break that rule tend not to last long."

"They're made examples of? By other vampires?"

"Or by the demihumans they were snacking on. Either way, those sorts of troublemakers get sorted out, and what passes for equilibrium gets restored. Vampires don't like it when demihumans kill one of their kin, but they'll turn a blind eye in certain cases. Anyway, back to the whole diet thing, vampires are omnivores like regular humans, but they can only replenish their mana by ingesting blood. Every species with magical abilities recharges differently, and that's how they do it."

"How powerful are they, really?"

"Very, but not in the way you'd expect. You know how vampires are typically portrayed? Powerful, graceful, beautiful, and absolutely lethal? Well, that's all a load of bull! Movie vampires are what you might call a vampiric power fantasy. It's what they *wish* they saw when they looked in the mirror each morning! Vampires can look like anyone, *be* anyone. They don't appear any different from everyday humans if their fangs are retracted."

"They cast reflections in mirrors?"

"Yeah, that ain't true, either!" Emma gave him a bemused headshake. "Now, all that said, they *are* dangerous. Very, *very* dangerous. They're stronger, faster, and more durable than regular humans, and they have a wide range of powerful magics at their disposal. The exact type of magic varies from one vampire to the other. They're also difficult to put down for good, capable of recovering from most injuries. If you need to kill one, go for the heart or the head. Those are both kill shots."

"What about sunlight?"

"Now that's an interesting one. Sunlight doesn't bother them directly, but it *will* interfere with their magic."

"Vampires are weaker in sunlight, then?"

"Yeah, but they know it, too. Which is why they normally take precautions when venturing out during the day."

"Why all the cloak-and-dagger if they're so power-ful? Why not rule openly?"

"Because there are so few of them. No one knows exactly how many vampires there are in the world; they work hard to keep it that way, but most estimates put their numbers in the tens of thousands."

"That's a *lot* of vampires."

"True, but when you compare that to the billions of humans on the planet, a few tens of thousands doesn't seem so large anymore."

"Why are there so few?" Clarke asked. "How are vampires created? Can you become one by being bitten?"

"No, it's not that simple. You don't have to worry about being 'infected' or anything like that. First, there are two basic categories of vampires: purebloods and risen. A union between two vampires of either kind will result in a vampiric child. Those vampires are considered purebloods. Next, you have vampires created through a combination of magic and vampire blood. Those are the risen."

"Pureblood and risen, got it. Am I right in assuming the purebloods are the more dangerous of the two?"

"Typically, yes, though the risen can get pretty darn powerful as they age. The big limit on risen is lifespan. They don't live any longer than regular humans, whereas purebloods can survive for centuries."

"What about—"

The doorbell rang, and Clarke turned sharply in his seat.

"Come in, Ash!" Emma called out. "It's unlocked!"

The door opened, spilling light into the living room. Ashley walked in, backlit by the sun, which rendered her hair as bright as golden fire. She strode in across the hardwood floor, clad in a cream crisscross halter top and matching slacks, a woven leather belt looped around her waist.

Clarke checked the wall clock out of curiosity. The time was exactly nine o'clock.

Ashley walked straight over to Clarke and placed a hand on his shoulder.

"A good morning to you, too," he said dryly.

"Morning," Ashley replied without much feeling, then closed her eyes. Her hairband grew brighter.

"What's she doing?" Clarke whispered.

"Checking out the hex."

"I can hear you two just fine," Ashley said, eyes still closed. "Also, I'm trying to concentrate."

"Sorry!" Emma clapped a hand over her mouth.

Ashley held her pose for over a minute, during which Clarke waited in patient silence. She withdrew her hand and nodded, her hairband dimming.

"I see everything went well last night."

"It went spectacularly!" Emma replied with a grin.

"I can imagine." Ashley turned to Clarke. "Then, are you ready to join Toothache?"

"Join *what*?"

"Our anti-vampiric resistance cell."

"You call yourselves *Toothache*?" Clarke turned back to Emma. "Seriously?"

"I told them." Emma put a hand to her brow and hung her head. "I *told* them we needed a better name."

"What's wrong with Toothache?" Ashley asked, sounding perfectly sincere in her question.

"*Everything.*"

"It's simple to remember and can be concealed easily in regular speech."

"It's lame as hell! We might as well say we spread minty freshness and fight cavities while we're at it!"

"Brooke and Sammy both seem fond of it."

"You know Sammy's just trolling us, don't you?"

"She is?"

"Yes, Ash! And as for Brooke, she only likes it because it was her idea!"

"Then come up with a better one."

"I already did! The Transplanar Vampire Killers!"

"Hard veto."

"Why? It says exactly what we are in the name."

"Which is a problem for an underground organization."

"Clarke, back me up here." Emma draped an arm over his shoulders. "Would you rather we be called Trans-planar Vampire Killers"—she glared at Ashley—"or *Toothache?*"

"I, uh, well …"

Both women watched him expectantly. It surprised him how being stuck between two beautiful ladies could make him feel this uncomfortable.

"Well, I think both options have some merits and, perhaps, some shortcomings," he said as delicately as he could. "Have you considered that, maybe, you haven't landed on the right option yet?"

"The suggestion box is open," Ashley said simply.

Emma leaned close, eyes bright, one breast smooshed against his arm.

"Got any ideas?" she asked.

Clarke frowned. Yes, he was being dragged into this whether he liked it or not.

He considered the matter.

Vampires, he thought.

Vampires all have fangs, right?

The ladies want to strike a blow against them. At least, that seems to be the case.

"What's your long-term goal?" he asked.

"To break the vampiric stranglehold on the world!" Emma declared with an excited shake of her fist.

"You don't aim low, do you?"

"Hey. It's good to have stretch goals."

"I suppose."

To break their grip on the world.

Breaking …

Breaking …

Breaking …

"How about … Broken Fang?"

He paused hopefully, eyes darting from Emma to Ashley and back.

"You know what?" the succubus said. "I like it. It's a little understated. Not quite as flashy as Transplanar Vampire Killers, but it works."

"I can tolerate it," Ashley said indifferently. "So, are you willing to join?"

"I still have a *lot* of questions," Clarke said.

"That's to be expected."

"But, the answer's yes. I'm on board with striking a blow against monsters who eat people."

"Drink their blood," Ashley corrected.

"Whatever. The important part is I'm in."

"Wonderful." She gestured toward the door. "Shall we go see the others?"

CHAPTER FIVE

"I'LL DRIVE!" Emma grabbed her keys and purse.

"I'll text the others, then," Ashley said, retrieving her phone. "Let them know to meet us there."

"Where are we going?" Clarke asked.

Emma waggled her eyebrows. "It's a *secret*."

"No, it's not," Ashley said, head down as she texted.

"It is if you're a vampire."

"None of us are vampires, Emma."

"Well, *obviously*."

"Is anyone going to tell me where we're headed?" Clarke asked.

"Just a quiet place beyond the city outskirts." Ashley pocketed her phone and looked up. "It's nothing special."

"Come on, Ash." Emma stopped by the door and

put a hand on her hip. "You can't talk about our secret base so casually."

"Whatever," Ashley sighed more than said. "Let's go."

"Also, Clarke? Might want to bring your spell book."

"Sure."

He grabbed the binder and followed the ladies out the door and to the apartment parking lot. They piled into Emma's car, a blue Volkswagen Jetta, which struck him as a typical college student's hand-me-down ride. Not all that different from his own wheels, though he noticed the exterior had been more recently washed than his and the interior was both free of trash and smelled faintly of lemon.

"Join me in the back?" Ashley asked.

"Sure."

He climbed into the seat behind Emma and buckled up. Emma started the car and pulled out of the parking lot.

"Let me see your phone," Ashley said.

He handed it over.

She switched it on, waited for it to boot up, then placed it in her lap and closed her eyes.

"What are you doing?"

"Replacing the spells infecting it. Don't worry. This won't take long."

"She's setting it up so you can use it freely," Emma said from the driver's seat.

"Yeah, I figured that'd be the case, given how you

two seem comfortable using yours."

"Still, I'd recommend staying off social media. All the big names are swimming with malicious spells, which can then get transferred to your phone and then to you."

"I'll keep that in mind." Clarke glanced over at Ashley, who hadn't moved since she started. "Anything else I should watch out for?"

"Tons, unfortunately. Social media's a recent addition to the vampiric control apparatus. Internet, television, movies, radio, newspapers, books, magazine. The list goes on and on. If it's something you read or watch, a vampire has used it. I even heard about vampires who'll use everything from restaurant menus to street signs to spread their spells."

"What do those spells do, anyway?"

"It varies, but most of them either suppress magic or work to keep people in the dark. You know how when you write a paper it's difficult to catch your own errors?"

"Don't I ever. I can read the same passage a dozen times, and every time I'll read a 'the' that isn't there. Why do you ask?"

"The control spells work on the same principle. It's just a difference in scope. People under their influence see and hear what their minds *expect* to be there, rather than what actually is."

"Then the vampires are essentially using everyone's imaginations and expectations against them?"

"Exactly."

"Kind of clever, if you ask me."

"The enemy is both cunning and powerful," Ashley said, opening her eyes. She handed the phone back to Clarke. "And they've had centuries to perfect their craft."

"That doesn't mean it's perfect, though," Emma said. "And some of their techniques can be used against them."

"What do you mean?"

"The spells Ash put on your phone? Basically, they're an inversion of the originals. The metadata being sucked off it will look like what the *vampires* expect to find, which will show you're just one more example of their ignorant cattle."

"Crafty." Clarke pocketed the phone. "How safe is it to use now?"

"Safe enough for most texts and calls," Ashley said. "But the risk isn't zero."

"How big a risk are we talking here?"

"You're on the wrong plane of existence if you want life to come with guarantees."

"Uh, excuse me?"

"Now, Ash," Emma said. "Be nice."

"I'd rather be helpful."

"You know you can be both at the same time, don't you?"

Ashley grimaced but didn't reply.

"Are you really from another plane?" Clarke asked.

"I ... think so?" Ashley's hairband dimmed, and she shrugged. "Probably?"

"You don't sound very certain."

"I'm not."

"That's just her crossed celestial wires talking," Emma said. "You think this is odd, you should have seen her a few months ago! She kept trying to go outside buck naked!"

Ashley crossed her arms. "I would appreciate it if you didn't mention that."

"Why not? It's a great story! Especially when you almost—"

"Please stop."

"Fine, fine." Emma glanced at her passengers through the rearview mirror. "Don't worry, Clarke. I'll tell you the story later. Next time you and I have some 'special time' together."

Ashley rolled her eyes.

Clarke observed her for a moment, trying to wrap his head around the concept that she was from another dimension. Somehow, he found it difficult to believe an angel—or whatever she was—could be this snippy. Still, he had to admit there was something ... otherworldly, for lack of a better term, about her beauty. Everything about her, from the luster of her hair to the complexion of her skin, was a little too perfect.

Both Emma and Ashley were undeniably sexy, but there was something grounded about Emma's allure. Something visceral and carnal and easy to grasp, even if it came with wings and a tail. In contrast, Ashley felt somehow out of his reach; he didn't really know why other than that's what his gut told him.

Who was she?

What was she?

"Hey, Ash?" Clarke asked. "Is it all right if I call you Ash?"

"I prefer Ashley, if you don't mind."

Emma chuckled.

"All right," Clarke said. "Ashley, then. How long have you been here?"

"You mean this city?"

"I was thinking more along the lines of this planet."

"I'm not sure."

"Years, maybe?"

"I'm sorry. I just don't know."

"Do you know where you were beforehand?"

"Somewhere else."

"That's pretty vague."

"I'm sorry." She frowned, looking genuinely disappointed in herself. "I wish I could share more, but my memories aren't entirely clear."

"All right. Maybe a different question, then. How

did you get so good at dealing with vampire magic?”

“I just am.”

“Just like that? Never learned the skill from anyone?”

“Maybe?” She shrugged her shoulders, an unsure expression on her too-perfect face. Her hairband dimmed.

“There are a lot of unknowns when it comes to Ash,” Emma said. “But one thing is for certain. She does *not* like vampires!”

“No, I don’t.”

“And a good thing, too, because she’s crazy good at countering their spells.”

“I know you may find some of my answers unsatisfying,” Ashley said, some of her confidence and poise returning. “But let me assure you of one thing. I know, with absolute certainty, that what the vampires have done to humanity—and *continue* to do—is wrong. And I give you my word that I will do *everything* within my power to stop them. To right this terrible wrong.”

“I believe you,” he said, and meant it.

“But.” She reached out to him, resting a delicate hand on his forearm. “There’s one thing I need *you* to understand.”

“What’s that?”

She looked straight at him, her blue eyes filled with a strange-yet-unmistakable vulnerability.

“Clarke, I can’t do this alone.”

Clarke gazed out the window, watching the scenery shift. Emma drove them through downtown Chester Creek, around a core of modest skyscrapers and past a long strip of quaint shops and local restaurants.

They'd stopped at a red light when something caught Clarke's eye. He leaned toward the window, staring at a group of teenagers waiting to cross the street. One of the guys possessed an impressive bulk, a shock of coarse black hair, and vividly green skin. He must have noticed Clarke staring because he spat on the sidewalk before extending his middle finger. His eyes were an unnatural red.

Clarke turned away.

"Noticing a difference, are you?" Emma asked. She must have caught his expression in the rearview mirror.

"You mean the guy with the green skin? The …"

"Orc. Yeah, that would be the one."

"Do his human friends know?"

"That he's an orc? Not anymore than you would have yesterday."

"Figured."

Clarke stole a quick glance back at the group of teens as they hurried across the street. No one else gave the greenskin a second glance. At least, no more than a group of unruly teens deserved.

"Did you catch his wood elf girlfriend?"

"No. Missed her." He watched the group duck into a frozen yogurt shop.

"She was the thin one with the beret that looked like a big, squashed tomato. You can tell by the shape of her ears. Pointier than yours, but not quite high elf sharpness."

The light turned green, and Emma drove on.

"I'm going to be playing catch up for a while, aren't I?" Clarke said.

"Don't worry. We'll help you through any rough patches."

"Thanks. By the way, you sure those two were dating?"

"Pretty sure." Emma tapped the side of her temple. "A succubus knows these things."

"But don't orcs and elves hate each other? Or is that another example of vampires making stuff up?"

"Nah, there's some old, bad blood between orcs and elves. It's a lot better than it was a century ago, but the tension is still there, simmering below the surface. I imagine their parents will have some choice words for the lovebirds when they find out. If they haven't already."

They cut through the suburbs around Chester Creek, past rundown homes only a few blocks away from gated communities with brick and stone mansions. The suburbs gave way to rolling hills dotted with old farmhouses, corn fields, and the remnants of once mighty forests.

"How much farther?" Clarke asked.

"Almost there."

Emma turned down a gravel sideroad and drove past the rusted remains of a guard kiosk. The windows were all broken, and the jagged end of its wooden barrier stuck out the side. The rest of the gate's beam lay in a ditch along the road, flaking red and white paint.

"I think I saw a 'no trespassing' sign back there," Clarke said.

"You don't say?" Emma replied.

They drove down the road, then turned onto an old parking lot with tall grass and a few small trees growing out of the cracks. Emma parked next to the only other vehicles on the lot: a gray Jeep Wrangler splattered with mud and a pristine, black-and-green Kawasaki Ninja. The parking lot ran adjacent to a collection of the buildings, some covered in rusted sheet metal, others with walls of brick and busted windows, all joined by covered bridges or walkways and dotted with towering stacks.

It looked like the kind of place parents in 80s movies would tell their kids not to sneak into, only for the kids to do just that and thus launch into a kickass and at least slightly horrifying adventure.

"We're here!" Emma stopped the car and climbed out.

Clarke joined her and Ashley beside the vehicle.

"What is this place?"

"An old steel mill."

"I feel like I'm going to contract tetanus just by looking at it. Maybe wake up a poltergeist or two."

"There are no poltergeists here. We'd know," Emma said. "It has the advantage of being a building no one uses anymore. I heard somewhere a bank owns the property. They've been trying to offload it for years but can't because no one wants to go through the hassle of clearing out the old structures."

Well, if Emma said there were no poltergeists, there were no poltergeists, which would have been a strange sentence except for his new perspective on the world. And *well*, he'd already decided to roll with it.

"How old is this place?"

"Not sure. The place went out of business before any of us were born." Emma glanced over at Ashley. "Well, us two at least. Ash, how old are you again?"

"Are you trying to get a rise out of me?"

"Come on." She gave the celestial a pat on the arm. "You know I'm just teasing."

"Who brought the crotch rocket?" Clarke asked, walking up to the Kawasaki motorcycle. It looked brand new.

"That's Sammy's," Emma said. "And before you ask, no, she doesn't let any of us ride it. You're free to try and ask her, though."

"I'll keep that in mind."

Emma led the way into the old mill, through a large set of double doors, one door swinging free at an angle off a single hinge, its base having carved a groove in the dirt. A heavy chain and lock lay on the ground, grass shooting up through its reddened links.

The interior was a nonsensical jumble of old, hulking machines, pipes, storage silos, elevated walkways, wheeled carts on rails, and other debris, all atop cracked concrete spackled with weeds. The sun's beams slipped through busted skylights, spilling across a central area free of most obstructions. Given the positioning of grassless patches on the floor, Clarke guessed the area had been cleared recently, though he wasn't sure how they'd managed to move all that heavy equipment aside. He glanced at a pipe segment large enough to crawl through, now resting against a concrete barrier.

Are those ... claw marks in the metal?

Brooke sat between the wheels of an upturned cart, and Sammy leaned against a silo. Brooke wore a baggy T-shirt with an artistic rendition of a boob window on the front over a pair of black, formfitting pants. A pair of comfy sandals bookended her casual ensemble.

Sammy sported a high-collared black leather jacket, black jeans, and a pair of black gloves. Her bike helmet contrasted those with a riot of colors, and her pixie cut had changed to purple with green highlights.

90

"Greetings, my fellow demis!" Emma said with a jubilant wave. "I bring you good tidings in our battle against evil!"

"Looks like it." Sammy took a moment to size Clarke up. "Should I assume last night went well?"

"*Very* well!" Emma slung an arm around his waist. "In more ways than one."

"He hex free?"

"Free and clear and already using magic!"

Sammy raised an eyebrow. "Already?"

"Just a little bit." Clarke held up his thumb and forefinger.

"Which is pretty good for his first day without a hex holding him back," Emma added.

Brooke and Sammy exchanged a quick look. Brooke gave the slime girl a shoulder shrug, but Sammy only crossed her arms and huffed out a breath.

"I thought you'd be more excited," Emma said.

"We are, don't get us wrong," Sammy said. "It's just Brooke and I have been talking. We have concerns."

"About what?"

"The plan. What else?"

"Hey there, Clarke." Brooke gave him a shy, little wave. "Nice to see you again."

"Nice to see you, too."

"Bet you didn't expect all this, huh?"

"You mean the magic, monsters, and a secret fight against vampires? Nope. Didn't see it coming."

"Oh, that reminds me!" Emma pointed urgently at Clarke. "He came up with a new name for our group."

"What's wrong with Toothache?" Brooke asked, sounding sad and a little offended.

"Uh, nothing, nothing," Emma replied quickly. "But this one is better."

"Let's hear it, then," Sammy said.

"Ladies and gentle knight"—Emma spread her arms—"we are now called … Broken Fang!"

"Don't we get to vote on it?" Brooke asked.

"Already did. Three in favor. That's a majority."

"Aww." Brooke slouched on the cart.

"You know, 'Broken Fang' is actually pretty good," Sammy said. "Consider it four to one. I even like it more than that planar nonsense you kept pushing."

"Transplanar Vampire Killers," Emma corrected stiffly.

"Yeah. That one."

"But I thought you liked the name Toothache," Brooke said sadly.

Sammy snorted out a laugh, which only made Brooke frown more deeply.

"Let's not get sidetracked," Ashley said. "What's this about concerns?"

"The plan." Sammy pointed to Brooke. "As in, our

place at the tip of the spear. You're asking us to do a lot of the heavy lifting. No offense, but we don't know what Clarke's capable of yet."

"We'll be taking most of the risks," Brooke added.

"You know we don't have any other choice," Ashley said.

"I know, but still …"

"Hold on a second." Clarke turned to Emma. "Does this mean it'll be just me, Brooke, and Sammy going after the vampires?"

"Pretty much."

"I thought we were all in this together."

"We are."

"Then what's Sammy talking about?"

"It means these two"—Sammy pointed at the succubus and celestial—"will be hanging back."

"I'm more of a lover than a fighter." Emma shrugged. "Sorry!"

"And I don't fight," Ashley said with finality.

"Okay, I guess it makes sense to send in your best combatants," Clarke said. "But I'm still not clear on what the plan actually *is*."

"Wait a second." Sammy stood up off the machinery. "You haven't gone over that with him yet?"

"There's been a lot of ground to cover," Emma replied sternly.

"Fine, sure, but the plan is a really important part of all this! How can he agree to help if he doesn't know what he's leaping into?"

"He knows—"

"This is a problem," Ashley cut in, "with a very simple solution. We'll start by reviewing the plan." She pulled over a rickety wooden chair. "I hereby call this meeting of Broken Fang to order."

"Clarke, would you like to sit down?" Brooke shuffled to the side and wiped off a spot.

He was about to turn her down when Emma gave him a little shove forward. He gave her a confused glance, but she only winked at him before she sat down on an upturned bucket.

"Thanks, Brooke."

Clarke joined her on the cart. She smiled warmly at him, her hands resting on her knees.

"Hey," she said, her eyes twinkling.

"Hey yourself."

"To start off," Emma began, "we're confident there are three vampires operating in or around the Chester Creek University. We suspect none of them have teamed up, giving us three distinct factions vying for control of the territory."

"Why's that?" Clarke asked. "Why wouldn't they cooperate?"

"Vampires are fiercely territorial by nature. They're secretive and tend to look out for Number One above all else. That doesn't mean there aren't exceptions, but a large vampiric organization almost always requires a powerful vampire at its head in order to force the others to submit. Fortunately, we've seen no evidence of such an individual, which means the three we're dealing with will be on their own."

"A fact we plan to take advantage of," Ashley said. "With three relatively isolated vampires contesting the same territory, we'll be able to move against them one by one."

"But won't our actions cause them to unite and come after us?" Clarke asked.

"Only if they realize what's really going on. With smart use of my magic, we should be able to remain undetected. Which means the vampires will suspect one of their rivals is making a move, not us. And that's if they realize anything is going on at all."

"That part's fine," Sammy said. "But tell him about the big problem."

"Right," Emma said. "Unfortunately, we only know who one of the vampires is. Doctor Otto Heinrich."

"*What?!*" Clarke blurted, almost bolting off the cart. "Our calculus professor?"

Emma nodded.

"*He's* a bloodsucking vampire?"

Emma nodded again.

"The same man who volunteers at the animal shelter?"

She nodded once more.

"But he seems so … so …"

"Harmless?"

"Yes!"

"That's exactly what he'd want people to think. Including his rivals."

Doctor Heinrich was a tall, thin man of German descent with white creeping into his blonde hair. He always showed up to class with a button-down shirt, suspenders, and a bowtie. He didn't speak with a pronounced accent—maybe the barest hint of one—but he had this strange habit of mispronouncing the word "squared," which he often mangled into "squid."

"Doc Heinrich." Clarke shook his head. "I even like his classes."

"We lucked out there," Emma said. "His facade is good, but with enough time around him, I was able to pick out the clues. He's one of our vampires; no questions there."

"Using that empathic sense of yours?"

"Exactly!"

"I guess I shouldn't expect the vampires to show up in formal wear sporting prominent widow's peaks."

"Yeah, they don't do that. Unless they're trying to be too clever for their own good."

"What do you mean?"

"What vampire in his right mind would dress like Bela Lugosi? So, obviously, some of them at some point figured that was the *perfect* way to stay hidden."

"That sounds like a really stupid way to stay hidden."

"Well, the thing to remember about vampires is they come in all varieties. Same as regular people."

"Including the really dumb ones?"

"Yep. Just a whole lot more dangerous."

"Getting back to the underlying problem," Ashley said, "what we lack most right now is information. We need to know who the other two vampires are before we can make a move on any of them. Which means our first priority is acquiring that information."

"How, though?" Clarke asked. "Load up Emma's schedule with classes until she happens to run across the other two?"

"Fortunately, we won't need anything so random. Heinrich will have a grimoire: a combination spell book and journal. It will contain any intelligence he's gathered on his rivals. We'll steal that first."

"A physical journal? Not a file on a computer?"

"The records will be handwritten. No vampire in their right mind would archive their deepest secrets in digital format. Not with the Big Tech vampires sucking in everyone's metadata. Heinrich may be a vampiric loner, but we haven't seen any evidence he's a fool. He'll have a physical grimoire."

"Okay. So, Step One is to grab his grimoire. What's Step Two?"

"Go after the three vampires and free the university from their control."

"Right. And then?"

Ashley grimaced.

"You do have a Step Three, right?"

Ashley and Emma exchanged an awkward glance. Brooke shifted uncomfortably next to him, and Sammy cleared her throat noisily.

"Say we take out all three vampires?" he continued. "What then? What's the next step we take to free the world from vampiric control?"

"We … don't really have that figured out yet," Ashley admitted.

"You see why we have concerns?" Sammy asked.

"Yeah," Clarke said. "I'm seeing it."

"All I can say," Ashley began, "is I know Chester Creek—and the university specifically—are important to my mission here."

"But what is your mission? Do you even know that much?"

"I … don't." Ashley lowered her head, and her hairband dimmed until it was almost black.

The old mill fell silent for long, uncomfortable seconds. Eventually, Sammy spoke up.

"Look, it's not that we're opposed to killing ourselves some vampires. And, I guess, Brooke and I agree that starting small, starting at CCU, is a smart way to approach this. Plus, stealing Heinrich's grimoire makes sense as our first step along that path. But the fact of the matter is we need to make sure this team has the wits and muscle to take on a vampire before we agree to help."

"Yep," Brooke said, nodding.

"We need proof we"—Sammy indicated all of them with a sweeping gesture—"have what it takes before I'm willing to stick my proverbial neck out."

"Me, too," Brooke said.

"Which means what, exactly?" Ashley asked.

"None of us have ever met a blood knight before. Who can say if they live up to the hype? So, what I want is proof Clarke is all he's cracked up to be."

Brooke nodded in agreement, then turned back to Sammy, who continued:

"Those are my conditions—*our* conditions—and we're sticking to our guns. You can either accept them or find yourselves some new muscle."

"What kind of proof are you expecting?" Emma asked. "It hasn't been twenty-four hours since we cleared his hex."

"I want to see him in action. Gauge for myself if he has what it takes."

"We both do," Brooke added.

"Wait a second." Clarke rose from the cart and stepped forward until he was in between all four ladies. "Are you talking about a fight? A *real* one?"

"It doesn't have to be all out," Sammy clarified. "Just enough for us to see what you're made of."

"I have a strict policy against hitting girls."

Sammy flashed a sinister grin. "In case you missed the news flash, we're not exactly your average girls."

"Don't worry," Brooke said. "We know you're still getting the feel for your powers. You can go at us with everything you've got."

"That's ..."

Beware my slowly moving butter tray! he thought sarcastically.

"You want me to fight both of you?"

"Yep," Sammy said.

"At the same time?"

"You've got it."

"This is a bad idea."

"Look at it this way." She stepped over to him. "This is as much for you as it is for us. If you can't handle the two of us when we're pulling our punches, then you've got zero chance against a full-power vampire. Best learn that now than when you're neck deep in dire rats and hellhounds."

"I suppose you have a point—" Clarke blinked as his brain caught up with his ears. "Wait a second. Hellhounds are *real?*"

"Yeah, and vampires can summon far worse than a few hellish mutts." Sammy placed a black gloved hand on his shoulder. "Think you're up for this?"

"Not really," he said with a sigh, but then straightened his shoulders. "But you only live once."

"That's the spirit! Can you summon a thirstblade yet?"

"Nope."

"That's going to be a problem."

"I can fix that," Brooke said.

She headed over to a tangle of thin, rusted pipes, maybe small air or water lines. She found one she liked and spread the fingers of one hand. Something glinted at the tips of her fingers, and she swiped at the pipe. Metal sang, and the pipe segment clattered to the ground. She picked it up and jogged over to Clarke.

"Here. You can swing this at us."

"Thanks …" Clarke accepted the pipe with a mild hint of trepidation. It was roughly the length of his arm. One side ended in decayed threads while the other sparkled from a new, clean cut.

She just cut through a metal pipe like it was nothing! he thought. *With her bare hands!*

"All right!" Sammy pumped the air with both fists. "Let's do this!"

CHAPTER SIX

"THIS IS A BAD IDEA," Clarke said, holding his pipe like a twohanded blade.

"Oh, it'll be fine," Emma said. "The worst they'll do is rough you up a bit."

"You're not helping."

"Just think of them as the tutorial boss. Like a skill check gatekeeping the rest of the adventure."

"Just so long as they're not trying to mimic one of those brutal FromSoft tutorials."

Emma chuckled, then gave him a playful pat on the butt. "Go get 'em, Sexy!"

"All right. All right."

Clarke took up his position on one side of the concrete pad while Brooke and Sammy prepared on the other. Sammy took her leather gloves off and stuffed them into her coat pockets while Brooke …

Concentrated?

"Are you all right?" Clarke asked.

"Never better!" Brooke strained like she was a shonen anime hero about to spend twenty episodes on a power up. Instead, her human ears morphed, shooting up into the tall, furred triangles while a tail sprouted from her behind, its fur matching the luster of her brunette hair. On the strength of that strain, he'd half expected her to go full wolf with exaggerated muscles, but he didn't mind this version at all. She stretched luxuriantly, arms high over her head as she cracked her knuckles, then she let her arms down, shook them out, and rolled her neck in a circle, breaking in her modified form.

Clarke raised a wary eyebrow.

"What?" Brooke asked, scratching behind a wolf ear. The whites of her eyes were now a vivid yellow, but she'd changed in more unexpected ways, too.

"Are you taller now?"

"A little. Heavier, too, though please don't ask me how much."

"That violates the conservation of mass."

"Eh." Brooke shrugged. "Shifter magic."

"You ready for us?" Sammy asked, flexing her fingers. "Just so you know, the gloves are off."

"Literally, I see."

"An important detail in my case." She flashed that ominous smile again.

"Right …" Clarke spread his feet, settling into a fighting stance.

A decade of Karate lessons meant he wasn't completely green when it came to fights. His parents had enrolled him in the local Karate club to help with his self-esteem issues, and the lessons had done just that. As an added bonus, the first truly terrible bully he'd faced in high school had quickly learned not to mess with him. Granted, it had taken blood-splattered knuckles and a nose hanging at the wrong angle to get the point across, but a win was a win.

He knew how to throw a solid punch and could keep his balance during a fight, distribute his weight smartly while on the move. He'd also dabbled in Kendo, but hadn't stuck with it the way he had with Karate. Still, those starter lessons meant he at least knew the basics of how to handle a sword. However, something told him all these skills were about to meet their match *and then some* against these two women.

"Ready when you are," Sammy said. "We'll even give you the first swing. As long as it's against Brooke."

"Hey, now!" The wolf girl gave her a cross look.

Clarke thought back to the campaign last night and how it paralleled his new reality in so many ways. He didn't doubt for a second Brooke could take a full-strength swing from him, even if she didn't bother to block. She'd been the party bruiser: strong, fast, and difficult to kill. In contrast, Sammy had lacked the wolf girl's raw power and stats, but she'd compensated with a plethora of dangerous abilities.

Such as touch-inflicted ailments.

Clarke's eyes darted to the slender woman's bare hands. Yes, indeed. The gloves were off for a reason.

There really isn't a good option here, he thought. *Guess I'll just have to wing it.*

"Here goes!"

He charged at Brooke and swung the pipe with all his might.

She caught it onehanded, and the shock of the impact reverberated back through his arms. It was like he'd slammed the pipe into a brick wall.

"Was that your best swing?" she asked, sounding genuinely curious.

"Uh, Emma!" he called out without turning. "That bad feeling is back!"

It came back harder when Brooke swiped at him with an open hand. He backpedaled; her fingertips lacked the earlier glint of claws, but her hands were still coiled with enough power that he didn't want to see what they could do to him.

"Use your magic!" Emma shouted.

"What are you talking about? She doesn't have a butter tray!"

"Not Telekinesis! The *other* one!"

"What other—?"

"You know! The other one!"

"Stop being mysterious!"

He backed away, and Brooke let him open the distance while Sammy surged forward from the side. She threw a punch at Clarke's face; he swung the pipe around to block. The pipe connected with her elbow, but it didn't stop. The joint bowed unnaturally under the fierce momentum of his blow, turning her arm into a misshapen U, and though he'd half-expected it—you know, slime girl and all—he couldn't help an internal cringe.

Sammy, though, didn't care one bit. She whipped her elongated arm back, not the slightest hint of pain on her face, and threw another punch. This time, Clarke managed to cut inside her guard and connect with her stomach, which rippled under her leather jacket.

She backed away, her torso and limbs sloshing back into their original places like a weird, cute, gelatinous river.

"Mm." Sammy sized him up. "A promising start."

"You think this is 'promising'?"

"You're not unconscious yet, are you?"

Brooke lunged forward, swiping again with open hands. Clarke tried to block, but the force of her attack knocked his pipe aside. He fell back, circling the room, working to keep both combatants in front of him.

His mind raced. What magic did he have? He could move small objects with his mind, but not without enough force or speed to be useful in combat. What was Emma referring to? He'd only managed the one spell before—

And then it came to him. He *did* possess another ability, one he'd already pulled off at least once.

He tried to recall the sensation from last night, the knot in the back of his mind. A presence resting against his thoughts, waiting to be activated by his will. A force akin to a mental muscle, relaxed but capable of tensing.

He tensed it now.

His body grew lighter, and he kicked off the ground, floating above the two ladies.

Sammy spun to face Emma. "You didn't say he could *fly*."

"Yes!" The succubus declared proudly, hands on hips. "He can fly."

"It's more of a lazy float." Clarke grabbed the railing of an elevated walkway about two stories up and swung himself over the edge. He released the tension in his mind, and his full weight dropped onto the corrugated steel platform.

"But blood knights can't fly," Sammy said, brow wrinkled in confusion. "Can they?"

"Ah, but that's where you're wrong." Emma flourished with one hand. "They can if they use Power Graft to absorb the powers of other demihumans."

Brooke and Sammy faced each other then turned back to Clarke.

"Oh, this suddenly got a whole lot more interesting!" Sammy sat down on concrete and began undoing her laces. "I need to take my shoes off for this one!"

Your shoes? Clarke thought.

"How stable is that walkway?" Brooke called up.

"Um." Clarke grabbed the railing and gave it a healthy shake. He then jumped up and down, jarring loose a light rain of dust that had accumulated over the years. "Seems pretty stable. Why?"

Brooke leaped into the air and caught the edge of the platform.

"Whoa!" Clarke grabbed hold of the railing as the walkway rattled, more dirt shaking off.

Brooke lifted herself up with one arm, her muscles bulging from the effort. She caught the top of the railing and hauled herself over the edge, eyes gleaming with ferocious purpose.

"Because here I come!"

She charged at him, ears flattened, arms to her sides, fingers spread.

"Later!" Clarke vaulted over the railing and gave it a

firm kick. He floated across the factory, limbs scrambling until he latched on to another railing.

Brooke cupped her hands around her mouth. "You can't run forever!"

"Just watch me!"

"Clarke!" Emma shouted from the ground. "Behind you!"

"What?"

He spun around to find Sammy scurrying up the wall like a four-legged spider, her bare hands and feet adhering to the sheet metal. It was kind of cool—until her head twisted around to face him over her back, like she was some demon-possessed babe or sexy supernatural monster in a weird-ass horror porn. She leaped off the siding and onto the platform.

"Surprise!"

Sammy rose from the ground, her limbs morphing to match her head's new orientation, even though her clothes didn't change. And with that goofy getup, it was hard to be freaked out by her.

"Your coat's on backwards."

"I'll manage."

She sprinted forward, and he swung the pipe. She dodged and the pipe cracked against the railing, shaking free flakes of paint and decades of dust. She dashed in, and he reversed his swing, scraping along the railing.

The pipe connected with her arm, bowing it inward again, but she pushed through, slamming into his body. He fell back, gasping when his back hit the platform—and Sammy pinned him in place.

"I'm very sorry about this." She grabbed his face with both hands and planted a wet kiss on his forehead. "Mwah!"

"Sorry about—"

His eyes bugged out. All the bad food decision he'd made in the past week reared their ugly heads like a vicious hydra made from indigestion and spite. His intestines roiled, his stomach gurgled, and bile threatened to rush up his throat.

Sammy climbed off him. "Guess round one goes to the girls!"

Clarke let out a dry heave, turned onto his side, and struggled to rise to his feet. The pipe clattered out of his fingers, and he hacked into a fist. He could feel … something spreading through his body. He wasn't sure what, though his mind interpreted it as dark and oily, almost as if he could see the contamination, whatever it was.

He clenched his eyes shut, tight enough for tears to leak from the edges. Sweat beaded on his brow as the shadow in his mind's eye spread throughout his body.

But he sensed something else in his addled state, a presence alongside the sickness, spreading with it but adding nothing to it. A tension he hadn't noticed before. A mental muscle he could flex. A tool to be used.

Magic ready for him to wield it.

"You sure you're pulling your punches?" Emma asked pointedly from the ground.

"Um, I thought so!" Sammy shouted back.

"He's starting to turn gray! You weren't supposed to hit him full force!"

"Well, it's not like I have this slime thing down to a science! I thought I was going easy on him!"

Clarke reached out with his mind and grasped this new presence, felt its shape, its texture, took full hold of it.

And *commanded* it.

A comforting warmth spread out from his chest— no, his heart, to be precise. Flameless heat exploded to fill his chest cavity and raced outward along his limbs. It scorched away the strange malaise, cleansing his body, healing it, reinvigorating it.

Clarke pushed off the corrugated steel and rose to his feet. He picked up the pipe and held it with both hands.

"Round one isn't over," he croaked.

Sammy took a step back. "Um, what just happened?"

"I think he used a Purify spell," Emma said.

"Sure felt like it," Ashley said.

The platform shuddered, and Clarke checked over his shoulder. Brooke had made her way up onto the walkway, sandwiching him between a werewolf and a slime. He could try floating to another part of the factory, and that was probably the best tactical choice.

But he chose not to.

His mind throbbed with fresh sensations and an awakening perception that whatever magic he'd just wielded was one of many abilities. He didn't know them well yet, but he knew of them, and that was a lot more than he'd possessed only a few minutes ago.

Neither Brooke nor Sammy looked eager to charge in, and so he concentrated, testing the texture of each ability, tasting their potential power until he found one that felt strangely familiar, even though he knew he'd never used it.

He used it now, commanding the flows of magic within his body as if they were his old friends.

The hairs on his skin prickled, and a sheen of reddish energy crackled into existence before turning invisible.

"A Sanguine Shield?" Emma shook her fist. "Yeah! You go, Clarke! You've got this!"

Brooke dashed forward, her boots thudding across the walkway. She swung at him, and this time he didn't block. Her fingers clawed through the air, and a sheen of energy crackled as she struck, absorbing her attack like a layer of invisible armor. Still, he felt the blow. Not physically, not with his body, but through the shield. The impact drew upon some resource within his being, something hidden and ethereal but still an integral part of who he was.

He brought the pipe crashing down on her exposed forearm and connected.

"Ouch!"

Brooke jerked her arm back. She shook out the limb, a shallow cut across her skin.

"He managed to hurt you?" Sammy asked, surprised.

"Yeah. That smarted!" Brooke sucked on the fresh wound, which was already closing up. "Cut me a bit, too."

"With a *pipe*?"

Clarke inspected the makeshift weapon. A snap of red energy danced up the length and then back down to his hands. He wasn't sure why, but he leaned the pipe against the railing and stared at his open hand.

The shape of the pipe remained: a ghostly, reddish echo of the weapon.

He focused once more, and the red shadow snapped into vivid clarity, now transformed into a fully realized scarlet sword.

"And my thirstblade, I presume." Clarke smiled as he held the weapon aloft.

"Wow," Sammy breathed.

"Hey, time out!" Brooke shouted, making a T with her hands. She leaned over the railing. "This is getting serious now. Can I go all out?" Clarke could have sworn he saw her tail wagging.

"Sure!" Emma replied with a wave. "Knock yourselves out! I'm sure he can handle it!"

"Wait, *what?*" Clarke blurted.

"All right!" Brooke punched her palm. "Time to *really* cut loose!"

"You said it!" Sammy replied, stripping off her leather jacket.

"Hold on a second!" Clarke exclaimed, suddenly worried. "Don't I have a say in this?"

All five of them reconvened on the ground.

"Your grasp of foundational blood magic is impressive," Ashley said, appraising his thirstblade and defensive aura with approving nods.

"Purify isn't base tier magic," Emma pointed out.

"He may have instinctively triggered that one."

"I think she's right," Clarke said. "I was ready to puke my guts out, but I could feel something else at the same time. Almost like the counter was within reach, and all I had to do was trigger it."

"Seems like everything turned out fine in the end," Ashley said.

"No thanks to *someone*." Emma gave Sammy a stern side eye.

"Yeah, sorry about that." Sammy looked down and

kicked a random pebble aside. "I let a little too much toxin slip. My bad. Sorry, Clarke."

"What would have happened if I hadn't magicked it away?" Clarke asked. "Would it have killed me?"

"No!" Sammy said urgently, holding her hands up, open-palmed. "Nothing like that!"

"You just would have been bedridden for the rest of the week," Emma said.

"Hey, I would have sucked the toxin out before that!"

"Oh?" Emma's eyes twinkled mischievously. "Was that your plan all along?"

Sammy's jaw moved as if she were trying to find the right words, but no sounds came out. She wagged an angry finger at the smug succubus, but eventually relented and crossed her arms with a huff.

"Come on." Brooke bounced on her toes. "We going to fight or not? I hardly ever get to go all out!"

"Clarke?" Emma asked. "You up for some more?"

"A question first. What, exactly is 'all out' for these two?"

"Can I show him?" Brooke continued to bounce on her toes. "Can I?"

"You go for it, girl," Emma said.

"Yes! Clarke, check this out!"

Brooke backed away and kicked off her sandals.

She clenched her teeth and flexed every muscle in her body. Her body bulged, veined biceps and engorged pectorals straining against her T-shirt, quadriceps and calves stretching her spandex leggings. She snarled, incisors lengthening, face wrinkling, nose and mouth extending, nails growing into heavy, scythed claws. Coarse fur sprouted from her exposed skin, puffing out around where the neck and sleeves constricted it.

Her feet and toes extended into digitigrade legs. Her shoulders broadened and her torso extended until the top of her head was at least seven feet tall. The T-shirt's flesh-colored boob window art looked terribly out of place on her full, furry werewolf body.

"The law of conservation of mass is *very* unhappy with you right now," Clarke said with fake indignation.

Werewolf Brooke brushed her long ponytail aside.

"You get used to it," she said, her voice lower by at least an octave.

"Hey, Clarke?"

He faced Sammy, and then performed a double-take. He'd been so engrossed in Brooke's shifting that he'd missed Sammy stripping down to her black bra and panties. Her skin now possessed a pinkish, almost liquid sheen.

"Wanna see a magic trick?" Sammy asked with a half-smile.

"Sure."

"Grab my bra." She pointed at her cleavage. "Right here."

"Um. Okay."

He pinched the join between the cups with two careful fingers, somewhat leery about touching her skin after the whole toxin experience. There were few things that could put a damper on touching skin proximate to boobs, but that was one of them.

"Now hold still."

Sammy stepped backward, and her bra *ploop*ed right through her torso, still hooked together to form a loop.

She spread her arms theatrically. "Pretty neat, huh?"

Clarke's eyes darted to the bra in his hand and then to Sammy's breasts, so perky he wasn't even sure why she wore a bra.

"Very."

"Being a slime has its advantages. Those hooks on the back can be so finicky!"

"I'll take your word for it." He didn't have enough experience removing bras to disagree.

Not *yet*.

"Now can I have it back, please? My nipples are cold."

"Sure."

He handed the bra over, and Sammy balled it up and jammed it into her chest. A bra-like shadow unfolded with her and surfaced in the traditional position.

"That's … one way to put a bra on."

"The best way, you mean!"

"Can we fight now?" Brooke asked eagerly.

"I'm still not sure of what 'all out' means," Clarke said.

"Exactly what you'd expect," Ashley said. "None of you hold back."

"But I have a sword."

"So?"

"Well …" He looked down at the blood-hued blade then at the two ladies he was about to fight. "It's a sword."

"You'll fight until one of you draws blood," Ashley said.

Sammy cleared her throat noisily.

"Or gets hit in your case," Ashley added.

The slime girl smiled. "That's better."

"Emma and I will call it out whenever someone scores."

"You don't have blood?" Clarke asked the slime girl.

"I do, but mine works differently from the rest of you. I don't bleed from cuts, for instance. Wouldn't want me and Brooke to have an unfair advantage."

"Right …" Clarke sized up his two opponents, both experienced demihumans. "What's unfair about any of this?"

"You say that, but we're about to take on a blood knight," Sammy said. "You don't realize how intimidating that makes you, even at this stage."

"Come on!" Brooke flexed her claws. "Let's do this!"

"You ready for us, Clarke?" Sammy asked, standing nonchalantly with a hand on her hip.

"As ready as I'll ever be." He settled into a lower stance, sword held before him. A snap of red energy crackled across his body's ethereal defenses before vanishing. "You only live once."

"You say that like you're expecting something bad to happen."

"Am I wrong?"

"Combatants set?" Emma raised an arm. "Round two, go!"

Brooke exploded forward like a runner leaving the blocks. She cleared the distance to Clarke in two massive strides and swiped at him with claws that were terrifyingly prominent now, gleaming with the promise of damage. He dodged to the side, claws and blade connecting in a snap of red sparks. She swung with her free arm, but her forward momentum and the angle of his dodge made the attack awkward.

She overshot him, and Clarke drew a shallow line across her forearm with the tip of his blade.

"Hit!" Emma exclaimed. "Point to Clarke!"

"Aww." Brooke backed away and licked a long tongue across her forearm. The wound was already closing.

"Maybe not rush in like an idiot this time?" Sammy said.

"Sorry." Brooke joined the other demigirl. "I just get so excited when I go full wolf!"

"Well, try to hold it in. I'll play fetch with you later."

"Hey! Why you got to be like that?"

"Because you make it too easy."

"Settle down, ladies." Emma checked both sides. "Round three, go!"

Sammy gave Brooke a quick hand gesture, and the two split off, their paths curving toward Clarke in a clear effort to flank him. He could have pulled back, trying to keep both in front, but instead he dashed in, rushing down Sammy.

The slime girl whipped an arm at him, the limb stretching and elongating. The attack hit him in the shoulder and rebounded off with a brief flash. He sensed his connection to the Sanguine Shield change, not so much weakening as straining. That hit had come with a cost, one he couldn't afford to pay out indefinitely.

But tanking that hit had brought him within reach of Sammy, and her eyes widened as he swung at her extended limb. He expected her body to bow around the attack like when he'd struck her with the pipe, but instead the thirstblade hissed through her flesh and cleaved the stretched limb off at the middle.

Half her arm plopped wetly onto the concrete.

"Oh, shit!" Clarke exclaimed.

"That's a hit!" Emma declared.

"I'm sorry! I didn't mean to—"

"It's all right." Sammy frowned down at her own severed limb. "Shit happens."

"I think you dropped something," Emma said.

"Yeah, I see it."

Sammy's chest contracted as if she were letting out a deep breath, and her stump sprouted into a full arm. She flexed her new fingers, let out a disappointed huff, and walked over to her disconnected arm. Clarke wasn't entirely sure, but her chest seemed to have shrunk by about the same volume her restored limb took up. She retrieved the severed part from the ground, balled it up, and jammed it into her chest. None of that, from losing the limb to shoving it back inside, seemed to cause her any pain.

"Okay. I'm whole again."

"What was that about rushing in like an idiot?" Brooke asked pointedly.

Sammy opened her mouth, but then paused as if reconsidering her words.

"Yeah, I deserved that one."

"Let's try to take him down together this time."

"Fine by me."

"Everyone ready?" Emma asked. "Round four, go!"

Brooke and Sammy charged straight in, forgoing any subtlety this time. Claws flashed against his thirstblade, and Brooke kept swinging in a frantic blur while Sammy lashed at him with stretched limbs, sometimes arching in from above or angling down down low to entangle his feet.

He met their attacks, holding when he could and pulling back when they threatened to overwhelm him. They advanced so ferociously he struggled to find any openings. Or any he could capitalize on, at least. Whenever he saw one, the other girl used that window to attack.

And they were getting hits in on *him*. His shield sparked from each glancing blow, and he sensed the barrier tiring right alongside the burning in his muscles. Sweat glistened on his brow, and his arms and legs ached. Finally, Brooke caught him hard on the shoulder, and the shield shattered into twinkling snaps of red lightning.

Sammy whipped a comically long arm at him and coiled long, thin fingers around his neck. He sensed the toxins entering his body, picturing them as a black cloud expanding out from his neck, clouding his head, infecting his chest and then his limbs.

His vision blurred, and his head began to fog over. He swung at her stretched arm with the thirstblade. She coiled back.

He backpedaled and cast Purify. This time, the spell came naturally, and comforting warmth spread outward from his chest. His head cleared, his eyes focused, and—

Brooke tackled him to the ground, and the thirstblade shattered into winking red motes.

"Gotcha!"

She gave him a quick, almost loving scratch on the cheek.

"Hit!" Emma said. "Point goes to the slime girl and the were-girl."

"*Wolf* girl," Brooke corrected, climbing to her feet.

"What's the difference?"

"'Were' means man. You literally just called me a 'man-girl'."

"Oh." Emma took on a thoughtful look, then shrugged her shoulders. "Whoops."

Brooke extended a hand to Clarke. He took it, and she pulled him up to his feet.

"How're you holding up?"

"Tired," Clarke said, sweating and panting. "You two are a handful and then some! I could use a breather. And maybe some water, too."

"Coming right up!" Emma hurried over to a backpack either Brooke or Sammy must have brought. She zipped it open and rummaged inside until she pulled out a bottled water. "Here you go."

"Thanks." He unscrewed the cap and gulped down half the bottle. He didn't even care it was lukewarm.

"Got enough energy in you for another round?" Ashley asked.

"Don't think so. My shield is drained, and it feels like I won't be raising it anytime soon."

"Then perhaps we should call it quits for now."

"Aww." Brooke's ears drooped. "But I was just getting started."

"Sorry," Clarke said. "Not happening. Not today."

"Still, you did great!" Emma said.

"Yeah, I'm sold," Sammy said. "With him on our team, this whole Broken Fang business has a real shot."

Clarke smiled at her.

"Need me to draw out those toxins?"

"Nah, I was able to purge them right before Brooke crashed into me."

"Hmm." Sammy tapped her lips with a finger, her eyes bright with mischief. "What a shame."

"You *sure* you can't go another round?" Brooke begged.

"Yeah. I need to stop being hit so much. Without my shield, I'm just a regular, squishy human."

"There may be another option," Ashley said carefully. "If you'd like to test it out."

"What's that?"

"Can you summon your thirstblade still?"

"Let me try." He held his arms out in a twohanded ghost grip and concentrated. A brief crackle of red lightning arced between his fingers, and the blade snapped into being.

"Good," Ashley said. "Now we just need a volunteer."

"For what?" Clarke asked.

"For you to syphon some health off of." Ashley glanced over at Brooke meaningfully.

"Sure, he can have some of mine." Brooke proffered her forearm.

"You want me to do what now?"

"Poke her in the arm and Drain some of her vitality," Ashley said.

"Won't that hurt her?"

"Don't worry." Brooke thumped her chest with a fist. "I've got plenty of stamina to spare on you."

Sammy sniggered.

"Hey!" Brooke said, "I didn't mean it like *that!*"

"Go ahead, Clarke," Emma placed an arm around his shoulders. "Insert your tip into her."

Brooke lowered her head. "Both of you are terrible!"

"But seriously," Emma urged. "Give it a shot."

"All right. Here goes."

Clarke sank the edge of the thirstblade about a centimeter into Brooke's furred forearm. In that moment, he felt a connection open, one full of potential and linked vitality. He could sense the wolf girl's inhuman, seemingly limitless reserves of energy.

And he drew some of that wealth to himself as if he were drinking raw vitality through a straw.

"Oh, wow." He pulled the sword back and stood a little straighter.

Brooke rubbed the shallow wound. "Feel any better?"

"I do. What about you?"

"Feel a bit tired. Nothing to worry about."

"It worked, then?" Emma asked.

Clarke closed his eyes to concentrate. A shimmer of reddish energy danced across his body, and the Sanguine Shield snapped into place at full strength.

He opened his eyes. "I'll say."

"Normally, you'll draw your strength from our enemies," Ashley explained. "Your mana reserves are shallow compared to a vampire's, and draw from your own life. But that weakness is also a strength, given your thristblade autocasts Drain on contact with an enemy. With that in your arsenal, every foe you face might as well be a combination magical battery and health kit."

"Nice! I'm beginning to see why blood knights are such a big deal."

"Up for round five?" Brooke asked hopefully.

The ladies looked to him, and he smiled back.

"Why, yes. I believe I am."

CHAPTER SEVEN

CLARKE WENT TO CHESTER CREEK UNIVERSITY Monday morning as if nothing had changed.

Except everything had.

He'd spent most of Sunday wondering how to approach the next day, and he'd settled on "act natural," which was easier said than done. Some of his classmates weren't even human—well, weren't *fully* human—and at least one of his professors was a bloodsucking vampire!

His first test came as soon as he left the parking deck. He passed a group of students hanging around outside the library, and realized all of them were demihumans! He guessed most were elves—judging by their ears and tall, slender builds—but one young woman must have been something else. A pair of ivory horns arched back above her ears and red scales crept up along her neck. Her eyes were black with gold pupils. Dragonkin, maybe?

He managed not to stare, and he was rather pleased with the results of this small exercise in self-control. He'd come a long way in just a few days.

His morning classes came and went without any commotion or drama, though he was keeping a rough tally in the back of his mind as the day dragged on. So far, it seemed that around a third of all CCU students were demihumans. That struck him as unusually high based on what he'd seen so far. Granted, he hadn't spent much time in the city over the weekend—sticking with Emma and the others mostly—but he hadn't noticed anywhere near those concentration levels outside the university grounds.

Additionally, his estimate could have been on the low side. All four ladies could pass as regular humans if they wanted to. How many of CCU's students could do the same? It would be impossible to identify some of them as demihumans by sight alone. At least for him at his current skill level.

His eleven o'clock class was his first real challenge and the moment he'd been dreading the most. He arrived early and grabbed a seat near the back of Professor Heinrich's Calculus 2 class. Emma arrived on time and sat next to him.

Heinrich showed up two minutes late, apologized for his tardiness—stating that faculty business had detained him—and then dove right to his lecture, picking up with the integration examples they'd reviewed on Friday.

Clarke studied the man more than the material during that hour, keeping an eye open for any sign the being before him was a vampire.

He saw none. Heinrich was, for all appearances, just another professor. A bit quirky, perhaps, but not in an alarming way.

Which horrified Clarke.

A true, honest to goodness monster stood before him. A creature with the cunning of a man and the blood-lust of a beast. A being that viewed humans like him as if they were vending machines with legs.

A part of him wanted to shout at the top of his lungs, to warn everyone in the class of the danger in their midst.

But what would his outburst have accomplished? Nothing, and only if he were lucky. His actions would have placed not only himself in danger, but Emma and the others as well, and he couldn't do that—*wouldn't* do that.

And so, he held his tongue. He took notes like the good student he wanted Heinrich to see and worked his way through the sample problems. The vampire dismissed class promptly at 11:50, and Clarke headed to the food court with Emma in tow. He ordered an Italian sub, grabbed a bottled water, then joined Emma at a table in the corner. She was already eating her boxed lunch.

"How are you holding up?" she asked.

"Fine, I guess." Clarke set his tray down, then

glanced around before sitting. The food court was thick with demihumans, just like the rest of the campus.

"What do you think of the view now that your vision's unclouded?"

"It'll take some getting used to."

"I don't doubt it."

He leaned close and whispered. "I couldn't tell Heinrich was a vampire."

"They're hard to spot, that's for sure."

"But aren't I supposed to be a vampire killer?"

"Yep. One of a rare breed these days."

"Then shouldn't I be able to spot them?"

"You will. Give it time. Your powers are still awakening. Can't expect to go from zero to full power in a weekend."

"I know." He sat back. "It still doesn't sit right with me. I should feel repulsed by what he is, but instead I don't feel anything. Can't sense *anything*."

"Have you sensed any of the spells around campus?"

"I don't think so. Should I have?"

"Maybe. Ashley and I can work with you on your magic sensitivity. We'll focus there over the weekend. Combat skills are important, but we need to make sure you build up your full kit. Given your blood knight heritage, you may become more attuned to magic than I am, and I'm no slouch."

"I'll do my best."

"And speaking of heritage, Ashley brought up a good question. Would it be worth our time to check on your parents? See if either of them has the talent?"

"I was adopted. No idea who my biological parents are."

"Really?" Emma's eyebrows pinched together. "Your adoptive parents named you Joffrey Baratheon Clarke?"

"Yep."

Emma wore a perplexed look for several seconds, then shrugged. "Never mind then."

"What's our next step?"

"Finding a lead on where Heinrich's stored his grimoire. That's Priority Number One for Ashley and me this week."

"Anything I can do to help?"

"Not right now, and the same goes for Brooke and Sammy. Just hang tight while Ashley and I sniff around."

"Got it."

The two settled in and ate in relative silence. Clarke worked through his sub while Emma munched on her boxed lunch: teriyaki chicken over rice, steamed carrots and broccoli with a light coat of butter and salt, and a fruit medley for dessert. For someone who got at least some of her nutrients from … other sources, it was surprisingly balanced.

Speaking of those sources, another question came to his mind:

"Emma?"

"Yeah?"

"I've got something to ask you. But first, let me start by saying I'm sorry for not bringing this up earlier. The weekend was … dense."

"No need to apologize. What's on your mind?"

"Are you and I … dating?"

"Would you like us to be?"

Clarke blinked. That wasn't the answer he'd expected.

"I know that look." She smiled sweetly and set her fork down. "Here's the crash course on how dating a succubus works. You see all this?" She gestured down the length of her body. "This is yours whenever you want it."

"Oh." His eyebrows shot up. "Whenever?"

"Within reason." She winked at him. "I'm many things, but an exhibitionist isn't one of them."

"Duly noted."

"If you'd like to date me on top of that, consider it a done deal. Easy as that. You want to date someone else instead—or someone else in *addition* to me—that won't bother me in the slightest."

"It won't?"

"Monogamy isn't a thing succubi do. Or most demi-human species, for that matter."

"Then, you'd want the option of seeing other guys?"

"Nah," she replied with a slow headshake.

"No?"

"Not interested." She placed a delicate hand atop his. "Not after my first night with you. I got a taste of the good stuff."

"Was it really that great for you?"

"Let me put it this way. Why would I ever buy store brand skim milk again when I can go directly to the cow?"

Clarke laughed. "I'm a cow?"

"The bull, then. A super sexy bull." She gazed at him with a dreamy look in her eyes. "One with the creamiest, most delicious milk imaginable."

He was about to make a comment on the implications of "bull milk" when he realized:

"Are you drooling?"

"Oh!" She grabbed her napkin and dabbed the damp corners of her mouth. "Sorry about that."

Yeah, she definitely knew the implications.

Clarke chuckled, shaking his head. "I get the feeling dating you is going to be a straightforward experience."

"I'll take that as a compliment." She finished wiping her mouth. "My question still stands, though. How do you feel about dating a succubus? Are you okay with that?"

"Yes. Yes, I am *very* okay with it."

"Wonderful!" She leaned closer. "Then, as my first act as your new girlfriend, how about I start making extra boxed lunches each day? One for me, and one for my sexy boyfriend? How's that sound to you?"

"That sounds great," he replied, smiling.

Clarke received a text from Brooke later that day, asking him to meet her in the stadium after his last class. By that hour, one side of the sky had darkened to a rich orange shot through with purple clouds, and the stadium lights shone across the football field and surrounding tracks.

About a dozen students were running laps, though Clarke got the impression they were close to finishing up for the day. Almost all of them were demihumans, many of them shifters in what he'd begun to think of as their hybrid forms.

Brooke spotted him almost instantly as he stepped onto the field, and he wondered how sharp her eyesight was. She waved at him as she ran past, completed one more lap, then jogged over to share a few words with the track and field coach. She grabbed two water bottles from an ice barrel beside the benches and joined him.

"Hey, Clarke." She offered him a bottle. "Want one?"

"Sure. Thanks."

He accepted the drink, twisted it open, and they picked a spot in the stands to sit down—not quite side by side, but close enough for him to feel the heat radiating off her in the cooling air. Sweat glistened on her skin and trickled down the firm arches of her breasts. She wore a red-and-white tank top with her name and the number 15 on both sides, along with matching shorts. The top pressed tightly against her body and left her firm midriff bare.

"Ahhh!" she exclaimed after draining half the bottle. Her tail swished contently.

"You wanted to see me?"

"Got an idea to run by you." Her wolf ears perked. "Been thinking about it since Saturday. It's how you floated around at the mill."

"You mean how I ..." He checked around them. They were the only two people on this side of the stands, and they were pretty far from the bench the rest of the track and field team was using. But unlike the food court, there wasn't any ambient noise to mask their conversation.

"It's all right." Brooke flicked one ear then wrinkled her nose. "I'd know if anyone was close enough to listen."

"I suppose you would." He smiled at her, and she almost seemed to blush before he continued. "I was about to bring up my Power Graft and how I gained some of Emma's magic."

"That'd be it! You also brought up an important problem during our sparring."

"Which is?"

"You're too vulnerable when your shield is down. That could bite you in the ass if we find ourselves stuck in a bad fight."

136

"You're not wrong. Not sure what to do about it, though, besides get better."

"Ah, but there *is* something we can do!" Her eyes glinted in the waning light. "You can use Power Graft on me. There's no reason for you to stop at just Emma. Between a succubus, a werewolf, and a slime, you've got a veritable buffet of abilities to choose from."

"What about Ashley?"

"I honestly don't know if it'd work with her. She's not actually a demihuman, you know."

"Her celestial nature might not be compatible?"

"Can't say for sure." She shrugged. "Your best bet is to ask her yourself. But as far as I know, me and Sammy are fair game, which means you should be able to absorb some of my shifter magic. We werewolves are pretty hard to kill, even when we have a hex holding us back. Some magical durability and regen could come in handy in a pinch."

"I wouldn't start growing fur or howling at the moon, would I?"

"No, no, nothing like that." She chuckled, shaking her head. "At least I don't think so. Granted, I don't actually know how your Power Graft works, but I did talk to Emma about it earlier today. She thinks at first you'll only pick up basic attributes or skills like her flying or my toughness, though weaker than the original's."

"At first?"

"She made it sound like you'll eventually grow powerful enough to mimic our abilities at full strength, and even target which attributes you want to absorb." She leaned in and grinned toothily, her canines glinting in the light. "Also, the whole howling-at-the-moon thing is way overblown in media."

"Vampiric propaganda?"

"More like vampires being total jerks! They never skip a chance to put us werewolves down."

"So that rivalry is overblown, too?" He recalled all the movies he'd seen that pitted vampires against werewolves in ages-old feuds.

"If there's a problem, it's because *they* keep provoking us." Brooke huffed, but then shook her head, as if to brush the irritation away.

"I see." He took a swig of water and watched the training session wind down.

"So." Brooke scooched an inch closer. "What do you say?"

"About the whole Power Graft thing?"

"Yeah."

"I think it's a great idea. The less dying I do, the better."

Brooke laughed.

"When do you want to try?" he asked.

"Whenever you're ready." She leaned even closer.

"All you and I should need is some time together with no prying eyes."

"I'm scheduled to meet Emma and Ashley at the mill this Saturday. Would that work?"

"That …" She sat back. Her ears drooped a little and her shoulders sagged. "Yeah. That'll work fine."

Something in the tone of her voice struck Clarke as off. Had he missed something there?

He glanced over at her, but she stared out at the field instead of meeting his eyes. Had this meeting been about Broken Fang business? Or something else? Or *both*?

Was Brooke coming on to me? he wondered. *All the ladies knew I'd spent Friday with Emma.*

That, by itself, should have set some boundaries. It certainly had in his mind. But then he recalled what Emma had said.

"Monogamy isn't a thing succubi do. Or most demihuman species, for that matter."

He'd been so focused on the first part that he hadn't fully considered the second, and what it could possibly mean for his future with his new friends. He hadn't noticed any interest from Brooke until now, but Sammy had been flirty as hell at the mill!

Perhaps I should ask Emma for a crash course on how to date wolf girls, he thought. *And maybe slime girls, too, while I'm at it. Because life isn't getting any less complicated for me.*

"Saturday then?" Brooke asked, somewhat distantly.

"Yeah," he said, determined to consider his words more carefully in the future. "Looking forward to it."

He didn't see much of the ladies until the weekend, except for Emma, and even she was relegated to classes and the food court. True to her word, she packed him lunches every day, and they were all delicious. She even went so far as to insert handwritten notes, signed with a kiss of lipstick.

He met Emma at her apartment early Saturday morning. He would have liked to have spent every evening over at her place, but she and Ashley were busy searching for Heinrich's grimoire. Ashley joined them promptly at 9 o'clock, and they drove out to the abandoned steel mill once breakfast had been demolished and cleaned up. Once there, they began his first formal lesson in magic.

"How about now?" Emma asked from somewhere in front of him.

Clarke sat with folded legs in the center of the huge room where he'd fought Brooke and Sammy. His eyes were closed, though he wore a blindfold to enforce the point as he concentrated on the magic around him. He'd spent most of the day like this, feeling out the currents of magic around him rather relying on sight or sound, only stopping for one of Emma's amazing boxed lunches. This one featured baby tomatoes and mozzarella chunks on skewers with balsamic drizzle, rolls of prosciutto, a slice of garlic bread, and fresh grapes. (He wasn't sure if this was a succubus-related skill or not, but either way, it rocked.)

Except for that brief break, he'd spent the majority of the day blindfolded and sitting on this one spot.

He focused on the nearby magical aura. His perception of magic had changed over the past week, or perhaps had slowly awakened. Like someone who'd been cloistered in a dark room suddenly walking out into the noon sun. It took time for everything to stop being a bright, milky blur.

The spell behind him felt … yellow, tall, and warm. He found it easiest to ascribe mundane descriptions to the magical sensations, to make them less overwhelming and easier to process. This one he recognized from earlier in the day.

"Illuminate."

"Very good," Emma said. "Can you tell where she is?"

"Um. I'm guessing about twenty feet away. Behind and to the left."

"She's a bit further away than that, but not bad. You're doing better. Next?"

"Go ahead."

The magic faded, like winking motes behind his eyelids. He covered his ears and counted to ten. Not much point to the exercise if he could hear where Ashley moved to each time.

He uncovered his ears and concentrated on the magic once more.

This one was blue, bold, wide. Perhaps a bit warm and fresh, too. Like a gentle breeze.

"Um. Not sure. Feels a similar to when I float around, but that's all I've got."

"You're closer than you realize," Emma said. "She's flying right now. Can you tell where she is?"

"Somewhere to the left, but that's as close as I can get."

"Take a look, then."

Clarke peeled back the blindfold and looked.

Ashley hovered up near the skylight, a pair of wide, feathery wings unfurled to either side. The feathers were so perfect and pure they seemed to sparkle, and her hairband glowed like a half-circle of gold.

She settled to the ground with delicate clicks of her heels, and the wings vanished in a brief shower of vanishing feathers. Her hairband dimmed back to normal.

"Not gonna lie," Clarke said. "That was pretty awesome."

"I'm surprised you weren't able to guess my position. You've been getting so close for the past hour."

"I bet it's because you were up in the air." He tapped his temple. "I wasn't paying attention to up and down. Need to start thinking in three axes when it comes to magic."

"It's a good lesson to keep in mind," Emma said.

"Some vampires can fly, and plenty of their summons can, too."

The sound of wheels crunching through gravel caught everyone's attention. Emma hurried over to a window.

"Brooke's here. And it looks like she brought food."

Clarke heard a car door slam, and then Brooke walked in with a pizza box in her hands.

"Hey there!" Her eyes met Clarke's for a brief moment, but then darted away. "I got the munchies on the way over, and since I was coming this way, I bought extra. Anyone want a slice?"

"I could go for a small bite," Ashley said, giving Emma a dirty look. "*Someone* forgot to pack a lunch for me."

"You didn't ask," the succubus replied.

Ashley opened the proffered box, but then gave the contents a disapproving frown.

"So much meat."

"What's wrong with that? You know I like meat."

"Are there even any vegetables on this abomination?"

"There might be a few scraps hiding under the cheese."

Ashley sighed and, with a little headshake, stepped away.

"Clarke, you want some before I dig in?" Brooke held out the box for him.

"That's fine. I just—"

Emma gave him a quick, stealthy nudge in the small of his back.

"Actually, yeah, I could go for a slice."

He grabbed one, and so did Emma. The three of them sat down on the available "furniture" while Ashley stepped outside.

Brooke practically inhaled her first slice. She must have been *famished*!

"How goes the training?" she asked, grabbing a second.

"Very well," Emma said. "His sense for spells is developing at a brisk pace. Ashley and I are having trouble stumping him."

"Have you tried out Power Graft yet?"

"Nope. We were waiting for you."

Brooke nodded, then ate her second slice quietly, followed by her third and fourth. The three of them polished off the pizza box, and Brooke handed out some napkins. Everyone cleaned up, and she took the empty box and trash out to her Jeep.

"Wow," Emma said softly once they were alone. "That happened *fast*."

"What's that?"

"Brooke. She views you as a potential alpha."

"Meaning?"

"She's interested in you."

"I was wondering about that, actually."

"Well, wonder no more. You have an empath sitting next to you, and one who's attuned to sexual desire. She bought that pizza for you, not us. Give it a little time, and she'll be wanting to taste a different kind of meat." Emma licked her lips. "A very deep, very thorough taste."

"And how do you feel about that?"

"Depends." Her voice became huskier. "When the time comes, would you like to do just her or have me join in?"

"Uh." He hadn't expected *that*!

Emma laughed sweetly. "I kid, I kid. Threesomes can be awkward. It's better to get to know a new partner before trying anything more advanced."

"Are you speaking from experience?"

"Actually, no. That's just a lesson my parents taught me."

"About how to correctly handle threesomes?"

Emma nodded.

"Wow. The sex talk must be *weird* in succubus households."

"Oh, you have no idea!" she said, eyes laughing.

Brooke returned, again hesitant to meet Clarke's eyes, and Ashley followed her in.

"Shall we give it a try?" Brooke asked.

"Sure!" Clarke said, making his enthusiasm obvious. "Been looking forward to this all week."

Brooke's shyness instantly flashed into a grin. Yes, that was definitely the right thing to say.

"Here." Emma rearranged two wooden chairs. "Start by sitting down across from each other. Nice and close."

Clarke and Brooke followed her instructions and took their positions, close enough that Clarke had to spread his legs to make room for Brooke's knees.

"Now take hold of each other," Emma said. "Physical contact is a requirement for this to work."

Clarke held out his open palms, and Brooke rested her forearms in his hands. They each grasped the other's wrists. She met his eyes this time, holding his gaze with more certainty than before. It was the first time he'd paused to appreciate her wolf eyes, how their yellow coloring imbued her face with a fierce, primal beauty.

"Brooke, your job in this is to be at ease."

The wolf girl nodded and took a few deep breaths, as if kicking off a meditative session. The muscles in her face and shoulder slackened, becoming more relaxed and placid.

"And now it's your turn, Clarke. Find the core of her magic."

He closed his eyes and focused his inner eye. Brooke was a pulsating presence before him. A heartbeat without a heart. A core of magical essence pressed into the shape of an athletic young woman.

He reached toward her without moving, touched the magic beating within her chest.

And …

Nothing?

He grimaced and tried again.

Again, nothing.

He shifted in his seat and huffed out a breath.

"Don't force it," Emma said. "Stay calm. Loosen up."

"I'm trying."

Clarke took a few deep breaths to regroup and then reached out once more. He touched Brooke's magic, caressed it as softly as possible, but found he couldn't press inward. Something impeded his progress. A barrier of some sort? No, that wasn't right. The problem wasn't on Brooke's side, but on his. He wasn't sure how he knew this, except perhaps that some instinct or sixth sense provided him with the necessary clarity.

But how was he blocking himself? He wanted to this to succeed, right? Why block his own magic? Why was this so difficult? He'd managed every task the ladies had put in front of him so far, even excelled at some. Why would this be any different? He'd already succeeded once, and by accident!

What could possibly be the problem?

"You're growing anxious," Emma warned. "You need to stay relaxed."

"I'm *trying*."

They worked at it for a whole hour, took a break, then tried again, failed again. As an experiment, Emma swapped positions with Brooke, but nothing came of it. He failed even where he'd succeeded before, and the two women swapped places again.

In the end, he realized it didn't matter what they tried; Power Graft wouldn't kick in, and all Clarke managed to succeed at was frustrating himself and disappointing the ladies.

"I'm sorry," he said at last. "It's just not happening today."

"That's all right." Emma placed a comforting hand on his shoulder. She stood behind him with Brooke seated in front. "We gave it a solid try."

"Is it because of me?" Brooke asked worriedly.

"No," Clarke replied quickly, eager to reassure her. "The problem's me, though hell if I know why. Maybe the first time was a fluke, and I need to sharpen my skills before I can make it work on demand."

"Could be," Emma said. "We'll try again next week."

"Yeah …"

Clarke stood up and stretched his legs. He rubbed his tailbone, which had gone sore from sitting in the chair too long. Brooke headed out first, and the other two followed soon after in Emma's car. She and Ashley were due to head back to the university that night to continue their search, so he said his goodbyes and drove home.

He struggled to fall asleep that night, his mind dwelling on the mystery behind his failure.

CHAPTER EIGHT

THE FOLLOWING WEEK proved to be uneventful.

Up until the point it wasn't.

Clarke's classwork had piled up over the previous week, and he found it rather refreshing to have a breather from the supernatural. All that changed when Emma sent him a text on Friday:

We found it. Meet at the usual place at 5?

He typed his reply: **I'll be there.**

He arrived at the steel mill about half an hour late thanks to a bad accident outside CCU's main parking deck. He was the last to arrive, and the sun had dipped into the treetops behind the mill, filling the parking lot with long shadows. Soft, orange light spilled out through the mill's broken windows.

He headed inside.

"There he is!" Emma said with a big grin.

"Sorry, ladies. Traffic was a mess."

"Glad you made it here in one piece, then," Brooke said.

"Hey." Sammy gave him a wave as she leaned against a pipe. She wore her black biker leathers, which Clarke had expected with her Kawasaki outside. He hadn't anticipated Brooke and Emma to also be dressed in black. Even Ashley had forgone her usual attire for dark grays.

"Is it just me, or did I miss the dress code memo?"

"Don't you worry. Got you covered." Emma handed him a black hoodie. "I bought this up for you on the way here."

Clarke slipped the garment over his shirt, pulled it snug, and shook the hood out.

"Fits perfectly. Thanks."

"It should." Emma danced her fingers across her chest and lowered her voice. "I pay close attention when it comes to a man's size."

Sammy snorted.

"Something funny?" Emma asked with a fake air of innocence.

"Just you being the Queen of Subtlety. As usual."

"It's not my fault I have an eye for details." Emma slung an arm around his waist. "I've missed you, by the way."

"You see him every day!" Sammy protested.

"Not in the evenings. I've worked up quite the appetite, you see."

Brooke blushed at the exchange while Sammy rolled her eyes.

"Come on, ladies." Ashley crossed her arms. "Settle down. We're here on business."

"You found it, then?" Clarke asked.

"Yep!" Emma said. "We caught Heinrich with his grimoire out, and Ashley managed to plant a Tracking spell on it. He keeps the book at a Cube4Rent just outside the city. Storage unit Green Five."

"A cheap self-storage site?" Clarke asked. "He doesn't keep it at home or at work? That seems odd."

"Which may be why he keeps it there," Ashley said. "Misdirection is as natural to a vampire as breathing, so don't let the innocuous location fool you. It *will* be defended."

"What should we expect?"

"Hard to say. Familiars, protective spells, perhaps even a thrall or two. We won't know until we're neck deep."

"That brings up a question I've had: what exactly is a thrall? I know they were vampiric servants in Ashley's campaign, but where do they come from?"

"They're regular people who've been brainwashed by a vampire," Emma explained. "Typically with a spell like Dominate or Enthrall. Sometimes Persuade will work if the human's mind is weak enough. The requirements vary from person to person, and vampire to vampire. Most of the time it's a difficult, complicated process, which is about the only good thing I can say about it. Thralls are victims as much as the people vampires feed on, and sometimes are one and the same."

"That's about what I expected. Is there any way we can save them?"

"Rarely is there ever enough left *to* save."

Clarke nodded grimly, understanding. "Then if we have to, we shouldn't hesitate to take them out."

"They certainly won't hesitate to do the same to us."

"Should one of us scout out the location beforehand?" he asked. "Gather some intel before we rush in?"

"Ideally, yes," Ashley said. "One of my Scrying spells would normally do the trick."

"I'm detecting an unspoken 'but'."

"Because there is one. The site is Warded. My Tracking spell broke as soon as it hit the threshold. It'll take a very strong Scrying to punch through that kind of interference. I can pull it off, but the spell will set off enough magical alarms to wake the dead. He'll know someone's snooping around, which could lead him to strengthen his defenses or relocate the grimoire entirely."

"Sounds like our best bet is to go straight for the grimoire," Clarke said, "even if we are heading in blind."

"That's my thinking as well."

Clarke turned to Brooke and Sammy, eager to gauge their reactions. He'd be facing Heinrich's defenses right alongside them, and he was relieved to see both women held themselves with a mix of confidence and eagerness.

"We can handle this," Sammy said.

Brooke nodded with a slim smile, ears tall, tail wagging.

"Then I say we go for it," Clarke said. "When do we bust in?"

"Tonight," Ashley said.

"No time like the present."

"Yeah!" Emma pumped the air. "Time to kick off this campaign for real!"

They took Emma's car to the self-storage site. Ashley claimed the front seat, which left the others to pile into the back. Clarke ended up sandwiched between Brooke and Sammy, though neither girl seemed to mind. Brooke kept her hands to herself, arms folded under her breasts, while Sammy rested a hand over his thigh. A gloved hand, fortunately.

Emma drove them to a strip plaza that ran parallel to the Cube4Rent and pulled into the employee parking behind the strip. A few lights were on, but theirs was the only car. They climbed out, and Ashley led them through a line of trees and up a hill that overlooked the self-storage site.

They crouched together in a patch of tall grass.

The storage cubes were arranged in contiguous rows with heavy rollup doors on either side, all of them numbered and color coded.

Emma raised a pair of binoculars to her eyes.

"Just one vehicle in the parking lot. But I don't see anyone walking around."

"Maybe they're inside one of the cubes?" Brooke asked.

"Maybe. Each row has a PTZ camera mounted beneath the floodlights, and there's a chain link fence around the site. Other than that, it's a clear shot from here to Heinrich's cube."

"Will the cameras be a problem?" Clarke asked.

"No," Ashley said. "The spells I put on your clothes will conceal your identities from any recording devices."

Clarke tugged on his new hoodie in lieu of a question.

"Yes, that one, too. I cast the spell before you arrived at the mill. Anyone watching you on video will know someone was here but won't know it was you. To regular humans, your image will appear too blurry to make out, and they'll assume it was an issue with the camera's focus or gunk on the lens. Something like that."

"What if a vampire looks over the footage?"

"Any vampire worth his fangs will recognize the Concealment spells but still won't be able to tell it was you."

"Handy. I'd hate to end up in jail before we get to kick our first vampire's butt."

"Still no one in sight," Emma reported, lowering her binoculars. "That car might be a clunker someone left in the lot."

"Then let's get to it!" Clarke said, summoning his Sanguine Shield.

"Here, for the book." Emma handed him an empty backpack.

Brooke kicked off her sandals and shifted into her full werewolf form, while Sammy stripped off her gloves, shoes, coat, and pants. Her skin glistened with a pale, pink sheen, which contrasted with her black bra and panties.

Clarke led the way down the hill and across to the fence. He glanced back over his shoulder.

"Brooke, you bring the bolt cutters?"

"Sure did!"

Brooke raked both claws downward, then swiped once across at waist height. Severed pieces of fence tinkled to the ground, and a rectangular section levered down. She grabbed it before it hit the ground then shifted it aside.

"After you," Brooke said, sweeping a broad arm toward the new hole.

"Perfect."

Clarke crouch-walked through the gap in the fence. Sammy followed him in, and Brooke took up the rear, replacing the fence piece once she was inside. Clarke took a right, followed the long row of rollup doors to its end, then cut across their colored fronts. He found the conspicuously green one and was about to check around the corner when Brooke grabbed his shoulder and jerked him back.

"Hold it," she hissed under her breath. "Some-one's there."

She bobbed her head to indicate the direction then tapped an ear.

Clarke nodded his understanding. He eased up to the corner and inched one eye into view. He stole a quick glance then backed away.

"One guy," he whispered. "A big fella, and he's standing right in front of Heinrich's unit."

"Think he's a thrall?" Brooke asked.

"What else could he be?" Sammy said.

"Let me check." Clarke lowered his head and focused his inner eye toward Heinrich's cube. He'd expected to find magic pouring off the building but sensed nothing remark-able about it. Perhaps the Ward was blocking him?

He shifted his focus to the man instead.

Iron, he thought. *The taste of iron. Like sucking on a rusted nail. Cold and sharp and maybe a bit brittle.*

He couldn't identify the exact spell, but he knew enough from his lessons to generalize. The iron was the key.

So close to the taste of blood.

"Yeah, he's got vampiric spells on him."

"Want me to take him out?" Brooke asked.

Clarke met the werewolf's gaze. He glanced down at her razor-sharp claws then up into her eyes.

"Won't that be messy?" he asked.

"*Knock* him out," she clarified.

"You two hang back here," Sammy said. "I've got this one. Clarke, hold this for me."

She pressed a bundle of something warm and soft into his hands. Her body liquefied and dropped into a pink puddle, which then oozed swiftly around the corner.

Clarke looked down at the undergarments Sammy had stuffed into his hands, and then he sighed.

"Her, too, I guess."

"Something up?" Brooke asked.

"I'll explain later."

He peeked around the corner.

The guard stood rigidly in front of a rollup door about halfway down the row, eyes forward, shoulders squared, hands clasped in front. He wore a tan windbreaker despite the pleasant weather, which made Clarke wonder if the jacket concealed a firearm. His nocturnal sunglasses did nothing to make him appear any more normal.

Sammy slithered up the wall and onto the roof without making a sound. Clarke lost sight of her until she reappeared, oozing down behind the sentry.

Her face took form in the pink slime, upside down and directly behind the man's own head. She licked the back of his neck, then recoiled upward.

The man smacked the spot as if trying to swat a fly. He rubbed the base of his neck, grimacing for a moment— before his jaw clamped shut and the muscles in his neck bulged outward. He staggered forward, both hands clenching his gut.

"Huk! Huk! *Hu-u-u-u-urk!*"

The man puked out his dinner. He collapsed to his knees, heaved again, and more chunks spewed from his mouth. His forehead smacked against the pavement, and he kicked his legs out, scrambling frantically in place as the contents of his gut fought to be free of his body.

Clarke cringed. "That does *not* look pleasant."

As if it wasn't dramatic enough already, the man twisted around and flopped onto his back. He groaned and gurgled before more vomit fountained out of his mouth. As his latest heave splattered on the ground, he began twitching uncontrollably, arms and legs and even his head thrashing for a whole minute until finally he stopped and lay still.

Clarke stepped out into the open.

"Uh, Sammy?"

The slime girl leaped off the roof and landed in human form, completely naked.

"You didn't kill him, did you?" He walked up to the sentry and prodded him with the toe of his boot. The man twitched, eyes rolled back into his head, mouth foaming.

"Nah. He'll be fine in a few days."

She took her bra and panties out of his hand and jammed them into her chest. Two cloth shadows unfolded within her body and floated apart before emerging at the normal locations.

"A few *days*?" Clarke asked.

"Yep. Why? You want me to put him down for longer?"

"No, no!" he replied quickly. "A few days is fine."

"Eww!" Brooke rubbed her snout. "He crapped himself, too!"

"Sorry?" Sammy gave her an indifferent shrug. "Not my fault."

"How is this *not* your fault?"

"Well, you see, when the human body needs to purge a foreign substance, it's not picky about the exit."

"Ladies, let's stay focused," Clarke said. "Brooke, would you mind getting the door?"

"On it."

She bent down and ripped the lock out with one quick jerk. Clarke grabbed the handle at the base of the rollup door and lifted.

His eyes widened when he saw what was inside.

Or rather, what wasn't.

"Well." He licked his suddenly dry lips. "Didn't see this coming."

"I know we didn't expect this," Ashley said over the phone, "but the bottom line is we need that grimoire."

"Then we head in?" Clarke asked. "This could take a while."

"I don't see any other option. Emma and I will keep watch from here. We'll let you know if we spot trouble heading your way."

"Understood." He pocketed his phone. "Ashley says we keep going."

"Fine by me." Brooke finished dragging the guard into the self-storage unit. She let go of his armpits, and he sprawled on the floor.

Clarke eyed the back of the cube.

The *missing* back of the cube.

Someone had removed the back wall, joining this cube with one on the opposite side of the row, then installed a flight of wooden steps that led down into unseen depths. He found a switch and flipped it. Lights flickered on, illuminating the sterile steps that leveled off about two stories underground.

Definitely not a standard subscription unit.

"I'll go first," Brooke said, closing the rollup door behind them. "I'm the toughest and who knows what's down there."

"Good idea."

They headed down the stairs with Brooke in the lead. The path widened into a large rectangular room at the bottom. The air was cool and dry, and the room furnished with thick, red carpeting and a long wooden table with a single highbacked chair. Three doors led out in three different directions through the cinderblock walls. Power conduits ran under awkward folds in the carpet to three wall-mounted junction boxes, one for each door.

"Pick a door," Brooke said softly. "Any door."

"Can you sense any magic?" Sammy asked.

"Nothing distinct or recognizable," Clarke said. "Maybe if I get closer."

"Then I guess we'll have try our luck."

"Guess so. Brooke? Start on the left. We'll sweep around, one door at a time until we find that book."

"You got it."

They bunched up outside the first door. Brooke cracked it open, sniffed the air, then swung it wide.

A blast of cold air hit Clarke in the face, and he shivered.

Brooke halted at the threshold and growled deep in

her throat. Clarke couldn't see the room past her.

"What's wrong?" he asked.

"Death."

"What, like literally? Is that a thing?"

"No, I mean dead animals. Poor things."

Brooke stepped aside to let Clarke pass. Cold air bit at his face, neck, and hands as he walked in—and a chill from a deeper place struck him when he looked inside. Frost encrusted the concrete surfaces while furred carcasses hung from the ceiling on meat hooks, most missing their heads. Long, metal basins sat underneath each row, collecting the dead animals' blood.

It resembled a butcher's freezer, except the goal wasn't to drain the carcasses in preparation for the next step; the draining *was* the purpose. He couldn't tell the different breeds apart without their heads, but they weren't pigs or cows.

Some of them were small.

Very small.

House pet small.

"Heinrich's pantry," Sammy whispered, her voice as cold and harsh as the air.

"This is sick," Clarke said. "The man volunteers at a rescue shelter!"

"And now we know why." Sammy gave his shoulder a tug. "Come on. I doubt the book's in here."

"Right." Clarke stepped out and closed the door, cutting off the chill. "Let's look elsewhere."

Brooke cracked the middle door open and sniffed the air.

"Nothing dead in here," she said, and swung the door wide.

This room featured a cozy recliner, the leather along its back and seat cracked with age and use. A stack of books sat atop the nightstand beside the chair, and more books filled the two metal bookcases bolted into the side walls. The racks along the far wall held dozens of jars, their labels yellowed with age. Intricate markings covered a circular patch of the floor.

"*Much* more promising!" Sammy said.

"What's all this?" Clarke pointed to the floor markings. "Feels like vampire magic."

"Could be part of a magic circle."

"Is it dangerous?"

"Don't know. Looks unfinished." Sammy poked the edge with her toe. Nothing happened. "Seems safe."

"*Sammy?*"

"What?"

"Isn't that the same as sticking your tongue in an electrical outlet to check if the wires are live?"

"Heck if I know. I don't do the magic stuff. Now, come on. Let's find that book!"

Sammy stepped around the unfinished magic circle. She grabbed a book off the shelf, leafed through it, then tossed it aside and pulled out another. Brooke joined her, and the two began working their way through the vampire's library.

Clarke walked up to the opposite case, since he didn't want to crowd the ladies while they worked. He pulled a book off the shelf, checked the spine—just a date and some German—and leafed through the interior.

An old ledger of some kind. Not the grimoire.

He tossed it aside and reached for another.

His fingers touched the top of the spine, but then he hesitated, his mind racing all of a sudden.

Was there a way he could speed up this process?

He wondered, closed his eyes.

And opened a different one.

The first thing he sensed was the magic circle, heavy with the taste of iron, but mingled with hints of raw meat, coarse hair, and teeth. He shifted his mind's eye elsewhere, letting it float about like an ethereal dousing rod.

He found his focus drawn to the stacks at the back, to the labeled jars. Why, he couldn't say, but he let himself be pulled toward them. He rounded the circle's inscriptions and walked slowly from one side of the racks to the other, a finger tracing dust off the top shelf.

None of the jars drew his attention.

He dropped his finger down a shelf and paced back the other way.

Something tickled at his mind near the center, and he stopped in front of two jars: one filled with small bones, the other some kind of powder. He pushed them side, revealing the cinderblock wall behind the racks.

He grimaced at the wall for long seconds, unsure why he was staring at it or what he was looking for.

He reached toward it, rested his fingers lightly on the block, and felt for the flows of magic.

Iron. Subtle, but present. Along with … wet ink? Yes, fresh ink—cool and crisp—but coupled with furnace heat and walls of volcanic glass.

He ran a finger along the block's cement groove, then pressed into it with his nail.

The "cement" gave to the pressure like soft clay.

"I found something!"

Brooke and Sammy joined him at the back wall, and he dug out more of the fake cement with his fingernail.

"Something's behind this block."

"I've got this." Brooke raked a single claw around the block, excavating the fake cement. She sank her claws into the block and pulled it out, revealing a hidden compartment.

And a heavy, leatherbound book.

Clarke pulled the tome out and opened it near the center. The pages were covered with tiny, blurred text. He flipped through it, but every page was equally muddled.

"A Concealment spell?"

"That must be Heinrich's grimoire," Sammy said.

"Can we be sure?"

"None of the other books are protected with magic. Plus, it was hidden behind a wall. What else could it be?"

"All right." Clarke stuffed the book into his backpack and zipped it up. "Guess we'll need Ashley to decipher this mess. Let's get out of here before—"

The magic circle began to glow with ghoulish light.

"Oh, shit."

All at once, the center of the circle blazed with greenish fire, its flames hot like a natural blaze but somehow containing all the welcoming warmth of a corpse left outside in the dead of winter. A bestial shape began to coalesce amidst the green corpse light, its four-legged silhouette bulky and low to the ground.

"We must have triggered a booby trap!" Brooke shouted over the roar of the flames.

"You *think*?" Sammy snapped.

"The door!" Clarke shouted. "While it's summoning! Go!"

They bolted past the magic circle, racing for the open door, but it slammed shut on its own. Metal creaked, and spikes shot into the surrounding walls and ceiling, anchoring it in place.

Brooke slammed her shoulder into it. The door buckled but didn't break. She raked her claws across it, and sparks flew into the air. The door refused to yield.

"It's coming through!" Sammy shouted.

"Get ready!" Clarke conjured his thirstblade. "We can do this!"

"Fuck!" Brooke swung back around, brandishing her claws.

The green flames snuffed themselves out, and smoke rose from a creature not unlike a Doberman, but much larger and more heavily muscled. It must have weighed over four hundred pounds at least.

The beast's body was covered in short, black fur. Its ears were two tall points, and steam escaped through its glistening teeth with every hot breath. The eyes burned two harsh, glowing points of green within its hollow sockets.

"Hellhound," Sammy breathed.

The beast bellowed, flecks of spittle flying from its gums.

Brooke let out her own savage roar and charged at the creature.

The hellhound leaped, powerful hind legs propelling it forward with all the force of a cannonball. It slammed into Brooke, knocking the wind out of her. Ribs cracked, and she folded over until her hands almost touched her ankles. She hit the ground hard on her side, and the hellhound bolted past her, eyes fixed on Clarke.

"Brooke!" he called out.

"I'm … fine …" she wheezed, struggling to her feet.

The hellhound galloped at Clarke, and he dashed to the side, slashing across with his sword. The blade cut into the hellhound's flank, and black ichor bled across the wound. It landed on all fours and swung around, once again locking its gaze on Clarke.

Sammy whipped an arm out and lassoed the creature's throat. The hellhound ignored her, running forward until it found its head jerked back. It wheezed steam, then howled. Green flames danced across its body.

"Ah!" Sammy cried, yanking her limb away. "Hot, hot, hot!"

"You ladies okay?" Clarke asked, backing away from the hellhound.

"Never better!" Sammy replied, shaking out her smoking wrist.

"Me, too!" Brooke sucked in a sharp breath, and her ribs cracked back into place. "Come on! I barely felt that, you monster!"

The hellhound ignored Brooke and dashed straight for Clarke. He again dodged at the last moment and scored a glancing blow across the beast's hind quarter. More dark fluid spilled of the creature's wounds, and it snarled in defiance, vile gobs of spittle splattering on the concrete floor.

"It seems to *really* not like me!" Clarke said.

The hellhound charged again, and this time the beast caught him with a paw. Claws scraped across his shield, and red sparks flew into the air. He backpedaled away, raising his sword once more.

"The book!" Sammy exclaimed. "It's going for the book! That's got to be it!"

"I'm not giving it back!"

"You don't have to. Just keep doing what you're doing. Brooke?"

"This mean we know its next move?"

"You've got it! Pincer attack!"

"Hell, yeah!"

Brooke and Sammy positioned themselves ahead and to either side of Clarke. The hellhound ignored them, almost to a comical degree, and bolted straight for the only target it cared about.

But this time the ladies were ready.

Sammy morphed her arms together, hands forming the head of a mallet, and smashed them into the hellhound's skull. Her attack cracked bone, and the hellhound's glowing eyes winked out for a moment.

Brooke lunged at it from the other side. Her jaws snapped into its back like a bear trap, and she sank her claws into its flesh. The hellhound howled; flames exploded from its wounds. Brooke's fur burned and her skin sizzled, but she pressed the attack, ripping her claws through the hellhound's guts.

The creature hit the ground with a thud and skidded forward, foul intestines spooling out of its body. Clarke shot forward, thirstblade forming a rising scarlet arc through the air. The blade hissed through the hellhound's face. Its eyes dimmed into blackness, and the top half of its head slid down onto the floor.

Brooke rose to her feet, her forearms and snout smoking, flesh writhing as she healed. She gave the corpse a swift kick to the ribs.

"And stay down!"

CHAPTER NINE

CLARKE JABBED HIS WEAPON into the defeated monster. His thirstblade drank in what remained of the creature's polluted lifeforce, and his Sanguine Shield snapped back to full strength.

"Ladies, I believe it's time we made our exit."

"You said it!" Sammy replied. "Brooke?"

"Way ahead of you."

Brooke stalked over to the door and began slicing through it with her claws.

While she worked, Clarke's phone vibrated. He and Sammy checked their messages at the same time.

The text read: **Heinrich is here! GET OUT NOW!**

"Brooke?" Clarke said urgently. "We need to hurry! Vampire incoming!"

"Almost through!"

With renewed intensity, the werewolf ripped into the door, tore back one of the spikes, and then bashed the tattered remains with her shoulder. The tortured metal dropped to the ground, and all three of them barreled through, back to the main carpeted room with the big wooden table.

"Hurry!" Clarke said. "Up the stairs before—!"

"Before what, human?"

Otto Heinrich descended the stairs one casual step at a time, as if he were merely strolling into his classroom. He nearly looked the part, too, in a red bowtie and matching suspenders over his crisp, white shirt, the kind of garb worn by quirky professors who had little fan clubs among the students.

This image was thoroughly wrecked by the long fangs peeking out over his lower lips and the annoyed scowl that said he was about to use them. Clarke and the others braced for battle—but he regarded them with eyes meant for flies or other minor pests.

"Hellhounds." The vampire shook his head like he'd just been disappointed by a student's half-assed program, then let out a little sigh. "Honestly, why do I even bother? Good help is so hard to summon these days. I suppose I'll have to deal with this mess myself."

"I wouldn't sound so confident if I were you," Clarke said. "It's three against one."

"So what if it is?" Heinrich eyed each of them in turn. "The werewolf and the slime should have known better, but *you*, human: Who freed you from your yoke, I wonder." He extended an upturned palm toward Clarke. "My grimoire. Hand it back."

Clarke couldn't get over how *normal* his voice sounded, even as he said things like "Who freed you from your yoke?" Another testament to how well the vampire could fool a person, even with his fangs obvious.

Still, Clarke managed:

"Over my dead body."

"Ha! Poor choice of words." The vampire's eyes gleamed with a faint light, and he snapped his fingers like a playful magician.

A wall of green flame erupted at the base of the stairs, forming a barrier between them and the vampire. The thrall Sammy had sickened earlier lurched down the entry-way—and bumped into Heinrich's back, which prompted the vampire to give everyone an exaggerated eyeroll, again as if pissed off by a dumbass student.

"What the hell are you doing?"

"Mmurrr …"

"Around me. Go *around* me! You're making me look bad!"

"Urrr …"

The thrall shuffled past Heinrich, slow walked against

the wall for a few seconds, then turned toward Clarke and the others. Clarke was almost tempted to laugh—almost—but then he realized the thrall's skin was deathly pale, and he passed through the corpse fire unharmed.

"What the hell is wrong with him?" Clarke asked.

"Oh?" Heinrich flourished with one hand. "Haven't you ever seen a zombie before?"

"A zombie?!" Sammy's eyes widened. "But I didn't kill him! He was alive when we left him!"

"Alive, but useless," Heinrich said matter-of-factly. "However, a zombie is far more resilient to your brand of mischief, little slime. I simply used the raw material at hand."

"You *killed* him so that you could *raise* him?" Clarke spat. All inklings of humor left him, repulsed by the vampire's casual attitude toward death.

"Correct." Heinrich pointed at Clarke. "Kill the human. Retrieve my book."

"Blurrrgh!"

The zombie drew a revolver from his shoulder harness and fired. The shot hit Clarke square in the chest. His shield flashed, and he stumbled back. He hadn't even rebalanced before Brooke rushed forward, blocking the remaining shots with her body. Three struck her with meaty *thunks*, and two more ricocheted wildly around the room. One of the rebounds punched a divot into the table while the other splashed into Sammy's abdomen, spawning a brief wave of ripples across her stomach.

"Ah!" Clarke cried. "Shit, that stung!"

"You okay?" Brooke asked.

"I think so." Clarke patted his chest. No holes. Not even in his hoodie. "How about you?"

"Pissed off. You, Sammy?"

"I'm fine. It wasn't a bad hit."

Heinrich stared at Clarke, some of his poise and superiority turning toward confusion.

"Now, what kind of magic was that, I wonder?" he asked, tilting his head.

"Uurrr!" The zombie dropped his empty six-shooter and shambled toward Clarke, both arms reaching.

Brooke grabbed the zombie by the neck and lifted him off his feet. His legs continued to pantomime a walk.

"How *dare* you hurt him!"

Her jaw gaped, almost like it had unhinged. She chomped down on the zombie's head from above and then jerked her mouth to the side, taking the head with it. Blood spurted from the zombie's neck. She threw the headless corpse at Heinrich's feet and chewed loudly, glaring at him.

"Brooke?" Clarke asked, slightly horrified by all the blood.

She swallowed. "Yes?"

"Did you really have to bite his head off?"

175

"He was already dead."

"Fair point, I suppose …"

"How unpleasant." Heinrich inspected his white shirt, found a splotch of blood, and frowned at it. "Well, that's another shirt ruined. I suppose it's my own fault for playing with my food."

"We going to kick his ass?" Sammy said. "Because I really want to."

"You better believe we are." Clarke pointed his thirstblade at the vampire. "Time to take him—"

"Silence!" Heinrich swept out his arm, and a wave of shadows slammed into the three of them, knocking them a step back. "Know your place. You think a hellhound is the worst I prepared for intruders?"

The vampire snapped his fingers, and a series of loud thunks echoed from the pantry. A strange gurgling, hissing, slithering chorus rose from behind the door, and then something huge and heavy slammed into it.

It struck again.

Then again.

"Oh, for fuck's sake." Heinrich rubbed his temples.

The door shuddered from another blow.

"You need to *pull* it open!"

The unseen beast roared through a dozen throats and slammed into the door again.

"No! Pull! The other way!"

The lock and hinges strained from another impact, and Heinrich sighed. Clarke got the impression he fancied himself the kind of vampire who'd rule the world, if only he could get some damn help that wouldn't do dumbass things in the shadows.

"Why the fuck do I even bother?" the vampire grumbled, moments before the door flew off its hinges, and a grotesque monstrosity pushed its way through the opening.

The patchwork of furred flesh writhed forward on two legs made from dead cats and dogs. A pair of arms swung languidly at either side, and a dozen severed necks undulated where the head should have been, each oozing fluids. The monstrosity faced Heinrich, for a certain value of the term, and extended a finger toward Clarke.

"Corpse golem, I command you to retrieve my book!"

The golem roared, blood spurting from its orifices. It lumbered forward, shoved the table aside as if it were made of Styrofoam, then brought a huge limb of corpses crashing down.

Clarke backpedaled to the wall, and the fist of dead cats squelched against concrete. He darted back in, slashed across the limb and circled around behind the monster. It followed him with its eyeless gaze, shambling ponderously around, which gave the others an opening.

Brooke leaped onto the golem from behind and began ripping its back apart with claws and teeth. Ragged chunks of dead animals hit the ground with wet thuds, and the golem grumbled deep within its many chests. It swung an arm at the werewolf.

The creature's flexibility wasn't limited by a skeleton—or rather, not a *single* skeleton—and the corpse-fist smashed into Brooke from the side, throwing her off its back. She hit the ground hard and rolled until she smacked against the wall, then snarled, baring her fangs as she scrambled back to her feet.

Sammy flung both arms forward like pink serpentine whips. She ensnared one of the golem's legs and tugged back hard. The golem staggered toward her, close to tumbling over.

"A little help!" she cried.

"I'm here!"

Clarke cut down through the other leg, his thirst-blade cleaving skin, sinew, and bone with ease. That limb bulked, and the golem dropped to the equivalent of one knee. It swiped at Clarke and thumped the side of his head hard enough for his shield to flare and for stars to swim across his vision. He struggled to keep his balance and almost fell over, but Brooke caught him, steadied him, and then rushed in herself.

The golem swung at her, but she caught the limb with both arms, her claws sinking into dead flesh. She jammed a leg against the corpse golem and yanked back on its arm. The limb began to break free, bones cracking, skin and muscle tearing.

The golem tried to punch Brooke with its free arm, but Sammy wrapped the appendage with her arms and pulled it back.

Clarke saw the opening, the stretched sinews and loose bones holding the weakened arm to its body. He swung his sword down into the fleshy connection and sliced straight through.

The limb broke free, and Brooke chucked it aside. She charged right back in, tearing into the golem's chest in a flurry of claws. Bits of meat and bone flew into the air as the golem struggled to free its remaining arm. It threw a ponderous kick at Brooke, but missed, too unbalanced by her relentless attack.

Clarke snatched the opportunity, sidestepping around the golem to thrust his sword into its side. The scarlet blade sank in deep. He wrenched it around in the creature's gut, then tore it up through the hideous torso of meat and bone.

Something slackened within the creature. Its movements slowed, became less certain, less powerful as it fought to free itself. Brooke tore through the creature, her claws rending its flesh in crimson blurs.

Clarke slashed through a leg, and the creature toppled. It thrashed on the floor, more a mound of corpse meat than the humanoid monstrosity it had been moments ago. Brooke ripped off chunks of dead animals, Clarke stabbed the central mass over and over, and Sammy joined in, hammering the animated flesh with fists like mallets.

Soon they'd hammered it enough. The creature shuddered, then relaxed as it sighed through a dozen broken orifices. The broken flesh mound seemed to deflate, what remained of its body separating into individual corpses that flopped aside—

—and ceased to move.

"What a fucking mess." Heinrich looked at the floor as if they'd just spilled an entire lasagna dinner all over this favorite white rug.

"You're … next …" Clarke panted, pointing the tip of his sword at the vampire. He wiped away the sweat beading on his brow.

"Oh, please! You? A human with a little magic? I'm a fucking vampire!"

Heinrich spread his arms, and the wall of ghoulish flame protecting him vanished. Green energy formed a flaming rod above his hands, which rapidly solidified into a huge, shining blade of obsidian. The summoned weapon dropped into his open palms. He took hold of the grip and raised the massive blade, large enough to be a zweihander—and Clarke couldn't help but feel a chill. Heinrich might still be in his quirky professor clothes, but the huge blade changed things.

Clarke held up his own sword and took a deep, steadying breath. The previous fights had worn him down, as much as he hated to admit it, whereas Heinrich was fresh and eager for action (on top of having a giant magic sword). Clarke glanced to either side; both Sammy and Brooke were still in this fight, but he could tell they weren't in top form. Brooke, especially, had taken some nasty hits. Her ribs had been broken, mouth and hands burned, and she'd been shot three times!

Her werewolf nature granted her inhuman vitality, but everyone had their limits. How close was she to hers? Most of her wounds had vanished, but blood trickled from her three bullet wounds.

"I'll grant you this one final chance," Heinrich said. "Return my grimoire, and you have my word I will *only* kill these two. As demihumans, they should know better. You, on the other hand, I can restore to blissful ignorance."

"Go to hell!"

Heinrich sighed with a little headshake. "Suit yourself."

He conjured an aura of green flame that about his body. Clarke and the others braced for this one, final battle.

"Tonight, I feast on your corpses!" Heinrich licked an obscenely long tongue across the flat of his sword.

And then he shot forward with inhuman speed.

He didn't get far.

His shoe caught on a rut in the carpet, and he stumbled forward.

"Wh-whoa!"

The sword flew out of his hands and arced ahead of him as he clawed at the air with flailing limbs. The sword landed hilt-first, and Heinrich's momentum carried him straight into it. The blade sank into his heart, and then the tip punched out his back as a little, bloody triangle.

Clarke cringed, not sure what to make of the spectacle.

"Fuck!" Heinrich squirmed on his sword, legs kicking out, but that only served to drive the blade deeper. He vomited up blood, soaking his collar.

In the face of a sight that absurd, Clarke thought it was safe to risk a little humor.

"You doing all right there, Professor? I think you dropped something."

"Fuck you!" he croaked. "Fuck all of you!"

"Right. Let me help you with that." Clarke grabbed a fistful of the vampire's hair and—slowly and deliberately—pulled the man all the way down his own sword.

Heinrich thrashed on the ground, stuck on the sword, blood pooling underneath the wound. He spat at them and swore, but the rest of his words were garbled by the blood gushing out of his mouth. He let out one last gurgling exhale and, finally, lay still.

The giant sword vanished into a twinkling rain.

And then the corpse shat itself.

Clarke sniffed the air.

"Brooke?"

"Yeah?"

"Did he just …?"

"Yup. A big stinker, too."

"I didn't expect this."

"Me neither."

Clarke glanced at Sammy.

"Don't look at me." She threw up her hands. "I'm as surprised as the rest of you."

He turned to Brooke.

"Maybe Heinrich was a second-rate vampire?" Brooke said with a shrug. "*Third*-rate?"

"Maybe."

Clarke regarded the dead vampire, recalling what Emma had told him about how hard they were to kill. Or, more specifically, how difficult it could be to make them stay dead. He stepped over to the side of the body, raised his sword and—with one clean stroke—cleaved off the man's head.

Just to be sure.

"Well," he said matter-of-factly, dismissing his thirst-blade. "That's that, I suppose. Let's get out of here."

"You sure this is the best we can do?" Clarke asked, eyeing the bottle of Absolut vodka with suspicion. Emma had driven him and the rest of Broken Fang back to the steel mill after they left Heinrich's secret lair. He sat next to Brooke, back in hybrid form with her shirt off. Sammy kept the flashlight trained on the werewolf's wounds while Ashley sat nearby, diligently studying the grimoire open in her lap.

"At this hour, it is," Emma said, standing behind him. "We could try our luck with a hospital, I suppose."

"I don't need a hospital." Brooke grabbed the bottle of vodka and took a swig. "Yeah, this'll do fine."

"That's for the bullet wounds," Clarke said.

"I'm sterilizing them from the inside."

"It doesn't work that way."

"Shows what you know." Brooke took another gulp. "Whew! This stuff has some serious kick!"

"It should," Emma said. "It's forty percent alcohol."

"We should *really* prep a better first aid kit for next time," Clarke said.

"He's right," Sammy added. "Just think where we'd be if someone other than Brooke got shot."

"What are you talking about?" Brooke asked. "You were shot, too."

"I was?" Sammy's brow crinkled as she thought. "Oh, right! Yeah, I forgot about that."

"You forgot being hit by a bullet?" Clarke asked. "How's *that* work?"

"Hey, a lot happened tonight."

"You can say that again," Brooke sighed, and took another swig.

Clarke picked up the needle nose pliers. "Sammy, you okay going second?"

"Hold up." She tilted her head back, eyes darting this way and that. "I think I found it."

"Found what?"

"Almost there." She swished something around inside her mouth, then bent over and spat into the bucket.

Clarke glanced inside to find a glistening bullet fragment.

"Well, that was easy." He raised the pliers to the bullet wound over Brooke's left breast. "You ready for this?"

Brooke set down the bottle of vodka. "Ready. Yank it out."

"Brace yourself."

Brooke clenched her eyes shut.

Clarke eased the pliers into the wound, then spread the head.

"Gah!" Brooke gasped. Her muscles flexed, and her claws extended, but she kept her arms down.

"I feel the bullet." He twisted the pliers around, clamped down on the unseen mass, and then eased it out.

"Shit!"

He inspected the flattened bullet in the light, then dropped it into the bucket.

"Two more. You good?"

"Just get this over with."

Clarke shifted his seat over to the next two wounds, both located in her abs, and went to work.

"Fuck!" Brooke cried after he pulled out the third bullet. "They're worse coming out!"

"That's all of them." Clarke smiled at her. "You did great."

"Here." Emma handed him a cloth soaked with vodka.

Clarke cleaned and dressed each of Brooke's bullet wounds, but he wasn't sure if he was helping at all, given how fast the wounds were closing. Emma offered Brooke a clean shirt, but she waved it away and took another gulp of vodka instead.

The succubus set the shirt aside and picked up one of the bullets.

"Well?" Clarke asked.

"Just what I thought." She held the bullet up to the light. "Hexed ammunition. A variant of Cripple, if I'm not mistaken. A good counter for demihumans with fast healing factors. Someone came prepared."

"Or got lucky," Sammy said.

"I think it was *us* who got lucky," Brooke said.

"Good thing we managed to pull them out," Clarke asked. "What would have happened if we hadn't?"

"Depends on the strength of the hex." Emma

dropped the bullet back into the bucket. "A powerful one could have messed up her natural healing for a while. Maybe even enough to threaten her life. These, though, don't feel nearly that strong to me. Her shifter magic would have worn them out in a day or so, and she would have healed just fine afterward."

"That's still enough to keep her bleeding in the middle of a fight," Clarke pointed out. "How you doing over there, Brooke?"

"Mellow and relaxed!" She took another sip, then set the bottle aside and flashed a happy smile his way.

"Well, you earned it." Clarke glanced over at Ashley, who'd been quietly studying the grimoire. "How's it going over there?"

"Could be better." Ashley didn't look up as she turned the page. "The Conceal spell protecting this book is surprisingly sophisticated. I'll need some time to break through it."

"Don't stay up too late." Clarke climbed to his feet. "I don't know about the rest of you, but I could use some Z's."

"I second the motion to adjourn," Sammy said, followed by an epic yawn.

"What time is it, anyway?" Emma asked, rubbing her eyes.

"Three in the morning," Ashley replied, still engrossed in the tome.

"Oh, gawd!"

"Brooke, you need a ride home?" Clarke asked.

"Nah." She smiled pleasantly, cheeks warm and rosy. "I've got my camping gear in the Jeep. I'll spend the night here. Thanks for the offer, though."

"All right. You take care of yourself." Clarke waved to his fellow members of Broken Fang. "I'm heading out. Ladies, call if you need anything."

Chapter Ten

Clarke collapsed in bed back at his apartment, surprised by how severely he'd crashed after the adrenaline wore off. He slept past noon and only stirred when Emma texted him.

"Hey," he grunted, still cocooned within his comforter, phone to his ear.

"Hey, Clarke. How you feeling?"

"A little sore. Especially where I got shot. You?"

"Had a pleasant night's sleep."

"Good, good." He rubbed his face. "Need something?"

"'Need' is … too strong a word." He could almost see her sly, flirty smile. "Let's go with 'want' instead."

"Sure. What do you want?"

"I think you know."

He did, and he wasn't about to turn down an offer

like that. After the exhaustion of last night, he could do with *multiple* forms of rejuvenation. He roused himself from bed, took a quick shower, threw on some clothes, and then drove to Emma's apartment.

"It's open!" she called out when he knocked on the door.

A rich, hearty aroma greeted him when he entered.

"Smells good!" He closed the door. "What are you cooking?"

"Clam chowder with a side of sourdough toast. I figured you wouldn't mind some food first."

"Not at all." He walked over to the kitchen, then slowed and smiled at the lovely view. "Now, that's a surprise."

"It shouldn't be," Emma replied, naked except for her apron and glasses. Her wings and tail were out as well. "Enjoying the view?"

"You know it." He leaned against the counter and let his eyes drink in her curves.

"I can serve it whenever you're ready," she said, stirring the vat of soup. "I'm just letting it reduce a bit."

"Take your time." He let his eyes linger on her shapely behind. "I'm in no hurry."

"But what if I am!" she replied, laughing. She stirred the vat some more, and her face turned serious. "I was worried about you last night."

"That makes two of us. Still can't believe what we just pulled."

"And this is only the start."

"I know."

"I spoke with the others this morning."

"How's Brooke doing?"

"Back to a hundred percent. Werewolves bounce back fast."

"Yeah, I figured."

"She really appreciates how you helped out last night. Sammy, too. They're not sure what would have happened without you there, but it wouldn't have been good."

"Glad I could help. We form a good team."

"They feel the same way." She ladled out two bowls and set them on the counter next to a plate of hot toast. "Want anything to drink?"

"Water is fine."

"With ice?"

"Yes, please."

"Coming right up."

She served him a glass of ice water, then joined him on the other side of the counter.

Clarke blew on the first hot spoonful before eating it.

"Mmm! What'd you put in this?"

"Besides the usual ingredients, I add bits of bacon, onion, celery, and just a dash of Tabasco and Worcestershire sauces to give it a subtle kick."

"It's delicious!"

"Thank you. I borrowed the recipe from one of my aunts."

"She a succubus, too?"

"Siren, actually." Emma leaned in, eyes laughing. "That part of the family tree can get a little weird, but she's my go-to when it comes to seafood."

They both finished their meals, perhaps faster than normal. When Clarke finished, Emma pulled the knot loose along her back and tossed the apron aside.

"Come here, you gorgeous hunk!"

Clarke pulled Emma into his arms, and they kissed hungrily, voraciously. He squeezed one of her breasts, and she moaned eagerly into his mouth. It was the only demand he needed to hear. He picked her up and carried her to the bedroom.

Clarke lost track of how many times they had sex that weekend. He'd shared his bed with women before, but none so eager, so comfortable—with her own body and with him. She trusted him, as a man and as a lover, and that trust came through in how she made love to him.

Emma started by climbing onto the bed on all fours and begging him to take her from behind. Later, he rolled her onto her back and pounded her with her knees resting up on his shoulders. She mounted him after that, riding him hard as he played with her firm, shapely breasts.

They took breaks when they felt like it, ate when they grew hungry, but beyond those basic needs, the day was filled with nothing but sex. Clarke surprised himself with his ability to keep up with Emma's ravenous desire. Whether this stemmed from his nature as a blood knight or from Emma's succubus magic, he didn't know. Perhaps a combination of both. Either way, it almost became a competition to see who could reduce the other to an exhausted heap first.

He learned a lot about women that day, and about Emma especially. She enjoyed sex the same way a sommelier savored fine wines. She was a connoisseur, open both to enjoying the tried and true and to exploring less well-known vintages. But she enjoyed being taken from behind the most. On all fours, draped over the edge of the bed, or pressed against the wall; it didn't matter to her. Even airborne with both of them casting Fly.

She relished surrendering her body to the rhythms of her partner, of trusting her pleasure to him, of letting him take her at his own pace, all while his hands explored her supple body.

Clarke learned a lot that night.

About Emma.

About himself.

And how he felt about her.

He lay in bed long after the sun had set, her head resting against his chest, rising and falling with each breath, her raven black hair tousled about. He stroked his fingers through the silken strands, and she smiled as she snuggled up to him.

He'd known her for such a short period of time, and yet his feelings for her felt so strong, so crystal clear.

Was that because of magic? His or hers?

Or was there something deeper here? Something meant to last.

He wasn't ready to vocalize how he felt. Not yet, not so soon.

Did he hold his tongue out of fear? Perhaps. Was he afraid of what she might say in response? Of course, he was. He'd known her for a fraction of a semester, and he'd known the real her for barely a blip of time. How could he, in good conscience, dump such a heavy word on her?

Love.

Was this the real thing?

Was this what it felt like?

He knew its darker partners—lust and infatuation—all too well. This was different.

Better.

More powerful.

Imbued with a sense of rightness he found difficult to describe.

Was there a logical reason for the sensation welling up within his chest? Was this some side effect of her nature as a succubus? A knack for cutting through the friction surrounding life and love?

Perhaps. Perhaps not, but he knew this was what his heart was genuinely saying. He was in love with Emma. He only needed the courage to listen to what his heart already knew to be true.

And to seize the beautiful opportunity life had placed before him.

Emma fell asleep with her head on his chest, and he drifted into a peaceful slumber soon after her.

She roused him the next morning with a blowjob and followed that by cooking breakfast. They talked over sausage, French toast, and freshly squeezed orange juice.

"I've been thinking," Emma said, smiling at him, her eyes bright.

"About what?"

"Why don't you move in with me?"

Clarke paused with a forkful halfway to his mouth. He hadn't expected this. Was this a sign she felt the same way as he did? He set the fork down and let her continue.

She glanced down and traced circles on the countertop with a finger.

"The place has room enough for two, and I'm sure your wallet wouldn't mind one less monthly payment."

"You've got that right. My place is an overpriced dump."

"Plus, I wouldn't mind the company."

He chuckled. "Me neither."

"You see? It'd be a win for both of us." Her eyes met his. "What do you say?"

"I like it! But we should split your rent."

"You sure?"

"I insist. I don't want to mooch off of you."

"Somehow I knew you'd say that." She knitted her fingers and rested her chin there. "When would you like to move in?"

"Depends. Got any plans today?"

She smiled. "Besides chilling with my boyfriend, I'm free and clear."

They finished breakfast, cleaned up the dishes, and headed out in two cars. Clarke started by boxing up his possessions while Emma ran them back to her place, completing a circuit roughly once an hour. He'd never been one to accumulate a lot of "stuff," and having an extra pair of hands made short work of the task. He filed a change request online with his apartment complex once they were finished and began unpacking before dinner.

He and Emma celebrated by having sex that night.

Because of course they did.

Heinrich's death never appeared in the news. Nor did that of his thrall, whoever the poor soul had been.

The university acknowledged the professor's absence, but only by stating he'd elected to take a well-earned sabbatical. Monday's class was canceled via email, and one of the other math professors shifted his schedule around to fill in for the rest of the week while a more permanent solution was prepared.

Clarke asked Emma about this over lunch at the food court.

"It's how vampiric magic works," she said. "Repeat a lie enough times, especially one buttressed by magic, and it becomes the new truth. It's how vampires have maintained control for so long."

"And the secret of their existence has never gotten out?"

"No, there've been breaches before. Vampires who've screwed up so royally the secret's gotten loose. But their control spells are too strong and too widespread."

"But Heinrich's dead. Doesn't *anyone* know or care about that?"

"Our human classmates won't bat an eye at the sabbatical news, and eventually, they'll forget Heinrich even existed. The lie will become truth, and life will go on."

"What about the demihumans in our class? The ones who can see past the control magic. They'll know something's up."

"Yes, but they also know not to make a fuss. Otherwise—" Emma ran a finger across her throat.

Clarke grimaced and shook his head.

"The other university vampires know, too," she continued. "Otherwise, we wouldn't have heard this nonsense about a sabbatical. They keep too close an eye on their rivals to not have noticed. But they also benefit from his death, and the vacuum it forms in their power struggles. The sabbatical story works in their favor."

"How so?"

"It keeps Heinrich's death secret from vampires higher up the food chain. That lie gives the local vampires time to absorb Heinrich's territory."

"You think they'll come looking for us?"

"Maybe, but I doubt it. The assumption will be another vampire managed to take him out. They'll be suspicious of each other, which gives us the advantage."

"Then there won't ever be a record of Heinrich dying?"

"Not unless the vampires want there to be one."

"What about the police? How do they factor into the death of a vampire?"

"They'll never find out about Heinrich's untimely passing unless the other vampires screw up. Even now,

I bet one of them has thralls clearing away the evidence. Vampires avoid scrutiny wherever possible, which is exactly what law enforcement can bring to their doorstep. Despite all the power vampires have, they do fear humanity's numbers, and rightfully so."

"It still feels strange," Clarke said. "Knowing he's dead but seeing everyone around us act as if he weren't."

"I know."

"And then there's the other side of this coin. If the vampires can make everyone forget one of their own, then they can do the same to regular people."

Emma nodded grimly. "That's one of the reasons why we're in this fight."

"Makes me angry just thinking about it. How they have the power to disappear people. How many lives have they harvested that way? Feeding on them like Heinrich drained those cats and dogs?"

"Too many."

"You know what else this does? It makes me eager to get back in the fight and kick some vampire ass. Heinrich was just the start."

Emma put a soft hand atop his and gave him a tender squeeze.

"We'll get our chance, Clarke. I promise you that."

"How's work on the grimoire going?"

"Slowly. Ashley's been sifting through it nonstop,

but she's been struggling with the protective magic."

"Then it seems we're in a holding pattern until she breaks that Conceal spell."

"There *is* one other thing." Emma smiled at him. "Brooke called. She wants to give your Power Graft another shot."

Clarke and Brooke's schedules didn't align until that Thursday. He headed to the abandoned steel mill with Emma that evening, and they set up two chairs across from each other for another go at the spell. Brooke arrived half an hour later.

Clarke sensed something different the moment the wolf girl stepped inside. She'd dressed fancier, for lack of a better term. No baggy T-shirt or ripped jeans this time. Instead, she wore a knitted foldover top that left her neck and shoulders bare, a cargo miniskirt, and a pair of tall, buckled boots. Her tail swished when she saw him, and something glinted in her one of her wolf ears.

"Hey, Brooke," Clarke said. "Glad you could make it."

"Sorry for being late." She set her backpack down next to a chair. "I had to stop home first."

"Is that jewelry I see in your ear?"

"You noticed?" The wolf girl smiled and touched the jeweled stud piercing the furred tip of one ear. "What do you think?"

"It looks great on you. Really accentuates your ears."

"Thanks!" Some of the penned-up tension left her shoulders. "Jewelry can be a nuisance for us shifters, but I wanted to change things up today."

Clarke wondered if Brooke had stopped home *solely* so she could fancy herself up. There weren't many reasons why she'd do that before a trip to an abandoned steel mill. He caught Emma's eye, and she gave him a knowing wink, which didn't help matters at all.

He knew what Emma had said about him dating other girls. But it was one thing to discuss the matter in theory and another for him to be on the receiving end of subtle wolf girl flirting with his succubus girlfriend a few steps away.

Dating demihumans should come with a manual, he thought, sitting down across from Brooke.

"Should we try it like before?" Brooke asked, holding out her open palms.

"Not quite," Emma said. "We're going to approach it differently, at least at first." She opened an app on her phone, switched on a soundscape of gentle rain, and raised the volume. "I want both of you to close your eyes and focus on relaxing. Start by taking a few deep breaths. Once you're in the right state of mind, take hold of each other's hands."

"Okay." Brooke closed her eyes and drew in a long, slow, full breath.

Clarke did the same, breathing in and out rhythmically. He let the worries of the world melt away, ushering in a state of serenity that filled him from the inside. It was odd what a little focused breathing could do.

"Good," Emma said, her voice soft, soothing. "Keep breathing like that. In, two, three, four. Out, two, three, four. In …"

His mind and body slid into a deeper state of relaxation and calm, almost as if his muscles were loosening, one by one, as he allowed all the unwanted tension to ooze out of his body.

"Now, Clarke, I want you to become aware of Brooke. Keep your eyes closed and your breath steady. Yes, just like that. Now stretch out with your mind. See if you can sense the presence of her magic."

Clarke reached out for her without moving, and the fingers of his mind caressed the boundary of her magic. The experience was similar to his first attempt, but his senses had sharpened since, and he perceived a richer tapestry of details.

He studied the pulsing aura before him. It radiated heat and strength. Like an animal's hot breaths—not unpleasant at all, welcoming in a strange way, like a faithful companion panting after having raced over to greet him. He smelled the musk of heavy fur, felt his fingers slip through a shimmering coat.

But that's as far as he could reach.

The surface, but no deeper.

Something impeded him, as it had before.

A barrier of some kind.

No, again "barrier" was the wrong word.

More like … shackles? But on his side?

Yes, the problem was with him. He'd been right about that the first time.

What was holding him back?

And how could he overcome it?

"Now," Emma said quietly, almost in a whisper, "stretch out your hand and touch her."

He did just that.

"Ah!" Brooke squeaked.

Those unseen shackles loosened, and for a bright, wonderful moment, his mind sank into the warm folds of Brooke's inner magic. This was working. It was working! He only needed to push deeper.

"Clarke?" Brooke gasped. "That's … ah!"

His concentration slipped, and the light of her magic retreated. Those shackles constricted around his inner perception, and he blinked his eyes open.

His hand rested on Brooke's breast, fingers pressed deep into her firm flesh.

"Oh, damn!" He jerked his hand back. "I'm sorry! I didn't realize I was—"

"Never mind that!" Emma knelt beside them, grinning widely. "Tell me what just happened!"

"I felt him touch me," Brooke said, struggling with her words. "I mean other than the"—she waved a hand over her fondled breast—"you know."

"I felt something, too," Clarke said. "I'm certain I made contact with her magic."

"Can you do it again?" Emma asked.

"What? Like …" He made a groping gesture with one hand.

"Whatever makes the magic work."

"It's not that simple."

"Why not?"

"Well, I mean." Now it was Clarke's turn to struggle with his words. "There's another person involved."

"So?" Emma faced the wolf girl. "You okay with him groping your boobs? In the pursuit of science, of course."

Brooke's cheeks reddened. For a moment, Clarke thought she'd object, but instead she closed her eyes and stuck out her chest boldly.

"Perfect!" Emma gave him a pat on the back. "Go for it, Champ! Two-hand those love pillows if you have to!"

"What's got you all worked up?"

"I'm just excited to see where this leads! I have a theory for what's going on, but that can wait. Now, come on. Grab hold and try again."

"All right," he sighed. "Here goes."

He grasped two wonderful handfuls of wolf girl, ignored the cute squeak that followed, then close his eyes. Brooke's magic pulsed in his mind's eye, as vibrant and strong as before, but this time the barrier holding him back had loosened, almost to the point of crumbling.

But it still remained, still held him at bay.

What was the secret to tearing down this wall?

Hands touched his face, and something warm and soft pressed against the back of his head.

"Uh, Emma? That you?"

"Yes."

"What are you doing?"

"Hold still. This is important."

He remained still as Emma held him against her breasts.

"I knew it!" she exclaimed, releasing him. "I just knew it!"

"Knew what?" Both he and Brooke opened their eyes.

"It must have happened when we broke your hex!" Emma smiled brightly. "The Power Graft! Don't you see? You absorbed more than just my Flight magic!"

"I …" Clarke regarded the succubus with a quizzical expression, but confusion slowly shifted into realization.

He'd absorbed magic from a succubus.

A *succubus*.

His eyebrows shot up.

"Yes!" Emma declared, grinning. "You see it, too, don't you?"

"See what?" Brooke asked. "Can he use Power Graft or not?"

"Oh, he can! He absolutely can!" Emma's grin became downright devilish. "But the spell must have become fused with my magic when the hex broke. Not sure if this is a permanent change or not, but for now, he'll need to cast this one spell differently."

"Meaning?" Brooke asked.

"Meaning, he can only cast Power Graft during sex!"

Brooke's mouth formed a perfect O.

Clarke rested his face in his hands.

"What's with the long faces?" Emma asked. "This is great! We've solved the puzzle of how to power you up!"

"Yes," Clarke said, looking up, "but there's a *slight* problem you may have missed."

"I didn't miss a thing." Emma rested a hand on Brooke's shoulder. "She already told me how much she wants to jump your bone."

Brooke's mouth clapped shut and her cheeks turned a fierce shade of red.

"Furthermore, as your girlfriend, I hereby give you permission to fuck the wolf girl's brains out."

"I, well, um ..." the wolf girl stammered, looking away.

206

Clarke wasn't sure how much redder her cheeks could get.

"Perhaps," he began carefully, "we should give Brooke some time to consider this new information. The last thing we want to do is pressure her into doing something she's not comfortable with."

"I *suppose*," Emma said with a dismissive headshake.

"Brooke, why don't you head on home for today?" he continued. "We can talk about this again whenever you're ready."

"Actually," Brooke said, not making eye contact, hands clasped in her lap. "I'm okay with this."

"You are?"

"Yes. But I have one condition."

"Name it."

"I would …" She finally met his gaze. "I would like to go out on a date first."

CHAPTER ELEVEN

—◆—

BROOKE PICKED THE TIME and place for their date: Friday, 5 o'clock at the Reed River Park. Casual attire recommended. Clarke showed up a few minutes early, parked his car, and headed for the shade of a pavilion overlooking the river. He set his backpack down on the bench and waited. A few couples and families were enjoying the park, some with pets, some not human.

He was surprised by how normal that last part felt now. A man with bluish-black skin, pointed ears, and a shock of white hair walked by with a poodle on a leash. Clarke barely gave him a second thought.

The air was warm with a pleasant, intermittent breeze. The sun arched lower in the cloudless sky, casting its yellowing light over the park. The river's crisp, clear waters rippled by, foaming around the rare rock.

Clarke had picked a dark blue polo shirt for their date. He knew Brooke had specified casual wear, so he expected the date to involve a hike through the park, but he didn't want to come across as too casual. A short-sleeved shirt with a collar struck him as a good compromise. The shirt bordered on being a size too small, but given how Emma had all but salivated over the way it hugged his muscles, this felt like the opposite of a problem.

"Hey, Clarke!"

He glanced over the back of the bench, caught sight of Brooke waving, then rose to greet her. She'd selected a pair of loose jeans, hiking boots, and a tan sleeveless shirt with a plunging neckline that showed off her the firm swells of her breasts. A few earrings glittered in her wolf ears.

Casual. But not completely.

Seems the polo was the right choice, he thought, greeting her with a smile.

"Great to see you, Brooke. You look lovely."

"Thanks!" She shifted the gym bag slung over her shoulder. "I know this was an odd request, but thank you for going along with it."

"Don't mention it."

"It really helps me feel more comfortable about … you know."

"Of course. I wouldn't want it any other way."

"I'm glad to hear you say that. I know Emma was all

gung-ho with this solution, but it made me happy how you left the decision up to me." She smiled, yellow eyes taking him in. "You look good, by the way."

"Thanks."

"This is another first for me. I never had a date wear a shirt with a collar before."

"*Really?*"

"Yeah. Ripped jeans and shirts with stains or holes every time."

"Seriously?" Clarke frowned. "At least wear a nice, clean shirt when you take a lady out."

"I know! Right?"

"That just shows a lack of respect for your date. What gives?"

"The werewolf dating pool isn't the greatest. At least around these parts."

"I'm getting that feeling."

"Anyway, shall we head out?"

"Sure." Clarke grabbed his backpack off the park bench. "By the way, I thought I was bringing dinner."

"That's the plan."

"Then what did you bring?"

"Oh, this?" She blushed, then gave him a pleasant smile. "Safety first and all that."

"I'm sorry. I don't follow."

"It's important to practice safe sex."

"Ah." He nodded as if he understood. "Yes, of course. Very important, that."

"Don't want to have any accidents."

"Certainly not!"

What kind of contraceptive takes up a whole gym bag? he thought, but decided to set the topic aside, at least for now. Dating demihumans came with surprises, and that was just that.

They took a wooden, covered bridge across the river, then started down one of the hiking trails. The dirt path cut through the Reed River Forest. Trees towered all around them, reducing the sun to the rare beams of light that penetrated the canopy, creating an almost-ethereal atmosphere, like they were walking through the kind of forest where enchanted things happened. Their boots crunched on dry leaves and fallen twigs as they followed the trail.

"You enjoy the outdoors?" Clarke asked, walking beside the wolf girl.

"I do. It's quiet out here. Serene. I can set all my worries aside, shut out the noise of modern life, and just … be. There's something pure about a good, long walk. Cleansing, even. How about you?"

"I tend to relax with a good video game."

Brooke laughed. "I'm not surprised."

"Hey, I know for a fact you like games, too."

"Guilty as charged. What's your favorite game of all time?"

"*Final Fantasy X*. It's almost perfect, in my opinion."

"Almost?"

"Those unskippable cutscenes hold it back. How about you?"

"I'm partial to open world RPGs myself." Brooke let out a content sigh. "It can be fun to lose yourself in a fictional setting."

"I know exactly what you mean."

"Though, to be fair, I tend to get distracted when I play. I enjoy messing with NPCs. Like putting buckets on everyone's heads in *Skyrim*."

Clarke laughed. "I remember coming across that one."

The trail began to climb upward, the canopy thinning as they progressed.

"Anything else you do for fun?" Brooke asked.

"I work out. My parents taught me the body and mind are connected in more ways than we realize. Fail to care for one, and the other will suffer."

"Solid advice. They sound like good parents."

"They are, though it took me a while to realize that. I had to grow up before I could see what they were doing for me, why they would drive home certain lessons."

"I think we're all like that growing up. We all think we know everything until it finally dawns on us what idiots we are. My family is, well …" She held up a hand, and her claws grew. "You know."

"Must be different from what I experienced."

"In some ways. Just imagine trying to raise kids who can wolf out at will."

"Can't be easy."

"My brothers and I were absolute terrors as kids. Especially when we grew rambunctious. We knew we'd crossed the line whenever mom or dad transformed to rein us in."

The path began to level off, and the tree coverage grew sparser.

"Clarke, I have a confession to make. I've … had some bad luck when it comes to dating."

"That's pretty normal for people our age. Why the big deal?"

"Because it's worse in my case. Things got serious during my last date. This was about two years ago, and I haven't seen anyone since. He and I agreed to part ways after … the incident." She let out a weary sigh that had nothing to do with the hike. "He hardly speaks to me anyone, and I really can't blame him. The whole thing was my fault."

"What happened?"

"Things started to get physical. We were making out, and I … I got swept up in the moment. I lost control and ended up hurting him."

"How bad?"

"There was blood. The guy needed stitches afterward."

"I see." He couldn't find any other words.

213

"I don't want something like that to happen to you."

"That makes two of us."

She hefted the gym bag. "Which is why we're going to practice safe sex."

"I'm still not sure what you mean by that."

"It'll make sense when you see the gear. Can't be too careful. Especially with it being that time of the month."

"Time of … Brooke?"

"Yes?"

"Are we talking about your period?"

"What? No!" Her face twisted with equal parts horror and amusement. "It's a full moon tonight!"

"Oh. Right." He gave his forehead a firm smack. "I should have guessed. Sorry!"

"It's okay." She laughed nervously. "It's my fault for not being clear with my words. But in case you're worried about that *other* monthly cycle, I don't have one. Female werewolves only become fertile once a year."

"Is that similar to a wolf going into heat?"

"Pretty much."

"Good to know." He nodded thoughtfully. "So, how *do* you respond to a full moon? Does seeing one make you transform?"

"No, we can control our shifting all month long, but we do experience a strong lunar reaction. Full moons bring forth a period of heightened activity. High energy. High

… sex drive." She blushed again. "The rest is Hollywood vampires trying to make us werewolves look bad."

"As they seem to enjoy."

"Yeah. Bloodsucking jerks."

They continued up the trail. The forest had been reduced to a few random trees scattered across the slopes.

"Heightened sex drive, huh?" Clarke said.

"Yep. That's me right now. Just one big ball of nerves and hormones. Sorry if I'm coming across a little out of sorts."

She looked down, but then her tail jumped when Clarke slipped his fingers into her hand. She looked up at him, ears perked, tail swishing.

"I need to correct you there," he told her warmly. "You're one big, *beautiful* ball of nerves."

She laughed at this, and they continued up the hill, hand in hand.

The path led to a cliff that overlooked a suburb west of the park. A green guardrail with flaking paint lined the edge, and three picnic tables had been arranged in a row beside it. They were the only two people around.

The sky was a blaze of orange lit by the setting sun.

"Stop here for dinner?" Brooke asked.

"Sure."

Clarke unzipped his backpack and pulled out a variety of Rubbermaid containers. Emma had packed the meal, so he knew it would be good. One big container held salad topped with pecans, tomatoes, cucumbers, and balsamic dressing. Two smaller containers were for the toasted bread and butter, and she'd stored the minestrone soup in the large thermos to keep it hot.

He served Brooke first, then sat down.

She held the bowl with both hands, as if warming her fingers, and gazed out at the sunset.

"You come here often?" he asked.

"When the mood strikes me. I enjoy the peace, the simplicity of nature. Granted, I wouldn't want to *live* out here; I love indoor plumbing, microwaves, and hot showers too much."

"I hear that."

"But it feels good to get away from it all." She let out a long sigh. "At least for a little while."

The sun sank beyond the horizon, and the breeze picked up, growing cooler as they ate their meals in relative silence.

"Clarke, can I ask you a question?"

"Always."

"What do you think of all this? Of us, the rest of Broken Fang, and of what we're doing."

"Honestly, it feels like a long shot."

She let out another sigh, and then nodded slowly.

"I'm glad Heinrich is dead," he continued, "but I have to wonder about the wisdom of what we're doing. If a chump vampire living off cats and dogs can give us that much trouble, what's it going to be like when we face a real threat?"

"The same thought has crossed my mind."

"Sure, we killed one vampire, and the world is a better place for it. But we're just five people. What can we really expect to change?"

"I guess we'll find out."

"Yeah. Guess so." He drank the dregs of his minestrone and set the bowl aside.

"I'm grateful, you know," Brooke said. "To Ashley and to Emma. I've tasted the true power of my kind, the magic the vampires are so keen to repress, and I don't ever want to go back. I could tolerate living with that hex up until the moment I tasted freedom. I was weighed down by chains I couldn't see."

"I know what you mean. I owe those two a huge debt, and I don't know if I'll ever be able to repay it."

"And I agree with you there," Brooke said, her ears flattening. "But sometimes I wish this wasn't my fight. We've killed our first vampire, and sure, seems like we got away with it. But Heinrich is just the beginning. Eventually, the other vampires are going to get a clue."

"You're wondering what happens then?"

"Aren't you?"

"Yeah. I am."

"What happens when we're suddenly the ones being hunted?" She gazed out at the setting sun for long seconds. Her ears relaxed and she flashed a quick, sad smile. "I'm sorry. Seems I've gone and killed the mood."

"It's all right." He reached out and gave her hand a tender squeeze. "I'm worried, too, about where this is all going to lead. I don't want to see you or any of the others get hurt."

"Thanks, Clarke." She turned her hand over and returned the squeeze. "That means more to me than you might realize."

"Don't mention it. What are friends for?"

"'Friends,' huh?" Her smile became playful. "Is that all?"

"Comrade in arms."

"True. But what else?"

"We're about to find out, aren't we?"

She chuckled. "Yes, indeed!"

"Shall we start back?"

"No need. My family has a cabin about half a mile from here. We own a patch of land adjacent to the park. It comes in handy when we need some privacy."

"Sounds perfect. Lead the way, then."

Clarke started to clean up, and Brooke helped him pack the leftovers and any trash. Once finished, she guided him off the path, up and around the nearby hilltop, and through a dark patch of woods. The fading light filled the woods with an oppressive gloom, and he silently wished he'd brought a flashlight. Brooke cut a path for them with surefooted ease, and he struggled to match her pace.

"How's your night vision?" he asked.

"About as good as a genuine wolf. Why?"

"Just having a little trouble seeing the ground."

"Whoops! Sorry!"

She stopped, let him catch up, then took hold of his hand. She held it for the rest of their trek through the woods.

The cabin sat in a broad clearing. It was a modest, ranch-style home with wood siding and solar panels on the roof. Brooke retrieved a keyring from her pocket and unlocked the cabin. She swung the barred outer door aside.

"After you."

The interior was utilitarian: heavy wooden tables and chairs, a kitchen that gleamed from all the stainless steel, and no electronics in sight except for the lights and appliances.

The windows were all barred, and at first Clarke wondered what kind of wildlife necessitated such measures.

But then he realized there were bars on the *inside*, too.

He set his backpack down in a chair, then ran his finger through one of several parallel grooves in the table.

Claw marks.

"Sometimes we feel the need to shift and let off some steam," Brooke explained. "When we do, we do it here."

"Makes sense."

"The cabin sits empty most of the time."

"Ever have an issue with squatters?"

"Once. Bunch of druggies thought they could move in, but we took care of them. Word got around after that."

Clarke grimaced, his mind conjuring a picture of werewolves "taking care of" trespassers. The image involved a lot of red censored behind mosaics.

"Those losers even went to the police!" Brooke said. "Can you believe that? Told them they'd been attacked by monsters! The nerve of some people!"

"Wait a second. They're still alive?"

"Should be as long as they haven't died from an overdose or something. Why?"

"Nothing. Just making conversation."

The image in his mind became significantly less bloody.

"Anyway, there are beers in the fridge, and there's harder stuff in the cabinet. Help yourself. I'm going to get ready."

She slung her gym bag over a shoulder and headed through the door to what Clarke thought might be the bedroom. His eyes drifted down to the sway of her hips—and the swish of her tail—as she disappeared into the room and closed the door.

"I'm ready!" Brooke called out through the closed door. "You can come on in now!"

Clarke rose from his seat by the kitchen and opened the door.

Brooke sat on the edge of the bed, clad in a bathrobe. She held the front closed with crossed arms, her eyes shy and unsure. The "safe sex" gym bag lay open beside her.

He took in the lay of the room. It contained a bed and, therefore—by virtue of this inclusion—qualified as a bedroom. But that was only half the story, because the rest of the room's furnishings didn't revolve around sleep.

Despite the allure of the beautiful wolf girl seated on the bed, Clarke found himself drawn to a myriad of cuffs, straps, and chains hanging from the walls and ceiling. He lifted one heavy cuff on the end of a strap and gave it a tug. It felt *very* secure.

The bed was equipped in a similar way, with four heavy metal poles that anchored into the ceiling, eyebolts screwed into them at regular intervals. The floor and walls were all padded, and claw marks had exposed the stuffing on a few panels.

"Now I understand what you meant by safe sex."

Brooke gave him a bashful shrug. "Dating non-shifters can be complicated."

"And dangerous?"

"Sometimes. For our partners. Are you okay with this?"

"Let me give you a proper answer."

He sat on the bed next to her and took her into his arms, brought her close.

And then he kissed her. Long, slow, and tenderly. Her canines were sharp, and they occasionally pricked his tongue, but other than that, it was like any other kiss.

No, not like any other. Brooke was special, and he wanted her to *feel* special.

His hand traced down her shoulders to the small of her back and tugged her close. Her breasts pressed against his chest, and she wrapped her arms around him, pulling him tight, devouring his mouth with growing enthusiasm.

His hands explored her. He couldn't see what she wore underneath the bathrobe, but the black collar around her neck was telling. A metal ring hung from it near the base of her throat.

Brooke placed a gentle but insistent hand on his chest, and he broke their kiss. She stood up and shirked the bathrobe. It collected at her feet, revealing the full ripeness of her young, athletic body: her creamy skin, firm muscles, and proud breasts. Her long hair cascaded down bare shoulders in a rich, chocolate wave, and her nipples were taut with anticipation. Restraints around her wrists and ankles tinkled as she moved, their empty rings clicking against the buckles.

More straps constricted her body, framing her breasts and crisscrossing her abdomen, empty rings dangling at various places.

Clarke rose from the bed, pulling off his shirt. He embraced her, the warmth and softness of her chest pressing against his, and he kissed her again. She ran her fingers down his bare back, and he felt the prickle of nascent claws. An anxious jolt ran through him, and he became more keenly aware of the danger.

Brooke really could rip him apart if she wanted to, and she might even do that by accident if he didn't restrain her.

"Are *you* okay with this?" he asked, softly as he kissed down her neck.

"Yes," she moaned, arching her chin, letting him enjoy more of her. "I want this. I want *you*."

"How would you like me to start?"

"With this."

She retrieved a blindfold from the gym bag. It was one of the tamer accessories visible inside. She stepped underneath a rope hanging from the ceiling, then set the blindfold over her eyes.

"Help me with this. Please." She gave him a bashful smile. "It makes me more relaxed somehow."

He circled behind her and pulled the strap tight enough to secure the blindfold, but not too tight he hoped.

"How's this?"

"Just right."

"And now?"

Just then, he felt a shift in her—both physically and in her mood. All inklings of tension melted from her muscles, and when her voice came this time, it was with a husky eagerness:

"I'm sometimes a bad girl. You need to make sure I don't misbehave."

She dropped to her knees and raised both arms, her breasts flattening slightly as her muscles stretched.

Damn, that blindfold really *did* relax her.

Clarke grabbed the end of the rope, tugged it down until the clasp on the edge reached her wrists, then fitted the clasp through both wrist rings.

"Do whatever you want to me." Her chest heaved with excited breaths. "Tonight is for you."

"That's where you're wrong." He knelt behind her and kissed the nape of her neck. "It's for us."

She smiled, and some of her tension and nerves melted away. Her muscles relaxed, shifting some of her weight to the ceiling rope.

He took hold of her breasts from behind, rolled her nipples between his fingers.

"Yes." She sucked in a sharp breath. "Like that."

He played with her, alternating between teasing her

nipples and kneading the firm mounds. Her teeth clacked together after a particularly aggressive pinch, and her canines grew more prominent. Her tail brushed across his abdomen and then curved around his waist, almost as an invitation.

He decided to take it, one hand gliding down her stomach.

And then lower.

"Ah!"

He rubbed his fingers across her hot sex, then pressed one of them inside.

"Yes!"

"You're so wet already," he whispered into her ear, then gave it a playful nibble. His finger made rhythmic squelches as it explored her moist depths.

"I can't help myself!" she cried. "I've wanted this so badly, I could hardly stand it! Please don't make me wait any longer! Take me! Take me now!"

"As you wish."

He kissed her on the cheek, then unbuckled his pants, letting his cock twitch to full readiness. He stripped off the rest of his clothes and let his eyes drink in Brooke's body once more, on her knees with her arms pulled high, chest heaving, legs spread. A clear, glistening trail ran down the inside of her left thigh.

Clarke grasped her hips with strong, confident

hands and pulled her back. She shuffled backward on her knees until her ass stuck out and the angle was just right. He placed the tip against her hot, lower mouth.

And then he eased himself into her, one thick inch at a time until his groin pressed against her butt cheeks.

"God!" she cried. "Fuck, it's big!"

"Would you like me to go slow?"

"No! Please don't tease me anymore! Fuck me, as hard and as deep as you can!"

He drew his cock back until only the tip remained inside her. And then he drove himself back in, fully and forcefully. He repeated the motion several times, steadily picking up speed. Her breasts bounced with each hard plunge, and she grunted with each stroke. He pounded her from behind, over and over again, her vocalizations growing deeper, almost animalistic as she lost herself in a sea of ecstasy.

His hands ventured up from her hips, took hold of her narrow waist, and then grasped her breasts. His fingers found her erect nipples.

"Yes!" she cried, her words almost a growl. "Like that! Harder!"

He pinched down on her nipples and pounded into her from behind, harder and faster.

"Fuck!"

Brooke threw her head back. Every muscle in her

body clenched, and her claws and canines grew. Her teeth grated against each other, but then she opened her mouth in a soundless howl, her body shuddering as the climax rippled through her in sublime waves.

And then she collapsed forward, a spent vessel held up by the ceiling rope, panting out each breath, her smooth skin glistening.

Clarke kept going, driving himself into her hard and fast, as if trying to thrust deeper with each stroke. His own excitement built, boiling within his gonads, eclipsing his mind of everything but his own animalistic need. He ravished Brooke's body, and she took it, took him, accepting all he could give her, even within the afterglow of her own orgasm.

He buried himself one last time and exploded within her, filling himself with sweet, sweet relief as he filled her.

But something else erupted within his mind. His whole being blazed with magic, and not just his. He felt the presence of Brooke's aura, distinct from his own, yet open to him now. Ready to accept him in ways both familiar and alien.

His magic opened in response, almost like an echo.

Their auras touched, mingled, and then broke away. An ethereal kiss of sorts, but one that left something behind. A new wellspring that bubbled up within his chest and flowed outward, permeating his limbs. Energizing them in ways he'd never expected.

"That …" Brooke managed between breaths, "was great …"

Clarke unclasped her wrists, and she collapsed into his arms, all her inhuman strength forgotten. He pushed her blindfold up, and she gazed into his eyes for long, tender seconds. And then she kissed him on the cheek.

"It worked," he said.

"What did?" she asked, sounding as if she weren't fully present.

"You know. The whole point behind this?"

"The whole—" Her yellow eyes lit up. "Oh, that!"

"Yes. That. Did you forget?"

"Well …" She traced out a circle on his chest with a finger. "I've been preoccupied. Do you think you're stronger now?"

"Let's find out."

He slipped one arm around her back and another underneath her knees.

And then he lifted, rising to his feet with ease.

"You are!" Brooke beamed at him.

"Let's try a little more."

He shifted one arm underneath her butt and then held it out so that she sat atop his extended elbow. He had to spread his legs to account for the awkward center of gravity, but that was the only concession required. His muscles hardly felt any strain.

"Wonderful!" Brooke gave him an excited clap.

Clarke pulled her back in, her legs dangling over one arm.

"Pretty sure the old me would have torn a muscle trying that stunt."

"What else? Do you feel any tougher?"

"Not sure."

"Hmm." Brooke poked him in the chest with a clawed finger. "How's that feel?"

"Like you're sticking a claw in me."

"You're not bleeding." She traced a diagonal line across his chest. The skin didn't break once. She tried again, pressing harder this time. Again, no blood. "That was plenty hard enough to cut through human skin."

"Improvement confirmed, then."

He set her down on the bed. She sat up, hugging her knees.

"What now?" she asked.

"What do you mean?"

"Well, you got what you wanted." She glanced away, and her tail flicked. "Mission accomplished, and all that."

"Brooke." He sat on the bed beside her. "What did I tell you earlier? I said this night is for us, and I meant it. I'm not the kind of guy who'll get his rocks off and then leave. When I spend the night with a woman, it means something to me. And, I hope, to you as well."

Brooke looked up, contentment on her face.

Followed by the flash of a wicked grin.

What happened next came in a blur. She grabbed him by the shoulders and swung him onto the bed, pinning him in place in one swift, fluid motion.

"Whoa!"

She straddled his waist and leaned close enough for him to feel her lustful breaths.

"You're as tough as me now, aren't you?" she whispered, yellow eyes glinting with carnal desire.

"Not sure. Close, at least."

"You know what this means, don't you?"

He grinned back at her. "Do tell."

"Means I can finally go all out."

CHAPTER TWELVE

CLARKE DIDN'T GET MUCH SLEEP that night, and he suspected the police would have received noise complaints if not for the cabin's remote location.

Brooke proved insatiable, her libido living up to her "go all out" declaration. Fortunately, Clarke soon discovered it wasn't only his strength and toughness that had improved, but his endurance as well. Yet for all his enhanced physical prowess, Brooke still surpassed him, even more so when it came to her raw enthusiasm.

Clarke offered to remove her restraints after their second lovemaking session, but Brooke demurred. It seemed she enjoyed both the roles of conqueror and conquered, and she alternated between the two long into the night.

Eventually, their sexual marathon reached its conclusion, and they collapsed into a sweaty tangle on the bed.

They both took quick showers and then snuggled up for some much-needed rest.

Clarke wasn't sure what time it was when he drifted into a deep slumber, but he knew *exactly* what woke him up.

The fire alarm.

"What the what?!"

He threw the covers off and bolted out of bed in nothing but his boxers. Smoke poured into the bedroom, hugging the ceiling, and he raced out to find the source.

"Brooke?" he shouted over the alarm, storming into the living room and kitchen.

"Sorry!" she shouted, dousing the stovetop with a fire extinguisher. The flames licking upward from the cast iron pan died down. She made a circuit of the room, opening every window to let the smoke out, which was somewhat awkward with the metal bars in the way.

The fire alarm eventually stopped screeching at them.

Brooke planted the fire extinguisher on the table and blew out a long breath.

"What happened?" he asked.

"I tried to make breakfast."

He glanced into the pan. It was hard to tell what it was supposed to be, given all the char and fire-retardant foam.

"Breakfast appears to have been unsuccessful."

"I'm sorry! This was my fault."

232

"You still haven't explained what happened."

"Well …" She slumped into one of the seats. "Emma told me how she likes to cook you breakfast, so I thought I'd surprise you with a meal of my own. Only"— she waved at the ruins of breakfast—"this happened."

"But how?"

"Well, the fridge had a pack of bacon, so I thought I'd give that a try. How hard could it be, right? Put the bacon in the pan, apply heat, remove when done."

"That's sounds pretty normal for bacon."

"But then I started feeling antsy, so I decided to take care of that by running a few laps around the property."

"While leaving a hot stove and a pan of greasy bacon unattended?"

"Yes?" She seemed to shrink back from his words.

"Did you really need to go for a run this early in the morning?"

"I don't know. Sometimes I get these overpowering explosions of energy that I just need to burn off. Don't you ever get those?"

"No, but that sounds like one of my parents' dogs who'd—" He stopped, the puzzle pieces slotting together in his mind. "Brooke?"

"Yes?"

"I don't want you to take this the wrong way, but I have a question. It's a sincere one."

"Yes?"

"Do you ever … get the zoomies?"

"Sometimes?" She shrugged and smiled bashfully. "More often during full moons."

"This explains a lot."

"I'm really sorry about breakfast!"

"You almost burned down the cabin with a grease fire. How often do you cook?"

"All the time."

He raised a questioning eyebrow.

"If you count using a microwave or toaster," she clarified.

"And if you exclude those two?"

"Maybe once? If you include today?"

"Then, perhaps, this wasn't the brightest idea."

"I *know*." She leaned back in the chair and eyed the aborted breakfast. "You want some Pop-Tarts instead?"

"Pop-Tarts would be great."

Brooke proved much more skilled with the toaster than the stove, and so they feasted on Pop-Tarts and Kool-Aid that morning. She even spoiled him with his choice of s'mores or strawberry filling. Truly, a breakfast for the ages.

Afterward, Clarke helped her wash the dishes and clean up the remains of the initial breakfast. They sat down at the dinner table, and part of Brooke's attire drew his eye. The loose T-shirt and faded blue jeans were normal for her, but the collar …

"You're still wearing the collar from last night."

"I am." Her fingers found the ring in front and played with it. "I thought I might keep this as a memento of our first night together. Do you like it?"

"It looks good on you. Gives you a bit of a bad girl edge."

"That's because I *am* a bad girl." She leaned toward him with sultry eyes. "And sometimes I need my alpha to rein me in."

"Your alpha?"

"My leader. And my lover. The male I'll follow anywhere. Even into a war against the vampires, if he asks it of me."

"That's some heavy stuff, there."

"It comes from my heart."

"I believe you."

He glanced at the collar, then up into her wolf eyes.

A collar on a werewolf, he thought, trying not to think of it as a dog collar. *Not where I thought this would go, but there it is. As long as she doesn't clip a leash to it and ask me to take her out for walkies.*

Maybe it'll help if I think of it in a different context. Like a ring. Yeah, that's the ticket! It's circular. That makes it a symbol of our relationship. Hardly any difference at all.

Right. Because nothing says "in a relationship" like bond-age gear.

"Do you accept me as your mate?" Brooke asked. "For more than just this one night?"

"You mean, like my girlfriend?"

"In non-werewolf terms, yes."

"What about Emma?"

"What about her?"

"Well …"

"Alphas are the pack leaders. They are the strongest, smartest, and bravest the community has to offer. And yes, I know I'm the only shifter in Broken Fang, and I can't apply my way of thinking to everyone else. But that's the lens I see you through. You *are* my alpha, until one of us dies or you reject me."

"And Emma?"

"It would be strange for an alpha to have only one mate, to restrict his strengths to only one bloodline. The fact that you already have a mate makes you all the more desirable in my eyes, not the opposite."

"That's …"

"A very shifter point of view, I know." She rested a hand on her chest. "This is who I am."

"And I appreciate your honesty."

"Then, do you accept me?"

He already knew the answer, and he met her yellow eyes, so beautiful and fierce and yet so vulnerable. He reached out to her, and she placed her hand in his.

"Yes, Brooke," he said softly, giving her hand a tender squeeze. "Yes, I do."

She smiled broadly, as if her face were the sun rising to greet the new day. Her eyes moistened.

And then she grabbed the edge of the long, heavy table and effortlessly shoved it aside, clearing the space between them. She dropped down onto all fours and padded toward him, hungry eyes locked with his.

"Let me show you how happy you've made me."

She unzipped his pants, stroked him to prominence, and then took him into her mouth.

They were cuddling in bed after another sexual marathon when Clarke's phone rang. He reached out from under the covers, grabbed it from the nightstand, and checked the ID.

"It's Ashley."

"I wonder what's up." Brooke tapped the Accept button for him and then switched it to speaker. "Hey, Ash."

"Brooke? What are you doing with Clarke's phone?"

"Just chilling in bed with him." She entwined her legs with his. "He's cozy."

"Good morning. Clarke, here."

"You two are … oh, I see. Emma's theory. I should have guessed. How did it go?"

"Power Graft worked. I now have a bit of were-wolf in me."

"And there was plenty of the opposite," Brooke added with a giggle.

"Uh huh. Look, as much as I'd love to listen to all the explicit details, I did call for a reason. There's been a development."

"What kind?" Clarke asked.

"The unexpected sort. Not sure if it's a problem or an opportunity, but at the very least we have a decision to make as a team. Are you free to meet at the usual place in about an hour? The others said they can make it."

"Got it. We'll be there."

Clarke took a detour back to his apartment to change and freshen up before driving out to the steel mill. Emma and Brooke were already there when he arrived.

"There he is!" Emma hurried over and gave him a big hug. "I'm so happy for you two!"

"Thanks." He extricated one of his arms and gave Brooke a quick wave. "Hey there."

"Clarke." She smiled sweetly at him, the collar still around her neck.

Emma held him at arms' length. "Brooke and I have been talking."

"Yeah? What about?"

"Oh, you know. Blood knights, sex magic, werewolf libidos. All the important stuff. There's only so much of you to go around, which is such a *shame*!"

Clarke laughed.

"Are you able to control which powers you gain?"

"No. It just sort of happens. I could feel our magics merging, but what I came back with seemed somewhat random."

"Hmm." Emma nodded thoughtfully. "Not ideal, but still a solid improvement on where you were. Blood knights are so rare that there's scant documentation on how some of your spells work. It could be that this spell has an affinity for certain kinds of abilities. Or perhaps you yourself have an innate compatibility with other specific magics, which governs which abilities you gain. Or perhaps it's completely random!"

"Did your Power Graft trigger more than once?" Brooke asked.

"No. Just the first time."

"Oh?" Emma glanced back at the werewolf. "There's more to tell? You've been holding out on me, girl! How many times did you do it?"

"I ..." Brooke hugged her breasts and glanced away. "I lost count."

239

Emma faced Clarke expectantly.

"Don't look at me," he said. "I didn't know I was supposed to keep a tally."

"But this is for science!"

"Somehow, I feel you're exaggerating the point."

"Perhaps." Emma tapped her lips thoughtfully. "I wonder if more control will come as you gain experience with your magic. It's also possible Power Graft's fusion with my magic has made the spell more difficult to target. How strong are you now?"

"Check this out."

He picked her up and raised her over his head. He held her aloft, arm rigid with one hand supporting her butt.

Emma clapped enthusiastically.

He let her drop into his arms, then set her on her feet.

"*Very* impressive." She pulled him close, their lips almost touching. "I'll need to inspect these powers more thoroughly first chance we get. For science, you understand."

"Of course."

The crunch of gravel drew his eyes to the parking lot, and the beams from a red BMW Z4 roadster slid across the mill before the vehicle came to a rest. Sammy stepped out of the driver's seat and Ashley from the other side, Heinrich's grimoire tucked under her arm.

"Congratulations, Clarke," Ashley said once everyone was inside. "And to you, Brooke. Both of you are to be commended. This success bodes well for our efforts. Clarke, every power you gain strengthens not just you, but Broken Fang as a whole. I'm grateful for how well this team is coming together, and for your efforts in particular."

"Thanks," Clarke replied, though he felt her praise was overkill. All he'd done so far was help stop one vampire in between having a lot of hot sex with a succubus and a werewolf.

The two women came up to him from opposite sides, both slotting their arms through his, almost perfectly in sync with each other. He smiled at Emma and then to Brooke, a pleasant warmth swelling in his heart. His relationships with these ladies weren't solely about physical attraction; both women possessed an inner beauty which he found deeply attractive, and that made him want to become a better man.

Because both Emma and Brooke deserved nothing less from him.

"Sammy," Ashley began, "when can you make your contribution?"

"My …?"

"With Clarke. After we're done here, why don't you two look at your schedules and pick a time to take advantage of his Power Graft."

"Wh-wh-what?!" the slime girl stammered, turning beet red. Quite literally as every exposed inch of her skin blushed. Even her hair brightened to a vivid shade of red.

"It's the next logical step," Ashley said, apparently oblivious to Sammy's discomfort. "Now that we know the steps to make it work, it only makes sense for us to load him up with all the abilities we can."

"But, I mean, that's—" Sammy brought her coloration under control and glared fiercely at the celestial. "Why's it got to be me?"

"Why not? You've been flirting with him nonstop since he joined."

"This goes a few steps beyond flirting! Why don't you go next if you think this is such a great idea?"

"Hmm." Ashley looked over at Clarke as if appraising him. "I'm not sure he would survive the encounter."

Clarke didn't know how to respond to that, and neither did any of the other girls. Everyone stared at Ashley as if expecting some explanation, but none came, and she eventually shrugged it off.

"I suppose it's not a pressing matter."

"What the hell kind of explanation is *that?*" Sammy snapped.

"What do you mean?" Ashley asked, sounding confused. Her hairband dimmed a few shades.

"Uh oh," Emma said. "I think Confused Ashley is back."

"Please don't call me that."

"Hell of a thing to say!" Sammy spat, folding her arms.

"It's all right, Sammy," Clarke said. "My opinions on all this are fairly simple. If you're not comfortable with trying, then we're not going to do it."

"But Sammy has a lot of abilities you would find useful," Ashley said. "I do think it's important you two give it a try."

"I don't care, Ashley. No one's getting pressured just so I can power up."

"But—"

"My decision is final."

Ashley frowned, a momentary look of confusion passing over her face. It vanished just as suddenly.

"And so it is," she said at last. Her hairband brightened, and she swept her gaze around the room. "Shall we get to it, then? We're here for a reason, after all."

Ashley took one of the available seats, which was her way of saying, yes, they were about to get to it. She set the grimoire on her lap but didn't open it. Clarke and the others sat down in a rough ring and waited for her to start the meeting.

"There's been a development," she began. "Chelsea Etcoff, an archivist at the CCU library, has suddenly decided to take an extended leave of absence."

"The same sort Heinrich took?" Clarke asked.

"I believe so."

"How certain are we?"

"I was already keeping an eye on Etcoff before this," Emma said. "She was on my short list for potential thralls."

"Then, if that's true, one of the two remaining campus vampires just lost an underling."

"That's precisely what we suspect," Ashley said. "We don't know how, but one possible explanation is the vampires are fighting over Heinrich's scraps, and Etcoff's apparent death is evidence of a skirmish."

"Which means tensions between the vampiric factions are escalating?" Clarke asked. "Sounds like a great thing to me! Any way we can stoke this fire? Maybe encourage the vampires to take each other out?"

"Not at the moment." Ashley's hand brushed across the grimoire's cover. "The problem is we don't know *where* to 'stoke the fire,' as you put it. We need better information."

"Which is why we snagged the grimoire in the first place."

"Yes, but the spell protecting the book has proven to be surprisingly robust." She opened the book and showed them the blurred pages. She closed the book and set it down again. "I can break through the spell, given enough time, but that's the thing. It'll take time."

"Time we may not have," Emma said. "If we're going to coax the vampires into doing the dirty work for us, we need to know where to prod them. That means cracking the, um, 'magical encryption' on the grimoire as fast as possible."

"Then how do we do that?" Clarke asked.

"We don't, unfortunately." Ashley let out a brief huff. "None of us have the right combination of skills and knowledge to break the spell quickly."

"Not even you?"

"All I've managed so far is to weaken the spell with brute force, which is why it's been such a time sink. Fortunately, however, there may be an alternative."

"We could enlist the services of a mage," Emma explained. "Someone with the expertise we need. And, as chance would have it, my father happens to be on good terms with one such witch. Her name is Lady Hepatica Grey, and she's no friend of the vampires, I can tell you that much. We can trust her."

"*If* we can convince her to meet with us," Ashley added.

"But if she's that powerful," Clarke began, "why haven't the vampires taken her out? Don't they view her as a threat?"

"They do," Emma said, "but doing so would risk uniting the mage clans, and that's one step away from open war with the vampires. The vampires would win in the end—I don't think anyone doubts that—but not without paying a heavy price. Therefore, as long as individual mages stay clear of vampiric business, they're left alone."

"But don't the vampires hex them? You know, to weaken or seal their magic?"

"They try, but for every new hex the vampires throw at them, the mages find a counter. It's a magical stalemate that has lasted centuries. Mages are considered … a neutral party in the overall balance of power."

"Sounds like this witch will be taking a big risk in helping us, then."

"Which is why we can expect her services will come with a hefty price. No telling what she'll ask for until we speak with her, though."

"Still," Ashley said, patting the grimoire, "we believe this is our best option. Seek the aid of Lady Hepatica Grey so that we can read Heinrich's grimoire and take advantage of the situation brewing at CCU."

"By kicking some vampiric ass!" Emma added with a fist pump.

"Yes." Ashley let out a weary sigh. "That, too. All in favor?"

Everyone's hands went up.

"It's decided, then."

"I'll speak with my father tonight and get the ball rolling," Emma said. "As soon as I hear something, I'll let the team know."

CHAPTER THIRTEEN

THROUGH HER FAMILY'S CONNECTIONS, Emma managed to arrange a meeting with the witch the following day. Everyone met at her apartment and piled into her Jetta for the trip. She drove them out of the city and through long, winding backroads to a development tucked in between dense patches of forest.

Lady Grey's house sat at the end of a cul-de-sac deep into the development. Clarke wasn't sure what he thought an honest-to-goodness witch's abode should look like, but a white two-story with dormer windows and a picturesque yard hadn't been on his list. No twisted, old trees or wrought iron fence or crows perched atop swinging gibbets. Not even a cauldron or smokestack with strange fumes pouring forth. A puffy Maltese dog with black button eyes lounged on the patio, tongue lolling in its mouth.

There were no cats in sight, least of all a black one.

But looks could be deceiving. The place *reeked* of magic, too many kinds for Clarke's beginner senses to pick out.

Emma parked the car on the curb, then twisted around in her seat.

"We're here. Let me do most of the talking."

They exited the vehicle and crossed a flagstone path to the patio. Emma tapped the doorbell, and they waited. The Maltese stared at them with wild, wet eyes, then barked happily when the door opened.

Clarke judged the woman to be in her late thirties or early forties. She wore a turquoise blouse over tan slacks, and a pair of halfmoon glasses hung from a strap around her neck. Her platinum blonde hair was bound in a chignon bun, and her eyes were a deep blue that bordered on violet. She must have been stunning back in the day, and much of that allure remained, but now fully ripened into a voluptuous MILF.

She smiled pleasantly enough when she saw them, but the expression came across as a formality. A nicety she extended to her guests as a matter of course, one that lacked any true warmth.

"I've been expecting you. Which one of you girls is Emma?"

"I am, Lady Grey."

"I should have guessed." Her smile became knowing. "You have some of your father in your face."

"I believe he spoke with you about our problem?"

"He did. Whether or not I can help remains to be seen."

"We'd very much like to discuss the matter with you. May we come in?"

"First, let's have a look at you. Can't be too careful." She brought the glasses up to her eyes and peered through them at each visitor. "My, my. Quite the eclectic group we have here. A succubus, werewolf, and slime, all hanging out with two humans. One must wonder what kind of trouble you might—"

She stopped, her gaze fixating on Clarke. She adjusted the glasses and leaned forward with wide eyes.

"But that's …"

The witch removed her glasses. She rubbed them clean on her blouse, then stuck them back on. Her brow furrowed as she stared at Clarke.

"Is there a problem, Lady Grey?" Emma asked.

"No, I don't think so." She pulled the glasses off again and let them dangle from the strap. "Well, come in, come in. Don't be shy. The dog doesn't bite, and neither do I."

The dog gave them a chipper bark as they filed inside.

"Thank you, Lady Grey."

"Please, no need to be so formal. Call me Hepatica."

The living room looked like any other, which somehow disappointed Clarke. Hepatica's eyes lingered on him, but soon she motioned for the group to follow her.

"This way."

The witch led them down the stairs to the basement. The chalked remains of a magic circle covered a patch of stone floor with the waxy remains of candles seated at five points. Bookshelves lined one wall, each weighted with heavy volumes, and various containers took up even more space. An entire science lab's worth of beakers, flasks, complex tubing, and Bunsen burners cluttered several workstations. Equipment for creating potions, perhaps?

Now this is more like it! Clarke thought.

"Is this a witch's basement," Sammy asked under her breath, "or a meth lab?"

Brooke snorted out a laugh before she caught herself.

"Shush!" Emma snapped through the side of her mouth.

If Hepatica heard the remark, she gave no indication. She sat down at the head of the table at the back and beckoned the others to join her.

"All right. Let's see what you brought."

Emma nodded to Ashley, who retrieved the grimoire from her satchel and placed it in front of the witch.

"My, my." Hepatica ran her hand across the leather binding then put her glasses back on and opened the tome. Her lips curled into a wicked smile. "It's not every day you see one of these. How'd you come by it?"

"We stole it from a Chester Creek vampire."

"And the owner?"

"No longer needs it."

"Truly?" Hepatica glanced up at them over her glasses. Her eyes darted to Clarke, then back to Emma. "Dead?"

"The official word is he went on sabbatical."

"In the middle of the semester?" Hepatica sniffed. "Vampires. They think they're so clever. Still, that must have been quite the fight. How old was he?"

"We're not sure. Risen within the last ten years, I'd say."

"No way." Hepatica tapped the blurred text. "You won't see a spell this good from newly risen trash. This is the work of a master."

"Perhaps someone helped him with the spell."

"Perhaps."

"You don't sound convinced."

"Because I'm not." She closed the book and pushed it forward.

"It doesn't matter how old he was," Emma said. "He's dead, and we have his grimoire. Can you help us read it?"

"That's the question, isn't it?" The witch pressed her hands together as if praying and rested her chin on her thumbs, all while staring at the book. "The short answer is yes."

"And the long answer?"

Hepatica's eyes darted back to Clarke before returning to Emma.

"It's going to cost you."

"How much?"

"That will depend. First, tell me why you need the information contained within the grimoire?"

"We're trying to find the other CCU vampires."

"And?"

"And kill them."

"I see. That does complicate matters." She set her phone on the table and placed a call.

"*Wha-a-at?*" The young woman who answered sounded both bored and annoyed at being disturbed.

"Ixia, dear, we have guests down in the basement. I need you to collect your sisters and come down here. Family business."

"Now?"

"Yes, now."

"But I'm in the middle of a match! I've got a nydus worm in my natural expand and zerglings eating my siege tanks. As soon as I clean up this mess, I'll be sixty seconds away from a two-two timing attack. I can't leave now!"

"Your games can wait. This is important."

"Uh. *Fine.* You clearly don't care about my rank, so why should I? I'll go grab the others."

"Thank you, dear." Hepatica switched off her phone, then knitted her fingers. "I can provide you with the magic circle you need. One that will crack this book's Concealment like a hammer striking an eggshell. But it'll cost you."

"What's your price?"

"First, I must confess to a mistake." The witch looked over at Clarke once more. "I was wrong about you when I said you were human, because you aren't. Not anymore. Not completely. There are bits of succubus and shifter magic swirling within you, and I know of only one spell that can pull off such a feat: Power Graft. Which means you, young man, are a blood knight."

"What if I am?" Clarke replied guardedly.

"Who you are matters a great deal. It matters that you're descended from vampire slayers and that your bloodline is both rare and powerful."

"Which makes it valuable to you?"

"Precisely. You catch on quick."

"What is it you want from me? Some of my blood?"

"Not … quite." Hepatica tilted her head ever so slightly. "What's your name?"

"J.B. Clarke. Don't ask what the initials mean. Also, I prefer to be addressed by my family name."

Someone tromped noisily down the stairs, footfalls conveying an air of exasperation. Clarke twisted in his seat to get a good look at the new arrivals.

The witch's daughters were dressed predominantly in black, similar to Emma's attire but also totally different. While Clarke considered Emma's style to be "goth adjacent," Hepatica's three daughters had leaped headfirst into the gothic fashion pool. There was black lipstick, eye-shadow, lace sleeves, bare midriffs, short skirts, stockings, a few tasteful tattoos and piercings, and far too many buckles. One daughter had retained her natural blonde hair, another had bleached her hair ghost white, and the third had dyed her hair black, leaving only a single streak of blonde.

"Well, Mom? We're here." The daughter with the white hair gave an exaggerated shrug. "What now?"

Hepatica rose from her seat and rounded the table.

"Clarke, allow me to introduce my daughters: Ixia, Dahlia, and Hyacinth. Fraternal triplets, and very close to your age, I'd wager. Ladies, this is Clarke. He's a *blood knight.*"

All three daughters perked up, eyes wide in a combination of surprise and amazement.

"Here's how I see it," Hepatica continued, speaking to Clarke more than the others. "You intend to go out there and slay some vampires. You may even be successful for a time. But eventually, you'll create enough pain that they will turn their attentions toward you, and when that happens, you will die. I don't blame you for traveling this path; it's in your blood, after all. But it *will* end in tears."

"I'm aware of the risks," Clarke said.

"Are you now? I wonder."

"Evil must be confronted."

"A noble sentiment. One that too often crumbles in the face of reality."

"Enough dancing around the topic. What do you want?"

"It's quite simple. *You* may be doomed, but we can still preserve your bloodline. Therefore, I would have you sire a child with one of my daughters as payment for my services."

The room fell deathly silent, and all three daughters gaped in shock at their mother. So did everyone else, except for Emma, who wore the widest, dumbest, happiest grin he'd ever seen. A pin dropping would have been the equivalent of an artillery strike.

Clarke cleared his throat after the lengthy silence. "You mean …"

"Exactly what I just said." The witch gave her daughters a casual wave. "You may select whichever one you fancy the most."

"Wow!" Emma exclaimed once they'd regrouped outside her car. She sat down on the hood. "My man Clarke is on a *roll!* Is there any problem your loins can't solve?"

"Emma, please."

"What? We're looking at a bill that's very easy to pay."

"Yes, but we're talking about a child here. *My* child, and I'm being asked to use future offspring as currency! Can't she just take credit like everyone else?"

"I knew the price would be hefty," Ashley said. "But this? This is unexpected."

"How'd she figure out I was a blood knight? Aren't your spells supposed to keep that fact hidden? As far as I could tell, she doesn't have a clue you're a celestial."

"I caught that as well. The most likely explanation is the magics you've absorbed gave you away. She did call those out, after all. I may need to adjust the spells protecting you to compensate."

"A little late for that, don't you think?"

"So, what do we do?" Brooke asked.

"As I see it, we have two options," Ashley began. "We can walk away from this deal, and I go back to cracking the grimoire the slow way."

"Which means we lose our window," Emma said. "If we want to trick the campus vampires into killing each other, we should act before they're done with Heinrich's old turf."

"Which then leads us to the other option," Ashley continued, "where Clarke pays the witch's price, and we move forward with our plan as quickly as possible."

The ladies all turned to him.

"I don't know about this." He glanced around the rough circle of young women.

"Honestly, I don't see the problem," Emma said. "A bloodline like yours should be spread as far and as wide as possible. The situation is a happy bonus as far as I'm concerned."

"You are such a succubus," Sammy muttered.

"And proud of it."

"Yes, we *know*."

"Well, I get the problem," Brooke said. "To put this in werewolf terms, the witch and her daughters aren't part of our pack and have shown no desire to join it. They aren't loyal to the alpha, and any child from this union will *also* not be a part of our pack. Will they keep the child from him? I don't know, but that could be Hepatica's intent."

The group turned to Sammy next.

"Don't look at me. I don't have a dog in this hunt. No offense, Brooke."

"None taken."

"A price is being asked," Ashley said. "And, since Clarke is the one who must pay it, the decision must be his. Do we all agree on this?"

Everyone nodded.

"Thanks," Clarke said. "I appreciate how you're giving me space to think this through. Still not sure what I should do."

"What about Hepatica's daughters?" Brooke asked. "Has anyone checked if they're on board with this?"

"Damn, you're right!" Clarke rubbed his temples. "What a mess!"

"Hold that thought." Emma pushed off the car hood. "I'll find out if they're willing. Sexual empath to the rescue. Be back in a jiffy!"

Emma hurried inside the house and came back a few minutes later.

"Okay, I have good news, and I have … news."

"Is the second part good or bad?" Clarke asked.

"Not bad. Just yet another wrinkle to consider. Okay, good news first. Your magic blood makes you super desirable. All of Hepatica's daughters are willing, Ixia especially. She's practically dripping at the thought of doing you."

"Which one was she?"

"Bleached white hair."

"Okay, good to know. That makes her the best choice. Now what's the wrinkle?"

"All three daughters are powerful magic users, which makes them candidates for Power Graft. And since Hepatica is asking you to knock up one of her daughters anyway, why not grab an upgrade while you're at it?"

"Do they know my Power Graft kicks in when I have sex?"

"I won't tell them if you don't." Emma winked at him.

"Okay, but if they're all magic users, where's the wrinkle come in?"

"Their areas of expertise are different. Dahlia is a natural when it comes to Fire spells, Hyacinth is all about protective Wards, and Ixia is more of a support spell generalist. Who you pick will affect the kind of magic you absorb."

"So, my options are offense, defense, or support?"

"Pretty much."

"Oh, for the love of—" Clarke put his face in his hands. "This is like a side quest where you can only pick one of the quest rewards!"

"Offense would be my choice," Sammy said. "Can't go wrong with setting vampires on fire. I say you do Dahlia."

"I thought you didn't have a dog in this hunt," Brooke said.

"I do now that upgrades are on the table. The stronger he is, the better all our chances are."

"I'm still not sure about this." Clarke lowered his hands. "And I'm *especially* not sure about some witch keeping my future child from me!"

"Then tell her that," Ashley said. "Make her put your right to raise the child in the contract. This is a negotiation, and you clearly have something she wants. That gives you leverage. Fight for what's important to you. And if you can't find a compromise you're happy with, just walk away. We'll support your decision."

Clarke nodded, Ashley's words providing the steel he needed to form a decision.

"We're with you," Emma said. "Whatever you decide, we're with you."

He smiled at her, then took in the rest of their expressions. *All* of them had his back.

"Thank you. All of you." He let out a long exhale. "All right. Let's do this."

"Have you come to a decision?" Hepatica asked.

Clarke sat down at the table across from Hepatica, the ladies of Broken Fang standing behind him. The witch's daughters stood nearby, all three stealing glances when they thought he wasn't paying attention.

"I have," Clarke declared in a firm voice.

"And?"

"We need to discuss how the child will be raised."

"A child of this nature necessitates certain safeguards. He or she will be secreted away shortly after birth, handed over to another family and kept safe until reaching adulthood, when the blood magic will begin to manifest."

"I'm to have no hand in how the child is raised?"

"No."

"Then we have no deal."

"Because you wish to raise the child yourself?"

"I do."

Hepatica leaned forward and knitted her fingers.

"Tell me, young blood knight, were you adopted?"

Clarke sucked in a sharp breath, the witch's words taking him by surprise.

"How did you know that?"

"I only suspected until now." Her violet eyes seemed to laugh at him. "But it makes sense. Look at what we're discussing here. A child, to be born of blood and magic. A child of hunted heritage, delivered in secret and kept safe from the vampires. How familiar does this portrait look to you, I wonder? Almost like a reflection in the mirror?"

"You're suggesting I came from a union between a witch and a blood knight."

"Or some variety of mage. Perhaps even a warlock and blood knight. Who's to say which one was the mother?"

"Then why haven't my real parents shown themselves by now?"

"It's possible some tragedy befell them. Perhaps a d-hunter found and killed them. I could look into it, if you wish. One of the mage clans may have a record of the contract and what became of the signees."

"And how much would *that* service cost me?"

"Well." Hepatica tapped her lips with a thoughtful finger. "I do have three daughters."

"Thanks, but no thanks."

"It's nothing but my own speculation, anyway. I'm interested in you, not your parents."

"And I'm interested in the right to see and raise my own child."

"Then it seems we are at an impasse."

Clarke drummed his fingers on the hardwood table.

What could he use to shift the witch's position? What other leverage he could employ?

"The child's safety is your primary concern?" Clarke asked.

"Correct. You, with your plans to confront the vampires, might as well be a lightning rod for death and despair. Wouldn't you want to spare your child that?"

"What would have to change for the child to be safe? Me, giving up this fight against the vampires?"

"You and I both know that won't happen. This war in is your blood. You will be drawn into conflict with the vampires, whether you realize it or not."

"Then what?"

"A child with your heritage will never be safe until the vampires' hold on humanity is broken."

"Then that's what goes in the contract," Clarke declared, pointing his finger down at an imaginary document.

"Excuse me?" Hepatica's eyes widened, her cool confidence melting into surprise.

"You heard me. If we manage to break the vampiric spell over humanity on a large enough scale, the child is mine to raise alongside your daughter."

"I ... well, yes, of course, I suppose that would be a reasonable condition. But would you really take this so far?"

"I will either achieve this goal or I will die trying."

His own words shocked him, and yet he did not

regret them. They rang true in his mind, resonating with the core of his desires for the world now that his eyes had been opened.

Hepatica studied him for long seconds, perhaps taking him seriously for the first time.

"I believe you will," she uttered softly. But then she recovered some of her earlier composure, and her face grew serene once more. "That you will make the attempt, at least."

You may believe this is impossible, Clarke thought. *And you may be right, but I have a feeling my destiny would guide me to this path one way or another. Why not embrace it?*

"Then are we in agreement on the conditions?" he asked.

"Almost. Have you selected your partner?"

"Ixia, if she is willing."

The young witch jumped at hearing her name. Hepatica snapped her fingers, and she stepped forward and bowed her head.

"Uh, yes. Yes, sir. I'm willing," she said, the slightest hint of a smile gracing her lips.

"Anything else we need to discuss?" Clarke asked.

"That's it." Hepatica rose to her feet. "I'll draw up the contract immediately."

CHAPTER FOURTEEN

CLARKE READ THROUGH THE CONTRACT one last time. The language was simple and the terms plainly stated, devoid of any legalese to cloud the matter. Emma had already reviewed the contract and given her approval.

He picked up the pen; Hepatica and Ixia had already signed the document. The senior witch sat expectantly at the other end of the table while the ladies of Broken Fang stood supportively behind him.

Meanwhile, Ixia toiled at one of the workstations with a rubber apron, safety goggles, and gloves over her goth outfit. She'd mixed a dizzying array of substances before grinding it all up with a mortar and pestle and heating the powdered mixture with a Bunsen burner. A pale liquid bubbled up from the beaker, spilling over into a tubed corkscrew that ended in a vial.

That vial was almost full.

"What happens if you break your word?" Clarke asked.

"I won't," Hepatica replied.

"But what if?"

"The penalty for breaking a vow of this magnitude is excommunication from my clan, the Coven of the Ashen Blossom."

"And if I break my word?"

"You will be blacklisted by my clan, and by any others we're allied with."

"Sounds like we both have strong reasons to make this work, then."

"That's the general idea."

"Any spells I should know about on the contract?"

"No," Hepatica said. "Just ink on paper."

Clarke glanced over to Emma, who confirmed the witch's words with a nod.

He took one last look over the contract, then signed it and slid it forward.

"It's done." Hepatica pulled the contract closer and began rolling it into a scroll. "Ixia, dear? How's your potion coming along?"

"Just about to finish up."

"What's the potion for?" Clarke asked.

"It's a fertility decoction strong enough to guarantee your success." Hepatica slid her chair back and stood up.

"I leave you to your task. You may use my daughter's room or take your business elsewhere if you prefer. Come see me when the deed is done. I'll have the instructions for the magic circle ready and waiting for you."

Hepatica headed up the stairs.

Emma gave him a pat on the shoulder then an enthusiastic thumbs up before following the rest of the team out.

Ixia stoppered the vial of pale green fluid and pocketed it. She took off her goggles and gloves, placed the apron on a hanger, then joined him by the table.

She wore her straight hair long and loose down her back. Her lipstick and eyeshadow were black, and the tear under her left eye may have been a tattoo or drawn there. Her ears, bellybutton, and one eyebrow were pierced with a variety of silver rings and studs, and more rings decorated her slender fingers, some with decorative skulls.

She was a slender woman, her firm, perky breasts constrained by a tight, high-collared top, itself decorated with silver buckles and necklaces. She wore a miniskirt over narrow hips and black stockings that led down to ankle-high boots with too many buckles.

She sat beside him and set the vial on the table. She shared her mother's violet eyes.

"Hello, Ixia." He wasn't sure what else to say. She looked uneasy, which he could sympathize with.

"Hey."

"Is the potion for me or you?"

"For both of us. At this dosage, the effects last about twelve hours." She pulled the stopper out and drank half the contents before handing it over.

He downed the other half.

"Mmm. Minty."

"I added extra ingredients for flavor. Otherwise, it tastes like liquid chalk."

"You've used this before?"

"During practice, to evaluate the potion. Not for … you know." She let out a nervous laugh. "I've never had a kid before."

"Me neither. This is new to me." He made a circular gesture to encompass the basement. "All of it, actually. I only became aware of vampires a few weeks ago."

"Oh, wow! Really?"

"Yep." He stuffed hands into pockets. "And now look at me. Already paying off witches with my firstborn."

"It's not that bad. And, really, I think my mom has a point. Going after vampires is dangerous, and that goes double for someone like you."

"So I've been told."

"This way, even if something happens to you, you'll have left a legacy behind."

"I know what you're saying makes sense—in a cold, detached sort of way—but it still feels wrong in my gut."

"Then why did you agree to this?"

"Because I'm beginning to realize why I'm here, what my purpose in life is."

"To kill vampires?"

"As many of the bastards as I can."

"That's not going to be easy."

"Nothing worthwhile ever is."

Ixia nodded sympathetically, then she let out an exaggerated sigh.

"Well? Shall we head up to my room?"

"Lead the way."

She led him up three flights of stairs to one of the rooms built into a converted attic. The entrance was decorated with a huge *Dead Space* poster.

"Sorry about the mess," Ixia said, opening the door.

The room's walls were barely visible under all the posters: *Starcraft 2*, plenty of *League of Legends* champions, *Resident Evil* and *Silent Hill* games both recent and classic, and many others adorned every inch of the place, often overlapping.

The back wall slanted downward with the roof, but the space left by the dormer window had been filled with an impressive gaming station. The bookshelf held no books, but a wide variety of figurines and models. The bed was a rumpled mess of checkered covers.

Clarke stepped over to the bookshelf and inspected her collection with the eye of a gaming enthusiast. He found that eye drawn to a life-sized model of a plasma cutter from the *Dead Space* franchise.

"Yep," Ixia said, flopping onto the bed. "I really did buy a lump of plastic shaped like my favorite zombie-killing weapon of all time."

"I'm not judging. I love the *Dead Space* games." He paused, then reconsidered his words. "Well, the first two."

"I hate zombies. Like, with a passion. You ever meet a zombie?"

"Once. Didn't end well for him."

"My mom thinks all of this is stupid. Keeps telling me to focus on the family business instead of pursuing my passion."

"Which is?"

"I want to go into esports. Like, as a pro."

"That's a tough field to break into. I've watched a few tournaments. Three hundred plus actions per minute? Got to wonder if those players are even human."

"Some of them aren't. Lots of elves in esports."

"*Really?*" He supposed the revelation shouldn't have surprised him at this point.

"Yeah, but my witchcraft lets me keep up. The right combo of spells and potions, and my reflexes become god-tier!"

Clarke chuckled as he sat down next to her. "Sounds like the family business helps you with your passion."

"I guess. It's not like I have anything against witch-craft. I know what it means for me and the family, how it protects us. Keeps us from becoming food for the vampires. I just … I don't know. I wish my mom understood me better."

"I get that. You still okay with this?"

"I wouldn't be here if I wasn't. Trust me, I'm not afraid to tell her no."

He chucked again. "I believe you."

She spread her arms across the sheets, a sea of white hair framing her face.

"Just to warn you, Clarke, I'm not what you might consider 'experienced.' You're in the driver's seat from here on out."

"Gotcha. I think I can handle it."

He bent down toward her, intent on starting with a tender kiss, but something made him stop a few inches from her lips. His thoughts drifted back to his time with Brooke, so fresh in his mind, and an idea sparked its way into existence, rapidly taking form.

He backed away, hovering above the young witch on both arms. He smiled down at her.

"Ixia?"

"Yes?"

"I know this might sound strange, but before we, uh, fulfill the contract, how would you like to go on a date with me?"

Her violet eyes lit up at the suggestion.

"I don't know about you," he continued, "but this is just so damned awkward. So, I thought why not have some fun together and get to know each other before—"

"Oh, God, yes! This is such a good idea!"

Ixia picked the time and location—eight o'clock that night at a club in downtown Chester Creek called Studio Nightshade. Clarke headed out to the car and explained the situation, to the surprise of some but to Emma's whole-hearted approval.

"That's our Clarke!" she said. "Always thinking about us ladies."

"Just trying to make her feel more comfortable. And myself, too, if I'm being honest."

Emma drove them back to her apartment, and Ashley cast a revised Concealment spell on him along the way. After that, everyone went their separate ways for the evening.

Clarke grabbed a quick bite, showered, and picked out what he thought were some stylish date clothes. But Emma took one look at his freshly pressed slacks and button-down shirt, and crossed her arms with a frown.

"Could be better."

"What's wrong with my clothes? This is way nicer than what I wore for my date with Brooke."

271

"True, but you're about to go clubbing with a witch, one who has a clear stylistic preference." The succubus rubbed her chin thoughtfully. "Come on. Let's see what we have to work with."

She led him to his closet, where she proceeded to rifle through his shirts. She selected a different button-down and set it on the bed.

"This one."

"Black? Paired with black slacks? Isn't that a bit predictable for a date with a goth?"

"We'll break it up with some accessories. Trust me; she'll love this."

She sidestepped over to her closet and sifted through her belt hanger before selecting a thick, black leather belt with metal studs. He slipped it on as she rummaged through one of her jewelry boxes.

"Aha! I thought I still had this one."

She handed him a necklace with a silver skull pendant, a large red stone gripped in its jaw. He put it on.

"How do I look?" he asked, spreading his arms.

"Like you're ready to fuck a witch's brains out." Emma licked her lips, and then sauntered up to him. She draped her body against his, breasts smooshed against his chest, revealing her firm, pale cleavage. "If you weren't busy tonight, I'd take you right here and now."

"Wouldn't that be risky? You know, with the fertility

potion fresh in my system?"

"Oh, Clarke, please don't tease me like that. Why, just the thought of bearing your child makes me wet!"

"You're incorrigible, you know that?"

"Would you have me any other way?"

Clarke laughed, then bent down and gave the succubus a long, thorough kiss. Her wings pushed out from under her shirt as the kiss dragged on, and her tail took form, swishing back and forth underneath her skirt. He started to pull away, but her tail whipped around his thigh and gave it a tug.

"One more." She made a pouty face. "Please."

"Always."

He kissed her again, one hand at the back of her head, holding her tight. She reached down and stroked his crotch.

"Later," he said breathily. "Once the potion has worn off."

"There's no need to wait that long."

"But—"

"We succubi have precise control over our fertility. I will only ever conceive a child with you when you're ready. You have my solemn word."

They shared one last kiss before he headed out.

He drove into downtown Chester Creek and left his car in a parking garage near the address. The path to the club took him down the main street to an alley lined with local restaurants and specialty stores. The club's entrance was at the far end, tucked into a shadowed corner under a discreet sign. A bouncer stood by the door.

An *orc* bouncer.

Clarke headed for the door.

"Sorry, Sport." The orc stepped in front of him. He might as well have been an impenetrable wall of meat. "This club's not for you."

"I'm meeting someone here. She's expecting me."

"Sure, she is." The orc pointed up the alley. "Two blocks down on the right there's a joint called Hank's Rhythm Club. You'll like it a lot more than this place. Trust me."

"Can I at least check if she's inside?"

"No can do, Sport. This is an exclusive club, and you don't fit our—"

"He's with me."

Clarke and the orc turned to find Ixia Grey walking over, heels clicking on the asphalt. She'd exchanged her top for a lacy long-sleeve number that did nothing to hide the black bra underneath.

"My apologies, Miss Grey." The orc shuffled aside and bowed his head. "I wasn't told to expect you."

"That's all right, Hershel. Our date is a bit spur-of-the-moment." She pressed a hand softly against the small of Clarke's back. "Please let the others know he's with me."

"Of course, Miss Grey." He swung the door open for them.

Clarke offered Ixia his arm, and she slipped hers through his. They descended side-by-side down the brick-walled stairs and into the club's dark interior. The path leveled out, and they passed through two sets of double doors lit by blacklights. Clarke began to sense powerful, overlapping magics as soon as they cleared the first door. Music thumped in his chest, growing stronger as they traversed the corridor.

"Sorry about that." Ixia let out an unsure laugh and gave his arm a quick pat. "I should have called ahead."

They pushed through one more set of doors. The corridor opened into a high-ceilinged dance floor, and Clarke had to pause at the threshold to soak in the sights.

Demihumans formed an undulating sea of bodies on the dance floor. Shifters in full beast mode danced alongside lithe elves, while succubi and incubi wrapped their wings around prospective partners. A green-scaled dragonkin lounged by the well-stocked bar, one of her wings draped around a horned man.

The shirtless werewolf up on the stage banged his furry dreadlocks to the strumming of his guitar. Another werewolf and what might have been a werebear backed him up with their own guitars while a heavily tattooed orc pounded away at the drums.

A banner above the band read: **THE ANGRY HAIRBALLS**.

The lead singer grabbed his mic and began grunting and howling into it in what sounded like the werewolf equivalent of screaming death metal. The crowd cheered, and one of the elves near the front took off her bra and threw it onto the stage.

"Now there's something you don't see every day."

I need to remember this place, he thought. *I bet Emma and Brooke will love it.*

"Can I get you a drink?" Ixia asked, speaking up over the music.

"They going to card us?"

"Not here, and besides we're legal in this place."

"Demihumans can drink at a younger age?" He chuckled. "That doesn't seem fair."

"It's more about when your magic wakes up than someone's age. That's what we use in these circles."

"Okay. Then, sure. I'll have a drink."

"What's your poison?"

He wasn't all that knowledgeable when it came to alcoholic beverages, but he recalled his father's preferred beverage and went with that.

"Gin and tonic."

He accompanied Ixia to the bar, where a redheaded succubus in a suit and tie smiled primly, ready to take their order.

An empathic bartender? he thought. *Sure, why not?*

"One Bloody Mary, and a gin and tonic, please."

"You've got it, Miss Grey."

The succubus served them, and he followed Ixia to a corner booth. They sat down and nursed their drinks while the lead werewolf grunted through the song. It sounded a bit like angry German.

He sipped at his gin and tonic. "I get the impression you're a big deal around these parts."

"Guess so. My family is, at least."

"Why's that?"

"It's because we don't play by vampire rules. At least, not fully. We're powerful enough to resist their hexes and chart our own path. That power has earned our place in this world. People both respect and envy us. Some even hate us, but they also know what we can do for them, so they stay on their best behavior when we show up."

"You do a lot of business with demihumans?"

"Not as much as you'd think."

"Why not?"

"You've seen what we charge people."

"Hmm." Clarke shrugged and drank some more.

"It's not as simple as you might think." She brushed her hair back over an ear. "Yes, we're powerful and we can do a lot for the people vampires take advantage of, but there's a fine line between providing a dash of magical help and drawing a d-hunter to our door."

"What's a d-hunter? Your mother mentioned the name as well."

"It stands for deviant hunter. It's what the vampires call their frontline enforcers. They're trained and equipped to kill people like us."

"Charming."

"They're one of the reasons why we mages don't oppose the vampires more openly, and why we charge such high prices for our services."

"Because of the risks involved?"

Ixia nodded grimly. "The vampires tolerate our activities, for the most part. But push too hard, and they'll push back. I'd love to set up shop right here in this booth and spend the next month clearing all their hexes." She pointed to the crowd. "But all that'll do is get me and my whole family killed."

"I get it." Clarke sipped at his gin and tonic. A pleasant warmth began to spread through his body. "There's a difference between liking the world we live in and knowing how to survive it."

"Yeah. Something like that."

The club fell into a lull as the band prepped for their next song. Their conversation did, too, Ixia's eyes going distant as her thoughts wandered. Finally, they came back to him.

"You really going to do it?" she asked with an odd, conflicted tenor of eagerness and caution. "Go after the vampires?"

"Yep."

"Any chance I could convince you not to?"

"Why say that?"

"I don't know. Because you seem like a decent guy. I … I don't want to see you get hurt."

"I have the feeling I'm going to be hurt plenty by what's to come."

"And you'll still go through with it?"

"Yep."

"Why?"

"Because someone has to stop them. Maybe that someone isn't me, but I won't know until I try. And I won't be able to live with myself, knowing what I know now, unless I do."

"Your chances aren't great."

"I know …"

Silence hung over their booth like a dark, foreboding cloud.

The music picked up again, this time slow and serene. Clarke glanced over to find the shirtless singer now in his hybrid form, hairless chest glistening, wolf ears tall as he sang softly.

"Oh, I love this song!" Ixia rose to her feet, their

gloomy conversation forgotten. "Dance with me?"

"It would be my pleasure."

They found an open patch on the dance floor, and she put her arms around his shoulders. He held her by the hips, and they slow-danced their way through the song, each sway drawing them closer until her head rested against his chest.

The song faded toward its soft finale—a sad tale of lost love and missed chances that ended in bitter regret.

Ixia gazed up at him, her eyes wide, lips parted. He bent down and kissed her, and she hugged him tight, his tongue exploring her mouth and her his. She broke their kiss and rested her head upon his chest once more.

"There are private rooms downstairs," she whispered softly.

Ixia opened the door to the VIP room with a fob on her keychain. The room featured a minibar, huge television screen, integrated sound system, and a curving sofa so wide and deep it could double as a bed.

In fact, that seemed to be the intent.

Ixia locked the door behind them, and they kissed once more, hands exploring each other's bodies with greater vigor. Clarke slipped his hands underneath her lace overshirt, and she pulled his shirt free, fingers gliding over his back muscles. They pulled each other's shirts off as they kissed, leaving him topless and her in her black bra.

He lowered her to the sofa and slid a hand up her inner thigh. She trembled as his fingers drew closer to the heat of her sex, her cheeks flush, chest rising and falling with anticipation. She reached behind her back, unclasped her bra, and tossed it aside. Her round, perky breasts bounced free, nipples hard as stone.

He bent down and took one into his mouth.

"Yes!"

He caressed the hot wetness through her panties, stroking the fabric as he teased her nipple, and she cried out, little gasps of pleasure squeaking out of her mouth. She bit her lower lip, her delicate hands rummaging through his hair, clawing at his back and making him hungry for more.

He pulled her panties down to her ankles, and she slipped one leg out, and then the other. As she did, she held him in her gaze, eyes moist, nervous and yet eager, her pale skin flush. He broke the gaze, kissed one breast, then the other, then down her smooth, flat stomach. As his motions took him down, his desire only went up.

She hiked her skirt up, in sultry invitation, and he took it, kissing one inner thigh, and then the other, before—

"Ah!"

He lapped at her, softly, slowly, tenderly. Her legs trembled around him, hips arching toward him, eager and willing. He pressed into her with his tongue, and she threw her head back.

"More!" she gasped between squeals of delight. "I want all of you!"

He rose from his meal. "Then you shall have it."

He undid his belt buckle and cast aside his slacks. He didn't need any encouragement for what came next, and pressed his tip against the hot, dripping mouth between her legs.

"Kiss me when you do it," she panted. "Please."

"As you wish."

He bent down, hand holding the back of her head, and he kissed her once more.

She moaned into his mouth, and moaned louder as he entered her, stretching her wide with his girth. She was so wet, he slid all the way in—down to the root—with the first stroke, but he knew he she craved much more.

He hooked his arms underneath her knees, raising and spreading her legs, and then began to slide in and out.

"Fuck!" she cried. He picked up speed, and her breasts shuddered with each deep, full thrust, her arms spread wide in glorious surrender. He pounded her, hard and deep and without mercy, all their earlier tenderness evaporating under the burning heat of their lust.

"I'm close!" she breathed between feverish pants. "Just a little more. Just a—yes!"

She squeezed her eyes shut and squealed through clenched teeth, her legs clamped around him like a vise as the pleasure took her. The orgasm shuddered through her, followed by aftershocks that wracked her body until she fell limp, reduced to a boneless figure on the bed that no longer had the power or will to do anything beyond lay there and accept him into her.

His excitement built, crescendoing deep within his loins until it reached a zenith, and he erupted within her. He buried himself deep within her and filled her up with each exquisite pulse.

His perception of the room changed, heightened. He saw her body spread beneath him but also the intense beating of the magic within her, like the revving of a hotrod engine mixed with floral scents and a gentle rain of petals. Delicate, yet intensely powerful in the same instance.

His own magic touched hers, entered hers, and their energies mingled like two fluids swirling together. He pulled back, but not before a part of her left its mark upon him. He didn't perceive the difference as sharply as with Brooke—more a knot within the corner of his mind than a new font of strength—but he knew he'd succeeded all the same.

He slipped out of her and settled down on the sofa beside her. A pearly river oozed out from between her legs, pooling on the sheets. It had to be the largest load of his life. An effect of the potion, perhaps?

Her chest rose and fell as he stroked fingers through her hair, then gave her a peck on the cheek. She glanced down at his crotch, still hard despite his recent release, and she turned to him with hungry eyes.

"Again, please," she uttered breathlessly.

CHAPTER FIFTEEN

"ANOTHER JOB WELL DONE, I SEE," Ashley said, accepting the manila envelope from Clarke which contained Hepatica's instructions for the magic circle. The celestial had driven over to Emma's apartment upon hearing of his success, despite it being the dead of the night.

"She seemed to think so," Clarke said.

"Ixia? Or her mother?"

"Both."

Emma sniggered, which prompted a quick side eye from Ashley. The celestial sighed tiresomely, then opened the envelope and spread its contents on the coffee table. Both she and Emma sat down to review the diagram and detailed instructions.

"Clever," Emma said after a while.

"Yes," Ashley agreed quietly, chin resting on a loose

fist. "Elegant, too. Do you see this part here? How it uses flows of Scry mixed with Illuminate? I would have never thought of that."

"Me neither."

"And then there's this bit. The circle is already tailored for three focal points. Perfect for you, me, and Clarke. She even thought of that."

"Worth it, then?" he asked.

"You betcha!" Emma sat back on the sofa. "How long do you think you'll need to set this up? Two, maybe three days?"

"That sounds about right." Ashley picked up the diagram. "We could do it faster if all three of us worked together, but three days isn't bad. Clarke, did your Power Graft work on Ixia?"

"It did. Not really sure what I gained, but it's there."

"Then how about this for a plan: I'll focus on the circle, while you two explore your blood magic more *thoroughly*. Sound good?"

"Works for me," Clarke said.

"Me, too." Emma flashed a scandalous smile. "I like exploring Clarke. Thoroughly."

Ashley cleared her throat.

"What? I mean in a professional sense. For science."

"Of course, you did …" The celestial sighed once more. "Clarke, I recommend you focus your attention on one or two spells to become proficient at. Maybe Blood Boil or Daze. Spells that are fast to cast and have a low cost. You may want to try your hand at more advanced magic, but be careful with ones that consume large chunks of vitality like Sacrifice or Scarlet Slash. We don't want you burning yourself out by accident."

"Got it. I'll keep that in mind."

"At this stage, it's better for you to have one or two spells you can depend on rather than become a mediocre generalist." Ashley gathered the documents and stood up. "I'm heading out to the mill."

"At this hour?"

"Sleep is overrated. I'll keep you and the others informed of my progress."

Monday at the university passed by without incident, though Clarke caught one of his human classmates talking about Professor Heinrich's sabbatical, to which his human friend replied, "Heinrich who?"

The control spells are already working their magic, he thought, *already worming their way through people's memories.* The incident left a dark chill in his mind that didn't leave until he was back at Emma's apartment.

They spent the evening studying magic, starting with a review of his spell list. Together, they narrowed down the spells he wanted to focus on and eventually landed on both Blood Freeze and Sacrifice.

Blood Freeze was an attack spell that caused the target's blood and muscles to solidify, inflicting both damage and paralysis, just as it had in Ashley's campaign. Like most of the spells in his arsenal, it used his own body for fuel, with the cost being proportional to the size of the target. But since he could heal himself by vanquishing enemies with his thirstblade, and Blood Freeze left them vulnerable to attack, the cost was usually worth it.

Sacrifice was a self-targeted support spell that increased the effectiveness of his next attack. Its variable cost made the spell flexible and dangerous—to his enemies *and* himself. He could drain himself to within an inch of death if he wasn't careful, but such a spell would turn his next sword strike into a killing blow against almost anything.

He understood Ashley's warning about Sacrifice, but the spell was too powerful for him to ignore. If he and the ladies came across a foe that totally outclassed them, they needed some way to fight back, some recourse to even the odds.

And that's where Sacrifice came into play. It would serve as his trump card.

Emma helped him practice casting Blood Freeze by zipping out to the supermarket and bringing home a few steaks, which served as dummy targets for the spell. And, given their diminutive size, each cast barely taxed him at all. He became lightheaded after two hours of practice, but beyond that hiccup the session went well.

Sacrifice was another matter entirely. The target was himself, and the cost could be varied. At first, he wasn't sure he'd be able to practice the spell without someone to replenish his vitality from—as he'd done with Brooke during their sparring—but it turned out he could cast the spell while draining *no* life. The damage bonus from the spell was equally nonexistent, but he *could* practice the spell in this manner.

He thought of it as something akin to a launch drill for nuclear missiles—going through all the motions up to actually launching the nuke.

Emma grilled the steaks with blue cheese crumbles for dinner, and then offered herself up as dessert. Clarke enjoyed both immensely. She urged him onto his back so that she could ride him, doing all the work for a change. Which he didn't mind, because casting Blood Freeze so many times consecutively had left him weary.

Her succubus magic coursed through his body as they made love, reinvigorating him, much to their shared delight. The effect wasn't as strong as a slash from his thirstblade—and impractical for actual combat (for obvious reasons)—but still served to recharge his body's "batteries" after a hard day's work.

Tuesday came and went, with the evening filled with more magical practice. He and Emma tried to figure out what ability he'd gained from Ixia, but none of their efforts produced positive results. The strange knot in his mind was there; he could feel its presence and even touch it in a metaphysical sense, but never trigger it. Emma suggested the witch's magic may have merged with one of his other spells—the same way her magic combined with Power Graft—and that they'd discover which spell in due time.

It was a nice theory, but they had no immediate way to prove or disprove it, which left him wondering what he *had* gained from Ixia.

Brooke came over for dinner that night—

—and then joined him in bed for dessert.

She brought her gym bag full of "safety equipment" and asked him to bind her arms behind her back and blindfold her before he made love to her. Emma slipped into bed after they finished, and he dozed off with a succubus in one arm and a wolf girl in the other.

Shortly after noon on Wednesday, Clarke and Emma were eating lunch at the food court when they both received a text from Ashley.

It read: **Almost done. Should be finished by 6. Meet tonight at the usual spot?**

Clarke replied for both of them: **We'll be there.**

Ashley had prepared the circle on a flat section of concrete within the abandoned steel mill. The grimoire sat within an equilateral triangle tipped with three small circles and then encompassed by a thick outer ring filled with runic script. Three beeswax candles in glass jars flickered within the design, and the runes glowed faintly, energized by Ashley's preparations.

"It's ready," she said as they joined her beside the circle.

"And a good evening to you, too," Emma teased with a smile.

"Yes. Good evening," Ashley replied without feeling. "Shall we start?"

"What do you need us to do?" Clarke asked.

"We'll each take a corner." Ashley indicated the triangle. "Kneel in front of your candle and open yourself up to the circle. I'll act as the primary focus. You'll feel me tugging on your magic. Don't resist; just let it flow out of you naturally."

"So, basically, we just sit there and let you use our magic to power the circle?"

"Pretty much. Preparing the circle was the hard part. Actually cracking the spell shouldn't take more than a few minutes."

"Great!" Clarke said. "Then, let's get started."

291

They took their positions, and Clarke did his best to relax, not sure how this was supposed to feel. Perhaps it would be like his magic mingling with another's? Like that, but minus the sex?

Ashley closed her eyes and rested her hands on her knees.

"I'm starting. Here goes."

"Ready," Emma replied.

Both ladies unfurled their wings—one angelic, the other demonic—their supernatural limbs pushing out through slits in their clothing hidden by seamlines or folds. Ashley's hairband lifted off her head and tilted until it hovered over her, now a cracked, spinning halo that gradually grew brighter.

The markings in the circle glowed, and Clarke felt the magical equivalent of a magnet tug him downward. He resisted the pull out of reflex, but then relaxed and let the circle drink in his ethereal strength.

A red aura glowed around him, and energy crackled up and down his limbs.

The grimoire shuddered, and Ashley's brow crinkled in an unspoken question. Was she worried? Had something unusual just happened? The book hissed as if it were sitting on a skillet, and whiffs of green smoke traced upward.

Ashley seemed to settle down after that, and the veil of green energy continued to wisp upward from the book, growing thinner by the minute.

"Almost done," she said softly. "Just one more layer to—"

The book shuddered again, and then snapped open. A howling wind blasted up from the grimoire, spiraling into a miniature tornado that snuffed out the candles and pulled the runes right off the concrete. Glowing characters swirled above them, and dark lettering vomited up from the book, filling the vortex.

"Is this supposed to happen?" Clarke shouted over the roar of wind and magic.

"No!" Emma replied. "No, it's not!"

"Get back!" Ashley flapped her wings once and lifted into the air. "Both of you!"

Dark words poured out of the grimoire in a thick stream, filling out the towering shape until it sprouted two long arms, their fingers nothing more than dangling sentences. Runes gathered in two spots high up the torso, forming eyes that burned with green fire, and a green maw opened to reveal ragged word-teeth. Its body ended in a funnel of characters where proper legs would have been.

"Ink wraith!" Emma shouted.

Clarke snapped his blade out to the side and summoned his shield. "Can I kill it?"

"By all means!"

The wraith swiped at Emma with long fingers but

missed as she vaulted up into the air, spreading her wings to float near the ceiling.

"Oh, no you don't!" Clarke spent a portion of his strength. He gathered his magic and cast Blood Freeze on the monster.

Nothing happened.

He blinked, unsure what had gone wrong.

The ink wraith spread its arms and bellowed at him. Tiny words flew from its maw like spittle, and one smacked against Clarke's face. It read SPITE in all caps. He pinched it off his cheek and flicked it aside.

"No blood in you, huh? Just words?" He raised his sword. "Fine, then. We'll do this the hard way!"

The wraith clenched a fist. Words traveled along its arm, gathering at the end, growing and solidifying into a black sphere. It roared again, pulled back its arm, and then threw the punch.

Clarke swung his sword to meet it. Blade and fist collided in a flash of scarlet energy, illuminating words like SOLID and HEAVY and STONE. The blade shattered into twinkling splinters, and the wraith swung into Clarke's chest. His shield flashed, and he flew back, tumbling across the concrete.

"Careful!" Emma shouted. "It can adapt!"

"Thanks for the warning," Clarke groaned, rising to his feet.

"But it can't all change at one!" Ashley added, flapping her wings.

The wraith glared up at the two winged women, then began to float up toward them. The balled-up fist stretched, forming something new.

Clarke summoned a new sword and sprinted toward the wraith with fury in his eyes. He cut through the creature's slender tail, and words burned across the arc of his blade. New words slid into place to close the wound, and the creature ascended toward the angel and succubus, ignoring the threat on the ground.

Clarke cast Fly—which might as well have been called Float at his level of mastery—and kicked off the floor with leg muscles enhanced by werewolf magic. He shot up at the monster and plunged the thirstblade into its back. More words flashed away into crinkling embers, and the wraith screeched. This wound didn't close quite as fast, and words like PAIN and AGONY bled through the gash.

Its eyes closed and reopened on its back, burning bright with rage, and its mouth split open into a maw so chillingly stretched it would have looked unnatural on any other creature. Clarke kicked off the monster, barely escaping a quick snap of its ragged word-teeth. He floated over to a raised walkway, caught the railing, and steadied himself on the rusted perch.

The wraith snatched at him, and words like ROPE

and WHIP curled around his legs. Clarke only managed a quick "Oh shit!" before the creature yanked him off and threw him to the ground.

He crashed shoulder-first into a ruined, hulking machine, leaving a Clarke-shaped dent as his shield fizzled away. He pushed a crumpled panel aside and climbed back to his feet.

"You okay?" Emma called out.

"Never better," he grunted, shaking his head to banish the stars dancing across it.

The wraith bled letters from its new wound, and words dripped off its body, vanishing in brief flashes. He'd hurt it, but it was still in this fight.

The wraith floated higher and spread its arms. Words within its torso clumped together into a solid line and then spun in a circle, almost like propeller blades, faster and faster until they blurred. The wind slammed Ashley against the wall. Her wings dispersed into a shower of feathers, and she fell, but not before the wraith darted forward, clasping her head with long fingers and then catapulting her toward the ground.

She slammed into a silo with a sickening crunch.

"Ash!" Emma dove to help her friend.

The wraith descended toward the two women, its arms forming a pair of huge, worded scythes.

Clarke jumped off the machine and dashed in their

direction, but he instantly saw the wraith would reach them first. Emma had her back turned to the creature, arms reaching for her fallen friend.

He needed to do something, and fast.

His mind raced, flashing through all the spells he and Emma had discussed, not just the ones they'd practiced.

He needed to stop the disaster unfolding before his eyes.

He needed to *kill* that thing.

And he needed to do it now. From *here*.

A spell came to mind.

Unmastered, but possible.

The potential rested within him.

He only needed to seize it.

He focused his energy, consumed a part of himself, and cast Scarlet Slash. He snarled as he swung his sword, which blazed bright, leaving a glowing gash through empty air.

An identical line cut through the wraith, and it howled. Sentences burned across the gash, and the monster collapsed to the ground in a swirling, writhing mass of words and magic.

Clarke's head swam from the expenditure. He staggered as he sprinted forward, and almost lost his footing, but gritted his teeth and righted himself. He charged at the abomination with renewed fury, sword held low, and cut a vicious groove in one side of the creature and out the other.

The mass oozed outward, leaking, fading, dissolving until only a smear of chalk remained on the floor.

Clarke stumbled forward and dropped to one knee. He turned sharply to see Emma crowding the spot where Ashley had fallen, her black wings obscuring his view.

"Ashley!" He grabbed the side of a cart and hauled himself upright. "*Ashley!*"

"Yes?"

The calm nonchalance of the angel's response stunned him into silence. Emma backed away, her face filled with surprise, as Ashley stepped out of the crack in the silo. Her clothes were torn in several places, and her halo had darkened to a deep gray.

But she didn't seem to have a scratch on her.

"Are you all right?" Emma asked, looking her over.

Ashley patted herself down before examining the rips in her clothes.

"Yes, I believe so," she said at last.

"Are you even *hurt?*" Clarke asked, making his way over to them on wobbly legs.

"No, I appear to be fine."

"How'd *that* happen?"

"Well, I—" The angel looked up at the ceiling, then back at where she'd landed. "I'm not sure."

Clarke turned to Emma, but the succubus shrugged.

"Beats me, Clarke. I guess Ash is tougher than she looks!"

"So it would seem." The angel sounded curious about the matter herself.

"Well, I'm glad both of you ladies are all right. What the hell was that, anyway?"

"An ink wraith," Emma explained. "A surprisingly advanced creature for someone like Heinrich. The book must have been boobytrapped with a summoning spell layered underneath the Concealment."

"You mean, like how that hellhound showed up when we swiped the grimoire?"

"Yes." Ashley grabbed her halo and fitted it back in place as a hairband. "A well-hidden trap, too. All of us, Hepatica included, missed it."

Clarke wiped his brow. "I guess it's too late to ask for a refund."

"You okay there?" Emma placed a hand on his shoulder. "You look a bit woozy."

"I'll be fine. That last spell knocked the wind out of me, is all."

Ashley picked up the grimoire and flipped it open. "Surprise monster aside, we have what we came for. Some of the book is now readable."

"Only some?" Clarke asked.

"The summoning interrupted our circle." Ashley ran her fingers over the open page. "But the good news is the spell's been greatly weakened. I can break through the rest."

"Better be careful with that," Emma said, letting her wings and tail shrink into nothingness. "Heinrich may have left more than one surprise."

"Hmm. I suppose it wouldn't hurt to err on the side of caution." Ashley clapped the book shut and looked up. "Clarke, mind if I borrow you for the night?"

Chapter Sixteen

---◆---

Clarke wasn't sure what he expected the apartment of an angel to look like, but its plain, spartan nature caught him off guard. The interior didn't strike him as something a person actually lived in. It felt off, in the same way the showcase home for a real-estate development didn't quite line up with a genuine lived-in space.

The apartment was furnished and impeccably clean. Everything was perfectly spaced, angled orthogonally, and devoid of clutter.

He grimaced as he closed the door behind them.

"Make yourself at home," Ashley said, setting the grimoire down on her desk. "I appreciate you spending the night, but I expect this to be a boring exercise in caution."

"Thanks. Mind if I grab a bite from your fridge? I'm starving! I feel like I haven't eaten all day."

"Your body needs to recover from the magic you cast, and since the wraith didn't possess a conventional life-force, your thirstblade failed to replenish you."

"Right. Figured it was something like that."

He made his way to the kitchen and opened the refrigerator, then the freezer.

"Ashley?" he called out. "Your fridge has nothing but ice in it."

"Sorry. I'm not used to entertaining guests."

"It's all right. I can place a delivery order. How's pizza sound? Maybe Papa Johns?"

"I'm not hungry."

"You sure?"

"It's fine, Clarke. Order whatever you like."

"All right."

He pulled out his phone and put together an order for a large pepperoni pizza on the app. His stomach grumbled at him, so he added a large cheese pizza and sent the order.

"Pizza's on its way." He left the kitchen and rounded the corner. "I ordered plenty, including one with no meat, so you're welcome to—whoa!"

"Yes?" Ashley looked up from the grimoire, completely naked with wings folded along her back, cracked halo turning gently over her head. An orb of light hovered above her desk in lieu of a reading lamp, casting its warm glow over her pale, perfect skin and the firm swell of her breasts.

"Uh …"

"Is something wrong?" She tilted her head as if confused.

"Why'd you take your clothes off?"

"We're not in public anymore," she replied, as if that explained everything.

"Okay. And?"

"And what? I'm more comfortable this way." She returned her attention to the grimoire as if she'd explained herself adequately.

"Okay." He let out his breath and walked past her. "Never mind me. Just going to sit down on your couch and try my best to ignore the stirring in my pants."

"You're welcome to strip down as well."

"No, I think that would make it worse."

"Whatever you feel works best." She flipped to the next page.

Clarke dropped onto the couch and waited for his pizza to arrive, occasionally stealing glances at Ashley, which led him to conclude that—no—she was not trying to flirt with him. She was engrossed in the book, which meant her nakedness was not an invitation, no matter how much the bulge in his pants disagreed.

He found the wait to be an interesting exercise in

restraint. He'd grown accustomed to a predictable sequence of events when a beautiful, naked woman was nearby, and this did *not* fit.

"Ashley?" he asked after the pizza failed to arrive on time.

"Yes?"

"I've been wondering about something you said recently. About a night with you being potentially fatal."

"That's right, which is why I have refrained from making advances toward you."

"Right." He glanced at her naked backside. "Because that's exactly what you're doing."

"It's better this way."

"I'm curious more than anything else. Why is it dangerous?"

She looked up from the book and turned on the stool to face him.

"Honestly, Clarke? I don't know."

"Then how do you know it's dangerous?"

"I just do." Her gaze lowered, and her halo dimmed. "If I could explain it better, I would. But I can't."

"Because of the holes in your memory?"

"That's not quite how I'd put it. A hole would indicate something is missing or was removed. This is different. It's more like ... I've been disconnected from some other part of myself."

"Because of this?" He pointed at the space above his head.

"Perhaps." She smiled sadly at him. "I know the way I act makes you and the others uncomfortable at times. I wish I could put your worries at ease by telling you why I'm this way, but I don't even know myself."

"That's got to be tough."

"It is." She sighed. "There are so many things I don't understand. About you and the others, about the world, about the people all around me. I know I have difficulty relating to you and the others, that I sometimes come across as cold and clinical. Please believe that I don't do it on purpose. It's just I find people confusing, and I'm simply doing the best I can."

"Aren't we all? Making our way through life the best we can, I mean."

"There's truth in that, but are you confused about yourself? I am. That's the hardest part for me. I can deal with questions and uncertainty on the outside, but here?" She placed a hand on her chest. "Here, I should feel certainty, and I don't."

"You know enough. You know evil when you see it and have heart enough to do something about it."

"You're right. I do feel a strong sense of purpose, even if the details aren't clear. There is great injustice here, and I *must* fight it. Almost as if I'm compelled to. But I have no way *to* fight it."

"Which is where we come in," he said with a grin.

"Yes, and all our actions gladden me. They really do, yours especially. We've asked a lot of you in a short time, and you've really stepped up to the challenge. You've become an integral part of this team, whether you realize it or not."

"You really think so?"

"I do. Broken Fang wouldn't be the same without you, and I can't thank you enough."

The doorbell rang, and he rose from the couch. He cracked open the door and crowded the entrance to protect Ashley's privacy.

Not that she seemed to care.

He paid for the pizza and included a good tip despite the late delivery.

"You sure you don't want some?" he asked, setting the two pizzas down on the dinner table.

She opened her mouth to respond, but then paused and seemed to reconsider her response.

"I'll have a bite, thank you."

She joined him at the table and selected the thinnest slice of cheese pizza.

"Do you need to eat?" he asked.

"I ... don't think so?"

"Sorry. Are my questions making you uncomfortable?"

"No. I just wish I could answer them better. So many questions. Who am I, really, and why am I here? So many questions; so few answers."

"We have answers enough, I'd say." He raised a slice as if making a toast. "And we have pizza."

She gave him a genuine smile. "We do, indeed."

They ate in silence for a time, and Clarke worked his way through his entire pepperoni pizza, astonished by the size of his appetite. He started on the cheese pizza before Ashley finished her first slice.

Clarke studied the angel as he ate: her flawless skin, the golden silk of her hair, the perfect symmetry of her face.

If angels exist, he wondered, *then ...*

"Ashley, do devils exist?"

"I'm not sure. I know I came from another plane of existence; I have a clear memory of the Transplanar Hex disrupting my transit. Logically then, other planes can exist. But what they or their inhabitants are like, I couldn't say. Does one of them fit some definition of Hell? Do its denizens resemble mythical devils? Perhaps. Mythology's roots stem from reality, as you have so recently learned."

He laughed. "Yeah, no kidding!"

"It's a good question. Like so many others, I wish I had a better answer."

"That's all right. Just curious."

Clarke ate all but Ashley's one narrow slice and felt

like he could eat even more—but also felt that might have been pushing it. He cleaned up the pizza boxes as Ashley returned to her studies.

"You pulling an all-nighter?" he asked.

"Yes."

"Want me to stay up with you and keep watch?"

"No, it's all right. Rest and regain your strength. I'll wake you if I need anything."

"All right. Then I guess I'll grab a shower and crash on the couch."

"You're free to use the bed, if you like."

"Thanks. I'll do that."

The shower hadn't seen much use. The shampoo bottle was full, and the bar of soap was still in its box. Likewise, the bed was either perfectly made or hadn't seen a warm body in ages. He pulled the covers free and slipped beneath them.

He drifted into a deep sleep almost immediately.

His dreams were filled with winged women and their firm, buoyant breasts.

Clarke's phone woke him up. He groped around for it in the morning gloom, found it, and brought it to his ear.

"Hello?" he murmured.

"Morning, Sexy!"

"Hey, Emma. What's up?"

"Just calling to check in on you two. How'd it go last night?"

"Fine, I guess, but I haven't spoken to her this morning. Did you know she walks around her place naked?"

"Yep!"

"And you didn't think to tell me?"

"Why ruin the surprise? She try to seduce you?"

"No, we just talked about her feelings over pizza."

"Aww." She sounded disappointed.

"You heard her. Sex with her might kill me."

"I remember. But if anyone can survive a night with a celestial, it's *you*."

"Thanks for the vote of confidence, but I'm playing it safe."

"Don't rule it out. Power Graft with her could be out of this world, and who knows? She might benefit from the experience. All that banging might dislodge some of her memories."

Clarke blurted out a laugh.

"Oh, come on! You don't seriously believe that! You want me to try fucking away her amnesia? That'd never work! That's like something you'd find in a cheesy harem novel!"

"Don't knock it until you try it."

"Yeah, yeah. In your dreams, Emma."

"Actually, you laugh, but I *have* had dreams like that. When I first met her, her habit of roaming her apartment naked sent me *all* the wrong signals!"

"I can imagine."

Nubile angel disrobes next to horny succubus, he thought. *Yes, that'll paint a picture.*

"Carnal curiosity aside," Emma said, "I wanted to check up on you, see how you're feeling."

"Pretty good. I was starving and a little lightheaded yesterday, but I feel fine now."

"You going to make it to class today?"

"I should. Data Structures doesn't start until ten."

"All right. In that case, I'll see you then."

"See you, Emma."

She made a kissy sound over the phone and closed the call.

Clarke got dressed and found Ashley at her desk. As far as he could tell, she hadn't moved an inch the whole night.

"Good morning," he said, walking over.

"It is most *definitely* a good morning."

"Oh?"

"We now have the information we need. Here, look." She shifted the grimoire over and flipped to one of several bookmarks she'd added. "According to Heinrich's notes, there are only two other vampires on campus, and now we know who they are: Jayden Rost and Gretchen

310

Plainsborough, the head football coach and head librarian, respectively."

"Interesting. Etcoff was an archivist at the library, right? Makes sense for her master to be hiding within the same organization."

"Agreed. We don't have anything conclusive to back up Rost as a vampire, but Emma and I have been keeping our eyes on one of the assistant coaches as a potential thrall. That's circumstantial evidence, to be sure, but it lines up with Heinrich's notes."

"What else did he have on his rivals?"

"Various pieces of intelligence he'd gathered over the years. Force estimates, magical profiles, and the like. Rost and Plainsborough are older risen, thirty years at least and perhaps in the fifties for Plainsborough. That makes them substantially more dangerous than Heinrich, both in raw power and experience. They also have more thralls and familiars at their command than Heinrich did."

"What about their magic?"

"Plainsborough comes out on top there. She has a strong affinity for fire spells. Rost is also a competent mage, but his repertoire consists mostly of support buffs. Still dangerous, especially if we need to face his minions."

"He can make them stronger and tougher?"

"Pretty much."

"You think Rost had Etcoff eliminated?"

"That seems the most reasonable explanation."

"Then Plainsborough must already be looking for a way to stick the knife in."

"Of that, I'm less sure." Ashley flipped to a different bookmark. "Of the three vampires, Plainsborough is the most powerful. She's the oldest, wields the most powerful magic, and commands the most thralls. CCU's library might as well be her fortress. Yes, she lost a thrall, but I'm not sure that's enough to instigate a full-scale reprisal from her."

"She might be viewing Rost as a nuisance instead of a threat? A lesser vampire nipping at her heels?"

"Or she considers Etcoff an acceptable loss for some gain we're not aware of. Both Rost and Plainsborough are surely moving to claim Heinrich's old holdings. We know about the self-storage lair, but there are possibly others. Plainsborough may have seized one and lost Etcoff in the process."

"We really don't know how the fight is shaking out, then."

"Not without inserting ourselves into the situation more aggressively."

Clarke crossed his arms and leaned against the wall. "So, can we use this to our advantage?"

"Absolutely, but not on its own. We'll need to rile up either vampire, and preferably both. To do that, we'll need more detailed intelligence. Fortunately, we now have Heinrich's list of their thralls. Even if that list isn't complete, it *does* let us focus our efforts. I can accomplish some of our surveillance with careful use of Scrying, but I should also pull Sammy into this."

"A bit of slime girl reconnaissance?"

"Exactly. You haven't seen her use this ability yet, but she can masquerade as other people, given enough concentration and prep time."

"Same as she could back in your campaign?"

"The same. And now that we have a list of thralls …"

"You want to snoop on them?"

"More or less."

"Sounds dangerous."

"It is, and there's only so much support we can provide her."

"She okay sticking her neck out like that?"

"That question's best left for her, but I'm confident the answer will be yes."

"Why's that?"

"Sammy is …" Ashley let out a sad sigh and looked up. "She has her own reasons for hating the vampires."

The entire team met at the mill that Thursday night. Ashley laid out all the new information while Sammy and the others listened intently. Once that task was complete, they began to put together plans to recon the two remaining factions on campus.

"I'll do it," Sammy stated without hesitation.

"Are you sure?" Clarke asked. "Brooke and I will stage ourselves as close as we can, but if trouble breaks out, you're going to be on your own until we arrive."

"I appreciate your concern, but if this is going to work, then it's got to be me. I'll do it."

Clarke swept his gaze across the others and saw they were all in agreement.

"Then it's settled," Ashley said at last. "I'll spend the next few days probing the factions with Scry. The library seems to be the best place to start, since we suspect it'll be tougher to provoke Plainsborough. Once I've hit a dead end, we'll shift to Sammy with Clarke and Brooke nearby as backup."

Sammy flashed a thumbs-up.

"Great." Ashley rose from her bucket-chair. "I'll get started as soon as I'm home."

Clarke pushed off the ground and dusted his butt off. He was about to leave when Sammy said:

"Hey, hold up."

Everyone else stopped and faced the slime girl.

"Not you, Ash," Sammy said with an apologetic smile. "Just the others."

"Is something wrong?" Ashley asked.

"No." Sammy stuffed gloved hands into her pockets. "Everything's fine. I just need a word with the others."

Ashley's eyes darted across the group in search of an answer. Clarke gave her a shrug, and she replied with her own.

"If you say so."

The angel left without another word.

"What's up?" Clarke asked once it was the four of them. "You not happy with the plan?"

"No, nothing like that. The plan's great." Sammy shook a clenched fist. "We're closer than ever to kicking the vampires out of CCU. So close, I can taste it!"

"Then what's wrong?"

"No-o-o-othin'." She looked down and kicked a stray pebble. It bounced across the concrete and *plink*ed against the sheet metal wall.

"Sounds like *something*'s amiss."

Brooke's ears were perked with curiosity, while Emma was trying and failing to hide her grin.

"Well, you see, Clarke, things are getting serious here." Sammy kept her eyes down and swung her leg back and forth like a pendulum. "We're about to instigate a feud between two vampires that make Heinrich look like a chump. We either bring our A game to the table or we call it quits and take our winnings home. You know what I'm saying?"

"I ... think so?"

"Our team needs to be in top form. *Top* form. And we need to be doing everything we can to attain that … uh, topness of form. You hear me?"

"I hear you."

"Our ship needs to be at battle stations. All pilots to their fighters. Shields up and missile tubes loaded."

"Okay?"

"Any preparation we can make that's within our power *to* make—and is within reason and everyone's consent, mind you—we *should* make."

"Sammy, are you asking if you can have sex with me?"

"No!" she blurted, eyes sweeping up to meet his. "I'm mean, *ye-e-es*. But only if you're okay with it."

"So, you're only asking me if I'll have sex with you on the condition I'm willing to say yes?"

"Yes!" She paused, her eyes darting back and forth. "I mean, no! I'm asking you, but my asking is not preconditioned on the condition of your answer. Does that make sense?"

"Sort of."

"Uh, why is this so hard?!" Sammy glanced over at Emma. "I should have gone with your suggestion."

"Yes, you should have."

"Okay!" Sammy spread her arms. "I'm starting over and going with the succubus' plan. Clarke?"

"Yes, Sammy?"

"Do you like big boobs?"

"What sort of question is that?"

"A very important one. Do you like big boobs?"

"Well, yes, I suppose I am partial to more generous curves."

"How about build? What's your preference? Slender or curvy?"

"I'd say both have their charms."

"You need to pick one. It's *important*."

"Curvy, then."

"Okay, how about hair? Got a favorite color?"

"Sammy, what's this about?"

"Pick. A. Color."

"Fine," he sighed. "I suppose I've always had a thing for redheads."

"Ooh!" Emma nudged Brooke. "We could try dying our hair!"

"That might work for you, but have you ever seen a werewolf with dyed hair?"

"No."

"There's a reason for that."

"How about style?" Sammy continued. "Long or short? Ponytails, pigtails, Princess Leia buns? The sky's the limit."

Clarke placed a hand on his hip and grimaced at her.

"On second thought, never mind," Sammy said quickly. "I'll pick out the rest for you."

"Would you please tell me what this is about?"

"Sure, sure, I'm getting to that." She stood a little straighter and squared her shoulders. "Here's my proposal. I'm going to prepare myself for a chill evening with you based on your specifications. Food and entertainment will be provided, and we will cap off the evening with Power Graft."

Clarke glanced over at the succubus, who was nearly bouncing on her heels with excitement.

"This was my idea," she told him, like a proud mother showing off her weird-ass baby.

"I can tell."

"Are you, um …" Sammy cleared her throat. "What do you think, Clarke? You okay with this?"

He turned to Brooke, who wagged her tail happily.

"You're my alpha, and Sammy is absolutely one of us. I'm only surprised it took her this long to ask."

Clarke nodded. He'd expected both Emma and Brooke to be fine with this, but it didn't hurt to check. Dating demihumans didn't follow the normal rules, but being respectful to his girlfriend—or girl*friends*, as the case happened to be—was important to him.

"Well?" Sammy shrugged with hopeful shoulders. "What do you say?"

"I say yes." He smiled at her warmly. "I would love to hang out with you."

CHAPTER SEVENTEEN

CLARKE HEADED OVER TO SAMMY'S PLACE that Saturday, arriving a little before six. Ashley was still probing the library with Scrying spells, so he and Sammy could afford to take the evening off from Broken Fang duties.

He'd expected an apartment—an upscale one, given what Sammy drove to school—but when he arrived, he had to check the address.

And then he checked it again.

He hadn't expected a house.

And he most certainly hadn't expected a sprawling two-story mansion with a massive, gated yard and its own turnabout. The address checked out and the gate stood open, so he drove in and parked his car next to what he assumed was Sammy's Z4 roadster.

He exited his humble vehicle and walked up to the

front door, feeling underdressed. Only a few windows across the bottom floor showed light, though, and he wondered how many people lived with Sammy. The mansion featured an expansive garage along its left wing, but the roadster and her Kawasaki bike were the only other vehicles in sight.

He tapped the doorbell.

Sammy greeted him at the front door, though it took him a moment to realize it was her. She was taller now, with a fuller figure and a long braid of red hair that reached down to her hips. Her face had remained the same, and she wore a cozy turtleneck, skirt, and stockings. All three bore overlapping splotches of color as if she'd been splattered with paint in an act of exuberant drive-by artistry. She also wore a pair of leather gloves, leaving her covered from the chin down.

"Hey there!"

"Evening, Sammy. You look great."

"Thanks!" She ran a hand down her generous curves. "I spent a lot of time getting it right." She gave her hips a firm pat. "Glad you appreciate it!"

"I do. You really do look fantastic. May I come in?"

"Sure, sure!" She eased the door aside, and he stepped into the foyer.

This place is so big it needs a foyer, he thought as he looked around. Twin curving staircases led up to a second-floor balcony.

"What a place."

"So, um, as you can see, the family's rich." She gave him an apologetic shrug. "We got our money in real estate, which is why the parents decided to loan me this place while I'm going to school."

"Who else lives here?"

"Just me."

His eyebrows shot up. "You live here all alone?"

"Mostly. Housekeeping and maintenance stop by once a week, but other than that, I'm on my own."

"Don't you ever get lonely?"

"No more than if I lived in an apartment."

"But this place is massive! Even in an apartment, you can sometimes hear your neighbors."

"Well, here I can crank my music as loud as I want. Besides, I barely use a fifth of the place. Most of it just sits there, empty."

"A *fifth*." He shook his head in disbelief.

"Would you like a tour? We've got some time before dinner arrives."

"Sure!"

Sammy stuck to the first floor as she led him through one of the building's wings. The first room she showed off was her digital art studio, equipped with a central computer station and both 2D and 3D printers. The walls were covered with fantastical landscapes, portraits, and creatures along with printed sculptures cluttering the shelves.

"You're studying to be an artist?" he asked.

"Yep, that's me. I've always had this itch in me, this desire to create. Plus, it's not something my parents can just hand to me. I have to *earn* my way to becoming a great artist."

"Sounds like you've given it some thought."

"It's because I have. I'm an only child, and my parents sometimes confuse raising me with throwing money my way. They love me, don't get me wrong, and I love them back. But sometimes they don't get that I want to earn my way in the world."

"Makes sense to …"

A series of digital paintings caught Clarke's eye. They featured demihuman males in various states of undress, sometimes in the same picture, sometimes kissing.

"Whoops!" Sammy bolted past him and yanked down the most explicit picture. She crumpled it up and tossed it into a waste can. "Forgot to take those down."

"You dabble in a bit of yaoi art?"

"Sometimes." Her skin reddened and the shade of her hair deepened to a rich cherry. "When the mood strikes me."

"You didn't have to throw it away, you know."

"It's fine. I can always print out a new one."

She showed him the bedroom next.

"For when the mood strikes *us*," she said with an exaggerated waggle of her eyebrows. "Also, pregnancy won't be a concern tonight."

"Slimes and humans aren't compatible?"

"No, you're perfectly capable of knocking me up, but I'll keep that from happening. I have a womb of sorts, but I also have precise control over what fluids reach which parts of me." She shrugged. "Can't have a baby if the sperm never meets the egg."

"Got it. Good to know."

He returned his attention to the room.

The shelves were stocked to overflowing with plushies: Pokémon, Digimon, Monster Hunter, generic fantasy monsters, and many others. There were even a few body pillows in the mix, all featuring video game characters, some not entirely in their costumes. Clarke spotted one with Ignis from *Final Fantasy XV* wearing an apron and nothing else. The caption read: **I've come up with a new recipe … for love!**

He was almost certain the other side of the pillow would feature Ignis' naked butt.

Sammy chuckled nervously. "Pretend you didn't see that."

"See what?"

"Yes! Just like that."

She showed off her anime and manga collection next, which filled an entire walk-in closet larger than his old apartment.

"Behold!" She spread her arms theatrically.

"Tonight's entertainment!"

"Oh, wow." Clarke looked around. "Where do I even start?"

"You like anime?"

"Sure, who doesn't?"

"Good answer!" She circled the room, fingers drumming across the spines. "Everything is in alphabetical order except for those." She pointed to shelves painted red and plastered with adult content warnings. "I keep the hentai separate, lest it contaminate the more innocent shows."

Clarke nodded thoughtfully. He'd never seen that much porn in one place before.

A few disc cases were open on the central table. He picked up one and read the title.

"*That Time I Got Reincarnated as a Slime*. Can't say that I've seen this one."

"I didn't care for it. *Very* inaccurate! Didn't help me at all."

"Help with what?"

"Don't worry about it." She made a shooing gesture. "It's not important. Come on, let's pick out our movie."

"Sure, um." He looked around, not sure where to begin. "Maybe a little help here?"

"What are you in the mood for? Sci-fi? Fantasy? Action? Romcom? Something serious? Something funny? I've got movies for all tastes."

"How about ... what's your favorite movie of all time?"

"That's easy. *Dirty Pair: Project Eden*. It's my go-to movie when I want something light, fun, and action-packed. It never fails to put a smile on my face."

"I've never seen it. Let's go with that, then."

"Perfect!" She knew where the case was without looking and pulled it out. "I'll get the theater set up."

The mansion's architect had a different definition for "home theater" than most people. The screen was an interlocked array of HDTVs that took up the entire wall, and the seating could be changed out depending on the number of guests and whether they were eating and watching at the same time. It was currently set up with a single large, half-circle booth and table.

Dinner arrived, delivered by a skinny elf girl in a Doordash uniform who needed multiple trips to drop off all the food. Clarke helped Sammy haul the half-dozen bags over to the theater. They unpacked the meal, laying out multiple trays of nigiri and rolled sushi, a plate of gyoza dumplings and takoyaki balls, edamame, seaweed salads, a big bowl of shoyu ramen, another heaping portion of pork cutlets over rice, plus one small bowl of miso soup, almost as an afterthought.

Clarke eyed the impressive spread like a climber gazing up at the slopes of a looming Mount Everest. He was hungry, but not *this* hungry!

"Don't worry," Sammy said, collecting the plastic bags. "I didn't forget dessert. There's plenty in the fridge."

"Plenty, you say."

"And I know what you're thinking. How's a big eater like me maintain a figure like this?"

"Well, I'd be lying if I said the thought never crossed my mind."

"It all comes down to calories. A slime girl's got to keep up her strength, and morphing burns a *lot* of energy. Even more than Brooke needs when she wolfs out."

"Hadn't thought of that. Does holding a form take a lot of effort?"

"Not really. You can think of it like holding a pose. It's the actual morphing that wears me out the most. On a training day, I can go through ten thousand calories, easy!"

"What sort of training?"

"Vampire killing, of course." She flashed a fiendish grin. "Brooke and I spar to hone our fighting edge or try out new techniques."

"I didn't realize that."

"You're welcome to join us any time."

"I may take you up on that." He smiled. "In fact, I think I *will*. Won't hurt for us to become more familiar with each other's fighting styles and capabilities."

"Hell, yeah!" Sammy pumped the air. "Watch out, you bloodsuckers! Here we come!"

Her enthusiasm coaxed a laugh out of him.

She started the movie, and they settled in for dinner. Clarke began with the miso soup while Sammy horked down the entire bowl of ramen in one long, continuous gulp.

"Ah!" she sighed, slapped the empty bowl down. "That hit the spot!"

"Wow. You'd wipe the floor at any eating contest on the planet!"

"You'd think, but most competitions bar slimes and other demihumans with big appetites." She stared into the empty bowl as if deep in thought, then cringed. "Whoops! Sorry! Did you want ramen, too? I can order more."

He chuckled. "Don't worry; you're fine. I'm going to have some sushi after I finish my soup."

"Okay. Whew!" She mimed wiping sweat off her brow. "I'm not used to having guests. Don't want you to think I'm being rude or something."

"It's all right, Sammy. Really."

She replied with a smile, then dragged the pork cutlet bowl over. "I know you might not think it, but I'm actually savoring this meal."

"Uh ..." His eyes darted over to the empty ramen bowl. "You are?"

"Sure am! On super-active days, I just shove the food in and let it dissolve. Don't even bother to chew or swallow. Here, I'll show you."

She grabbed a dumpling with her chopsticks, stretched her turtleneck down low enough to show off her enhanced cleavage, then pushed the dumpling through her sternum.

Or where a regular human's sternum would be; he wasn't sure how Sammy's skeleton worked, or if she even had one.

The dumpling sank beneath her skin, and she let go of her collar.

"Like that. I just take my shirt off and start shoving food in. That method *is* faster, but I prefer to taste my food." She picked up the cutlet bowl, but then she paused and set it back down. "Clarke, am I weirding you out?"

"Why would you think that?"

"Because I'm, well … I'm less human than your average demihuman."

"You're wondering if that bothers me?"

"Yeah, guess so." She tilted her head. "Does it?"

"Not in the slightest," he replied honestly. "First of all, my 'weirding out' tolerance has been increased *substantially* by recent events. And second, everyone has their quirks, me included. Yours are just more unique than most, and there's nothing wrong with that."

"Okay, good! Whew!"

"Do I really make you this nervous?"

"It's not you, Clarke, it's …"

"Yes?"

Sammy frowned and sat in silence for long seconds, then she grabbed the remote and muted the movie.

"Clarke, can I be honest with you?"

"Always."

"I'm scared." She stole a quick glance his way. "About tonight."

"Why would you be scared?"

"Because of what I am."

"You mean because you're a slime?"

She nodded slowly. He waited, quiet and attentive, for her to build up enough courage to continue.

"What do you know about my family?"

"Just what you've told me. That they're rich and you're an only child."

"There's more to it than that. I'm also the only demi-human in my family."

"Were you adopted?"

"No, my mom pushed me out the old-fashioned way."

"Then how could your parents not be slimes?"

"I'm not sure. It has something to do with recessive traits—both genetic and magical. The right factors came together, and here I am." She shrugged. "Emma could probably give you a better answer, but the important part is my parents both see only what the hexes allow them to see."

"They don't know you're a slime."

"Yeah. Which is bad enough by itself, but it gets worse. I started … changing during puberty. Can you imagine that? My body was changing in all sorts of ways, and no one could provide the answers I needed. Not my teachers, not the dozens of doctors who examined me, and certainly not my parents.

"I broke my bones all the time back then. Everyone assumed I'd developed some type of degenerative bone disease, but the doctors only made things worse. They would see things that didn't make sense—like my blood turning into a pink sludge—and they would forget! I would show them some new symptom, and they would nod and take dutiful notes, but then forget all about it an hour later!

"I didn't know what to do, couldn't make sense of what was happening. I thought I was going insane! Was I imagining these things? Was I sick in both my body and my head? I felt trapped, and there was no one I could turn to for help.

"I eventually figured it out on my own. One day, I had a nasty tumble down the stairs. The worst I'd ever had. Broke pretty much everything there was to break. But it didn't *hurt*, and that was the strangest part. My mind latched on to that fact, even as they rushed me to the hospital.

"I started to experiment, to test the limits of my body. One day, I turned my hand, over and over and over until my wrist looked like a spiral of pink Play-Doh. And then I managed to return it to normal without untwisting it. I learned a lot while I sat 'recovering' in that bed, but most importantly of all, I figured out why medical science had failed so spectacularly with me.

"It's because I wasn't sick in the first place. That's when it hit me."

"What did?"

"The realization that I was a monster."

She laughed, but it was a sad, joyless sound.

"You're not a monster." Clarke tried to put his arm around her shoulders, but she held up a hand, and he stopped.

"I know you mean well, but there's more, and you should hear it before you touch me."

"All right." He settled back on his side of the booth. "Go on, then."

"My parents visited me at the hospital often, but it was my dad who I saw me most. He was scheduled to spend a month in France for business meetings, but he canceled the whole thing. Can you believe it? Just like that! I saw him every day. He'd hold my hand during the day and give me a kiss before he headed home. Some nights, he'd stay in my room, a blanket draped over his legs, just trying to comfort me with his presence."

Sammy took a deep breath to gather herself.

"I didn't realize until later that I was slowly killing him, that my very presence is a poison." She laughed again, cold and jaded. "You know the phrase, 'you make me sick'? Well, I'm its poster child. I couldn't control the toxins back then, didn't even know they existed, and my father grew deathly ill because of them. Until one day he collapsed in my room."

"Did he …?"

"He began to recover once we were separated. The doctors thought they were protecting me from whatever *he* had. Except the opposite was true."

She turned to him, eyes moist, trails of pink fluid running down her cheeks.

"I almost killed my own father. Out of *ignorance*! Because no one knew what was happening to me. Because vampires have brainwashed the whole fucking planet! They hurt me, hurt my family, and I will *never* forgive them for it!"

Clarke fought the urge to reach out and comfort her. He wanted to hold her, to let her feel his presence, the warmth of his embrace, but he also remembered how a single kiss to his forehead had nearly driven him to vomit up breakfast.

"You want to know the worst part?" She wiped away her pink tears. "What happened to me is happening to other boys and girls right now. Kids who are either hurting or being hurt because the vampires need to keep everyone in the dark. I don't want people to have to go through that. To suffer like I did. I can't stand the thought of it, which is why I'm in this fight. 'Til the bitter end."

"Hey, now."

She tried to back away, but he slid forward and draped an arm around her shoulders, careful not to touch her skin.

"I'm here for you," he said softly, his lips near her ear.

She looked into his eyes, tears of slime trickling down her cheeks, and she sniffled.

"Clarke, do you … do you think you could put up with someone like me? A monster who brings only pain to those dearest to her? Could you learn to accept a creature like this? Accept me, as terrible and as flawed and as hideous as I am?"

"I don't need to learn." He leaned forward. "I already do."

He kissed her.

She wept as she kissed him back.

She wept, but they were tears of joy.

Clarke carried her to the bedroom, then laid her down on the sheets.

"How do you feel?" she asked, arms spread to either side, her long braid coiled above her.

He thought about sugarcoating his words, reassuring her the kiss had failed to affect him. But she'd know he was lying, and his dishonesty would sting more than the facts. He didn't want that for her. He trusted her and wanted her to trust him, and so he told her the plain truth.

"My mouth is a little numb. Like I just came from the dentist. Otherwise, I'm fine."

"Sorry."

"Don't be."

"I swear I'm trying to keep my toxins in check."

"It's all right. I'll manage." He put on a brave smile. "I have some of Brooke's vitality now."

"You shouldn't have to worry about this at all."

"Hey, now." He took hold of her gloved hand and gave it a squeeze. "Don't beat yourself up. I'll be fine."

"Thank you, Clarke. Just … only touch me when you have to. I don't want to hurt you."

"I understand."

"And … be gentle." She rested her head to the side, skin flush. "It's my first time."

"I will be. I promise."

He took hold of her large breasts and kneaded them through her turtleneck. They felt perfectly natural, as if he'd grabbed two handfuls of Emma's bountiful chest. She let out a content sigh, then reached over to stroke him through his slacks. His cock stiffened at her gentle caress.

He crawled onto the bed, kneeling between her spread legs as he continued to massage her breasts. Her hands explored him, gloved fingers riding up his sleeves to his shoulders, then across his broad chest. She moaned as he worked her over, and her legs twitched. She wrapped them around him, pulling his pelvis against her skirt.

She began to grind against him, the heat of her sex teasing him through layers of cloth. He gripped her nipples through the turtleneck and pinched.

"Yeah," she breathed contentedly. "That feels good."

There was nothing monstrous about the woman beneath him. Nothing that made him second guess his actions—or hers. She was radiant in her uniqueness, and he welcomed their coming union.

She undid his buckle, pulled the belt out of the loops, and tossed it aside. Her gloved fingers found the zipper and pulled it down, relieving some of the strain on his dick.

He placed his hands on her knees and spread her legs, then stroked down her inner thighs. His fingers touched the supple skin above her stockings and sent a quiver through her body. A numbing tingle spread across his fingertips. He rested two fingers atop her panties and stroked up and down them, pressing into her sex.

She reached into his pants and pulled him free. His cock stood at attention.

"I'm ready," she uttered softly.

"You sure? Is it wet enough?"

She giggled, her skin rosy, all her worries forgotten in the moment.

"Who do you think you're talking to?" She smiled up at him. "Lubrication won't be a problem."

"Oh, I see!" He grinned back at her and peeled aside her panties.

He placed the tip against her sweltering lower mouth—

—and pushed in, gliding deep into her in one slow, steady stroke. His skin tingled wherever they touched.

"How is it?" she asked.

"Perfect."

"How's the tightness? Should I—"

"You don't need to change yourself to make me happy. You're wonderful just the way you are." He bent forward, taking her head in his hand, accepting the faint numbness spreading across his palm.

And then he kissed her. Long, full, and deep as he began to rock in and out of her.

She moaned into his mouth, her tongue dueling with his. She grabbed fistfuls of his shirt and tugged him closer, urged him deeper. She broke their kiss, and her eyes locked with his, legs crossed behind his back, breasts shuddering with each stroke.

"I want this," she gasped, twisting fistfuls of his shirt. "I want you. All of you. Give it to me. Harder! Faster!"

He obliged, slamming into her with each full and complete thrust, wracking her body with pleasure as he bottomed out inside her. His own excitement built, a furious burning in his loins that yearned for release, for an outlet.

His head swam, growing foggy from the prolonged contact, but he kept thrusting into her, his pace unrelenting, his strength unwavering.

"More," she cried. "More!"

Her body squeezed around his shaft, and that drove him over the edge. He slammed deep into her one last time, and his body exploded with pleasure, flooding his mind as he flooded her womb.

An ethereal sense heightened, and he became aware of the shape of her magic, the mercurial eddies that composed her body. They shifted before his mind's eye with dizzying speed, nesting within each other like an insane ball of yarn—but instead of string, *sensations* formed the building blocks of her aura.

Soft and hard. Pale and dark. Hot and cold.

Hers was a magic of contradictions. So many contrasts swirled within her, all except for one lonely concept floating about without its sibling. Touching that one was like dipping his hand into a pool of liquid death, and yet it, too, seemed to yearn for its missing half. To thirst for life and vitality.

Their magics merged, their combined essence mingling for a brief, wondrous moment before they pulled away.

Clarke slid out of her and sat back on his legs. Sammy lay on her back, legs spread, arms wide, chest heaving in the aftermath of delicious release.

"That," she uttered between breaths, "was awesome …"

Clarke studied his hand, flexed his fingers. The numbness in his fingertips was melting away, like candle wax before a flame.

"Was it good for you, too?" she asked cautiously.

"How's this for an answer?"

He crawled over her on his hands and knees, then bent down and kissed her.

This time his lips didn't tingle.

CHAPTER EIGHTEEN

◆

CLARKE LAY ON THE BED, his arm around Sammy, her head on his chest, one leg draped over his. Her fingers explored his chest muscles in the serenity of their postcoital bliss, both of them completely naked.

"How do you feel?" she asked.

"Like I just made love to a beautiful woman."

"You know what I mean."

"I do, and I'm being truthful. I can … I guess you can say I'm aware of the toxins. But they don't bother me anymore."

Sammy closed her eyes and rubbed a cheek against his defined pectoral.

"You must have absorbed some of my resistances."

"Seems so."

"Lucky me."

"Why do you say that?"

"The dating pool for us slimes is ... shallow. Who wants to fuck a poisonous puddle?"

"Don't put it like that." He ran his hand down the generous curve of her hips. "You're all woman from where I sit."

"You say that now, but you haven't seen me when I'm asleep."

"And why should that bother me?"

She didn't answer, so he approached the topic from a different angle.

"How rare is your species?"

"Very. I'm the only slime around these parts."

"Must be lonely."

"Yeah. Emma and the others help, though." She hugged his chest. "You, too. A *lot*."

"It is a pleasure to be of service."

She laughed and kissed his chest. "You have no idea how good this feels."

"Sex *is* pretty awesome."

"Well, yeah. That, too. But I was referring to the simple pleasure of holding someone in my arms, and of being held. No clothes to get in the way. No phobias about accidentally touching them. Just the feel of another person beside me, free from all my hangups."

She snuggled up to him tighter, her legs entwining with his, arms squeezing his chest tenderly.

"You don't mind, do you?" she asked.

"Not at all. I enjoy a good post-sex cuddle. Makes me feel more connected to my lover."

"Mmm," she murmured into his chest. "Love-*ers*, in your case."

"Does that bother you?"

"I've been asking myself that question, trying to discover my own feelings. I like Emma a lot. Brooke, too, even if I tease her more than I should. But that's friendship, and now we're talking about something else. This is the first time I've thought about those two in the context of a larger relationship, all centered around one guy."

"And? Any conclusions?"

"Yes, though I don't know if what I feel is typical for my kind. It's not like I know all that much about my species, and the few slimes I've met over the years weren't eager to help me."

"There could be more of them than you realize," he said. "Could be some are just really good at blending in and don't want to draw attention to themselves."

"Maybe. Either way, I can't ask them *right now*, so it's up to me to figure out my own head, my own feelings." She sat up beside him on the bed and gazed into his eyes. "I want to be with you, Clarke. As long as I have that, I'll be happy."

"Come here then."

He pulled her down and kissed her, stroking her back.

She nestled her chin into the crook of his neck. "And, on a practical level, where else am I going to find a guy who's immune to me?"

"Lucky me," he said, echoing her earlier words.

"You still in the mood?" She straddled his legs. "I'm game for one more if you are."

He chuckled. "You're incorrigible!"

"Hey, I need to make up for lost time." She stroked him, and his erection firmed. "Well? How about it? One more go?"

"Absolutely, though I do have a request."

"Anything."

"Can you change your look a bit?"

"Of course!" She spread her arms. "I will happily customize my look however you want. Just think of me as a character design screen."

"In that case, I want to see the natural you."

Stunned silence fell over the bedroom, and she lowered her arms.

"No holding a particular shape or style," he continued. "No customization for my benefit. Just relax and be yourself. I want to spend the rest of the night with *that* Sammy."

"But my default shape is so plain." She grabbed her breasts. "And you said you like big boobs."

"If I'm making you uncomfortable, you can stick with this."

"It's not that, it's just …" She lowered her gaze. "I rarely show anyone that side of me."

"I want to see it." He raised her chin. "If you're willing."

She didn't say anything for long seconds, but then nodded.

"All right. I'll show you."

She closed her eyes and let out an unnaturally long exhale, slimming down to the body shape she used on campus. Her skin developed a glossy sheen as it turned pink, became uniform in color and texture. Her hair shortened into a damp, fiery pixie cut, and her skin became faintly translucent.

She opened her eyes, and they were glowing swirls of red and orange.

"This is the real me." She glanced to the side, as if afraid of his reaction. "This is the monster underneath the mask. Do you … still want to do this? I can switch back if you like."

Clarke ran both hands along the tops of her thighs, then settled his grip around her waist. She felt slippery, as if her entire body were oiled, but the boundary of her skin held firm against his touch. He took hold of her wrists and pulled her down to him gently.

"You're so beautiful," he said, and kissed her once more.

Clarke awoke the next morning to the most curious of sensations.

He was floating on his back, but not in water. The substance was warm and cloying, supporting the back of his head, enveloping every inch of his body up to the neck.

He stirred and tried to rub the sleep from his eyes. The syrupy fluid gave to his arm, clinging greedily to it, but then it resisted and pulled his arm back down.

He frowned and tried again.

Again, his arm was pulled back into the fluidic embrace.

He blinked his eyes open and stared at the ceiling. The light of morning filtered through the blinds.

He blinked again and raised his head.

A pink cocoon encased his body.

"Uh, Sammy?"

"Hmm?" The sound vibrated across his skin.

"I think I'm inside you."

"That's because you are. You're just so cozy! Way better than Ignis."

"Who?" Clarke asked, still groggy.

"This fella." A pseudopod reached over the side of the bed and retrieved one of her body pillows. "Sorry,

Ignis. You've been replaced!" She tossed the pillow toward her plushy collection.

"Ah. That Ignis."

"Good morning, by the way!" she said brightly.

"Mornin'."

He tried to wiggle free, but she held him tight. He was sure he could have broken free at any moment, though; Sammy was strong, but he was stronger now. Still, he figured a softer touch would work best.

"Sammy, my face itches, and I need to scratch it."

"Sorry!"

Splo-o-o-ork!

The slime girl congealed on top of him, back in her humanoid form. Fiery hair framed her face, and she gazed down at him with bright swirling eyes.

"Guess I got a little carried away there."

"It's okay." He rubbed the sleep out of his eyes. "Just so long as you don't smother me by accident or something."

"Hey now!" She gave his chest a playful pat. "I have more control over my body than that!"

"I'm sure you do. Just saying that safety is important when it comes to demihuman relationships. Trust me. I speak from experience here."

"Did one of the other girls hurt you?"

"No, but Brooke could have if we hadn't taken precautions."

"Oh, right. She told me about that."

"She did?"

"We girls compared notes." Sammy raised her arms over her head and crossed her wrists. "Sorry, but bondage play won't be as fun with me. Too easy for me to slip out."

Clarke laughed. "I'm sure you and I can think of something else to try."

"Who says I haven't already?"

"Oh? What's on your mind?"

"Not. Telling." She tapped his forehead with a finger. "It's going to be a surprise."

"Looking forward to it."

His stomach growled, and they both glanced down at his midsection.

"Right back at you," Sammy said. "We skipped most of dinner, so I'm *famished*. What do you want for breakfast?"

"Besides you?"

The slime girl blushed with her entire body.

"What are my options?" he asked.

"Whatever you like." She stretched an arm to grab her phone off the nightstand. "I'll have it delivered."

"Something hearty. Maybe Cracker Barrel?"

"Sounds good to me. How would you like your eggs?"

"Let's go with sunny side up."

"Will do!"

She started to enter the order but didn't get off him. Clarke cleared his throat. She didn't seem to notice.

"Um, Sammy?"

"Yes?"

"Would you mind letting me out? I'd like to take a shower before breakfast."

"Sorry!" She dismounted him. "My head is in the clouds this morning."

"Don't worry about it. Which way to the bathroom?"

"The closest one is through the door to your left."

"To the left. Thanks." He gathered up his clothes and headed through the door.

The bathroom included both a walk-in shower and a bathtub. The latter saw more use judging by the bottles along its lip and the pile of bookmarked manga nearby. Clarke wondered if Sammy found the tub more relaxing, given her semiliquid nature.

He showered, dressed, and rejoined Sammy in her room. She'd thrown on a fresh set of clothes, and her appearance was outwardly human.

"Breakfast is on its way."

"Great."

They waited for the delivery in a room by the foyer.

"Clarke?"

"Hmm?"

"You want to make it official?"

"You mean us?"

"Yeah. Got room in your harem for one more?"

"My 'harem'?" He couldn't help but laugh.

"What else are we going to call it?"

"I don't know." He shook his head, still chuckling at the absurdity of it all.

"Come on. No dodging the question."

"If it's you, then yes. Absolutely."

She smiled at him, then reached out and took hold of his hand. He slid his fingers between hers.

Breakfast arrived, and it was as colossal as Clarke had expected: plate after plate after plate of eggs, pancakes, bacon, sausage, French toast, hash browns, biscuits, and muffins, along with a jug of orange juice.

"You're going to spoil me for choice if I keep eating with you."

"I have no problem with this," she said, and gobbled a biscuit whole.

Clarke's phone rang toward the end of their meal.

"It's Emma." He answered the call. "Hey, Emma. I have you on speaker with Sammy."

"Morning!" Sammy added.

"Hey, you two! Everything go all right?"

"Oh, my God, yes!" Sammy exclaimed, leaning into the phone. "He was so good!"

"And Power Graft worked," Clarke added.

"Yes, yes." Sammy waved vaguely with one hand. "And that."

"Fantastic!" Emma said. "You'll have to spill all the sultry details later, because we've got news of our own. Ashley had a breakthrough last night, and we're all meeting at my place to discuss. Can you be here in half an hour?"

"We'll head right over."

"Great! See you then."

Emma ended the call.

Sammy stood up and stuffed a muffin into her mouth.

"Han I Ee Oor Eeeth?"

"I didn't catch any of that."

Sammy swallowed. "Can I see your keys?"

"Why?"

"It'll make sense in a moment." She held out her hand. "Please?"

"Sure, I guess."

He rummaged in his pocket and handed his keyring over. She added two items to the ring and offered it back. He took it back with a curious expression and examined the two additions.

One was an RFID card with ELOISE ESTATES printed on one side. The other was a BMW key fob.

"This is …"

"For the house and the roadster. They're both yours

349

whenever you want them."

"You sure about this?"

Sammy laughed. "Clarke, you're my boyfriend now! You've seen this place. Did you really think dating me wouldn't come with some perks?"

"Didn't really consider that until now. Thank you, by the way."

"You are very welcome. Now, come on." She pointed a thumb over her shoulder. "You can give me a lift in your new wheels."

Clarke joined the others around the coffee table, picking a spot on the couch next to Emma. Heinrich's grimoire sat on the table.

"What have you got for us, Ashley?" he asked.

"A lucky break. I was Scrying the library when I saw one of the thralls moving stationery into the basement."

Clarke waited for her to continue, and when she didn't, he leaned back on the sofa.

"A thrall?"

"Yes."

"Moving stationery?"

"Yes."

"Into the *library*?"

"Yes!"

"I must be missing something here, because I don't get it."

"Wait a second," Brooke cut in. "Are we talking about *stationery* stationery or regular stationery?"

"The former," Ashley said.

"Ooooh!" Brooke grinned wolfishly. "Is this going where I think it is?"

"Probably!" Emma echoed the werewolf's grin.

"Hold up." Clarke raised both hands. "The team's blood knight is confused. What's so special about this stationery?"

"It's what most vampires use to communicate with each other," Emma explained. "They rarely correspond with each other electronically."

"Because they don't want the Big Tech vampires snooping on them?"

"Exactly. Same as their motivation for keeping physical grimoires. Instead, they use handwritten missives. But they don't use just any old paper; vampires produce special stationery as an added security measure. Some of them produce their own, but most outsource the production, and Plainsborough just received a shipment."

"Then, if we get our hands on this stationery, we can fake a message from one vampire to another?"

"Precisely!"

"What's so special about the stationery? Is it like

paper soaked in the blood of virgins, or something?"

Emma grimaced. "You're not as far off as you think."

"The important part is we can send *any* message," Ashley said. "Including letters of challenge. What I propose is we steal at least two pages and use those to send the 'right' messages to both Rost and Plainsborough."

"And, on top of that," Emma added, "we're going to write the letters in *rat's blood!*"

"Oh ho!" Brooke's ears perked up. "That'll rile them up!"

"Rat's blood?" Clarke asked.

"The cheap stuff," Emma explained. "Signifying the recipient isn't worth even the most basic of courtesies. Our aim is to make these messages as offensive as possible. The vampiric equivalent of a flaming bag of poop on the porch."

"Vampires write to each other in blood?"

Emma nodded.

"Even human blood?"

"You better believe it. Especially if they're being extra polite, such as when they want to placate a more powerful vampire."

"Disgusting." Clarke grimaced. "Okay, so we need to grab this stationery. But the library's basement is going to be big and cluttered. It's mostly used for storage, right? How do we find the stationery?"

"It'll have a distinct smell." Brooke tapped her nose.

"A leftover from the manufacturing process. I can track it down based on that."

"Sounds good. That should keep the time we need down to a minimum." Clarke thought for a moment. "But won't Plainsborough know the paper is missing? Won't she be suspicious of any messages she receives after the theft?"

"That's why the plan is to only take two sheets," Emma said. "And then hide the theft by wrecking the place. Make it look like an attack from Rost."

"Got it. When do we make our move?"

"Tonight," Ashley said, eyes sweeping across Clarke, Brooke, and Sammy. "Either that, or we wait until next weekend. The library's closed on Sundays, so the chances of encountering Plainsborough or her thralls is low."

"But not zero," Clarke pointed out.

"Unfortunately, not. There's also a very real risk of traps and other magical defenses. The library's basement is Warded, so I can't tell you what's waiting for us."

Clarke shrugged. "Nothing ventured …"

"Nothing gained," Ashley finished. "Exactly."

"You two up for this?" he asked the werewolf and slime girl.

"You bet!" Brooke cracked her knuckles. "Bring it, I say!"

"Same here," Sammy said. "This is what we've been waiting for. Let's go for it!"

"Emma and I will hang back and support you," Ashley added. "Same as before."

"Sounds good," Clarke said. "What about after we have the stationery? What then?"

"I'll forge the letters of challenging." Ashley rested a hand on the grimoire. "Heinrich kept records of both Rost's and Plainsborough's missives, including their signatures. I'll use his notes to forge our own messages. It won't be perfect, it should be enough to fool a cursory inspection."

"I can handle the deliveries," Sammy said. "I'll disguise myself as one of the opposition's thralls and drop off each letter."

"And I can provide the rat," Brooke said. "Shouldn't be too hard for me to track down a suitable specimen."

"Sounds like this plan is really coming together." Clarke smiled at them. "Great work, everyone."

Brooke's tail wagged, and Sammy blushed a little.

"Ashley, you've had eyes on this place for a few days," he said. "What's the best time to hit it?"

"After ten o'clock tonight, I'd say."

CHAPTER NINETEEN

"THAT'S NOT GOOD." Emma lowered her binoculars then slid back down the hill to join the others. "There's someone guarding the exterior basement access."

"A thrall?" Clarke asked.

They'd gathered behind a hill near the edge of the CCU campus. The huge, concrete block of the library was visible over the rise, each of its five levels lined with tall, tinted windows.

"If she is, she's not on Heinrich's list," Emma replied.

"Could be one he wasn't aware of," Clarke said.

"Could be."

"Can you sense a control spell on her?"

"Nah. Too far away."

"Doesn't matter if she's a thrall or not." Sammy began stripping down. "I'll get rid of her."

"Hold up." Brooke sniffed the air, still in her hybrid form. "You smell that?"

"Smell what?" Sammy asked.

"Something's off."

Clarke sniffed the air experimentally, but all he picked up was the hill's freshly cut grass.

"Brooke?"

She crawled up to the hill's crest and breathed in deeply. Her ears flattened, and she slid back down.

"That's no thrall. She's a *zombie*."

"Well, there goes my idea." Sammy put her bra back on. "No way a zombie'll pass out from explosive diarrhea."

"Is that what you were going to hit her with?" Clarke asked. "Explosive diarrhea?"

The slime girl shrugged. "I made the last guy puke his guts out. Thought I'd change it up a bit."

"The presence of a zombie concerns me," Ashley said.

"Why?" Brooke asked. "She's one zombie. I'll rip her head off, and that'll be that."

"Because it's a sign Plainsborough is on guard, and where there's one zombie, there are often more. Zombies may not be much of a threat on their own, but vampires can make them fast, and in large numbers if they have access to a morgue."

"Or a shovel," Emma added.

"That, too. Bottom line, this site is more protected than I thought."

"Which means we need to be on our toes." Clarke grabbed his backpack. "Got it. We'll take it from here. Brooke?"

"Yes?"

"Remove the obstacle."

"No problem!"

Brooke shifted into a full werewolf, torso and neck straining against her hoodie, arms and legs bulging with fur and muscle and claws. Her snout lengthened, and she snarled, clacking her teeth together as if eager for even this easy hunt. She scurried up the hill, caught sight of the zombie, then dashed down the other side like a dog after an ugly squirrel.

The zombie turned to face the huge mass of fur, fangs, and claws barreling in.

"Urr?" A line of drool leaked from the side of her mouth. "Nurrh—*hk!*"

Brooke tackled the zombie with enough force to empty her lungs. The two hit the ground with the crunch of broken bones, Brooke on top, one arm locked around her target's throat. She twisted the zombie's head around in a full circle and then ripped it off in a sickly splash of fluids.

"Let's go!" Clarke cast Sanguine Shield and ran out to join the werewolf. Sammy followed only a few steps behind.

"Obstacle. Removed," Brooke growled.

"Great work. Get that door open. Sammy, help me with the body."

The door was at the bottom of a short flight of stairs. Brooke slashed through the lock and shoved the door open while Clarke dragged the corpse down the stairs and Sammy collected the head. They found themselves in a wide storage area, rows of metal racks filled with computer desktops, monitors, keyboards, mouses, and mounds of Ethernet and power cables. Old chairs and folded tables were stacked next to boxes piled up to the ceiling.

It was all so ordinary.

Clarke didn't buy it for a second.

He could practically taste magic in the air the moment he crossed the threshold: iron and the roughness of old parchment mixed with hot embers smoldering in some unseen fireplace. This was a vampire's lair, all right.

Sammy found a rack of collapsible storage bins.

"Here. For the body." She unfolded one of the bins and chucked the head in. Clarke crammed the body inside and placed the entire bin on a high shelf.

He summoned his thirstblade.

"Lead the way, Brooke."

"Checking." She sniffed the air, snout bobbing this way and that. "The place reeks of zombies. I'm having trouble differentiating the two."

"Zombies smell like vampire stationery?"

"More like the other way around, but yeah."

Clarke cringed. "What the hell do they put in that paper?"

"It's not paper." She sniffed some more, then shook her head. "Fuck it. Too much zombie B.O. This'll take forever."

"Can you tell where the zombies are?"

"Sure. That part's easy."

"Then we head there next. We find the zombies, we find what they're guarding."

"I like it!" Brooke drew in a deep breath. "Yeah, I've got your scent, you walking stink factories. This way!"

She led them across the basement to a pallet stacked with bins.

"The stench is coming from behind this." She grabbed the top bin and lifted it an inch before setting it back down. "Huh. Nothing inside these. Hang on." She grabbed the pallet and shoved the entire stack to the side—

—revealing an unremarkable patch of the wall and floor.

"Nothing," Sammy said.

Brooke sampled the air. "The smell is coming from here, all right."

Clarke placed his hand against the bare concrete, except it didn't feel like concrete.

"Conceal magic. But the effect is only visual." He felt around, found a hidden doorknob, and turned it. The illusion shimmered as he pulled the door open, revealing a dark set of stairs leading down to a level that shouldn't exist.

"Spell couldn't hide the stink, either." Brooke grinned, revealing rows of teeth. "Zombies down below. No mistake."

"Then that's where we're headed." Clarke readied his sword. "Let's go, ladies."

An elderly zombie with ghost-gray skin lurched toward Clarke, arms extended, jaw hanging slack. He cleaved the creature's head off with a swift stroke, then kicked the shambling corpse back.

"Wasn't expecting quite so many!" Brooke snarled, mauling another zombie. Her claws shredded his chest, turned meat and bone into red mist. She grabbed hold of his ribcage and spine, lifted the corpse into the air, and ripped him in half.

"How many *were* you expecting?" Sammy looped a stretched arm around a zombie's neck and then jerked the appendage back. The creature's head whirled around with a sickening crack, and he faltered, collapsing to the ground.

Another zombie clambered over the fallen corpse, indifferent to the carnage. More shambled up behind him, crowding the corridor, shuffling and moaning as they advanced.

"Keep at it, ladies! We're making progress!"

Clarke consumed a portion of his own life and cast Blood Freeze. The closest five zombies shuddered to a halt. He cut one in half, and his thirstblade drank in whatever foul lifeforce sustained the zombie, topping off his health.

"You say that like there's an end to them!" Sammy formed one arm into a mallet. "What the hell are we up against? The ghosts of library past?"

"They're corpses, not ghosts!" Brooke corrected.

"Whatever! Just keep fighting!" Sammy brought the mallet down on a zombie's head, crushing her skull.

Brooke picked up a zombie by the sternum and threw him, bowling over three more. The fallen tangle of zombies struggled back to their feet.

"This place built on a cemetery or something?" Brooke growled, then chomped down on a zombie's face. She ripped it off with a sharp jerk of her neck and shoved the rest of the body back.

"'You son of a bitch!'" Clarke quoted. "'You left the bodies, and you only moved the headstones!'"

"Ha! *Poltergeist*, right?" Sammy asked.

"Yep!"

"That movie freaked me the hell out when I was a kid. I'm still mad at my parents for letting me watch it!"

"Then you can think of this as exposure therapy."

"I just might! But if a creepy clown doll shows up next, you two are on your own. No way I'm putting up with that shit!"

Sammy swung an arm in a wide arc, tripping several zombies. Brooke pounced on one and mauled it to pieces. Clarke could finally see the end of the corridor through the shambling horde.

"Their ranks are thinning. Keep at it, ladies!"

"About freakin' time!"

Clarke advanced through the horde and cut down two more. He spent part of his lifeforce and cast Blood Freeze again, locking down another batch of zombies.

The average human armed with a pistol or rifle would have stood no chance against the mass of corpses Plainsborough had raised, but Clarke wasn't average. He was a blood knight, a vampire slayer, and these zombies would *not* stop him!

He pushed through, cutting and slashing as Brooke and Sammy advanced on either side. Broken corpses and spilled entrails littered the floor, blood and guts splattered its walls, and the three of them pushed forward, forming a whirlwind of carnage.

They cut and smashed and mauled.

Until there was nothing left to face.

Clarke stopped at the end of the blood-slick corridor, stance low, legs spread for stability. His chest heaved from exertion, face slick with sweat and spackled with blood, thirstblade glowing at his side.

He checked on his comrades—his lovers.

"Any of that your blood?" he asked Brooke.

"Nope!"

"How about you, Sammy? You good?"

The slime girl inspected the blood drenching her skin, which quickly faded away.

"Yuck! Zombie blood tastes like rusty nails and old shoes."

"We can go out for ice cream when this is over."

Her eyes lit up. "You promise?"

"Promise."

"That was actually kind of fun." Brooke brushed someone's intestine off her shoulder. "Let's never do it again."

"I second that." Sammy *schloorp*ed her arms back to normal size.

"Come on. We still have to find those papers. Brooke?"

"My nose won't be much help out here." She gestured back down the corridor. "Too much zombie funk."

"Then we press on."

Clarke pushed through the double doors at their end of the corridor and stepped out into a wide, circular space. The walls were lined with bookshelves and storage containers, and three magic circles had been drawn on the floor, each in various states of completion. One circle cast a faint greenish glow from its edges. Metal sliding doors led further in, branching out to either side.

"Brooke?"

"On it." She began a circuit of the room, sniffing the shelves and containers while staying clear of the magic circles. "Hmm. Yeah. There's a whiff of vampire stationery in here."

She opened a filing cabinet and rifled through folders.

"No good. These have already been used. Must be old correspondence."

She closed the filing cabinet and continued around the room.

An itch in Clarke's mind snapped his gaze over to one of the doors. He stared at it, focusing intensely.

"What is it?" Sammy asked.

"Magic, I think. Not sure."

"A spell, perhaps?"

"Could be."

"What kind?"

"Don't know. Feels strange. Like a steak left on the grill too long."

He turned to the slime girl, hoping the description would help, but she only shrugged.

"Sorry, Clarke. You're asking the wrong girl."

Brooke's ears stood upright. She faced the same door.

"Something's moving," she said softly. "Coming toward us."

"Get ready," Clarke whispered, raising his thirst-blade.

They took up positions around the room, keeping their distance from the door while staying clear of the magic circles in the center.

Metal scratched frantically against metal on the far side, almost as if a creature were scrabbling against the barrier. A loud clank followed, denting the door outward, followed by more scrabbling.

The door slid aside, and an exhale of freezer air plumed through, revealing a chamber that reminded Clarke sickeningly of Heinrich's pantry. Bodies—both animal *and* human—hung from meat hooks in neat rows, but they weren't the room's only occupants.

A shroud of heavy, chilling mist parted, and a creature crawled forward on all fours. At first Clarke thought it was another zombie, and perhaps it was, but it wasn't like the others. Its hips were backward, and its shoulders pivoted the wrong way, allowing the creature to move about the ground with an absurd approximation of grace.

If anything so hideous could be called "graceful."

The tattered remains of its skin clung to a well-muscled body, as if it were a grotesque butterfly that had shed its chrysalis mere moments ago. Meat hooks embedded in its hands clicked against the floor with each step, like grotesque claws. Its head rotated on a too-flexible neck, staring at them with wide, lidless eyes. It clacked its lipless teeth together then licked them with a long, dripping tongue.

Two more of the creatures padded out into the open.

"What the hell?" Sammy winced. "This is some *Attack on Titan* bullshit right here!"

"At least they're not sixty meters tall and farting steam," Brooke replied.

"What do you even call these things?"

"I vote for 'meat zombies.'"

"Careful," Clarke said. "We don't know—"

One of the zombies shot forward with a startling burst of speed. It leaped at Clarke, and its meat hooks sparked against his shield as it hurtled by. The other two zombies snapped their jaws and rushed the others.

The meat zombie going for Clarke landed behind him, then scurried across the floor, rounding him rapidly, skinless head tracking his every motion with harrowing precision. When it judged the perfect moment, it sprang into action again, and Clarke swung his sword around to meet it.

Too slow!

The zombie slammed into his chest, throwing him back. He hit the ground on his back, horrible jaws snapping at his face, meat hooks digging into his shoulders. Red lightning danced across his body, then sputtered out as his shield collapsed, and the meat hooks sank into his flesh.

Clarke gritted his teeth as he punched the zombie in the ribs. A satisfying *crack!* gave under his fist. He brought his thirstblade around and slashed toward the creature's flank—but it darted off him the moment it felt the kiss of his blade. Its hooks tore through his shoulders, and he bled from the wounds. Still, he fought through the pain, scrambling to his feet.

The zombie seemed to size him up, eyes flitting from him to his sword and back. It bounced on its feet and meat hooks, juking left and right, not yet ready to commit to an attack.

"Screw this."

Clarke gathered his strength and cast Blood Freeze. Stars danced across his vision.

The zombie shuddered, limbs shaking, and its head twitched its way through a full rotation.

Clarke charged, sword rising in a scarlet arc.

The zombie lurched into motion at the last moment, skittering away from his blade, even as the edge cleaved through its wrist. One of its hands flew off in a spray of blood—and the thirstblade drank in enough vitality to grant Clarke's head the relief of much-needed clarity.

The zombie landed on its feet and remaining hand,

nursing its injury. It clacked its teeth at him, muscles tensing, legs coiling, then launched itself like an ugly meat missile, jaws wide.

Clarke brought his sword down through the center of its head.

The thirstblade cut through the monster's flesh like butter, but the two severed halves refused to obey the Rule of Cool. Instead of splitting to either side and landing behind Clarke, they followed Sir Isaac Newton's instructions to the letter and thumped into his wounded shoulders, knocking him back—

—straight into Brooke's huge, furry arms.

"You okay, Clarke?"

"Yeah, I—"

He checked left, then right, but only found the scattered pieces of two more meat zombies. Both Brooke and Sammy had dispatched their respective foes. He put a hand on Brooke's shoulder to steady himself and stood up straight, shoulders healing thanks to the vigor stolen from his kill.

"I'm good," he finished. "You?"

"The meat zombie gave me some trouble, but I caught it in the end."

"Same here." Sammy walked over, the silhouette of a hand floating in her chest. "They actually don't taste all that bad."

"I'll take your word for it," Clarke said.

"Oh! Right! What we're here for!" Brooke hurried over to the wall and resumed sniffing the shelves and containers.

"Your shoulders okay?" Sammy asked, shifting aside one of the bloody rips in his shirt.

"Good enough. Drain and a bit of shifter magic go a long way, apparently."

He recast Sanguine Shield, and the defensive aura crackled back into existence.

"Glad to hear it." Sammy checked their surroundings. "I've had about enough of Plainsborough's hospitality."

"You and me both."

"At least these magic circles are duds." Sammy rubbed one with her foot. All three had been trampled during the fight with the meat zombies.

"So it would—"

"Found it!" Brooke held up two pale, grayish sheets. She hurried over and handed them to Clarke. The sheets gave with a bizarre softness, almost like soft leather, or …

"This isn't paper!" he exclaimed, lips twisting in revulsion. "It's human skin!"

"Yup," Brooke said with a sad nod. "That's why it smells like zombies."

"Vampires use this stuff to write memos? What the actual fuck!" He stared at the pages in his hands, his fingers itching with a sense of unease just from holding them. He buried those feelings and placed the stationery in a folder from his backpack, then zipped everything back up.

He slung the pack over a shoulder.

"We're done here. Let's scram before—"

The magic circle under his feet flared bright with green light. All three of them dashed out of the way, their senses freshly alert. The double doors leading out slammed shut, and green flames licked across the metal.

"Oh, what *now*?" Sammy said, morphing one of her fists into a hammerhead.

The circle's perimeter blazed brighter, acting as a shield as the summon began to coalesce. Magic swirled upward, forming bones and muscles from nothing. A lithe, graceful creature took shape, resembling a leopard or puma but with pale flesh and green flames for fur.

The outer circle of flame died out, and the creature padded forward, leaving paw prints of corpse fire.

"I know this one!" Brooke pointed at the creature. "It's a pyrelynx!"

"Stop gawking," Sammy snapped, "and start fighting!"

"Game faces, ladies!" Clarke readied his sword. "Let's do this!"

They spread out around the pyrelynx, sizing the beast up as it did the same. It padded forward, eyes tracking from one target to the next. The sleek body blazed with green fire, heat radiating off its muscled flanks. Its gaze locked onto Sammy, and it began turning toward her.

"Uh, Clarke?" Sammy said, backing away.

"What?"

"I probably should have mentioned this earlier, but I have a confession."

"Is this really the time?"

"It's about my body. I'm *slightly* more flammable than most people."

"How much is 'slightly'?"

The monster's throat bulged, and then it vomited a stream of fluorescent green ichor. Sammy dodged to the side, but several gobs splashed across her left arm, igniting the limb with a loud *WHOOSH!*

"Aah! This much! *This much!*"

"Oh, shit! Stop, drop, and roll, Sammy! Stop, drop, and roll!"

Sammy hit the deck for all she was worth and rolled across the room like a runaway log, trailing smoke that reeked of charred bubblegum. She smacked into the wall, and a few books toppled onto her back.

"Ow ..." She pushed off the ground, smoke rising from her arm, its flesh blackened and crispy.

"You okay?" Clarke asked, stepping between the monster and the slime girl.

"I'll live," she groaned.

The monster hawked up more phlegm, and its throat swelled.

"Sammy, get clear!"

She rushed to her feet, but Clarke saw she wouldn't be fast enough, and so he held his position, covering his face with his arms. The glowing phlegm splashed against his shield, wreathing him in fire. His shield protected him from the worst of the burns, and he shook the rest of the goop off his arms and chest. His cheeks felt like he'd been baking on the beach all day without any sunscreen.

The pyrelynx spat again, and this time both Sammy and Clarke cleared the firing lane. The arching stream splattered across a bookshelf, setting them ablaze.

"Who the hell summons a fire monster to guard a *library*?!" Sammy spat, nursing her arm.

The eldritch flames roared through the books, embers jumping to the next shelf. Heat washed over Clarke as he circled around the pyrelynx. He spent a part of himself to cast Blood Freeze, but the spell evaporated against the raging furnace within the monster.

"We need to take this thing out," he said, "and fast!"

"On it!" Brooke rushed in, claws flashing.

The pyrelynx spun to face her, but that only provided it with a better view of charging werewolf. The two slammed together, and both hit the ground, kicking and clawing, flames licking across Brooke's fur. She tore into the monster's belly and ripped fiery chunks out of its guts.

The pyrelynx kicked at her, slashed her arms and face, but she didn't back down, didn't pull away. Instead, she dug in, shoving her claws deeper, then raking them through its flesh. Her teeth glistened in the green firelight as she chomped down on its throat.

The pyrelynx wailed in pain and thrashed about, desperate to break free. Werewolf and pyrelynx rolled about the floor like an agonized eight-limbed creature. Brooke slammed its head into the ground, stunning it briefly, and Clarke saw his opening.

He charged in from behind the creature, and his sword cut up through its haunches, across its belly, and then up out the back of its neck. Whatever resistance the creature had left faltered, and Brooke raised it by the neck, still gripped in her maw, then slammed it onto the floor with the crunch of breaking bones.

The pyrelynx let out a long, wheezing death gurgle, and then lay still.

Brooke climbed to her feet, much of her fur charred. She patted down a smoldering patch on her shoulder. A gash ran through one of her eyes, and blood dribbled from the ruined socket.

"Brooke, your eye," Clarke said softly.

"It'll heal," she grunted through clenched teeth, her voice strained.

He nodded, and rested a hand on her shoulder as he walked past her.

"Let's get out of here," he said, and began slicing through the door.

CHAPTER TWENTY

"HOW BAD DOES IT LOOK?"

Brooke, now in her hybrid form, put on a pair of Emma's sunglasses. She tilted her head back and thrust out her chest as if modeling for a catalog. She'd replaced the burnt remains of her hoodie with one of Emma's shirts, which was—perhaps not surprisingly—a great fit for the werewolf's chest, despite the overall difference in size between the two women.

"Well …" Clarke frowned.

"Don't hold back. I know I'm a mess."

"I can still see the cut through your eye."

"That'll be gone in the morning. Anything else?"

"Your ears look like they've been chewed on."

"Gone in the morning. And?"

"What about the eye itself?"

BLOOD KNIGHT

"A few days to regen. Hence the sunglasses."

"You planning to wear those at school?"

"Yep."

"*Indoors?*"

"He's got a point there," Emma said, on the couch beside the werewolf.

All five of them had returned to her apartment after leaving the CCU library—and the smoke pouring out of its basement. Clarke had ditched his smoky clothes for fresher attire and then applied an entire tube of burn ointment to Brooke. The ointment seemed to provide her with some relief, if only minor and temporary.

Sammy had retreated to the shower to rinse her wounds with cold water, and Ashley sat in the corner, grimoire open next to the sheets of—Clarke shivered—*human skin*. Ashley had retrieved a fountain pen and syringe from her satchel, along with a bottle of something called enoxaparin.

"Plainsborough and her thralls will be on high alert," Emma continued. "You show up tomorrow with a missing eye, the wrong people are going to notice."

"Today," Ashley corrected without looking up. "It's already Monday."

"And I'm starting to feel it." Clarke ground his palms into his eyes.

"Want me to brew some coffee?" Emma asked, standing up.

376

"That'd be great. Thanks."

The succubus rounded the kitchen counter and switched on the coffeemaker.

"We need to be careful," Ashley said. "The fire you started is going to draw a lot of attention, including from the vampires."

"*We* didn't start *anything*," Brooke said. "We're victims of circumstance."

"The point still stands. Plainsborough might blame Rost for the attack, but then again, she might not. Until we put a letter of challenge in front of her, we need to keep a low profile."

"Which means you, Brooke," Clarke said.

"I know …" Her ears drooped and her tail sagged against the couch. She took off the glasses and set them on the coffee table.

Her left eye looked terrible. Clarke found it hard to believe it would return to normal in only a few days. Cuts, bruises, and broken bones were all one thing; they healed naturally in everyone, only much faster for certain demi-humans. Compared to that, regenerating an eye was on a whole other level.

"Hey, everyone." Sammy rounded the table and dropped heavily into a recliner. She'd borrowed a T-shirt and shorts from Emma. "I don't know about the rest of you, but I'm beat."

"How's the burn?" Clarke asked.

She held up her arm. The surface turned pinkish and translucent, revealing the slow flow of shadowy flakes inside.

"I swapped my outsides for my insides. It'll mend eventually. My healing factor isn't on the same level as Brooke's, but the way my organs work makes it difficult to deal me a crippling blow. Gotta deal with all of me if you want to take me out."

"Like setting you on fire?"

"Yeah, that'll do it." She sighed and slouched lower. "Hurt like a bitch, too."

Brooke's ears stood up.

"Sorry, Brooke. Poor choice of words."

"I just hope it was all worth it," Clarke said.

"It was." Ashley looked up from the grimoire. "I can start as soon as I have some rat blood."

"Right, I'll get on that." Brooke rose from the couch, but grimaced and rubbed her back, still halfway bent over. "One second. I think something isn't lined up right." She pushed into the small of her back and snapped upright with a loud crack. "There we go! All better!"

"Need a hand?" Clarke asked.

"Nah, I'll be back before you know it. Later!"

She headed out the door.

"Sammy," Ashley said, "have you reviewed the list of thralls and picked your impersonation targets?"

"Why, *yes*. I took care of that during my copious amounts of free time today. After all, I've only been preoccupied with infiltrating a vampire's lair, fighting through hordes of zombies, and being set on fire by a cat!"

Ashley's hairband darkened.

"No, Ash. I haven't looked at it yet." Sammy draped her arms over the armrests and let them stretch until her knuckles reached the floor.

"Would you like me to pick two names out for you, then?"

"Please."

"Then I'll take care of it."

Emma finished brewing the coffee and served three cups: with cream for Clarke, and with cream and sugar for herself and Sammy. She offered a cup to Ashley, but the celestial declined politely. Clarke wondered how long it had been since Ashley had slept. Days? Weeks? *Years?* Did she even need to sleep?

"I believe I have your targets," Ashley said after a while. "Claudia Butler is a library page and one of Plainsborough's thralls. Nicolas Lindbeck is a benchwarmer on the football team. He's a thrall under Rost."

"*He?*" Sammy retracted her arms and sat up. "You want me to impersonate a guy?"

"Is that a problem?" Clarke asked. "Are there restrictions for what you can mimic?"

"Not exactly. You've seen my natural state, so you can think of that as a base I shapeshift around. The further I deviate from that baseline, the more difficult the morph."

"Okay, I get it."

"Impersonating a guy is a matter of assuming the right outline. Creating a skinsuit of sorts that I plasticize the rest of my body into. All I'm doing is wearing a facade. But I don't mess with *all* the details, if you catch my meaning."

One particular detail immediately came to Clarke's mind.

"Ah, yes, I believe I do."

"Basically, when I morph into a guy, I have all the functionality of a Ken doll. Also, beards and mustaches give me fits. Don't know why; they just do. Ask me to mimic them at your own peril."

"Lindbeck's cheeks are baby smooth," Ashley said, once again engrossed in the grimoire.

"Good." Sammy slumped back and let her arms stretch out. "Bottom line is it's *much* easier for me to masquerade as women, but I can do guys in a pinch. Got pictures for me, Ash?"

"Already in your inbox."

"Perfect. I'll study up and be ready sometime this evening." She leaned back in the recliner and closed her eyes.

Brooke came back less than half an hour later.

"Got one!" she declared, stepping through the door with a laden plastic bag in one hand.

"Brooke, uh …" Clarke made a wiping gesture on one side of his lips. "You've got something on you."

"I do?" She wiped her free hand across her lips and studied the smear of blood. "Whoops! Guess I got carried away. Poor guy took one look at me and bolted, so I gave chase and, well, caught him."

"With your mouth?"

"Yes?" She smiled guiltily.

"I'll take that," Ashley said.

Brooke handed the bag over to her.

"Thank you." Ashley set it down next to her fountain pen, syringe, and chemical bottle. She peered into the bag and picked up the syringe. "Two letters of challenge coming right up."

The campus buzzed with news of the fire, and the administration swung into full damage control mode.

Yes, there had been a fire in the library's basement, and yes, some property had been destroyed, but the losses amounted to nothing more than a few spare computers and some old furniture. Hardly worth the mention at all. The university takes the safety of all its students very, very seriously and will be launching an investigation into the cause of the fire in conjunction with local law enforcement. Expect more news to follow, but the initial findings reveal the cause to be faulty wiring in the basement. As a precautionary measure, power to the basement will be switched off for the foreseeable future and blah-blah-blah-blah-blah.

Clarke found it almost comical to watch.

The days passed much as they had before Emma and Ashley had opened his eyes. His human classmates in Calculus 2 no longer remembered Heinrich—they thought the substitute professor had been there from the start, that no one with the name "Otto Heinrich" had ever taught at CCU—and the demihumans among them kept their mouths shut.

Monday night, Sammy delivered both letters of challenge without incident. Clarke and Brooke provided her with an overwatch of sorts, keeping their eyes—and, in Brooke's case, ears and nose—alert for any signs of trouble, but none came, and both vampires received their "flaming poop bags" through their proxy thralls.

After that, it was simply a matter of waiting and watching for the results.

They didn't have long to wait.

"Did you two see the news?" Brooke asked on Tuesday, meeting up with Clarke and Emma at the apartment after school. Her ears and face were already looking better.

She took off her sunglasses, revealing her still-missing eye, and sat down across from them.

"You mean how half of Rost's coaching staff suddenly decided to 'retire'?" Clarke asked.

"Yeah, they on the list of thralls?"

"All but one," Emma said. "Trevor Walton, the cornerback coach. He could have been a thrall Heinrich didn't know about. Or an unlucky bystander. No real way for us to be sure."

Brooke's ears drooped. "You really think that may be true? That we're responsible for an innocent death?"

"We knew something like this could happen, and besides, *every* thrall is innocent when you get right down to it. But what can we do about that? We can't ignore them, not when they're so brainwashed they'll die protecting their masters. They need to be taken out of the picture if we're to have a clear shot at the vampires."

"But …"

"I wish there was a better way. I really do."

"Brooke, I hear your concerns." Clarke leaned in and spoke softly. "But we're up against monsters. Inhuman killers who view people as nothing but food, who feel no remorse for the lives they take. You saw all the bodies strung up in Plainsborough's meat locker. *That's* what we're trying to stop. We rid this campus of vampires and we'll have saved—I don't know how many lives, but it'll be a lot!"

"I know. I just …"

"You wish no one had to get hurt."

"I guess so." Her fingers traced around the healing eye. "At least, no one besides us."

"You know that won't work. We either fight the vampires with every ounce of our strength, or we sit back and accept the status quo. Accept their dominion over us. We try to half-ass this, and it'll be *our* names that pop up in the news next."

"I know, Clarke." Brooke took a deep breath. "I know."

"And it's not like we put a gun to the man's head and pulled the trigger," Emma added. "Whether or not he was a thrall, he died because a vampire or an agent of one killed him."

Brooke nodded slowly.

Clarke thought he understood why this one death bothered her so much when all the others hadn't. Monsters were monsters, zombies were already dead, and thralls weren't too far behind either. Yes, they were living, breathing human beings, but their brains had been turned into cottage cheese by the vampires. What was the worse option: condemning them to a life of slavery or granting them release through death?

Clarke didn't have a good answer, but he *did* know killing vampires would make the world a better place, and he took solace in that.

"What now?" Brooke asked after a long pause.

"The fighting will likely grow worse," Emma said. "Plainsborough has made her first move, which indicates she's blaming the library attack on her rival. I doubt Rost will take her counterstroke sitting down. He's going to strike back, and strike back hard."

"Is there a chance he'll flee?" Brooke asked. "Maybe try and reestablish himself in less contested territory?"

"That's possible, but Plainsborough's forces have been weakened thanks to us. She's in a vulnerable state, and Rost may smell blood in the water. He may decide to go for her throat, even with the recent loss of so many thralls."

"Whatever happens next," Clarke said, "we need to be ready to act. You still up for this?"

"Absolutely." Brooke sat up straight. "Clarke, you're my mate and my alpha. I go where you go. I fight who you fight. I may not be perfectly at ease with everything that's happening, but I'm yours until the day I die."

The university posted more "retirements" in the following days.

"At this rate," Clarke said, scrolling through the news on his phone, "Sports and Library Services are both going to be ghost towns before the month is out."

"Yeah," Emma said, reading the same updates on her phone. "Those two are really going at it."

"Couldn't have happened to a nicer pair of killers." Sammy tossed her phone onto the coffee table and sank back into the recliner. It was Thursday, and everyone had dropped by Emma's apartment after school to discuss the latest news.

"How's the arm doing?" Clarke asked.

"A lot better." Sammy pulled back her sleeve and let her skin turn translucent. A scattering of dark particles clouded the interior. "Almost as good as new."

"It looks the part. Beautiful as always."

"Thanks." Sammy blushed as she rolled her sleeve down.

"What about me?" Brooke asked eagerly, eyes wide, face forward. "What about me?"

"The eye looks great. You can't even tell it was ripped out by a fire cat."

Brooke grinned at the compliment, showing her fangs.

"The number of attacks and casualties …" Emma shook her head. "Rost and Plainsborough aren't bothering with subtlety anymore. They want each other dead, and they don't seem to care how they achieve that. I think we're looking at a full-scale vendetta between the two vampires."

"Good," Sammy said. "The more they tear into each other, the easier it'll be for us to take down the winner."

"Any idea who's winning?" Brooke asked.

"Hard to say." Emma set her phone down on the coffee table. "Mind you, we lack the complete picture, but it feels like Rost is pulling out ahead. He consolidated after his losses earlier in the week and is really bringing the pain to Plainsborough. Honestly, I'm surprised. I thought Plainsborough would wipe the floor with him."

"This could be the result of their different magical affinities," Clarke said. "Sure, both of them have lost a lot of minions, but Rost can use his magic to buff up what he has left, making each creature or thrall that much more deadly. On the other hand, Plainsborough needs to be present in the battle to use her Fire magic. Advantage, Rost."

"Good point," Emma said. "I hadn't thought of it that way."

"And if we continue along that train of thought," Clarke added, "then Plainsborough must see the same problem. Sure, she started with more fodder, but Rost is putting her troops through a grinder. She can't keep fighting the way she has been, which presents her with a problem she needs to solve."

"You think she'll be motivated to challenge Rost directly?"

"The thought had crossed my mind." Clarke shrugged. "Hard to say with the snippets we have, though."

"Hold on. What's this?" Ashley looked up from her phone. "Did any of you catch the news about the stadium?"

"No," Emma said. "What's going on?"

"Every event for the weekend has been canceled.

Apparently, the administration decided *today* to replace some of the bald patches on the field."

"They make the call to cancel everything two days before the weekend?" Sammy rolled her eyes. "Yeah, right. I know the administration's bad, but they're not *that* incompetent!"

"This doesn't make any sense," Brooke said. "Sure, the field could use some work, but why close down the whole stadium instead of only part of the field? And why wouldn't they give students more notice? Don't these sorts of projects need to be planned out ahead of time? Budgeted, bid upon, awarded, and then scheduled?"

"*Very* irregular." Sammy sat forward on the edge of the recliner. "What do we think? This has got to be a cover story, right?"

"Right. But for what?" Brooke frowned as if deep in thought.

The apartment fell silent as everyone considered what they knew so far.

"Clarke, maybe there's a connection to your theory," Emma said at last. "Let's say Plainsborough sees the problem the way you do, that she now needs to involve herself directly in the fighting. One option open to her is to challenge Rost to a duel. This would be more specific than the letters of challenge we created, and it makes sense on more than one level. The two vampires could use the duel to settle their grievances, and in the process, deescalate the conflict. The terms of the duel would resolve the vendetta instead of open bloodshed."

"But if Rost is winning, why would he agree?"

"Because he knows he'll have to face Plainsborough eventually, and with her issuing the challenge, he gets to set the terms and location. He'll see this as an opportunity to carve off a piece of Plainsborough's holdings, perhaps the best he's ever had. And since Sports is his turf ..."

"He picks the stadium," Clarke finished for her. "It fits."

"Okay, say you're both right about all this," Brooke began. "If the vampires really are going to duel it out at the stadium this weekend, what's our move?"

"Isn't it obvious?" Emma smiled wickedly, her eyes turning to Clarke, who nodded knowingly.

"We stake out the stadium and, once they've worn each other down, we crash the party."

CHAPTER TWENTY-ONE

THEY BROKE INTO THE STADIUM before sunrise Saturday morning, entering through one of the forty gates that ringed the open-air structure. They picked the one farthest from the main parking deck, hoping to reduce the chances of either vampire passing through the same gate where they could spot Brooke's "lockpicking" job.

CCU Stadium's seating formed two rounded tiers around the playing field. Press boxes and suites rested along the northern side, arranged in two arches: one nestled in the gap between tiers and one across the top. The stadium lights were all off, though the moon cast its pale glow over the surroundings, providing just enough light for Clarke not to trip over his own feet.

They made their way to the upper press boxes, and Brooke "lockpicked" the door by ripping it off its hinges.

"Can you make any more noise?" Sammy snapped under her breath.

"Sorry," Brooke whispered, leaning the door against the wall gingerly, as if that would somehow hide the fact that it was no longer in the standard door position.

They filed into the unlit press box. A long table and four chairs sat in front of the windowed wall overlooking the stadium.

Clarke and the ladies hunkered down for what they expected would be a long, boring wait, punctuated at the end with terrifying violence. Everyone took turns keeping watch, with Brooke going first thanks to her werewolf eyesight. Emma and Sammy had collaborated on the food prep, and the menu consisted of stir-fry boxed meals, an entire backpack of food bars and snacks, bottled water, and two thermoses of coffee.

The sun rose, cresting over the tiered seating, and the stadium remained still as the grave.

Clarke felt surprisingly alert despite the odd hours he'd kept recently. Sammy and Emma drained most of one thermos, and Ashley took a few sips—perhaps out of politeness—but neither he nor Brooke required a pick-me-up. Did the shifter magic he now shared with her explain his added pep?

The day dragged on, and he joined Emma by the window. He sat on the floor next to her as she scanned the stadium with her binoculars. They'd made a point to stay clear of the windows as much as possible and to keep a low profile.

"Looks like those plans to rework the field were bogus," Clarke said.

"It was a lame cover story anyway." She lowered her binoculars.

"Think the vampires will show?"

"If they do, it'll be long after dark. They're not going to duke it out in the sun."

"Guess it's a case of hurry up and wait for us, then."

"Yep." Emma sighed and sat back. "I don't mind keeping watch, but now I'm getting hungry."

"Want me to grab you something?"

She glanced back at him and smiled slyly. "Wrong kind of hunger."

"Ah. Then not something a boxed lunch would solve."

"Nope!"

"You're insatiable."

She giggled.

"Sorry, but you're going to have to tough this one out. At least until tomorrow."

"Oh, but, Clarke"—she ran her hand across his thigh, tracking inward—"my meal is sitting right next to me."

"Aren't we trying to keep a low profile? You know, stay out of sight; not make a lot of noise."

"I can be discreet."

Clarke raised an eyebrow.

"Really, I can."

"Perhaps you should keep an eye on the stadium for now."

"If you *insist*."

She raised the binoculars and began another sweep of the stadium, but then stopped all of a sudden.

"Oh!" She shifted onto her stomach, chest propped up by her elbows. "Got something. A man coming up the stairs on the eastern side."

Clarke turned over onto his hands and knees and crawled up beside her.

"Where?"

"There." She pointed.

"Okay, I see him. What do you make of him?"

"Not sure. Maybe a scout from Plainsborough? Here to scope out the dueling pitch? Or one of Rost's boys sent to check on it."

"A thrall, then?"

"That's my guess. We're too far away to be sure, though."

Clarke waited quietly next to Emma as she tracked the man. Whoever he was, he walked out onto the field and began a slow circuit around the tracks.

Sammy oozed up to the window and then *splorp*ed

into human form wearing only underwear.

"What are we all staring at?" she whispered.

"There's a—"

"Hey!" Brooke crashed next to the trio. "Something out there?"

Clarke grimaced at the interruptions, then said, "Possible thrall on the field."

He pointed the man out.

"He doesn't look familiar," Brooke said. "I don't remember him from Heinrich's list."

"He's up to no good," Sammy said. "I can tell. Want me to get rid of him?"

"No," Clarke replied. "Let's all hang back and watch for now."

The man completed his circuit around the field and then hurried out of the stadium through one of the eastern gates.

"There, see?" Clarke said. "The problem took care of itself."

"Still would have been more fun to give him explosive diarrhea."

Three more people showed up during the day, but even with Brooke's eyesight and Emma's binoculars, they only managed to identify one: a thrall from Rost who switched on the stadium's main lights before leaving.

The sun set, and everyone made sure they were fed, hydrated, caffeinated, and ready for action. Ashley and Emma tag teamed surveillance duty while Brooke and Sammy stood by at the back of the press box. Clarke lay on the floor between Ashley and Emma; he wanted to see what they were up against before heading out.

A ripple ran through his senses, and for a moment, he thought he'd bitten his inner lip and drawn blood.

"Emma?"

"I feel it, too," the succubus replied, lying on her stomach next to Ashley. "Damn, that's strong!"

"It would seem the newcomer isn't interested in hiding," Ashley whispered. "I'm sensing Armor, Strength, Resist Fire, Speed, and maybe a few others in the mix. That's Rost all right, and he's prepped for war."

"He's the weaker of the two?" Clarke asked. "Damn!"

"Here he comes now." Emma offered him the binoculars. "Get a good look."

Rost's party of four marched onto the field through one of the western gates and stopped in the home team's endzone: a swath of red grass with the fearsome name of CHESTNUTS written in bold white letters. No one liked the name—least of all the students—and the mascot costume was just an embarrassment to everyone involved.

Rost was a middle-aged man with broad shoulders, thick arms, no neck, and a shaven head. He kept his beard trim and wore a pair of sports glasses secured by a flexible band, and walked with a swagger so pronounced it was like he wore it as a shield against the lameness of his employer's mascot. But because he *was* a vampire, after all, mere swagger wasn't enough.

He set an obsidian war hammer on the ground and rested his hands atop the shaft.

A golem composed of rebar and warped I-beams trudged alongside him, and two humans brought up the rear—not zombies but thralls judging by how fluidly they moved. Both men were armed with revolvers and swords.

A dozen women shambled out onto the field to join the vampire, all of them clad in red-and-white tops and skirts, but with decidedly less pep than Clarke was accustomed to seeing from them.

Clarke couldn't believe his eyes.

"He turned the cheerleader squad into *zombies?*"

Emma pulled the binoculars over and stole a glance.

"Don't think so. They look too decayed for that. I'd say he and his thralls dug up this lot to bulk up their numbers."

"So he raised a bunch of zombies and dressed them all in cheerleader outfits? What kind of a twisted mind would do that?"

"Maybe he really likes cheerleaders."

Clarke had barely shaken off the chill of that uncomfortable imagery when a second spike of magic shuddered through his being—this one heated and raw, yet tinged with that universal taste of blood.

"And there's his opponent," Ashley whispered.

Plainsborough and her feline companion entered the stadium from the eastern gate and walked out onto the visiting team's endzone. She was an old, shriveled stick of a woman, with sunken cheeks and a frizz of gray hair. The knitted sweater she wore gave her a homely, welcoming appearance, but the burning sickle she held told a very different story. She wasn't trying to fight off any lame associations like Rost was. Even in that stereotypical cardigan, she knew she was bad as hell, and ready to fuck up anyone who thought otherwise. The sickle was just an accessory.

And because a librarian could never be without her library cat, a single pyrelynx followed her onto the field, its hide ablaze with corpse fire.

"Time to move into position," Clarke said softly, backing away from the window.

Clarke led Brooke and Sammy down through the stadium to a tunnel that exited onto the field. They stopped at the end and peered out at the two vampires, ready to do battle, but blissfully unaware of the real threat lurking in the shadows.

"What?" Plainsborough shouted from her endzone.

An indistinct murmur responded from across the field.

"*What?*"

The murmur repeated, only louder.

"Rost, I can't hear a fucking word you're saying! Speak up!"

The vampire on the other side of the field waved an arm angrily, and one of his thralls ran off the field. The man came back with a megaphone.

"I said—" The megaphone squawked from feedback, and he paused before continuing. "I *said*, in accordance with the customs laid down by the Academy of Silence, and under the aegis of the Throne of Shadows, we hereby pledge to settle our dispute through ritual—"

"Oh, pull your head out of your ass, Rost! We know why we're here!"

"Don't interrupt me!" Rost shouted, his megaphone squawking again. "I've got a lot to say to you!"

"That makes two of us."

"Anyway, where was I …?" The megaphone magnified a paper shuffling sound. "Damn it. I've lost my place."

"You've always been in the dark, Rost. You should be used to it by now."

"Would you give me a moment, *please*? We're supposed to follow the steps!" The vampire shuffled more papers around. "Ah, here it is. Says here we're required to try one final time to resolve our dispute peacefully before we engage in ritual combat."

"Great! I'll accept your apology and tribute now."

"I'm not apologizing for anything! *You* killed my favorite thrall!"

"*You* killed *my* favorite thrall!"

"You burned my grimoire!"

"You burned down my lair!"

"What the hell are you talking about? That wasn't me."

"Yes, it was!"

"No, it wasn't! You did that to yourself! Seriously, who guards a library with fire monsters?"

"It's what I'm good at!"

"Are you also good at not setting your own place on fire?"

"Fuck you, Rost!"

"Well, fuck you right back!"

"Fuck you times infinity!"

"What the hell does that even mean?"

"It means we're done talking!"

Plainsborough bared her fangs and hissed, levitating off the ground. Rost hissed right back, but the effect was somewhat less intimidating because he was still holding the megaphone. He realized this and handed the megaphone back to a thrall, who tried to juggle it with the pistol and sword but only succeeded in dropping all three.

Rost gave the thrall an exasperated look and waited for him to pick up his weapons. Then he took hold of his war hammer and pointed it down the field. The cheerleader zombies launched themselves into a chaotic, shambling run reminiscent of a weird-ass, terrible halftime dance routine, limbs flailing as they almost tripped over themselves. The metal golem exhaled green, glowing smoke from its chest and lumbered forward.

"Zombies, Rost? Am I supposed to be frightened?"

Rost shouted something back, but his words were drowned out by the moans of his troops.

"I can't hear you!" Plainsborough stroked the pyre-lynx's burning hide, and the creature shot across the field, leaving a trail of smoke and embers.

Clarke leaned back from the archway and spoke softly to Brooke and Sammy.

"Both of you head that way." He pointed down a side passage. "Try to reach Rost's endzone. We'll catch them from both sides. Wait as long as you can before attacking, but use your judgment. When one of us jumps into the fight, we all do. Got it?"

Both of them nodded.

"Good. Now go!"

They took off down the passage, and Clarke turned back to observe the battle.

The two forces began to converge with Rost and Plainsborough both trailing their frontline forces with the leisurely pace of commanders confident of victory.

The pyrelynx reached the cheerleaders near the 50-yard line and vomited all over them. Four zombies lit up like dry underbrush soaked in gasoline. They wailed, foul smoke billowing upward until they dropped to the ground in flaming heaps.

The remaining zombies shambled on, indifferent to fear or pain—

—or any sense of tactical awareness.

They marched straight over the lit bodies, igniting themselves in the process. The center of the field blazed with a dozen flaming, moaning cheerleader zombies who collapsed one by one.

"I'm not impressed, Rost!"

Plainsborough conjured a ball of fire and flung it with a sidearm throw. The ball struck Rost's golem in the chest and exploded with a sharp, fiery crack, enveloping the construct. It marched through the fire, its chest scorched but otherwise unharmed.

Rost shouted something down the field.

"Still can't hear you!" Plainsborough spat, readying another fireball.

Rost picked up the megaphone. "Neither am I, you hag!"

"Neither what?"

"Impressed! I'm not impressed! That much should be obvious!"

Plainborough bared her fangs and threw the second fireball. It cracked against the golem in a brief snap-flash of arcane energy.

"Shoot her down!" Rost ordered.

His thralls opened fire with their pistols. None of the shots even came close, and one zinged off the arch over the visiting team's tunnel. Clarke's heart leaped into his throat as he ducked inside.

"Not from here, you idiots!" Rost shouted to his thralls, the megaphone blaring into their ears. "She's an evasive airborne target! Get closer first!"

The thralls obeyed, though one covered his ears as he advanced.

The pyrelynx spat phlegm all over the metal golem, but all that seemed to accomplish was turning it into a *flaming* metal golem. It stomped toward the pyrelynx and swung at it with a clenched fist made of rebar. The pyrelynx darted away from the ponderous attack.

Rost's thralls reached the midfield and rattled off more shots. Plainsborough dodged back and forth, leaving shadowy afterimages in her wake. One lucky bullet hit her, and she glanced down at the hole in her sweater. She stuck a thumb through the hole with … less irritation than Clarke had expected, actually, given librarians' love of their cardigans.

Still, as if in revenge, her pyrelynx rounded the metal golem and pounced on one of Rost's thralls, digging into flesh with superheated claws and teeth. The man screamed—briefly—before the lynx tore out his throat.

"Damn it!" Rost shouted, still using his megaphone. "I really liked that one!"

"Then you shouldn't have picked this fight!"

All surviving combatants had collected near the center of the field. Clarke eased out of the tunnel, then scaled a wall up to the bottom tier and used a row of seats for cover as he advanced.

Plainsborough raised a clenched fist, green light leaking through her fingers. She made a sharp throwing gesture, but only a fine, sparkling mist came out, settling upon the field like a swarm of tiny, harmless fireflies. A pistol shot hissed past her head, and she hovered back.

Rost's remaining thrall ran after her, feverishly reloading his weapon. Which was how he discovered the truth of the pretty green sparkles. He stepped onto the glittering grass, which erupted into a great green fireball. Scorched pieces of the thrall rained down all across the football field.

"Did you like that one, too?" Plainsborough spat.

"Eh. He was kind of middling."

Rost chucked the megaphone over his shoulder and twohanded his war hammer. The pyrelynx charged him like a green comet, and he swung for its head, war hammer shattering the monster's skull. The monster collapsed onto its side, and the golem stomped over, crushing its exposed belly under one massive, metal boot.

"You're looking a bit lonely up there!" Rost taunted, resting the war hammer on his shoulder.

"I'm more than enough!"

"You think?" Rost pointed his hammer at the golem. "I sank every buff I've got into this guy."

"He's got to reach me first."

"I thought of that, too," Rost said, and the golem dropped a harpoon connected to its forearm by a long, heavy chain.

Plainsborough eyed it, her face a serene mask.

"You want to keep going?" Rost rested his war hammer on a shoulder. "Or shall we talk?"

Plainsborough sneered at him, but then her face relaxed, became placid. She floated to the ground.

"Fine, Rost. Let's talk."

With Plainsborough's back turned to him, Clarke saw his chance and decided to take it. He crouched at the end of a row and summoned his thirstblade. The sword formed a shaft of bloody light in his hands, hungering for more, thirsting for life—his or that of his enemies, it didn't matter.

He fed the summoned weapon, let it grow fat on his own lifeforce. The effort drained him, dangerously so, to the point where stars flitted across his vision. But the blood payment opened the right doors, gave him access to the right spells. He needed to strike a decisive blow, from here and without warning, and he knew exactly which spell to cast.

He swung the sword, cutting across with enough arcane force to leave a livid wound upon the air itself. A line of red energy formed across Plainsborough's neck, glowing and pulsating. She turned to face the source of the attack, perhaps instinctively, but her head kept turning, no longer moored to her shoulders, no longer restricted by skin, sinew, and bone.

She spent her last moments staring down her own back, her eyes wide with terror as her head toppled off.

The thirstblade vanished, and Clarke collapsed to his hands and knees, sucking at the delicious air. His weapon couldn't reap a foe so far away.

"*What?!*" Rost whirled around, trying to look in every direction at once.

Brooke blasted onto the field, galloping toward Rost with Sammy sprinting behind her. Brooke leaped at the vampire, who swung his war hammer around and struck her hard in the chest. Bones crunched, but Brooke pushed through, closing with Rost until she sank her claws into his forearm.

The vampire bared his fangs, hissing at her, spittle flying from his gums. Brooke roared back and ripped off one of the vampire's hands. He backpedaled, still holding his weapon, and Brooke dropped to her knees, one arm clutching her ribs.

Rost raised the war hammer singlehanded, ready to bring it down on Brooke's head, but Sammy lashed out, ensnaring the weapon in two overstretched arms. She yanked on the hammer, but Rost yanked back harder, pulling the weapon free.

The metal golem lurched around, facing Brooke.

Clarke grabbed a seatback and hauled himself upright. He told himself he'd found his second wind; even if that was a lie, he ignored the fog in his head, vaulted over the barrier at the bottom of the stands, and ran across the field. The thirstblade snapped into existence in his hand once more, and he sprinted toward the golem from behind, gulping down air the whole way.

The golem either didn't see him or ignored him entirely as it trudged after Brooke. Clarke slashed through one of its legs, cutting cleanly through rebar wrapped around an I-beam "bone," and the creature toppled.

Rost swung his war hammer in a wide, continuous arc while Sammy and Brooke held their distance.

"Do you have *any* idea who you're dealing with?" Rost snarled, fangs long and glistening. "I will reap your entire families! I will bathe in the blood of—"

"Now!" Clarke shouted, casting Blood Freeze. The spell taxed his already strained body, but the effect rippled through Rost, immediate and devastating. It didn't stop the vampire—he was too powerful for that—but his muscles spasmed, launching the weapon from his fingers mid-arc.

Sammy snagged one of his arms and tugged him off balance while Brooke lunged at him. Her claws sank into his belly, and her teeth punctured his throat. She ripped his abdomen open, spilling out his intestines, then crunched down on his neck.

"I! Cannot! Die!" the vampire rasped, blood pulsing from his ruined throat. He thrashed against Sammy's grip and beat on Brooke with his bloody stump.

"I think you can." Clarke shoved his sword into the vampire, burying it to the hilt.

"I ... I ..."

The life leaked out of the vampire, and the thirst-blade drank it in, flooding Clarke's body with renewed vigor.

"Prove us wrong."

"I ..."

Rost's eyes rolled back into his head, and his body slackened. The war hammer on the ground splintered into a thousand tinkling, obsidian shards. Green steam exhaled from the fallen golem, and its many parts collapsed into a junk pile.

An electric silence settled over the carnage of the stadium, startling in its contrast to the moments before. No one moved, as if afraid movement would draw out some hidden surprise—but soon the tense quiet settled into uneasy after-battle caution.

Brooke stood up straight and her broken ribs cracked back into place.

"You okay there?" Clarke asked.

The werewolf spat out blood. "Vampires taste like shit."

"Then don't swallow."

"That's not what you asked me to do earlier."

Clarke opened his mouth to respond, but he failed to find the words. He caught sight of Ashley and Emma hurrying down the stairs.

"Lightweight." Sammy spread a hand over her chest. "Clarke, just for the record, I'll swallow *anything* you ask me to."

"Ladies, I hardly think now is the time to—"

He was interrupted by the sound of clapping. The noise echoed across the empty stadium. Not a celebratory clap, but one with a slow, perhaps even a sarcastic cadence. All five of them turned to face the source.

There it was—the hidden surprise.

Otto Heinrich walked leisurely out onto the field, applauding them with a huge grin on his fanged face.

Chapter Twenty-Two

"Marvelous!" the vampire declared. "Simply marvelous! I couldn't have hoped for a better outcome!"

"*Heinrich?!*" Clarke recast his shield.

"The one and only."

"But we killed you!"

"Did you now?" The vampire brushed something off his shoulder. "I seem to have missed the memo."

"You were impaled through the heart. I chopped off your head!"

"No, no, no." He wagged a finger. "You beheaded my *decoy*. A young, risen vampire in my service, wrapped in spells to make him appear as if he were me. A rather disturbed specimen, actually. He won't be missed."

Brooke bared her teeth, a growl emanating from deep in her chest.

"Get ready, ladies!" Clarke summoned his weapon. "Looks like we've got one more vampire to kill!"

"Yes, yes. We could fight." Heinrich sighed. "But consider this: If I wanted you troublemakers dead, I would have already struck. I love theatrics as much as the next bloodsucker, but this would be a bit too stupid, don't you think?"

"Then why are we talking and not fighting?"

"Because I wish to talk." He stopped a healthy distance from the party. "Care to hear what I have to say?"

The vampire was too far away for anything but Scarlet Slash and would undoubtedly be on guard. Clarke glanced to his companions, but all four looked as confused as he was. How had they missed the presence of a fourth vampire? How had Heinrich fooled them? Had there been any warnings, any clues they'd missed?

"The spells," he said, every muscle in his body tense and ready for action.

"Pardon?" Heinrich replied.

"The spells embedded in the grimoire. They were too strong, too skillfully crafted. We should have known something was wrong back then."

"Yes, you should have." The vampire chuckled. "Does this mean you've decided to talk? Or are you still hellbent on challenging me?"

"Fine. If you want to talk, then get on with it."

"Splendid." He gestured to the corpses, carnage, and small fires littering the football field. "I have been following your little group's progress with great interest."

"Following us? How?"

"Through my grimoire, of course." He twirled a hand vaguely. "Well, one of them. I prepared *that* volume with a host of protective spells, including Far Sight."

Ashley gasped.

"Missed that one, didn't you?" Heinrich's eyes gleamed. "I've been watching you through the book ever since you stole it. And what did I spy with my little, bookish eye?" He extended both arms to Clarke. "Why, a blood knight, in the flesh!"

"Congratulations. You found us out. So what?"

"Naturally, I could have used this information to eliminate all five of you. But I didn't. Why? Because I see your potential." He grinned toothily. "Consider this business with Rost and Plainsborough as your final exam. One that you passed with flying colors."

"An exam? For what?"

"To determine if you have what it takes to become my servants." The vampire held up a finger. "Not thralls, mind you. *Servants.* Agents of my domain."

"Us? Work for a vampire? Ridiculous!"

"Is it now?"

"What makes you believe we'd ever serve you?"

411

"Because we all want the same thing."

"What? More dead vampires?"

"Precisely!" Heinrich spread his arms. "And I can help you achieve that goal. As many corpses as you want!"

Clarke shook his head in disbelief. "You want us to kill vampires?"

"Indeed, I do."

"Just not you, I take it."

"Naturally." He dipped his head.

"What? Are you hoping to move up in the world or something?"

"Ah, there it is! Your gray cells are starting to rub against each other, and the friction is birthing new thoughts. You're close to the truth. My goals are ... more immediate. More local. It's why I'm here, at this university, disguised as I am."

"Disguised?"

Heinrich smiled. "Appearances can be misleading."

"Like your decoy?"

"Ha! Quite so!"

"Why us?"

"Why not? You're a blood knight, after all. A slayer of vampires."

"And I see a vampire standing right in front of me."

"True, true. But, as I said, I can help you kill so many more. All I ask in return is your cooperation. Doesn't that sound like a fair exchange?"

Clarke looked to his companions once more and gauged their responses. None had spoken up during the whole conversation, and now he saw why. They were all conflicted, unsure what to make of this Faustian deal.

So was he, but a decision had to be made, and if no one else was willing to step forward, the decision fell to him.

He knew deep down, in both heart and mind, which call he needed to make.

"You're right about one thing," he told Heinrich.

"What's that?"

"We do have one goal in common, but that's where it ends. Our ultimate goal is to free humanity, even if we can only achieve it one dead vampire at a time. We're fighting to free people from the horrors of your kind. You don't want— No, you *can't* want the same thing, and that simple fact makes us enemies, no matter how much honey you pour over your words."

"I see," Heinrich replied stiffly, then swept his gaze over the others. "Does this man speak for all of you?"

"He does," Emma said without hesitation.

"He's my alpha," Brooke added. "Oppose him, and you oppose me."

Ashley's hairband glowed fiercely. "We will chart our own path, vampire."

"Come on!" Sammy bounced on her heels and raised her fists like a boxer. "Let's trounce this sucker!"

"Very well." Heinrich sighed and spread his open palms. "This, too, is an acceptable result."

A magic circle lit up beneath his feet.

"You should know, young blood knight, that you won't be facing a risen this time."

The corpses around them began to stir, to converge.

"I am pureblood, born over two hundred years ago. In my homeland, they called me Nachtpirscher." He grinned malevolently. "The Night Stalker."

Two corpse golems rose to their feet on either side of the vampire, but they were nothing like the golem from the decoy's lair. Their limbs were crafted from the bodies of dead humans, but their cores came from Rost and Plainsborough. One of the corpse golems raised a fist made out of five hands and conjured a glowing ball of green fire. The other summoned a giant war hammer and cast Strength and Armor upon itself.

"Try not to die too quickly," Heinrich taunted. "I enjoy playing with my food."

The fire golem launched its spell, and the party scattered, Ashley and Emma taking flight.

The explosion threw Clarke back, and his barrier shimmered. He steadied himself with one hand on the turf then ran to the side, circling the two corpse golems. The Rost-thing stomped toward him, while the Plainsborough-thing readied another spell. Heinrich turned his back to the action and casually walked away, which Clarke was fine with; two super golems were trouble enough!

"Sammy, distract the hammer golem! Brooke, on me! We'll tag team the caster!"

"Got it!" the ladies replied in stereo.

Sammy sprinted one way while Brooke galloped toward him. His path converged with the werewolf's as they circled the golems. The fire golem unleashed another attack, but missed, and the green bolt exploded against the stands.

"Now!"

Clarke and Brooke rushed the golem, splitting to either side at the last moment. His thirstblade hewed through one of the golem's corpse-legs, and it staggered forward as Brooke mauled its casting arm with teeth and claws. The werewolf's arms became savage blurs that sent chunks of flesh flying.

Still, barely hindered, the golem raised its undamaged arm, clenched its finger-hands together, and pale light bled through the gaps.

Clarke hacked the arm off at the creature's "elbow." The appendage thunked heavily to the ground, and its arcane light faded to rising sparks.

Brooke snatched the chance to leap onto the golem's back. The creature tried to throw her off, but she sank her claws in deep and began to rip it apart. Someone's arm arced through the air, followed by a lifeless head and organs slick with blood. Clarke sliced across the chest, and more of its ramshackle body parts spilled out.

He and Brooke hacked and ripped and slashed and chomped and tore until the air stank of blood and the ground turned crimson. The golem faltered, sinking to what remained of its broken limbs. Brooke reached deep into the creature, her fur matted with blood up past the elbows. Her back and shoulder muscles flexed, and she snarled.

Bones cracked, muscles ripped, and she sundered the golem's main body into two. Both halves collapsed to the ground with Brooke crouched on top, triumphant.

"Now the Rost-thing!" Clarke shouted. "Converge and attack!"

Brooke snarled, her maw dripping with blood as she leaped off the broken golem. She hit the ground on all fours and galloped toward the second. Clarke ran after her but couldn't match her speed.

Sammy held one of the golem's arms in the tentative grip of her stretched arms—but the creature brought its hammer around in a brutal arc, forcing her to let go and whip her limbs back. She was still well within its range, though, and the golem raised its hammer, stomping forward, ready to bring the weapon down on her.

Clarke cast Blood Freeze, and the hammer shuddered at its zenith. It didn't stop the weapon, but it granted

Sammy the precious moment she needed to dash clear. The golem followed through, and its hammer struck earth, blasting grass and dirt into the air.

Brooke tackled the golem from behind. She lashed at its back, but her claws struggled to find purchase. Weaves of magic toughened its flesh and fortified its bones. The golem's arm bent in an unnatural direction, and it swung the hammer at its own body.

"Brooke!" Clarke shouted, too late.

The hammer head slammed into the werewolf, throwing her clear. She hit the ground hard and tumbled across the turf until she stopped herself, rebounding onto all fours. She bared her teeth at the monster.

The golem raised its hammer and stomped toward her.

Sammy whirled her arms into a lasso, snared the weapon, and yanked back, slowing the creature.

"Now!" Clarke shouted, charging in. He cut into the monster's flank, and guts from its many bodies spilled out.

Brooke rammed her shoulder into one of the golem's legs, and the creature lost its footing. It toppled forward, landing with a wet crunch. She leaped onto its back once more and thrashed at its meat with her claws. Clarke carved through one of its shoulders, and the arm gripping the hammer stopped moving. Sammy formed her hands into mallets and pounded at the opposite arm, pulverizing the appendage until it was nothing but crimson pulp.

"Clarke, watch out!" Emma shouted from high above. "It's getting back up!"

He glanced up at the succubus, saw where she was pointing, then spun around. The Plainsborough golem was reforming, broken and bloody chunks pulling together like iron filings next to a magnet. A magic circle glowed underneath it, while a second point flickered amidst the stands.

Clarke's eyes tracked up and across to the second glow, only to find Heinrich lounging in a seat, feet propped up on the next row down. The vampire gave him an insulting little wave.

A second circle lit under his feet, and the arm he'd just cut off slithered over to the main body. Bones and tendons reached out in either direction, and the joint reknit itself with a grotesque series of cracks and squelches.

Clarke and the others backed away from the Rost golem as it rose back to its feet. An explosive bolt flew over their heads and detonated against the stands.

"We can't keep this up forever!" Sammy shouted, backpedaling.

"It's Heinrich. We need to take him out!" Clarke stole a quick look toward the stands.

Heinrich blew them all a kiss.

"What about these two things?" Sammy asked urgently. "We're going to get pulverized and exploded if we ignore them!"

"Hold them off," Clarke said. "I'll take down the vampire."

"What? *Alone?*"

"You have a better idea?"

"But …" Sammy couldn't find the words.

"Go, Clarke." Emma flew in low, unfurling her bat wings. "Let us ladies handle the golems."

"What are you thinking?" Sammy snapped. "You can't fight!"

"No, but we can distract them." Ashley joined Emma, her halo shining like a broken ring of liquid gold. "Go! We have your back!"

The fire golem readied another spell. Emma and Ashley swooped toward it.

The hammer golem lumbered forward. Brooke and Sammy charged it head on.

"Thanks," Clarke said, too softly for any of them to hear. He locked eyes with Heinrich and crossed the field, arms and legs pumping. He cast Fly, and took one long, floating leap up to the stands, landing in an aisle. His opponent looked at him like he was a ball or souvenir t-shirt thrown into the crowd.

"Oh, I suppose I should stand up for this." Heinrich swung his boots off the seat back and rose to his feet. He rounded the seat at a casual pace and stopped opposite Clarke in the aisle.

The vampire smirked at him and spread his hands, summoning an obsidian longsword in one and a dagger in the other. He crossed his arms over his chest and bowed.

Clarke took no time for theatrics. He cast Scarlet Slash. The thirstblade tore through the air, and a matching rip cut across Heinrich.

Except it didn't.

The shadowy afterimage of the vampire dissolved. The floating slash vanished, and the vampire walked calmly over to take its place.

"Nice try, blood knight, but I've faced your kind before."

The cost of the spell slammed into Clarke, and he almost dropped to one knee. His heart raced, fear prickling across his skin. Scarlet Slash was his best shot at taking Heinrich down, but this time it had backfired, weakening him against the most terrifying foe of his life.

Heinrich raised his weapons into a two-handed fighting stance.

"Gotten that out of your system? Good." The vampire shot forward, leaving a streak of shadow in his wake. He cleared the distance with inhuman speed, and Clarke barely brought his sword up in time. Their blades clashed, sparking with arcane energies, and Clarke tried to shove the vampire back.

It was like pushing against a mountain.

"You're starting to see it now, aren't you?" Heinrich thrust with his dagger, forcing Clarke back.

"See what?"

"That I'm toying with you." The vampire advanced on him, and their swords clashed again.

Clarke tried to bring his sword around, to come at the vampire's side, but Heinrich was too fast, too skilled. He parried the attack, still advancing, dagger darting this way and that, flashing against Clarke's shield, draining his defenses one prick at a time.

Clarke struggled to keep track of both weapons. He'd never faced a fighting style like this; hell, he had almost zero experience with a sword! What was he supposed to do against a two-hundred-year-old vampire?

"You have potential. But your technique?" Heinrich made a *tut-tut* sound. "It doesn't impress."

"What the hell do you care?"

"That's not the question you should be asking!" The vampire lunged, and his dagger struck once more. Clarke's shield splintered into a shower of red glass, and the blade cut across his thigh.

He backpedaled, a fiery blight spreading through his leg. He fought the urge to scream.

"Marvelous." Heinrich raised the dagger. Its sheen of dark liquid caught the light. "To think you still stand, even after tasting Agony's bite. The slime girl's influence, no doubt. Oh, you have such beautiful potential."

Clarke knew he was running out of options. He couldn't let the vampire pick him apart, and so he went on the offensive, swinging furiously. Heinrich blocked each attack with almost contemptuous ease. The vampire's eyes flashed, and he became shadow, swooping around Clarke.

The dagger slashed at him, again and again, cutting across his arms, legs, and the back of his neck. Fresh pain blossomed across his entire body, and he dropped to his knees. He gritted his teeth and cast Purify, but it only dulled the symptoms.

Heinrich stood before him, the dagger at his throat. He gazed down at Clarke as if appraising him.

"We will have to do something about your technique."

"What are you getting on at?" Clarke growled.

"Still don't get it? Well, I suppose you have been a bit distracted. The question you should be asking yourself is why you aren't dead? Why are none of you dead?"

"Because you want something."

"Correct." Heinrich dipped his head ever so slightly. "And that something is my very own blood knight. I will mold you as I see fit, forge you into my executioner." He smiled, fangs gleaming. "You will kill so many vampires for me."

"I refuse!"

"Oh, come now. Whose blade is at whose throat? Your life is too valuable to be thrown away on a whim. And besides, yours isn't the only life at stake." The vampire's eyes darted toward the field and the sound of battle.

"You keep your hands off them!" Clarke spat.

"You care for them, don't you?" He pressed the dagger in. "What if I told you they need not die? That none of you need to die."

Clarke leaned back from the tip.

"If you won't enter into my service willingly—if you refuse to be my servant—then I will make you my slave. Those women shall be your chains. I will spare them, even protect them for you. All I require is you on your knees. Are you willing to fight for them?"

"Yes," he grunted through clenched teeth.

"Would you be willing to die for them?"

"Yes."

"And why is that? Tell me. I wish to hear it."

"It's because I love them!" he shouted.

His voice rang out across the stadium, so loud it shocked him, clear enough to eclipse the raging battle behind him. The entire field held its collective breath, and he felt four gazes upon his back, fleetingly given in the chaos, but each distinct.

He didn't understand how he felt this, how he knew each woman had turned her eyes toward him in that moment.

But it had happened.

He knew this to be true.

And he knew he couldn't let them down, couldn't exchange them like coins with this monster. They were all beautiful to him, both outside and within, and he would never betray them.

He would protect them.

Even at the cost of his own life.

"Very good." Heinrich removed the dagger and took a step back. "Now, my young executioner, swear allegiance to me."

The battle on the field stopped, and he sensed their gazes again. They saw him, defeated and on his knees before the pureblood vampire, and it hurt to think he'd let them down, that they believed this fiend had broken him.

But he was not broken.

He would not betray them.

He would fight for them. For as long as he still breathed.

Clarke made his decision.

He gathered what remained of his strength—

—and cast Sacrifice.

The total sum of his life poured into the thirstblade, draining him to within an inch of death. That much he'd expected, but something else happened. Something alien to his blood magic. A kernel within his mind opened, blossoming like a flower, its ethereal vines reaching out, intertwining with his thoughts.

He remembered the last time he'd seen that magical flower petal motif.

It was the magic he'd gained from Ixia; it had fused with Sacrifice, just as Emma's magic had fused with Power Graft, and the transformed spell blazed in his mind like the sun.

The thirstblade ignited with enough force to throw Heinrich back. Lightning crackled across Clarke's body, and red steam rose from his skin. His eyes became two points of fire, and he rose, swinging his sword in a swift arc.

Heinrich was off balance from the blast but not defenseless, and he brought his longsword down to meet Clarke's stroke. The two blades met in a flash of red and green lightning that snapped outward, blasting away chairs and chunks of concrete.

The obsidian longsword trembled in Heinrich's hands, blurred like a tuning fork, and then shattered. Clarke cut upward. He cleaved Heinrich in two from hip to shoulder, the stroke leaving a glowing fissure that expanded, spreading veins of red light throughout the vampire. His flesh crisped, bulged—and then he exploded into a shower of blood and viscera. Snaps of red energy arced across the ground where he once stood.

The two corpse golems collapsed into ugly piles of meat.

The light around Clarke faded, manifesting for a brief moment like a rain of blood-soaked petals. He dropped to his hands and knees, and the women of Broken Fang raced toward him. His thirstblade drank in the vampire's vanquished life, replenishing all that he'd given and more, but the seesaw toward death and back left his head spinning and his body shaken.

"Clarke!"

He grabbed a seatback and hauled himself upright. His clothes were soaked with Heinrich's blood.

"CLARKE!"

Emma reached him first, flying over the stands to throw her arms around him. Her shoes touched the ground, and her wings wrapped around him. She pulled him tight, her head pressed against his neck.

"Oh, Clarke!" She was almost crying.

Brooke caught up and joined the embrace, squeezing Clarke from behind. Sammy was about to follow her lead, but she hesitated when she saw the tangle of arms and wings already present, and she held off. Ashley landed next to them, a happy smile on her face.

"Hey there," Clarke said softly. "Are all of you all right?"

"Are *we* all right?" Emma held him at arm's length, a sad, almost scolding look in her eyes. "Are *you* all right?"

"I think so. Just don't let go. My legs are a bit wobbly."

"I'll hold you for as long as you need," Brooke said from behind him, her arms tight around his chest.

"Did you mean it?" Sammy asked. "Really mean it?"

"Mean what?"

"The L-word, of course!"

"Oh, that."

"Yes! That!"

Clarke glanced around, taking in their expressions. All of them watched him with nervous anticipation. Except for Brooke. He wasn't sure what to make of her face, but then again, he still struggled to read werewolf expressions besides angry and not angry.

"Yeah, I did." He gave them an apologetic smile. "Sorry."

"Whatever for?" Sammy asked.

"Something like this deserved a more appropriate moment. A candlelit dinner, maybe?"

"Oh, for crying out loud, Clarke!"

"I don't know about the rest of you," Emma said, "but shouting it in a stadium before bloodsploding a vampire is just about the *perfect* way for a blood knight to say 'I love you'."

Clarke chuckled. "I'll take that under advisement."

"You know what else?" Emma said, her eyes moistening.

"What's that?"

"We love you, too."

She kissed him. Long and with feeling.

Brooke followed her with a wet lick of her werewolf tongue. Emma stepped aside, and Sammy planted a deep kiss on his lips. Even Ashley gave him a playful peck on the cheek.

All he could do was grin like a fool.

"All of us do." Emma said once they'd all taken their turns. "Where would we be without you?"

CHAPTER TWENTY-THREE

CLARKE AND THE LADIES OF BROKEN FANG headed back to the steel mill, where they burned his bloody attire in a barrel and washed up as much as possible.

"What are the police going to make of the stadium?" Clarke asked, pulling on a fresh shirt. "Between the bodies and the craters, I don't see regular control spells keeping this quiet."

"They won't," Emma said. "But as soon as this hits social media, one of the Big Tech vampires will take notice. Remote spells will be deployed to control the masses, and this event will drift into obscurity. You'll see."

"You sure about that?"

"This isn't the first time vampires killed each other over territory. Local demihumans and mages will know what happened, or at least suspect the truth, but the city's humans will once again find themselves in the dark."

The team headed their separate ways and stuck to a low profile on Sunday. Clarke and Emma kept their eyes on the local news, which first manifested as speculation of a "wild animal attack" at CCU Stadium, prompting police to initiate a search of the surrounding area.

"A wild animal," Clarke scoffed.

"That's just for starters." Emma tapped her screen. "This article is loaded with spells. Ashley's magic is protecting us, but everyone else who reads them is going to get hit. Just wait and see. By the end of the week, there won't be a human in the city who remembers this, with you and mages as the only exceptions."

Sunday night saw Emma's "hunger" come to a head. She'd let Clarke rest since the battle at the stadium, but her needs and the proximity of his magical aura had combined to make her "as hot as a supernova and as wet as the ocean."

While both were obvious exaggerations, they weren't all that far off. She was deeply aroused, even for a succubus, and his recent confession only served to stimulate her more, to the point where she nearly begged him to do her.

Clarke had been so focused on the situation on campus that he hadn't realized how he'd neglected her needs, and he committed himself to rectifying this unfortunate oversight.

Repeatedly.

And vigorously.

He lost track of how many times they had sex that night, but even her overcharged libido met its match with his enhanced stamina, and eventually he sated her needs.

For a few days, at least.

Maybe?

Monday came, and "wild animal attack" became "several missing persons" due to the police being "misquoted." The stadium remained closed, and numerous events were canceled, resulting in a lot of angry, confused students.

Clarke and the others attended their regular slate of classes, keeping their eyes open for anything unusual. He saw a few police officers pass through campus, but even that presence tapered off by the end of the day.

Brooke dropped by Tuesday night, and this time she didn't bring her restraints. She said his confession had made her want to "cut loose," and then she showed him what that meant. The results were somewhere between sex and a car crash: loud, bone-jarringly violent, and a textbook example for why seatbelts exist.

Something broke in the bed halfway through the night, and Clarke wasn't sure what to do about the two big dents they left in the wall, but Emma didn't seem to mind. He was pretty sure she spent the night pleasuring herself to the sounds of their sexual rampage. She even managed to placate the angry neighbors when they came knocking sometime after midnight.

He snuggled up with both women after that, sore but thoroughly satisfied.

Wednesday arrived, and "several missing persons" transformed into "structural damage to the stadium" due to "faulty construction materials." Apparently, the university planned to launch an inquiry aimed at one of the site's building subcontractors, and the stadium was being closed until further notice.

Sammy stopped over Thursday night, which was when Clarke began to suspect the ladies had discussed some form of schedule in his absence, not that he didn't approve. Quite the opposite, in fact. He had secretly dreaded being asked to pick favorites, so if the ladies managed to sort all that out amongst themselves, then it was another sign this unconventional relationship—to him, at least—would go the distance.

He and Sammy finished watching *Dirty Pair: Project Eden*, which was as fun and frenetic as she'd led him to believe, then spent the rest of the night having sex. Later, he reflected that his night with Sammy was the most vanilla of the week, if anything about having sex with a shape-shifting slime girl could be called "vanilla."

Perhaps that said more about Emma and Brooke than anything else.

Sammy offered to head home after Clarke had sated her; she didn't want to expose Emma to her toxins if she rolled over in bed the wrong way, but Emma refused to hear any of it. The succubus simply grabbed her pillow and spent the night on the couch, leaving the slime girl to cuddle up with Clarke without any fears she might hurt someone.

Both she and Clarke slept like rocks.

Or a semiliquid polymer, give how he quite literally left an impression in her during the night.

By Friday, any mentions of "structural damage" had vanished, leaving only a few brief, boring mentions that the stadium had been closed for "renovations." In other, unrelated news, Head Coach Jayden Rost accepted a lucrative transfer to a competing university. Meanwhile, Head Librarian Gretchen Plainsborough tendered her resignation with the intention of spending more time with her family.

Clarke found it all so surreal how the news morphed from one narrative to the next, becoming more and more benign with each iteration.

"Unbelievable," he said, skimming the news with Emma that Friday evening. "From animal attack to remodeling in a week."

"That's how it goes sometimes," she said, seated next to him on the couch. "But it's a good sign it took this long to change. Remember when Heinrich's decoy died? That got covered up *a lot* faster."

"Because of Rost and Plainsborough?"

"Right. And we're not seeing the same pattern this time. Big Tech is having to scrub the feeds themselves, which means there isn't a local vampire left to cover their tracks. Those three vampires—four when you count the decoy—were it, and they're all dead."

"We did it, then? Cleared CCU of all its vampires?"

"Sure looks that way." Emma sighed thoughtfully. "It's a temporary state, though. Any power vacuum is. Other vampires will catch wind of the vacancy and see this as an opportunity to move in. But for now, for this moment in time, CCU is vampire free."

"But we saved lives by doing this, right?"

"Absolutely, and a lot of them too. But this achievement is important in more ways than you might realize. Freeing the area of vampires, even if it's temporary, gives our group some much-needed breathing room. Not sure what we'll do with it, but it gives us a chance to think bigger, reach farther."

"Maybe hit some vampires outside of CCU?"

"For sure, but I was thinking more along the lines of finding allies. We're still only five people, after all." She placed her hand on his thigh. "And while we do have the resident blood knight on our side, there's only so much we can do."

"Makes sense to me. From what I've seen, plenty of demihumans and mages aren't happy with the way things are. Did you have any particular groups in mind?"

"Not really. I'd love to get a mage clan or two on our side, but that's going to be a tough sell. We can ask the others what they think."

"They still coming over?"

"Yep. Should be here in about an hour."

"Hey, bitches!" Brooke said, barging through the door with three bags loaded with fast food. "And Clarke, of course. I'm here, and I brought food! Also, you'll be proud of me, Ash. I remembered your salad."

"Thank you," the celestial replied primly.

"Here, let me help you with that." Emma took one of the bags and began unloading cartons onto the kitchen counter alongside Brooke. She'd already set up their selection of drinks.

"You all know I'm totally cool with catering our meetings," Sammy said, lounging in a recliner. "I eat more than the rest of you anyway."

"We know," Emma said, helping Brooke with the second bag. "But it's the principle of the matter. We all agreed to pitch in, and so that's what we're going to do."

"Clarke, what would you like?" Brooke asked.

"I'll start with a Big Mac, please."

"Coming right up!"

"Me, too," Sammy said. "And make that three."

Brooke doled out the burgers, along with a salad for Ashley.

"Oh, can you grab me some McNuggets, too?" Sammy asked.

"Sure!"

"Brooke," Ashley said, "only give them to her if she promises to eat them correctly this time."

"Fine, fine." Sammy waved a hand. "I promise. Can I have my nuggets now?"

"Why?" Clarke asked, opening his carton. "What'd she do last time?"

"She neglected to take them out of the carton."

Clarke glanced over at the slime girl with a raised eyebrow.

"Whatever. They were still delicious."

Emma sat down next to Clarke.

"Don't you want anything, Emma?" Brooke asked.

"No, thanks. I couldn't handle another bite. I'm still full from this morning." The succubus draped an arm around Clarke.

"Which mouth were you eating from?" Sammy asked.

"You know which."

The slime girl snorted out a laugh then chomped down on her first burger.

Ashley opened her salad, speared a single baby

tomato, and placed it delicately in her mouth. She chewed and swallowed before speaking up.

"There's something that's been bothering me. And now that things have calmed down, I thought we should address the elephant in the room."

"Why are you looking at me?" Sammy asked.

"I'm not, I—" Ashley grimaced, suddenly uncomfortable. "I just happened to be looking your way. I'm talking about Heinrich."

"He was definitely a cut above the others," Clarke said. "We're lucky to be alive."

"Which brings me to my point. *Why* was a such a powerful vampire here at CCU? And, furthermore, why was he disguised as a lowly risen?"

"Have you come across anything in his grimoire?"

"No, and I don't expect to, unfortunately." Ashley set her fork down. "From the way Heinrich spoke, he created the grimoire we have specifically for his decoy, so I doubt he would reveal his true intentions in it."

"Something drew him here," Clarke said. "And something about it made him pretend to be much weaker than he actually was."

"It seems clear he wanted to avoid attention," Ashley said. "That is, until we drew his attention."

"At which point, he became interested in using me as his 'executioner'."

"Worst. Job offer. Ever!" Sammy said.

"Too true." Clarke sat forward, thinking. "Ashley, you once told me Chester Creek is important to your mission."

"Yes, and the university especially, though I still don't understand why."

"Could the reason this place is important to your mission have also drawn Heinrich to it?"

"Hmm. I suppose that could be." The celestial huffed out a breath. "I wish I could say more. You raise an interesting point, though. It's a possibility we should keep in mind as we plot our next moves. And speaking of which—"

"Stop!" Sammy cut in, and everyone turned to her. "Stop right there, Ash!"

"What? Something wrong?"

"You better believe it. All of us have been going nonstop for weeks. We've faced"—she began counting with her fingers—"zombies, golems, thralls, summoned monsters, *flaming* monsters, flaming *golems*."

"You realize your hand has six fingers now, right?"

Sammy ignored the angel as she added a seventh.

"And let's not forget the vampires, including one pureblood, all while trying to keep our grades from swirling down the toilet. On top of all that, many of us have been shot, stabbed, bludgeoned, chewed, partially blinded, and set on fire. Don't you think we've earned a breather, at least for one weekend?"

Ashley sat back with a frown.

"She does have a point there," Clarke said.

"Yes, I suppose she does." The angel collected herself. "Very well. Perhaps we should postpone Broken Fang business until next week. All in favor?"

Everyone but Ashley raised their hands.

"I seem to be in the minority." She sighed. "We'll continue this discussion at our next meeting."

"Great!" Sammy rubbed her hands together. "Now, let's talk about how we're going to celebrate our victory!"

"Sounds like you have something in mind," Clarke said.

"I do! You should all come over my place tomorrow and binge-watch the new Gundam series with me. It's been streaming for a while, and I need to get caught up before I run into spoilers. Also, there'll be tons of food."

"That seems a bit … you-centric."

"I'm open to suggestions."

"Oh!" Emma raised her hands. "I have an idea! We could have a good, old-fashioned slumber party."

"You mean a sex party, don't you?" Clarke asked.

"Aren't they the same?"

"Not last I heard."

"Hold it," Sammy said. "Got a counteroffer for the succubus. I'll match your slumber party and raise it with a *Stringendo* marathon."

"Hmm. Tempting, tempting," Emma replied, licking her lips. "I do love that show."

Clarke's brown creased. "*Stringendo*? The show have something to do with music?"

"Not really." Sammy gave him a mischievous grin. "Something's getting accelerated, but it's not music."

"Anime?"

"A subgenre of it, yes."

"Does the name of this subgenre start with an H, by any chance?"

"Good guess!"

"Hmm."

"We could all go camping?" Brooke suggested with an unsure shrug.

"Question," Emma said, raising her hand. "Would this camping excursion include a visit to your family's bondage hut?"

"Uh … I suppose it could."

"I feel like these suggestions are all gravitating in the same direction," Ashley said dryly. "Perhaps we could pick an activity I'm free to join?"

The table fell silent, everyone bowing their heads in thought.

"I got nothing," Emma said after a while.

"You sure you don't want to just hang back and watch?" Sammy asked the celestial.

"I would prefer to participate, if it's all the same."

"Oh!" Clarke leaned in. "I've got an idea."

Everyone waited attentively for him to continue.

"I was just reminded how all of this got started, at least for me. What if we had another pen-and-paper role-playing session?"

"Yes!" Emma thumped the air. "Great idea!"

"I'm already in love with this," Brooke added, smiling ear to ear.

"Me too," Sammy said. "Which rules? Want to continue Ash's campaign?"

"Actually, how about we start a new one? I figured we've all had our fill of vampires for a while. Any of you familiar with Titan Mage?"

The ladies all shook their heads.

"It's a steampunk setting. It has big, stompy robots fueled by magic."

Sammy's eyes went wide. "Clarke?"

"Yes?"

"I loved *every word* that just came out of your mouth. I would kiss you right now if my mouth didn't taste like a McNugget."

"I second that," Emma said. "Steampunk mecha and magic is just one of those chocolate and peanut butter combinations. Also, my mouth does *not* taste like a McNugget, so I'm very kissable at the moment."

Clarke laughed. "How about the rest of you?"

"I'm intrigued," Ashley said, her hairband gaining some luster.

"Me too," Brooke said, tail wagging. "Great idea, Clarke!"

"In that case, ladies, give me a minute to grab my sourcebook." He rose from the couch, feeling like the luckiest man alive. "Got a few ideas percolating in my brain already. What comes next should be fun!"

END OF BOOK ONE

READY TO CONTINUE THE ADVENTURE?

PRE-ORDER BOOK TWO HERE:
https://edieskye.com/book/scepter-of-bone/

OR JOIN MY PATREON TO READ IT EARLY:
https://www.patreon.com/edieskyeauthor

DEAR READER

If you've reached this page, congratulations! After all, out of all the spicy harem books you could have chosen to read, you chose *my* spicy harem book, and if you ask me, there are few better indicators of good taste.

That said, if you liked what you read and would like to see more, **be sure to leave a review on Amazon, Goodreads, or Bookbub.** The more reviews a book gets, the more likely I am to say, "Hmm, maybe I should write a sequel." (Plus, It's Just fun to hear back from readers.)

Also, if you'd like to receive updates on what else I'm writing, be sure to follow me on:

Patreon: https://www.patreon.com/edieskyeauthor
Facebook, Instagram, Twitter, and TikTok: @edieskyeauthor
Amazon: https://www.amazon.com/Edie-Skye/e/B09X3PQFXX
Goodreads: https://www.goodreads.com/edieskyeauthor
Bookbub: https://www.bookbub.com/authors/edie-skye
Website: https://edieskye.com
Mailing List: https://edieskye.com/newsletter

And finally, if you're looking for more harem lit, **be sure to join the Harem Lit, HaremLit Readers, Harem Gamelit, Pulp Fantasy, Harem and Romance for Men, Monster Girl Fiction, and Dukes of Harem groups on Facebook!** For more lit that may or may not be harem, but is definitely fun, join **SuperLit Book Club, Club Kaiju, and LitRPG Legion.**

Again, thank you for reading *Blood Knight: Vampire Slayer*! And don't be shy! I love to hear back from by readers, and you can reach me at all the sites above, or directly at **edieskyeauthor@gmail.com.**

Best,

Edie Skye

ABOUT THE AUTHOR

Edie Skye wrote Titan Mage as a joke and, in doing so, discovered that while she really likes writing smart stuff, she also likes writing smut stuff. Pretty spicy smut stuff, too, 'cause if you're gonna do it, you might as well do it hard.

Specifically, she likes to spin fun (and funny) adventure fantasies about badass women and the equally badass dudes who want to do them. There's action and monster-punching galore, sometimes with airships and mech upgrades, sometimes with monster girl gamers, but always with a substantial side of harem and fun-for-all-involved graphic spice. (Which is to say, it's super NSFW. Unless your workplace is, like, really cool.)

A WEREBEAR AT WIT'S END?
A NECROMANCER IN DIRE NEED?
A BONE SCEPTER THE VAMPIRES WILL KILL FOR?

SEND IN THE BLOOD KNIGHT TO SORT THIS MESS OUT!

J.B. Clarke and the lovely ladies of Broken Fang have won their first victory against the vampires who secretly rule the world. But their fight is far from over. To defeat the vampires once and for all, they'll need to rally powerful allies to their cause. But before they can do that, they need to make a name for themselves amongst the hidden underworld of monsters, mages, and vampire slayers.

Clarke makes a deal with the Coven of the Ashen Flower: his services as a blood knight in exchange for a steady stream of work. The coven agrees and assigns him to Ixia Grey, a young witch and aspiring esports player. Ixia proves to be a deft hand at lining up jobs for Broken Fang, and Clarke soon finds himself up to his elbows in monsters to slay—

—and fat paychecks to earn.

But all is not well in the city of Chester Creek. The vampires have unleashed a terrifying new monster, one more powerful and deadly than anything Clarke has ever faced. A ghostly killer now roams the shadows, an embodiment of fear and death that shreds its victims' minds as it drains their bodies.

But Clarke is a blood knight, heir to the greatest line of vampire slayers who ever walked the Earth, and he will face the coming darkness no matter what form it takes.

WARNING: *Blood Knight: Scepter of Bone* **is a fun urban fantasy adventure with a healthy side of heat: ravishing succubi, submissive werewolves, cosplaying slime girls, flirtatious witches, and saucy language to match. (So don't read it and then complain about the spice. Y'all know exactly what you're getting into.)**

COMING SUMMER 2024

IN eBOOK, PRINT, AND AUDIO

HTTPS://EDIESKYE.COM

A RED HOT, FIERY DEMON GIRL.
A GOBLIN GIRL OBSESSED WITH WOOD.
AN ONI GIRL WHO LOVES TO GRIP
A BIG SWORD.

AND THEY'RE GOING TO HELP HIM SAVE THE WORLD ... HOW?

Axel Hunter Radcliff has trained his whole life to be a hero. Once every generation, someone in his family is called upon to be a Chosen One, and Axel's prepared himself extensively, just in case it's him.

He just wasn't prepared for the portal.

Now he's in another world brimming with dangerous monsters beneath a sky full of magic portals ... and with no idea what he's been summoned to do. All he knows is that every Chosen Radcliff has been aided by a support staff of skilled women: a *tactical harem.*

When mysterious monster girls start wreaking havoc in this new world, Axel is ready to answer the call. He'll have to draw upon insight borne from every tabletop RPG he's played and every harem novel he's read to face them, because these are either the women he's destined to gather ... or the force he's been summoned to stop.

Either way, these monster girls need to be *tamed!*

WARNING: *Monster Girl Tamer* is a fun LitRPG fantasy adventure with a healthy side of heat: sensuous demons, lustful goblins, voluptuous oni, and saucy language to match. (So don't read it and then complain about the spice. Y'all know exactly what you're getting into.)

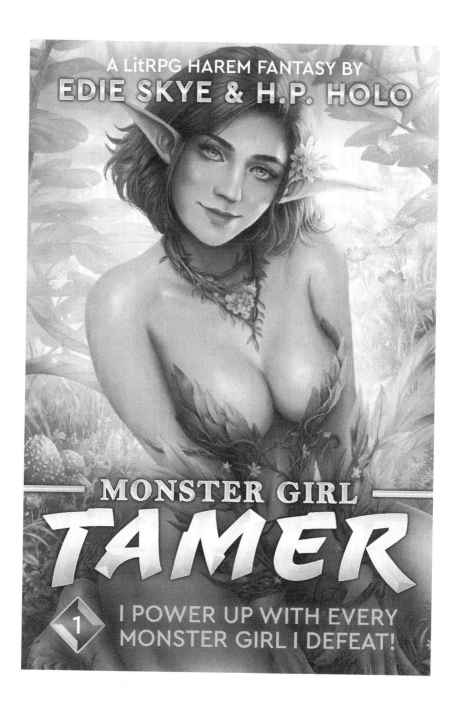

MAGIC POWERS?
HIS OWN MECH?
A WHOLE AIRSHIP OF GORGEOUS WOMEN DESPERATE FOR HIS GENES?

YES, PLEASE!

Paralyzed by a drunk driver, let go from his job, and stuck in a sad, stagnant town in the middle of nowhere, Joseph Locke was having the worst day of his life.

And then he *died*.

But considering that he wakes up with a brand new body, in the cockpit of a badass steampunk robot, on an airship of nothing but hot babes, his next life may not be all that bad. Especially when he learns that he's a void mage—the rarest and most powerful of all mages on the world of Haven. And his shipmates want to help him make *more*.

WARNING: *Titan Mage* **is a fun fantasy adventure containing steam both punk and smutty: raunchy sausage-obsessed mechanics, lusty airship captains, prurient mech pilots, and saucy language to match. (So don't read it and then complain about the spice. Y'all know exactly what you're getting into.)**

SERIES 1

NOW COMPLETE

IN EBOOK, PRINT, AND AUDIO

HTTPS://EDIESKYE.COM

Made in the USA
Middletown, DE
04 September 2024

60264056R00267